The Fortune Teller

Also by Donald James

Monstrum
The Fall of the Russian Empire
Penguin Dictionary of the Third Reich

THE FORTUNE TELLER

Donald James

CENTURY · LONDON

Published by Century Books in 1999

1 3 5 7 9 10 8 6 4 2

Copyright © Donald James 1999

Donald James has asserted his right under the Copyright, Designs and
Patents Act, 1988 to be identified as the author of this work

First published in the United Kingdom in 1999 by Century
Random House UK Limited
20 Vauxhall Bridge Road, London, SW1V 2SA

Random House Australia (Pty) Limited
20 Alfred Street, Milsons Point, Sydney,
New South Wales 2061, Australia

Random House New Zealand Limited
18 Poland Road, Glenfield
Auckland 10, New Zealand

Random House South Africa (Pty) Limited
Endulini, 5a Jubilee Road,
Parktown 2193, South Africa

Random House UK Limited Reg. No. 954009

A CIP catalogue record for this book is available from the British Library

Papers used by Random House UK Limited are natural, recyclable
products made from wood grown in sustainable forests. The
manufacturing processes conform to the environmental regulations of the
country of origin

ISBN 0 7126 7959 6 Hardback
ISBN 0 7126 8032 2 Paperback

Typeset by Palimpsest Book Production Limited,
Polmont, Stirlingshire
Printed and bound in Great Britain by
Mackays of Chatham PLC, Chatham, Kent

Of the many people who have helped to bring *The Fortune Teller* to the press, I hope it is not invidious to single out Oliver Johnson, my editor at Century, to thank him for his real efforts on behalf of the book.

PROLOGUE

THE FIRST ONE was washed in from Lake Michigan, rolling along the shoreline of Chicago's Lincoln Park. The body, a girl of perhaps fourteen, had been in the water several days. The cause of death was strangulation by ligature; there was evidence of violent sexual abuse.

The second body was recovered, nearly two years later, from a burning house on Brattle Street, Cambridge, Massachusetts. There was a little more to know about this second victim. Neighbours reported that she was the thirteen-year-old niece of a Dr John Pollinger, a member of the English Faculty at Harvard. She had been seen in the yard of the Brattle Street house several times during the summer, although nobody reported having had the opportunity to speak to her. When found, asphyxiated by smoke and fumes, examination showed she had been subject to severe sexual assault over an extended period. Later the same day, John Pollinger, who police believed had, himself, started the fire, was discovered dead in his Elliot House office, killed by a self-administered gunshot wound, the .22 bullet travelling through the roof of his mouth to lodge in his brain.

The third body, another girl, was found in New York City six months later, in a little-used alley in SoHo. Her death, the result of a sustained beating, had taken place elsewhere. A Hallmark greetings card for a fourteenth birthday read in a large looped hand: Happy birthday T – from your crazy lover, MJ.

Police and FBI investigating the deaths established that the clothing, in each case, differed greatly in quality, price and place of origin. No reason was found to think that one single man was responsible.

But the unifying factor in the three deaths was a crudely executed, pale green tattoo high on the upper arm of each girl, the single letter K. This was identified as a five-year fade-tattoo used in

Juvenile Penal Colonies in various parts of Russia, principally Krasnoyarsk, Kolyma and Kola, all of which were known as areas with a concentration of camps for young offenders.

A report was passed to Charles Fearless, the FBI Special Agent in Moscow at the height of the recent Civil War. There, within weeks, it had disappeared beneath the rubble of the American Embassy when the Novinsky Boulvar was destroyed by Nationalist bombing in the summer of 2015.

Russia, April, 2017

The Arctic province of Kola, in the centenary
year of the Russian Revolution

I

S CENES FROM A Russian policeman's day. Do you have days like this, I wonder? It's a dark early morning and I am leading a squad of men across the frozen lake. The stars are out and a necklace of lights glistens on the city shoreline perhaps a kilometre or two away. God forgive me, but at this distance, under the soft cap of Arctic darkness, the seaport of Murmansk looks almost picture postcard.

Our object is the big ice-locked cargo boat before us, an iron monster, victim of the recent Civil War, its plates twisted, its sides patched with frost and rust. Now it squats at a strange angle as if about to slip quietly through the ice.

We climb silently aboard. No cursing, no cries of pain as a frozen hand slips on an icy rail. We are professionals. In the belly of the boat we move, with our pinpoint flashlights, through the studded, steel-plated chambers. The rats terrify me – but I should be more afraid of the splits and twisted rents the bombs have left in the iron decking. It is a few degrees warmer down here and you can hear below us the heave and suck of frozen water. You can smell it too – a strange mix of fuel oil and fish.

We stop and listen. This is life, a Russian policeman's life, at its least edifying. This battered hulk, one of several cargo boats sunk in Lake Polkava by Anarchist air strikes, is inhabited now not only by rats and a dangerous statuary of rusting machinery – but by *children*.

Yes, brothers, we are hunting *children*. In Russia today we have so many orphaned and abandoned children we don't know what to do with them. The whole land is adrift with them, undersized, swaddled figures who live among the ruined areas of our cities or hang around the bus stations and airports, begging, stealing, renting themselves out for a living. The sad flotsam of civil war.

Again, I signal my men to stop. To extinguish lights. I can hear voices. A yellow gleam of lamplight precedes two children, a boy and a girl at the far end of the ship's hold. They pick their way forward. The girl is no more than six; the boy a little more, eight or nine years old. Narrow-shouldered and stunted, he may even be as much as ten. He is holding a tin lantern and he raises it, pausing at the foot of the companionway just in front of us.

I crouch in the darkness at the top of the companionway. I can hear the slosh of sea water below me and I can see my breath rising against the light from the boy's lantern. The six men behind me make no more noise than the rustling of rats.

'What made him come down here?' the little girl asks. She is dressed in rags and large boots. Her blonde hair falls in dirty ringlets.

'He came in out of the wind, fuck your mother,' the boy says. 'There he is, down there at the end.'

The light disappears behind a piece of shattered machinery. We stop at the foot of the companionway. From here I can again see the children. The lantern stands next to the corpse of a man, a tramp, a *clochard*. Yellow light falls on his battered head. The children are crouched as children do. The boy is going through his pockets. The girl is unlacing his boots.

Perhaps the boy has killed him while he slept. Perhaps the man slipped in the darkness and crashed his skull against an outcrop of torn iron or a piece of machinery. The truth is it doesn't matter. We have two more children saved, two more children who might be saved, can possibly be saved.

I switch on my big flashlight, full beam. Two of my men pound and slither forward. The children squeal. In another place, another time, you could see it all as some sort of schoolyard game.

It's afternoon now. A twilit, Arctic afternoon, and the Street Offences Patrol is on the other side of Lake Polkava, this time among lights and music and the smell of roasting reindeer steaks. In the last years, the Murmansk Ice Fair has become famous throughout the Kola Peninsula and even attracts a few Norwegians from across the nearby border. The region has an unusual characteristic. Thanks to the Gulf Stream's magic touch, Murmansk is an ice-free port. But every one of the region's thousand freshwater lakes are frozen solid in winter. For nearly six months of the year a finger of frozen freshwater lake, jutting into the land just below Murmansk, is taken over by coloured tents and every kind of brightly painted, fanciful wooden structure. The sheer ramshackle tackiness of the construction gives it a character all its own. Open-air stages are built for rock concerts. We have a ten-metre-high Leaning Tower of Pisa and London's Big Ben. We have the Statue of Liberty and miniature onion-domed Russian churches. Anton Badanov himself, Governor of Kola Province, initiated the fair. Now its rides and stalls, its music and coloured lights, its droves of mingling whores, its sex parlours and gambling clubs raise revenue for the city coffers. Everything goes: you can play war games with girls dressed as Hitler's generals in a papier mâché dug-out, or violate a nun or two on a gilded altar, to the soaring voices of a convent choir.

Sin City, it's called by all those who disapprove. They see it, not surprisingly, as a sort of vicious Disneyland. In Murmansk we argue fiercely over the rights and wrongs of our winter appendage, but Sin City pays for much that makes life tolerable up here at the frozen edges of the world. Its revenues enable us to run the Lermontov Infirmary, Arctic Russia's best-appointed hospital; they enable Governor Anton Badanov to pay the police and keep rapacious gangsterdom almost at arm's length.

As inspector in charge of Street Offences in District 18, Sin City is my patch. The maintenance of any real order in the City's sprawling, multicoloured alleys is beyond possibility, so my resources are concentrated on the children. If I can save even one child from rape or rent, I'm happy. Or happy enough. What's important in Russia today is to retain the *idea* of a decent future for our kids. Against all likelihood.

This afternoon we'll roll up a good twenty or thirty youngsters under twelve or thirteen. Many of them, with parents who work the fair, will be recognizable by being reasonably well-cared-for. They'll be released. The rest, thin and often diseased, we'll take into custody and ensure they get placed at the American Society's Orphanage on Festival Street. We have a minibus waiting. But for the moment I have sent the men off for a sausage and a warming pepper vodka before we get to work. For a few minutes I am alone.

I take a very deep breath and exhale it, pluming chilled droplets. I look one way, then the other. I hesitate a final moment longer in the narrow alley of coloured tents. Of course I hesitate. I can hardly afford to be seen. But I am driven. Obsessed. I tread furtively, one, two more steps towards the entrance of the tent and the flinchingly gaudy sign above. I glance over my shoulder. What in God's name am I doing here? What am I doing, even thinking about going in?

I go in.

Light strikes my face. 'Come in, come in quickly,' she says. 'That wind's like a knife.'

I enter the tent and let the hanging canvas fall behind me. It is a small space with worn southern carpets on the floor, already black with trodden snow. The light is from a dozen squat scented candles burning in metal holders suspended from a rusted iron chain.

Behind a table fringed with green chenille cloth sits an old woman with the heavy, Asiatic eyes of Uzbekistan. She watches me, drawing on her rolled cigarette until her cheeks collapse inwards, then releasing the smoke in a great cloud around her head.

A low drum thuds a hypnotic beat. I look round, puzzled, until I realize that, below the level of the table, the old lady is tapping with her free hand. For a long moment her dark eyes rest on my face. She is surveying me, mapping my features, working her rubbery lips so that the ash from her cigarette falls about her indiscriminately. The chenille cloth, I notice, carries a scattering of cigarette burns.

'Sit down, your honour,' she says in a voice with an accent of the south.

I sit on the three-legged stool beside her table. In front of me the glass ball picks up the candle flames, concentrating their brightness. The drumbeat stops.

'What do you use?' I ask her. I am trying to take control.

She gestures to the glass ball, to the packs of cards beside it and then to the tattered charts of the heavens that hang on one canvas wall. 'I've no favourites,' she says. 'The ball sometimes. Mostly the cards. And the lines in your hand.' She lays out two cards, face down.

So I'm doing my best, brothers. I'm trying to explain. I'm saying this is how it all began. It was, I believe, at this moment that I stepped or stumbled into the nightmare. At least I date it from this moment. Listen.

'What do you want to know?' she asks me.

I've no answer to that. 'Anything,' I say. 'Everything.'

The old woman smiles. When the wind rises outside, she cocks her head. 'The wind has words for us, too,' she says. She stretches out her hand from within the wide sleeves of yellow and black silk. It is scarred and big-knuckled like a working man's hand. She takes my fingertips and bends them back till it hurts. For a

8

moment she stares down at the lines criss-crossing the palm of my hand. 'A grille on Jupiter,' she murmurs, 'indicates tyranny. You have suffered in the past. In the recent past.'

'In the Civil War who didn't suffer? What Russian didn't?'

She sniffs. With her other hand she begins prodding at the base of my middle finger. 'This is the area of Saturn,' she murmurs. 'Generous phalanges indicate a depth of character, a sense of proportion . . .'

I dip my head to one shoulder. A modest concession to her skills. I suppose it's true I feel I've reached a certain maturity now, as I leave my fourth decade.

'On the other hand,' she says in the same toneless voice, 'a short Saturn signifies imprudence, rashness, an inclination to act on impulse.' She smiles thinly. 'A short Saturn like yours.'

I tell myself she's just a fortune teller, for God's sake.

But she hasn't finished. 'There's more,' she says. 'A grille on Saturn indicates misfortune.'

'I came for the good news,' I said. 'Misfortune?' Instinctively I pull at my hand but she holds on.

'You're afraid to hear?'

I stare her down. Of course I'm afraid to hear. But I have no choice. It's an obsession. I confess it. An unburied fear. 'Afraid? Not at all,' I say in answer to her taunt. 'Of course not.'

'Perhaps your honour does not believe in all this anyway?'

I pull in a quick breath. 'Let's say I've still to be convinced.'

She smiles. 'I see a woman in your life.' A long pause. 'Blonde. Capable. A lawyer maybe. An engineer?'

'My wife's a doctor.'

'There . . .' As if she'd just said so. She looks up at me and purses her lips. 'But something's not quite right. Troubles?' She pauses, staring at me with her black eyes. 'Marital troubles, perhaps?' She pokes the air between us. 'You and your doctor wife?'

'No.' I leave no room for doubt. Natalya, of course, had lost a child last summer. Barely three months pregnant when she slipped and fell, treating the victim of a train crash at Kreshnets. But that's behind us now. 'No troubles.' I shake my head vigorously.

She smirks. 'No ghosts from the past? Very well. But I see troubles still to come.' She pauses melodramatically, a crudely fearful look on her face. 'Danger perhaps.' She turns over the two cards. Ornate pictures that mean nothing to me. 'The cards agree,' she says, her tone firm now. She sits back, staring at a point above my head. 'Another man. A Scorpio, could he be? Shadowy for the moment – weak but passionate, self-willed, demanding . . . Yes, a Scorpio.'

'You see nothing of the sort.' I feel I'm betraying Natalya even by being here.

'I swear I see another man . . . ?'

'No, you don't.' I get up, angry with myself. The stool tips behind me and lies on the wet carpet. 'I'm going.' I pull a roll of roubles from my pocket and count off five. 'You could do a lot of damage with talk like this, old woman,' I say. 'Do you ever think of that?'

'It was your choice, Inspector. You could have stayed away.' The tone was quiet, almost apologetic, but the words were like a slap in the face.

'Inspector? Who told you I was a police inspector?'

'You,' she said. 'Surely?' She looks at me innocently. Deep folds of skin move across her cheeks. A sly smile. 'Of course, I know you don't believe. How can there be anything to it? Cards, glass balls, lifelines . . .' She spreads her brown arms and the yellow and black silk falls away to her wrinkled elbows. 'Here, take your money back. I don't want it.'

I push her hand away. I'm afraid now. 'Tell me,' I say. 'Do you read the cards for yourself?'

She relights the end of her cigarette. I can smell the weed in it. 'It's my living,' she says. 'But understand it? How can anyone understand it? Look . . .' She reaches down and picks up the tarot pack. 'I deal the cards again and this time they read long life and happiness for you and your doctor wife. Who can tell?'

'But do you *believe* it?'

'What else is there?' she asks. 'Even Stalin crossed himself before stepping onto thin ice.' She gets up and is moving me towards the entrance. When she pulls back the hanging canvas, the freezing wind sweeps around my legs. 'If you choose not to believe, I'll not press you.' She pushes the five roubles into my top pocket. 'There, go with God.'

Less than an hour later I am running like a madman along the quayside. Smoke and sudden showers of sparks pour through the darkness to muffle the flashing blue lights of ambulances and police Kamka jeeps.

I stop a blue-uniformed Port Militia sergeant and wave my badge at him. 'What's happening?'

His face is shining with sweat and spattered with black oil spots. 'Ship on fire, Inspector,' he says, pulling his greatcoat collar open and gasping for air.

'A tanker?'

'No, no. A small cargo. Port provision ship. Ten men at most. They've got the crew off. A couple of salvage tugs have attached a line. They're towing it out to sea.'

I run into the thick smoke. Some fire-fighters are being helped back by green-coated paramedics. I can read the words *Lermontov Infirmary* stamped on their backs. I run forward between a jumble of parked ambulances from another hospital. I cross a narrow iron drawbridge connecting two quays. On this side the smoke suddenly seems to thin. I can see the burning ship now, about fifty metres off the dockside, moving slowly away. Steel hawsers smack the water and rise streaming to take the strain again as the invisible tugs, obscured by smoke and dark flames, manoeuvre their burden towards the open sea.

On the quayside five or six men sit against a wall wrapped in blankets. Police and paramedics are attending them. A blonde woman in a green Lermontov overall and blue and white neck scarf is standing apart, watching the ship from the quayside. Her hair is smeared with oil; her hands with blood. I slow down and take the few paces necessary to bring me close. I stand next to her and touch her arm. She turns and reaches up slowly to kiss me on the cheek. 'What are you doing here, Constantin? I thought you'd booked an afternoon at Sin City.' She smiles.

I put my arm round her. 'I heard there was a fire at the docks . . .'

'It could have been worse,' she says matter-of-factly. 'Some oil products stowed on deck exploded. The crew jumped clear. All except one man trapped in the wheel-house.' She pauses. 'I had to amputate his foot.'

My stomach lurches. 'Jesus.'

'It was either that or leave him to die. He took the decision himself.' She looks over her shoulder. The burning ship is moving out past the Portmaster's tower now. Already it is disappearing into the grey of the sea-mist and its own unfurling smoke.

Be honest with me, brothers. Do *you* have days like this?

2

F OLD. LOOP ... PUSH through. Yes ... I step closer to the mirror to examine the result. I like it. Not bad. Not bad for a first black tie without assistance. Maybe less a butterfly than the flapping wings of a dying crow – but a little careful tweaking should deal with that. My day has taken a turn for the better.

The black trousers with the satin stripe fit well. The jacket ... I slip it on and wriggle my shoulders ... fits *really* well. Don't think for a moment that I'm one of those couldn't-care-less Russian dressers. If I borrow a dinner-jacket it should fit. And this does.

I pour a thumb of lemon vodka and carry it to Natalya in the bath. She has twisted up her hair and is about to step out of the steaming water. I hand her the glass.

Her look carries a smile. She stands naked but for the gold chain around her neck. Slowly, she sips her vodka, her eyes on me. 'Well ...' The intonation tells me she approves.

I look back at her. 'Well ...' I echo approval.

While she is dressing I put on a little Gerry Mulligan. California Concerts, *Blues Going Up* ... *A Bark for Barksdale*. I pour myself a thumb and consider the surprise invitation *To Militia Inspector Constantin Vadim and Dr Natalya Vadim from the Governor of the Kola Region*, which stands, gold-embossed, on the mantelshelf. I pick it up and feel the rich stiffness of the card and wonder why we've been invited. To a private dinner at the governor's apartment. A puzzle.

But for the moment I prefer to think of Natalya rising naked from the bath, of the trickle-rivulets that stop and start as they round her breasts and furtively traverse her hips. I take my vodka and cross to the window. A big ore tanker, with lights blazing, moves with infinite slowness across the black water below. Its huge bow swings, inches at a time it seems, into line with an invisible berth. I turn from the window, drumming my fingers to the Gerry Mulligan beat on the satin stripe on my pants. A few jive steps carry me into the centre of the room. Things are not bad, Constantin, I tell myself. Things are going your way.

First and foremost I have put Moscow behind me. That short disastrous episode in the capital is over. I am back in the sprawling, rotting-fish-stink Arctic city where I was born. To be candid, brothers, apart from the fact it's the capital of Kola province, there isn't much to say for Murmansk. We've a football team, Murmansk Dynamo, for whom the last winning match is only preserved in the oral tradition. We've a power station that people talk about in whispers, and a huge, mysterious, eye-watering brown cloud we call Anastasia which hangs permanently just above ground level, ten kilometres to the south of the city. Up river, at the naval port of Sevoromorsk, we have the once mighty Soviet Northern Fleet in mothballs. They say there are up to 150 rusting submarines there, most of which glow in the dark.

Since the Civil War two years ago a hundred thousand people have left the city, voting with their feet against darkness at noon and temperatures to shatter a bottle of vodka. Mostly born southerners, I suspect, from Moscow and Petersburg. Our city is now a half empty shadow of its former self.

But this town is home to me. I love the unrepentant provincialism of the place. I love the cold and the long weeks of darkness in a Kola winter and the surly bad humour of Murmanskers. In a muddled way, I even love Anastasia and Murmansk Dynamo.

So tonight I'm on top form. The Gerry Mulligan is down and dirty the way I like my jazz, and I can hear from the bedroom the seductive rustle of Natalya getting dressed, even catch a waft of the application of foundation or lipstick. Moments like this, I can *feel* my luck is changing. Maybe even the whole desperate, mafia-ridden country's luck is changing, slowly edging round in a new direction like one of those giant ore tankers changing course.

And then suddenly fears, triggered by this wave of optimism, leave my spine tingling with dread. Worse, I remember the toothless fortune teller in the candle-lit tent this afternoon. Naturally, there's nothing to it. I know that as well as the next man. I knew when I entered her tent this afternoon. But, all the same, there's no denying she's left her mark. A shadow, rather, just the slightest sense of unease when I think about her. A shiver, as I said, that passes down the spine.

Of course, I'm more given to such moments than Natalya. She

strides through life, that's the difference. I'm more the soul who pauses and checks the corners, hesitates before an unusually deep, dark doorway.

So you can guess that what might be seen as a second warning, as we left the car that night on the way to the governor's private dinner party, had more effect on me than on Natalya. I had parked my mid-blue Fiat Tolstoy in front of Murmansk's newest and tallest development. The tower itself is the administrative centre for Kola Province, with an undisclosed number of private apartments for our most senior elected dignitaries. And a penthouse in which the governor of the region is housed. As part of the complex we also have the biggest shopping mall north of the Arctic Circle (don't smile, brothers, we compete with Norilsk, northern Siberia and even Fort Yukon, Alaska, here).

I had just stepped out of the car and sniffed the air. The meteo forecast was as bad as it could be but the snow blizzard was still lurking somewhere out at sea. It would be well after midnight, the forecast said, before it struck Murmansk.

Natalya had reached the pavement beside me as I locked the car. We turned and began to cross a forecourt cleared of snow towards the wide smoked-glass doors that rendered the interior of the City Hall lobby warmly obscure and desirable.

Let me just add that, once out of the distinctly modest Fiat, we didn't look like a middle-ranking policeman and his overworked doctor wife. I'd borrowed the dinner-jacket for the occasion from the black-marketeer Vassikin (did I mention that?) and Natalya was looking . . . well, what can a man say about a wife like Natalya?

I saw the black bundle, crouched against the low wall enclosing the forecourt, moments before she did, by training perhaps. I saw it move and rise before us, releasing the sweet stench of poverty. The mouth opened in the grey head and screamed words I didn't fully understand. A long dirty finger pointed in Natalya's face.

The security guard appeared from outside my range of vision. His black gloved hand punched the old man in the chest and, with an explosive screech, the whole reeking bundle of rags fell rolling across the sidewalk. I stopped the security guard as he drew back his foot to kick out and he scowled, diverting his contempt towards me as the tramp scuttled clear.

Natalya had stepped swiftly across to where the old man crouched. Taking a few roubles from her purse she bent quickly, placing the coins in his palm, ignoring the scowl of the security man. It was all over in seconds.

I joined Natalya and we walked hand in hand towards the plate-glass doors. I tried to keep the tremor out of my voice. 'A slow death, he threatened you with,' I said.

'Only if I don't mend my ways.' Natalya took my arm as the door opened and a great waft of warm scented air enclosed us. 'He cursed me for a Jezebel.'

'Is that biblical?' I had enjoyed a Soviet education in my early years. Holy Writ had not figured large.

We entered the mirrored lobby. A uniformed militia sergeant took our topcoats. Trained as he was, he still couldn't resist a quick, swooning glance at Natalya's minimalist black dress. A second sergeant conducted us to a waiting elevator. Holding open the sliding door, he reached forward and pressed an unlabelled button once we had stepped inside.

'Jezebel,' Natalya said as we were borne upwards. 'Phoenician princess. Wife of can't remember who. Got herself a bad name with the scribes for her lap-dancing and general whoring around.' Hitching her skirt high, she kicked a leg in the air, and had just time to let it fall to her knee before the lift door slid open.

This was a good thing. Because we found ourselves facing the wide reception room of the governor's private apartment. The two dozen dinner guests, cocktails in hand, had fallen silent, turning to see which distinguished members of Kola's glitterati the private elevator was delivering next into the bosom of the party.

Within moments Natalya had been drawn away in the midst of a group of admiring middle-aged Americans and Russian business-men. Curiously, I found I enjoyed it. I enjoyed seeing these rich Americans and *racketiry* and local government officials buzz-ing around her. I even enjoyed seeing Osopov, the mayor of Murmansk, virtually an appointee of the governor, his huge neck fatly swollen, bending over her hand.

There were more men than women. A few knots of professional girls sipped drinks and chatted to each other in the corners of the big room. At official receptions like this, discreetly available girls were expected to be provided by the host. They were decoration, like fresh flowers arranged in vases about the room. None of the male guests was paying any attention to them at the moment. But their time would come. It was recognized that at the end of the evening a guest might choose to take one of the hospitality girls home.

For myself I moved about the periphery of the room, dipping into trays of canapés on the polished tables – and accepting glasses of champagne from white-jacketed waiters. In the bright light of the chandeliers, the sly innuendo of the old woman in the dingy tent seemed ridiculous. I was so relaxed I didn't even try to duck away from the matronly figure in the glittering turquoise dress who was bearing down on me.

'You're thinking what a dreadful mob of *racketiry* and war-profiteers the governor has invited to dinner,' she said. She had one hand extended and I took it, about to give my name when she lifted her chin in a pleasantly peremptory gesture to silence me. 'Inspector Constantin Vadim,' she said, 'who made his reputation with the recent murders in Moscow.'

'Who very nearly *lost* more than his reputation with the recent murders in Moscow,' I said.

'And I am Mariya Badanova. One-time Soviet swimming champion. Bronze medallist at the Montreal Olympics, although you'd hardly think so now.'

One-time Olympic swimming champion – and currently the governor's wife. I produced my faint bow of acknowledgement. The American actor Cary Grant is my model here.

'*I*,' Madame Badanova said, with a pout of her heavily lipsticked lips, 'am the reason you're here tonight. My husband didn't tell you that?'

'No, madame,' I said, puzzled.

'I chose you for your looks of course, Constantin. That was the first consideration.'

This floored me. It floored Cary Grant too.

'It was bound to be, in the circumstances,' she said with a kittenish movement of the heavy shoulders which made her bare upper arms shudder. 'Was it not?'

Many Russian women are known to be insatiable, to suffer from a sort of female priapism. 'The first consideration? I'm not sure I understand.' I knew my smile looked fixed in place.

She smiled back at me and massaged the lines in her neck. 'I'm embarrassing you, Constantin.'

'You're mystifying me, madame,' I said cautiously.

Then suddenly she laughed. 'Oh my God!' She threw her arms wide and the great bosom lifted towards me. 'Of course! He hasn't spoken to you yet. My husband hasn't even broached the subject.'

'Not a word.'

'So you thought this roll-necked old bird was aiming for a quick peck at your vitals.'

'You're embarrassing me *now*, madame,' I said, more at ease than I was a moment ago.

She took my arm. 'Let's get ourselves another glass of champagne. You must sit next to me at dinner. My husband will demand he sits next to your sparkling wife.'

'But I still don't know what I've been selected for. Are you going to tell me?'

'I must leave Anton to tell you in his own time. I'll just say that there were two candidates put forward. You were by far the most beautiful so I persuaded my husband to see you first. Until he does, let's just get drunk and flirt a little. Use your imagination, Constantin. Narrow your eyes until the vision blurs. Think of me as a slender young creature forty or fifty years my junior.'

I liked him a good deal less than I liked her. He was short, beak-nosed, with shaved hair above his ears and a thick, curly black topknot. He had once been a military man, an armchair air-general in the late Civil War while his wife had kept on their thriving business making uniforms for the Nationalist Army. Today his cheap Texas-Badanov brand of jeans dressed a large part of the working male population of Murmansk. Yet the essential Governor Badanov was a politician. Looked like, dressed like, spoke like one – though the word was that he was basically honest. And in Russia today honest politicians should be prized like buttercups in an Arctic spring.

'I start from the proposition that this city is bleeding to death,' he said, striding to the great window that lined one wall. We were in the library, away from the other guests. 'Come here, Inspector. Look across the river at those tower blocks up on the hills and tell me what strikes you.'

'North Bay? They're all empty.' I looked out at the dark towers of concrete rising towards the bright stars. 'The people have left.'

'Exactly. It's my ambition to rejuvenate the city,' he said. 'Rome was built on seven hills, did you know that?'

'I seem to have read it somewhere, sir.'

'Count those hills out there, Vadim. Seven, you make it seven?'

'More or less,' I said, staring out at the clusters of tower blocks on the surrounding hills.

'It's an omen, Vadim. As capital city of the reborn province of Kola, Murmansk will rise again. Lights will shine afresh from those dark hills. At the moment Kola has untold mineral wealth – and less than half a million people.'

'I think change is on the way, Governor. My impression is that we have Americans flooding in, businessmen and engineers . . .'

'Vultures,' he said brusquely.

'I thought you'd said publicly that we need all the American help we can get.'

'Not help, Vadim, *aid*. We need all the American *aid* we can get. We'll accept a limited number of their engineers and advisers, but we must remember we are Russians. It is we who come from the superior culture, is it not?'

I thought about that. 'Frankly,' I said, 'I'm not sure our twentieth century culture is much of an example to anyone, Governor.'

'You're not one of these Westernizers are you? Ready to open the floodgates to an American low-class tide of rubbish? Is it true that some of our citizens are already beginning to call the province *Koka*-Kola?'

'I think there's some pride in the idea we've attracted so much attention from across the Atlantic.'

'I won't have it, Vadim. Koka-Kola? It's outrageous. You policemen should be ready to stamp on the term whenever you hear it.'

He turned and walked towards a side-table. 'Now, to the matter in hand. An unusual task, you might think . . . His tone had changed abruptly. 'In selecting someone for this task, an ability to speak English was the prime consideration.' He poured us both after-dinner brandies. That wasn't, of course, quite what his wife had said but I smiled encouragement. He looked up, his heavy grey eyebrows raised. 'I understand you speak the language exceptionally well.'

'I studied languages at university, Governor Badanov. English and French. I then did a special radio-surveillance course in idiomatic American-English during my Navy service.'

He nodded towards the phone. 'I want you to take the next call that comes through,' he said. 'It will be a video call from Moscow.' He didn't seem about to tell me any more.

He handed me the brandy. I sniffed in the way universally considered appreciative and allowed my eyes to wander over the leather-bound fake books that covered the walls. But my mind was on the phone call.

We seemed to have little more to say to each other until the call came through. I followed him to the big window and again looked down on the city but he had nothing to add to his vision of rejuvenation.

Murmansk, I have to say, is not a city that lends itself easily to the idea of rejuvenation. The Gulf Stream, as I've said, ensures our sea waters steam gently even in the depths of a polar winter when all the freshwater lakes around us are frozen solid. Built on the right bank of the Kola river twenty kilometres from the sea, today the city is a Stalinist mass of cracked concrete buildings sliced through by wide boulevards like the Lenin Prospekt, now called Union Street. We have myriad problems of which depopulation is only one. Pollution is certainly another, not the mildly inconvenient pollution the West worries about but the deadly, invisible pollution left by Soviet nuclear profligacy. Vodka is yet another of our problems, always present, seldom dwelt upon. And then there are our tribes of abandoned children, but those you know something about already.

When the phone rang, I jumped. He nodded to me and I crossed to pick up the receiver. The screen in front of me jerked in a frazzle of grey lines. A woman's voice said in English: 'Inspector Vadim?'

'Speaking.'

'My name is Cunningham. Abby Cunningham. Governor Badanov will vouch for my credentials as an agent of the United States Federal Bureau of Investigation.'

I turned to the governor. 'I have a woman speaking English here . . .'

'An American FBI officer.' He smiled broadly, pleased that his chess-play seemed to be working out. 'Very senior. She's just taking over as Head of FBI at the American Embassy in Moscow.'

I turned back to the phone. The bottom part of the screen resolved and a woman's hand became visible, long fingers, tastefully beringed and a pale coffee-brown colour. 'I can only see from the wrists down,' I said. 'Is there a body attached?'

'There's a body attached,' she said flatly. 'The ass is the same colour as the hands.'

The screen clicked and filled with a smoothly dark-skinned young woman in a cream-coloured suit seated behind a desk. She had a sharp European nose and a well-shaped African mouth. Her black hair was smooth and slightly curled but held in a chignon which I didn't see until she leaned forward to rest on her elbows and clasp her hands. She didn't need her horn-rimmed spectacles or the American flag behind her to look imposing.

'You're full screen now, Miss Cunningham,' I told her.

'Agent Cunningham,' she said briskly. The screen lightened and her skin with it to a mid-honey colour. 'Captain Vadim,' she said.

'Yes.'

'Are you ready?'

'For all I know,' I said. I glanced quizzically towards the governor.

'Please complete the American expression,' she glanced down at a pad on the desk, 'it's the squeaky wheel . . .'

'. . . that gets the grease,' I said without thinking.

'What's the boodle?'

'The loot?'

'A high-five?'

'A salute. Sporty.'

'Where are you if you're in your seventh heaven?'

'Wherever I am,' I said, 'I'm having a whale of a time.'

She almost smiled, lips pursed. 'Not bad, Captain. Tell the governor we're checking the other details. But on language you pass muster.' She rang off and her picture faded.

I put down the phone and turned back to the governor. 'She asked me to tell you I passed.'

'Good.' He sucked in his bottom lip, released it and looked up at me. Pleasure loosened his facial muscles into a slow smile. Whatever it was – I could feel this was it. 'You've heard about the rumours, of course.'

'The whole of Murmansk is awash with rumours, Governor,' I said. I had heard nothing.

'Remember what we were talking about, Vadim. Not help – Aid.' He looked at me with undisguised satisfaction. 'The visit of the American Trade Mission is one of the most important events in the modern history of Murmansk.'

'It must be.' Historically, I knew the competition wasn't intense.

He lurched forward. With every gesture, every clenching and unclenching of his hands, he exuded energy and determination. 'We're fortunate in having this insoluble nuclear waste problem.

As a province, Inspector, we stand every chance of Kola being designated a Special Aid Region.'

'And that means buckets of American aid.'

He frowned at my terminology, not at the idea. 'A great deal will undoubtedly flow our way,' he conceded gravely. 'And to the position of Governor, a special aid designation for Kola will bring a new respect among all other regional governors in Western Russia.'

Meaning Kola had beaten its rivals to the trough. I nodded encouragement.

'All this . . .' He struck another pose, frowning, hurt even. 'All this depends on the clearing-up of a certain matter. A brief investigation and a report. That's all I'll be asking of you.' He walked quickly to the door and left the room. I stood in the middle of the broad Scandinavian-weave carpet, staring at the closed door. Had the interview ended? Was a certain decisive abruptness the essence of Governor Badanov's executive style? Or was he coming back to tell me more?

I paced along the blue-and-yellow-patterned edges of the carpet like a schoolboy kicking leaves. It was almost five minutes before the door opened again to allow the governor to usher in a middle-aged couple, both tall and with a sleek, well-cared-for look.

'I don't know if you've met?'

We all smiled and shook our heads politely.

'Very well. This is Mr Miles Bridger, the American consul in Murmansk, a very good friend to the Kola region. And the beautiful Mrs Bridger.'

'Please call me Isobel,' she said straight away and I think I detected an English accent there.

'And this, Mr Bridger, is the militia officer we discussed to help us in this little matter.'

'Good to meet you Vadim,' Bridger said. 'It won't surprise you to know we're depending on you.'

I liked the smooth, grey hair, the slim, fit build and the generally unhurried ease of the man. *He* didn't have to check the fit of his dinner-jacket. In seven or eight years' time I might have to desert Cary Grant and take on Miles Bridger as a role model. 'The governor mentioned an investigation and report,' I said.

While Isobel Bridger lifted her hand to decline, Bridger accepted a mimed offer of brandy from Badanov. 'Let me fill you in, Inspector,' he said. 'Beginning this month we have a change of Head of FBI in Moscow. Old Charles Fearless was a lazy time-server but he knew his Russians.'

'You make us sound like a special breed of dog, Consul,' I said.

'I'm sorry.' He laughed. 'No. God forbid. Charlie was an admirer, as I am, of all things Russian. Totally devoted to fighting the Russian corner. But things may be somewhat different with the new head of section?' He raised his eyebrows.

'Special Agent Abby Cunningham.'

'Yes. New broom and all that sort of thing. Her colour, of course, makes her even more anxious to succeed.'

'Does it?'

He flicked his eyes towards me in quick appraisal, then continued. 'Cast your eyes over this.' He drew a folded paper from his pocket and handed it to me. I began to read it as the governor poured his brandy. It was an FBI report on a number of unidentified girl children found dead in various parts of the United States, all with a pale green K tattooed on the shoulder.

'It's a tragic story, isn't it?' Isobel said. 'Spread across the USA. And they simply don't know when they'll find the next one.'

'What does it mean to you?' the governor said, his head inclined towards me.

'As I'm sure Mr Bridger knows, there are many children's penal colonies sited up here on the Kola Peninsula. It's always been a favourite place for Moscow to hide away its unsavoury activities.'

The governor frowned. The consul looked embarrassed. I wasn't making a hit here.

'There is absolutely no reason to connect these children to Kola,' Badanov said with great firmness.

'Except we use a tattooed K on the upper arms of both children and adult prisoners.'

'But isn't it equally the case, Inspector,' Bridger said reasonably, 'that the same system is used in camps in Krasnoyarsk, Kolyma and a dozen other places in Russia beginning with K.'

'Perfectly true,' I agreed.

'Good.' Governor Badanov took centre stage, striding the room like a bantam cock. 'So give us an investigation making clear that the K tattoo could come from any of a dozen areas of Russia – if Russian at all. An investigation emphasizing that our region has had no child escapees in the last five-year period. Print the official statistics to back it up. Give us a summary that says the children were most probably runaways from American Red Cross orphanages in the United States – and are more likely to come, originally, from a less well-run penal area than Kola.'

I was frowning. The governor hadn't noticed but Miles Bridger had.

'The governor's suggesting a general line of attack,' Bridger said earnestly. 'This is categorically not just a rubber stamp we're looking for.'

He didn't know Russians as well as he thought.

'You are to be taken off Street Offences,' the governor said, 'and given your own office staff straight away. Select your ten best men to join you.'

'Governor Badanov . . .'

He silenced me with a look. 'You'll be working in this building, with your office on the floor below. Which is why my wife insisted on a certain type of man. No bull-necked creatures hanging around all day, she specified.' He looked me over. 'You look personable enough to me, nothing out of the ordinary, but nothing that a decently fitting tuxedo wouldn't put right.' He ignored my glare. 'My wife assures me you're an attractive man. Your militia speciality is in the children's department. You speak English. So be it.'

At last he sensed my reaction. Very slowly he lifted the brandy to his lips, watching me over the glass. 'Well, Inspector?'

'Governor Badanov, this is an honour.'

The appalling treatment my country hands out to its children is something I live with in my job every day. But what we were talking about here was a rubber-stamp inquiry, despite the American's assurance that they were looking for more. This inquiry was aimed at a quick cover-up, so that the American aid that the governor was looking forward to should not dry up in an open inquiry into the substandard children's camp conditions on Kola. There was no alternative but to put it to him, quick and blunt. 'I'm sorry, Governor Badanov, but I'm not your man.'

He stood back in surprise at my undiplomatic directness. Miles Bridger pretended to study a porcelain figure of Pushkin on a side-table. He lifted it, turned it in his hand and set it down again. His back to the governor, he gave me a quick wry smile. He wasn't surprised I'd turned down the job. Isobel Bridger was picking lint from the sleeve of her green silk dress. They both knew, despite

Bridger's insistence, that I was being asked for a rubber stamp. Their expressions were saying I don't blame you if you turn the job down.

For the moment the governor said nothing. 'We must look towards our own futures,' Badanov said pointedly. 'Do you have children?'

I shook my head. What else was I to do? What else to tell him? That I once had a child? May still have a child for all I know. A boy, Mischa, disappeared among the flood of abandoned children in the Civil War. 'No, sir,' I lied.

'But you're an ambitious man, Inspector, are you not?'

And how can you answer that question in a line and a half? Such a question goes to the heart of morality. Are you ambitious enough to steal, to take bribes, to kill? Are you ambitious enough to lie, to dissemble, to sleep with your mother-in-law? What do any of us know until the moment is presented to us? Ambition is a big number. Like the fool I am, I began to quote George Eliot. '"There is a great deal of unmapped country within each of us . . ."'

'Yes, yes.' The governor cut me short. 'For some reason, you think rounding up street urchins in Sin City is more rewarding than ensuring that Kola will be designated a Special Aid Region. So be it.' He glared at me and nodded briskly towards the door. I was dismissed.

Yet there was, as I left the inner office at a little after midnight, a certain glow of triumph and good brandy about me, despite the way I had bungled things in the governor's study. Writing whitewash reports was not for me. Natalya would be pleased I'd turned him down.

I was moving through the dinner-jackets and satin dresses looking for her when Mariya Badanova, the governor's wife, came up to me. 'Your beautiful lady has just been called away, Constantin. Her pager sounded from the hospital a few minutes ago. An emergency.'

'Did she say where?'

'No. She asked me to apologize to the governor. And to tell you not to expect her back until morning.'

'I don't know what's worse,' I said. 'To be a doctor's husband. Or a policeman's wife.'

'Perhaps these absences make the heart grow stronger,' Madame

Badanova fluttered her eyelashes. 'Before you leave to go home to your empty bed, share a nightcap with me, Constantin.'

'Gladly,' I said. As we crossed the room I noticed the hospitality girls were no longer in a gaggle by themselves. There were plenty of men with them now. Men stood with their hands round their waists or shoulders, staking out their claim for later. The governor of Kola knew how to throw a modern party.

'I still have to thank you,' I said to Madame Badanova, 'for putting my name forward to the governor, but . . .' I was wondering how to tell her that I'd turned the job down. Or been turned down.

'I only hope you'll want to thank me in a month's time,' she broke in. 'You're entering Kola politics, my dear Constantin. There'll be plenty of knives out seeking broad backs like yours.' She ran the palm of her hand across my back. 'Look on me as a friend,' she said. 'You won't find too many others at court.'

'Madame Badanova,' I coughed apologetically. 'I said no.' I gestured towards the governor's study. 'I turned down the job. Or perhaps I made it clear I wasn't the man your husband was looking for. Either way he'll be looking for someone else.'

Her features broke into a broad and surprised smile. 'Really?'

'Really.'

'I'm sorry, Constantin, because it would have meant you'd be about a lot. I'm sure he made you a tempting offer? And possibly a few mild threats about your future if you declined the job, if I know my husband. So I'm doubly impressed.'

She had not seen my fumbling performance. She glanced down. 'Sometimes, to say no takes real balls.' Smiling, she made a grasping gesture with her right hand.

Mariya Badanova was not everyone's idea of a high official's wife.

3

O NLY IN THE lift going down did it occur to me to wonder if Natalya had taken the Fiat. In fact, when I got outside City Hall and stood absorbing the first blast of tooth-cracking cold, I found myself looking straight at an official car with a uniformed sergeant driver holding open the door for me.

Sitting in the back of the big comfortable Mercedes as the bright lights of Pushkin Boulvar moved steadily past, I could easily imagine myself in some Western city. The whores adopted the Amsterdam shop-window approach here. It was too cold, until at least the month of July, to parade the streets. Mercedes and even the occasional Rolls-Royce were parked outside the clubs and restaurants. The windows of the clothes shops with French or Italian names glittered with displays of lifelike models wearing outrageously expensive clothes. Groups of foreign businessmen, with their uniformed militia escorts to protect them against casual mugging, moved from bar to bar to assess the drink and girls.

Here in the car, I am momentarily part of that world. The reminder that I am driving through Murmansk and not Oslo or Helsinki comes not so much from the shop-window hookers, but with the big rebuilt 1950s open-topped American cars that cruise past us – pink, purple or electric blue and open-topped despite the intense cold. Their occupants, five or six men usually, wear their trade-mark black furs and explode champagne bottles directed at the feet of passers-by. These men are the enforcers, employed even by respectable firms as a 'legal department' to exact payment or delivery of promised goods. Lacking a law of contracts, the wheels of Russian commerce would not turn without them.

Affluence *à la Russe*. But affluence, I suppose, all the same. Governor Badanov would defend it as a necessary stage in Russia's slow climb to a decent society. Perhaps. And certainly I can feel how easy it is, with the sweet-smelling leather of the Mercedes enclosing me, to forget the world I work in. The world of deserted children, of sleeping rough in capsized ships or half-ruined buildings, of stealing or selling yourself to live. The gaudy, painted world of Sin City.

The blizzard that the meteo predicted hit us five minutes after Pushkin Boulvar, moving in on the city with ominous speed. Snow squalls rushed at the car from every angle. Gusts shook and rattled the goose-neck lighting stands along the roadside. A hoarding flapped from a high wall at one corner and I watched it rip off, float through the air, buckle and land like a crashing plane in the roadway.

I got my driver sergeant to drop me off at the entrance to the underground car park of our apartment block. Letting myself through the protective grille, I walked down the steep slope towards the double line of parked cars. I saw that my blue Fiat was now parked in the empty space reserved for Natalya's hospital Kamka jeep. This is our usual practice if she receives a call when we are out together. She takes the car home and switches it for her much more sturdy jeep.

I stopped to check that Natalya had locked the doors of the Fiat (and she had) and continued up the narrow concrete staircase to the lobby of the Gorshkov Tower. From there, I rode up to our tenth-floor apartment and let myself in.

In the hallway I stood a moment as the heat seeped into me. My thoughts were for Natalya, plucked at by the wind, under powerful blue emergency lights as she tried to work in a mess of blood and ice and torn metal. Major accidents on the main Murmansk–Kanevka highway happen almost every other day in severe weather conditions like these.

It's a thought I put aside. There's nothing I can do with it except worry and fret. I take off my coat. I am drawn to the bookcase. A line of militia college books I hardly ever consult now. *Alcohol and Crime Statistics in Provincial Russia. Serial Homicides in Russia Today.* But I am not looking for the crime manuals. Behind them, there's a small volume of astrology that I keep hidden. Natalya would not approve, would laugh rather and divert me with a hand slid down my trouser front. I flick through the pages. Scorpio, I'm looking for. Here we are. Born in the cold month between October and November's end, the lunar Scorpio, moon mad, a prey to secret lusts. I can feel my eyes bulge. A Beast ruled by Pluto, lord of the Underworld. But wait, philosophical too, with, often enough, a deep experience of life's problems . . . That's better. So, it's a mixed bag. From my magnanimous Leonine birth-date I tend to look down on such unfortunates.

I put the book away and notice, for the first time, that the green light on the phone is signalling messages. Three. One from Fanya, a colleague of Natalya's, one irate wrong number – and one from Roy Rolkin: 'Costya, my old friend. How are you? Why is it so hard these days to get to talk to you?'

I move to erase the message but for some reason don't and stand, lips pursed, hearing it through. 'We're still friends, aren't we?' the gravelly voice goes on. 'Of course we are. Nothing can alter that. Nothing. We knocked salmon on the head together before we were ten years old. No, we're not friends, fuck your mother, we're brothers, blood brothers and always will be—'

I switch off there. Roy Rolkin drunk is not what I want tonight. Long reminiscences of our childhood and teenage years together are always precipitated by vodka – or whatever he drinks in exile in Budapest. And tonight, I could hear the slur in his voice. Tonight he was very drunk. I wipe the tape.

I shall have to tell you about Roy. I think he must be down on his luck because he's been calling me a lot lately. Natalya can't stand him. Puts the phone down when he calls. And I understand why. Roy is the sort of friend most people would sooner *not* have. In the very bad old days, a secret policeman with a certain flair for the black arts of his profession, Roy made general before backing the wrong power group at the very end of the Civil War. Now he lives in exile under a false name and runs a small football team in Budapest. And when he's very drunk or very homesick, he rings me.

I slept badly that night. I'm not claiming it was any sort of premonition – or perhaps I am, I don't know. But when I awoke sometime after seven, I stretched my hand out quickly across the bed. Before I'd opened my eyes I knew that Natalya was not there.

I got up and put some coffee on. Of course it had happened before. A dozen times or more. A late-night emergency that carried on into the early hours of the next morning.

I dressed in jeans and a sweater and went down to the lobby to collect a copy of the *Kola Pravda*. I was back in the apartment drinking a glass of tea as it struck eight. It's a small two-bedroom apartment, and I sat with the living-room door open to give me a clear view through into the hall. I didn't want to miss that first sight of her at the front door.

I was conscious of the clock ticking the moments away, conscious of having part of my mind on the sound of Natalya's key in the lock. I read a lead story about the governor of the Rostov region being found dead from an overdose. That would mean another election. Rostov's third in two years.

In today's Russia elections are our new tyranny. The *racketiry*, the mafia as it's called in the West, has discovered democracy pays. To be mayor of a big city, or better still a regional governor, can be more profitable than striking oil. Thus elections proliferate. They are fought over with ferocity, the results contested on every excuse. Here on the Kola Peninsula judicious citizens have elected our middle-of-the-road Governor Badanov and have the good sense to reject any attempt to eject him. Perhaps he elevates his nephews, perhaps he revels in fine official automobiles and aspires to a personal protection squad, but he is not *plundering* the citizens. So, with what revenue we are able to collect from the gold and nickel mines on the peninsula, and the Sin City rents that flow as steadily as the Kola river, Murmansk is not doing too badly. It pursues the middle way. And all without an election since the one that brought in Anton Badanov at the end of the Civil War.

At ten past eight I put the paper down, lifted the phone, began to dial the Lermontov Infirmary number, then stopped, the fingers of my right hand splayed like a pianist's over the keys. Natalya says I worry too much.

I put down the phone, stared at it, picked it up again and dialled. The hospital answered quickly enough. I asked for the emergency unit. 'I'm Constantin Vadim,' I said.

'Dr Vadim's husband.'

'The same. The emergency last night. Where was it?'

As the silence extended on the other end of the line, the sickness deepened in my stomach. 'Emergency?'

'The emergency call-out. About midnight. For Christ's sake, you must have a record there.'

'Emergency,' the girl repeated. 'There wasn't one.'

'You're sure? Nothing?'

'The street patrols brought in the usual quota of drunks and homeless. Mostly hypothermia cases from North Bay.'

'But there was no surgical emergency?'

'No.' I could hear the rustling of papers. 'Surgical last night was remarkably clear. Six or seven slip-on-ice broken limbs. Five domestics, women with jaws to be reset, that sort of thing . . . Three shootings, Dead on Arrivals. There, Inspector. A quiet Saturday night in the city of Murmansk. Or at least our part of it. No call-outs. As I say, quiet night.'

'Listen,' I said. 'The surgical unit was called out last night. My wife was paged.'

At the other end of the line there was a long pause. 'Dr Weber was on surgical last night, Inspector. I have the night report in front of me. He signed it off as incident-free at six thirty this morning. I can't see why Dr Vadim would have been called out anyway.'

I could. Peter Weber was almost seventy. Scrambling about in freezing temperatures while they cut somebody out of a truck which had jackknifed on the Murmansk–Kanevka highway was not something a dispatcher would ask him to do. 'OK, thank you,' I said to the girl. 'Just tell me: who was the dispatcher last night?'

'I can't say, Inspector. But he won't be here until six this evening. Dispatcher shifts are six to six.'

When I rang off I walked slowly into the kitchen and made myself some coffee. I really had drunk too much last night. I could feel it in my head. I cleaned the small glass coffee-pot. So last night's dispatcher knew Dr Weber wasn't up to this particular emergency and decided to call out Natalya instead, then had problems deciding whether to enter the call . . . I poured boiling water into the coffee-pot. But there'd been emergencies in the past that Weber couldn't handle and Natalya had gladly covered for him. All officially recorded. Then again, perhaps the dispatcher was new and didn't know that.

Obviously that was the way it was. I stared down at the clear water in the pot. I had forgotten to put in the coffee.

4

T HE RULE BOOK says that for senior inspectors Sunday is a day
of rest, but the rule book says a lot of things. Half an hour
later I drew up at the series of portable offices, arranged like a fort
in Indian territory, which made up our Station 18 offices in Sin
City. I stamped the snow off my feet as I climbed the temporary
wooden steps to Reception and pushed at the swing door. Sergeant
Bubin, heavy, good-natured and smelling of fried onions, was just
coming off Saturday night shift. 'I put them in Interview 3, Chief,'
Bubin said.

'Do we have names?'

He shook his head. 'She calls the boy Borya. I don't think he
calls her anything. No papers of course. No ages. Maybe they
don't even know their family names.'

'If they've been on the streets for a year or two,' I said, 'why
should they? The girl's hardly more than a baby.'

Bubin had taken the necessary precaution of locking the two
children in. When I let myself into the bare room they were
sitting on the floor playing fivestones with bits of hard, inedible
biscuit. The rule book also says that children cannot be interviewed
unless an adult woman is present. I asked Bubin if any of the
station militia women were free. He shook his head. 'But there's
a volunteer on the way from the Orphanage,' he said.

I nodded and closed the door behind me. Leaning against the
wall I watched the children, the boy perhaps about nine, the girl
maybe six or even younger. Somehow they already looked more
like real children than they had yesterday in the dark belly of a
cargo ship.

It is 2017, one hundred years since the Communist Revolution
which was to bring Russia social justice. To me it seems that the
achievements of that centenary here in Kola can be seen in the fact
that we have become the land of children's work camps, a sad and
brutal Children's Gulag buried up here in the silent north.

Found guilty of theft (often enough, to eat), or of being without care and protection, a euphemism for homeless, there is little chance of escape from the isolated frozen camps on the Kola Peninsula. But, before they are tattooed with the system's green K, many children snatch back their freedom on the long journey up from Moscow or Petersburg or in transit from train to truck in the marshalling yards of Murmansk. Then they live free, but more like animals than humans, often enough in the alleys of Sin City and the ruined tower blocks of the North Bay. A frighteningly high percentage have already contracted disease, diptheria or even Aids. But then tuberculosis, in the children's penal colonies, is endemic.

My official task is to sweep these children out of sight. Privately, my task, as I see it, is to pluck a few children a week out of this inhuman system and install them in the American Orphanage on Festival Street.

So that oddly enough, *anonymity* is what I hope for the children the Street Offences Patrol picks up in Sin City. If they refuse to give their names and have no papers, they can't be identified and I'm not obliged to hand them to the penal authorities for whom they were undoubtedly destined. This gives us the opportunity to provide them with new papers and, hopefully, a new life through the American funded orphanage where Natalya sits on the committee.

The two children had barely looked up at me before going on with their game. The girl weighed the five pieces of biscuit carefully then threw them in the air, turning the palm down to catch the pieces on the back of her splayed hand. But the fingers were too tiny to retain more than one or two pieces. As they fell back to the floor she screeched an oath fit for a barrack-room.

I drew up a chair, and moved the water-jug so that I had an unimpeded view of them. They had been washed and given clean clothes. They were lucky. Neither carried the grey pallor of TB. The girl's hair shone under the bare interview-room light. The boy's face was clean, his hair cut. I knew both recognized me as their captor. 'Where do you come from?' I asked them.

The boy turned his back, scooping the pieces of biscuit, throwing and catching all five on the back of his hand.

'We're going to find a place for you to live.' I said. 'There'll be a lot of other children there. It's called an orphanage.'

'I've been to one. I know what they do to you at orphanages.'
He made an obscene gesture.

'This is different,' I said. 'You'll be treated decently.'

The boy snorted, throwing, and catching on the back of his hand,
all the five pieces of biscuit several times in quick succession.

'You know you can be charged with what you were doing down
in the ship?'

The boy looked deliberately blank.

'Robbing a dead body.'

'I've got a fistful of charges against me already, Chief,' he said.
'What's one more?' He flicked his hand and the pieces of biscuit
rattled against the wall. The girl looked at him in blue-eyed
admiration.

'Where are you from?'

'Petersburg,' he said. 'Where else?'

'So you were sentenced there for some sort of offence and sent up
here to serve your time. How did you escape from the boxcars?'

'The men came and broke the locks on the outside . . .' He
was talking about the violent drunks who roam the marshalling
yards. 'They tried to grab the older girls. The rest of us ran
like rats.'

'Listen, if you don't want to be sent to labour camp,' I said,
'don't give anybody your family name. Say you've forgotten it.
Say you've lived rough for years.'

'For the militia, he's not bad,' the boy said to the girl.

The truth is, brothers, I live for such small moments of recognition. I had made some contact. 'Now, are you hungry?'

They were suddenly children again, nodding in unison. There's
something marvellous about children, something direct and honest.
You ask them if they're hungry and it drives every other thought
from their minds.

I turned to the door and unlocked it. I had it half open when I
felt a sharp pain in the back of my leg. I was down on my back
before I identified it as a kick. Skull cracking on the metal-ribbed
floor, I stared up, mouth open.

I heard the girl squeal in excitement as I lifted my head to
speak, saw the lip of the water-jug tip and suddenly I was choking,
retching, gasping for breath.

I rose spluttering, coughing water, hearing, beyond all the noise
I was making, the scamper of two pairs of feet down the corridor.
I rubbed water from my eyes as the footsteps skittered across

Reception and I hawked water from deep in my throat as the outer door screeched open and slammed shut.

I was sitting at the table playing knuckle-bones with broken biscuits as the woman from the Orphanage arrived. Fanya Karpova was an old friend of Natalya's, a surgeon colleague who worked with her on the Orphanage committee in her spare time. She had obviously heard the story from someone in the front office. 'I find it hard not to laugh,' Fanya said, her mouth working to cover her grin. 'Downed by a nine-year-old boy. Whooa!'

'It was a vicious, underhand kick,' I said. 'He knew just where to place it. In any case there were two of them.'

Fanya nodded gravely. 'Of course. Two to one. The odds were stacked against you, Constantin.' She nodded towards my knee. 'You want me to take a look at the leg?'

I grunted a refusal and flipped the pieces of biscuit onto the back of my hand. They all tumbled off.

She sat down. We lost so many children, from dormitory windows, through narrow holes in orphanage fences, that both of us knew it would be sheer hypocrisy to make a fuss about two more.

'I'm sorry they called you out,' I said. 'Did you just get home?' Fanya was a junior doctor on Natalya's surgical team.

She looked blank.

'Last night's emergency,' I said. 'Standing in for old Dr Weber.'

Her back straightened. 'I didn't get a call.'

'You didn't?'

'No. In any case, I'd signed myself off. I'd just done twenty hours straight. What time was this call?'

'Natalya was bleeped just after midnight. I thought it must have been something big, something that took the whole team because she's not back yet.'

'Check with Weber. That must be it.'

'Sure.' I didn't say the Lermontov dispatcher had no record of anyone standing in.

She stood up. 'I'll be getting back home.' She was looking down at me. Her tongue clicked twice. 'Are you worried about something, Constantin?'

'No.'

'Something about Natalya. Something you're not telling me?'

'No. Of course not.'

She wouldn't let go. 'You're sure?'

'No. Of course not,' I said again. I got up and flexed my leg.

'Are you worried because she stayed out all night?' She lifted her eyebrows to make a joke of it.

'For Christ's sake, Fanya,' I said. 'It was a hospital call. To her pager.'

'I was joking,' she said. 'Of course I was joking.' She smiled.

I grunted acknowledgement. I was never entirely happy with Fanya's sense of humour.

'Listen,' she said. 'You want to stop off for a coffee somewhere? We can talk about it.'

I shook my head. 'Thanks, Fanya, but there's nothing to talk about.' I looked across the empty room at the bare scratched wall. 'Anyway, I have to get back to make breakfast for Natalya.'

Back home I called old Dr Peter Weber and got my head bitten off by his wife. The doctor had been on duty all night. He would be sleeping until lunch-time. Call him after one o'clock. I switched on the television to see if there was any local news of a medical emergency. Instead, the coverage was all for Governor Badanov as he toured the city announcing the coming visit of the American Mission. Thanks to his efforts, Badanov was saying, Murmansk would become one of the Russian cities eligible for funding from the American ERA, the Environmental Relief Agency. Dollars.

Then we swung into *Kola Round-up* and I sat glassy-eyed, in something close to a trance. This is the sort of time when my tinnitus hisses quietly in the background, an inducement to sleep. I dozed and woke to hear that something grim had happened in a nickel mine at Trelov; that Katerina Somebody had again taken first place in the floodlit skating competition at Silova and the winning catch had mysteriously slid back down the hole in an ice-fishing competition at Sin City. I got up and switched off.

Restlessness seized me by the collar. From the kitchen window at the side of the building I could crane my neck and look down ten floors to where a blue and white hospital Kamka jeep might pull over to turn into the garage. During the next twenty minutes I stood at that window as many times. I looked back down the road and counted off vehicles coming round the bend. She'll be in the next ten. The next twenty. The next thirty.

I put on boots, topcoat and fur hat and went out. There was a bar where I sometimes spent a spare few minutes on the edge of the port area, an interesting enough place for me where whores and foreign seamen from the International Seamen's Club provided most of the custom. I used it a lot to keep my English up to scratch. It was nothing much in the way of appointment. A corner shop in a Fifties development which had long ago begun to crumble. Soviet cement has not proved too durable against northern temperatures. Inside, the bar had a bare wooden floor blackened with snow that had been trodden in, a little dim light and comfortless Fifties furniture. This early in the morning it was almost empty. A glassy-eyed British merchant seaman was telling an Indian colleague how his grandfather had sailed in convoys from Liverpool to Murmansk during the Great Patriotic War, World War II as the Westerners call it.

I sat down with a half-litre of Budweiser and thought about Natalya. I was worrying unnecessarily. That much was obvious. She might even be home by now. I sat there, sipping beer, and counted off a full two minutes before I got up and called the apartment. It was her voice that answered – but only her recorded invitation to leave a message.

The British merchant navy man was recounting one of his grand-father's stories, the German air attack on the convoy code-named PQ17 as it rode the Arctic waters on its way to Western Russia's only ice-free port. I had heard of it in my own Navy days. Of the massive convoy all but thirteen British ships were sunk with the loss of all hands in the freezing waters off the Norwegian coast. At another time I would have happily joined the two mariners and taken the opportunity to speak a little English, but this morning the idea had no attractions.

I have only a snapshot memory of how I passed the time until one o'clock. I wandered about the port in the mid-morning Arctic half-light, occasionally singling out a lamp on the far side of the docks to stare at until my eyes misted. I was forcing my mind to remain blank. Had I been able to look out to a distant horizon it would have been more comforting. But it would be another six weeks or more before that was possible. And there's no point in pretending I'm the sort of beached seafaring man who draws any depth of real comfort from being at sea. I suffer from acute seasickness. All my best memories of the sea are watching it from the shore.

By the time I began to make my way back my hands were so badly chilled I found it difficult to call the apartment. At a phone booth I struggled with a coin, dropped it in the snow and made such a performance of picking it up again that a passing babushka mistook me for a drunk and did it for me. But there was still no Natalya.

I didn't hurry from there. I stopped off at a couple of bars and drank coffee and a thumb of vodka. By midday I was back home pretending to chop beetroot for a salad for Natalya's lunch. By one o'clock I'd set the table in the kitchen with two places; I'd beaten eggs for an omelette; I'd opened a bottle of Bulgarian red and drunk nearly half of it. On the dot I called Dr Weber's number.

I recognized Weber's voice, a touch aristocratic in its intonation.

'Dr Weber,' I said, 'this is Natalya Vadim's husband speaking.'

'The policeman.'

'Only among other things. I wonder if you could help me with a few questions.'

'Ah-ha,' he said as if he'd won a point.

'You were on surgical duty last night at the Lermontov.'

'I was.'

'Were there any emergencies? Call-outs I mean.'

'No. A very quiet Saturday night.'

'Dr Weber . . . From time to time Natalya has covered for you.'

'Yes,' he said, cautiously now. 'In the past, yes.'

'And last night?'

'There was *no* emergency last night, young man.'

I spent the afternoon calling other hospitals in the Murmansk medical area. It was Sunday and receptionists seemed to feel it was an intrusion on their meditation time to have someone call with a question. After a dozen mostly fruitless calls I put some herring and beetroot in a bread roll and started for the garage. I was pulling on my coat, the roll held in my teeth, when the phone rang.

'Vadim, Vadim speaking,' I mumbled and transferred the bun from my mouth.

'I thought they'd pulled all your teeth, fuck your mother,' Roy Rolkin's voice came down the line from Hungary. 'Mumbling like an old spaniel.'

'Listen Roy, I'm busy. I'm hanging up.'

'Costya, you fleabag. What sort of a friend hangs up on a friend? What's going on there?'

'Roy, I've got problems, worries. Just leave it.'

'Worries? What sort of worries? Anything I can do anything about?' And then, with that flash of intuition that comes when a man has conducted many, many interrogations, 'Is it Natalya?'

'Roy, for Christ's sake . . .'

'It's Natalya. I can hear it in your voice. Anybody you want the shit beaten out of? I can still pull in favours in our home town, I promise you, even though I can't walk across Union Square without being bounty-hunted.'

'I believe you, Roy. But it's not like that.' I held the phone away for a second, then my spirit seemed to collapse. Roy Rolkin was probably the last person in the world at that moment that I wanted to confide in – but he was the only voice on the line. Nobody could accuse me of being a strong, silent personality. Within minutes I'd let it all out.

Now Roy genuinely is not like any other friend I have. I detest everything he stands for, yet I still find myself mysteriously responding to some things about him. Vicious, foul-mouthed braggart that he is, he's also capable of listening with a shrewd sympathetic ear.

'I think you're right to be worried, Costya,' he said, when I'd finished. 'There's something weird here. Sit tight for twenty minutes while I make some calls. Find yourself a football match. It's Sunday, Murmansk's playing somewhere. They're always good for a laugh.'

'Look Roy, if you're going to call hospitals . . .'

'And get some big-tit receptionist too busy to speak? Trust me, Costya. We're old friends, right?'

I sat slowly sipping beer from a can for ten, fifteen minutes. It was as if I'd handed over to Roy. Apart from waiting for him to call back I could think of no useful step to take.

When he rang I grabbed at the phone. 'What did you get?'

'The whole picture,' Roy said slowly. 'I got this straight from the horse's ass.'

'Who?'

'The mayor. Osopov.'

'You know him?'

'I know that Sunday afternoons he always spends with his niece. In bed at the Tsar Nicholas Hotel. I called him up there. Told him I badly needed him to make a few calls. It took a moment to sink in but he finally got the message.'

'He must have liked that.'

'He *had* to get the message. She's fourteen, fuck your mother.'

'What was his answer?'

'Last night there were no major medical emergencies in the Murmansk city region. There was, however . . . are you listening Costya? There *was* an oblast-wide call to the Trelov nickel mine where twenty-six miners were trapped. Two dozen men who escaped the fall were rescued in need of varying levels of medical care. A number of surgical cases. They've set up an emergency operating theatre underground. To staff it, the medical unit at the mine called several hospitals in the city. Sometimes, even, the call was made direct to known surgeons. Got that? Looks like your answer, Costya. Your lovely Natalya can't call you because she's working her ass off . . . because she's working *underground*.'

A great wave of relief flooded me. 'Roy,' I said. 'If you could get here without being arrested at the airport . . .'

'You'd plant a big smacker full on my upturned lips.'

'I'd draw the line at that, Roy,' I said. 'But I've got a lot to thank you for.'

'Listen, Costya, a friend in need . . . You know all that stuff,' he said quietly and put down the phone.

I threw away the beer can, opened a bottle of Glenmorangie Scottish malt whisky which I'd been saving for an occasion and switched on the football match. At half-time the blue-shirted Murmansk side was only losing 4–0 to Rotor Volvograd. This was not entirely bad. I took a deep comforting mouthful of malt. I could persuade myself the blues were in with a chance.

5

I AWOKE AT MIDNIGHT in an empty flat. A series from the last century was playing on television. It was called *The Avengers*. An immaculate bowler-hatted Englishman was standing by, resting on his umbrella, while a beautiful and acrobatic girl worsted two (obviously Russian) agents. When a third Russian appeared, the Englishman tipped his bowler in greeting while the beautiful girl delivered a kick that must have been a foul even in a blindfold mud-fighting competition. I yawned and stumbled over to turn it off. The bottle on the coffee-table was down to the top of the orange label. Had I drunk that much Glenmorangie? I went yawning into the hall where the message-machine was kept. Natalya must have emerged from her nickel mine by now.

I stood by the door. Where I had confidently expected to see a green light flashing on the machine, there was only a small dark window.

You know how it is, brothers. Waking up at midnight with a quarter-bottle of malt whisky inside you is a low spot in any man's life. I was suddenly no longer so sure of Roy's explanation of Natalya's absence. The words of the fortune teller came back and sandbagged me with renewed worry. And the old man's imprecation outside City Hall last night only seemed to confirm the words of the toothless woman in the tent.

I did what I should have done three hours ago. I called the emergency services for the River Trelov district where the mining accident had taken place. My rank and number punched me through to the Emergency Director.

'The Trelov mine emergency was cleared two hours ago,' the Director's voice said. 'We're just picking up the pieces here.'

'Director.' I tried to keep my voice calm. 'Did you need to call on surgical help outside your district?'

'At one point it seemed as if it might be necessary.'

'But you didn't?'

'No. It remained an option. Your wife would certainly have been one of my first calls.'

'But you didn't call Natalya?'

'No, Inspector. I didn't.'

I went down to the garage, got into the car and drove straight through a falling screen of snow to the Militia Central Office on Union Square. I was a policeman but I hadn't been acting like one. Drunk, sleeping, I had lost vital hours. One thing every militiaman knew was that, in a disappearance, it was vital to get the widest possible publicity at the earliest possible moment.

And that meant the Murmansk Missing Persons Office. It was by now nearly two o'clock Monday morning. Only through Captain Boris Pasko would I be able to get Natalya's face and Kamka number broadcast quickly enough to . . . Quickly enough for what? I didn't form a sentence. Or an image. Instead I shuddered with fear. Quickly enough. I couldn't complete the thought.

This wasn't the first time in the course of my duties that I'd come up against Captain Pasko from the City Central Militia Office. Long ago he had been Roy Rolkin's deputy in the Cheka, the now disbanded secret police service. I didn't like him. I didn't trust him. But this was the man I had to make an official report to.

Missing Persons Officer Boris Pasko was tall, with a hard, raw face with big cheekbones, a big dominant nose and grey chin. His ears looked like crumpled flour sacks stuck on the shaved sides of his head. At two o'clock in the morning he wore a militia overcoat and a pair of sweat-smelling long johns under it, the legs tucked into his high boots. He stopped when he saw me sitting at the interview table and closed the door behind him. 'It's two o'clock in the morning, fuck your mother,' he snarled at me. 'What's wrong with you, Vadim? Who's so important you call me out at this time of the night?'

I stood up. Taller than him but not by much. Fifteen years younger counted for more if I was going to reach out and strangle him across the interview table, which is what I wanted to do.

Instead, I looked down. I placed my hands flat on the scarred surface of the tin table. Then I raised my eyes slowly. 'Captain Pasko, I am reporting the fact that my wife Natalya Vadim has been missing since midnight Saturday. Enter it, that's all I want from you. Send it out on the General Listing straight away. She's a well-known face in the city. Someone will have seen her.'

He made a dismissive gesture.

'Enter her name in the listing. Please, Pasko. Straight away. When you've done that you can go back to bed. And my thanks for coming down here in the middle of the night.'

'Somebody's going to pay for this. I was told it concerned a VIP.'

As if Natalya weren't worth a thousand VIPs. 'That was my doing,' I said. 'No-one else to blame. I apologize, Pasko, but I knew it was the only way to get you down here.'

His upper lip curled. 'So your wife didn't come home Saturday night . . . Could be any number of reasons. She's staying with her mother . . .' He didn't mean her mother.

I shook my head.

'No?' His dull eyes lightened. 'I mean could be she's being shafted by some vek . . .'

I must have moved towards him because he quickly held up his hands. 'You're a policeman, Vadim. You've got to recognize it's an investigative possibility. Yes or no?'

'I'll recognize it as a possibility.' It was like a sword in my gut to say it. To him it was a victory. He knew how badly I needed him. He grinned.

I sat down on the interviewee's side of the desk so that he could look down on me. 'Listen Captain,' I said respectfully. 'Can we get on with it. I'll owe you a thumb or two. I won't forget.'

He liked my attitude. The humility of it. He pulled a notebook from his overcoat pocket. 'OK, give me details.' He sat down.

I spoke quickly. 'Natalya Ivanova Vadim. Age thirty-one. Born Saratov. Russian citizen. Profession, doctor. Address: 107, Admiral Gorshkov Tower, City Street.'

'Last seen?'

'At just before midnight last night. Saturday.'

'Where?'

'At Governor Badanov's apartments. Private function.'

Pasko lifted his cropped head. 'She was at the governor's apartment? At a private function?' He spoke slowly, trying to evaluate this. His secret-police training went back to Soviet days. Suddenly he had sniffed the possibility that he might put a foot wrong.

'I was present as well,' I said. 'We had been invited to give the governor a chance to discuss a new appointment for me.'

Caution narrowed his eyes. 'A promotion?'

'That too.'

He felt in his pocket for cigarettes while he wrote in his note-book. His tone changed now, lost that underlying aggression when he spoke. 'She left the governor's function before you, you say?'

'Yes. In response to a call on her hospital pager.'

'Who from?'

'I'm not sure yet.'

He lit a cigarette and pushed back his chair. 'So, no offence, com-rade Inspector . . .' He hesitated and corrected himself. 'Inspector Vadim. But if your wife's a doctor and is called out at midnight, maybe she worked all night somewhere. All day Sunday. Maybe she's catching up on a little sleep at the hospital – and just forgot to call in.'

'Enter her on the list, Pasko,' I said. 'I spoke to Governor Badanov less than an hour ago. The list was his suggestion.'

Our eyes met and he looked away. He was almost certain I was lying. But in Russia almost certain isn't good enough if authority is being invoked against you. And he had no means of checking. 'OK,' he said. 'It's yours.' He stood up. 'I'll send it out now. Wait here. We can go through the full story when I'm done.'

The full story. I sat alone in the dingy white-tiled interview room, wondering what in God's name the full story could be.

I grant that when Pasko returned to the interview room where I was waiting, he was as polite and even considerate as a brute like him knew how. I gave all the details he needed. Perhaps unwisely, I gave him too many details. When I told him I'd turned down the governor's job offer, I could sense the shift in his attitude towards me.

And towards Natalya. He asked for a list of her men friends but I waved the question aside.

'A beautiful woman,' he said stubbornly. His heavy bottom lip thrust independently. 'She must have men friends at work.'

'You're on the wrong tack,' I said shortly.

'I check out everybody,' he said.

I had to go. I had called Pasko in. I had needed him to put Natalya on the list. But by calling on him, I had also given this gross figure in the militia greatcoat and the sweat-stained long johns authority to invade any area he chose of Natalya's private life. I gave him a list of doctors she worked with, a few friends, men at the American Orphanage.

Within an hour I was back at my apartment, roaming from room to room, wondering what to do next. Reckless in my anxiety, I rang the governor's private number, taken from the invitation card. It was now nearly four o'clock in the morning and the number rang for what seemed five minutes. Then a sleep-laden woman's voice answered. 'The governor's away until tomorrow,' she said. 'In Petersburg or Kirovsk inspecting something or other.'

I caught her as she yawned. 'Madame Badanova, this is Constantin Vadim,' I said hurriedly. 'I am truly sorry to call you at this time of night but I have to ask you some questions.' I heard a few sleepy grunts as she came awake. I heard a cough as she cleared her throat. I was terrified she was going to put the phone down. Terrified she'd forgotten who I was. 'It's Constantin Vadim,' I said desperately. 'I was at your apartment for the party on Saturday.'

'Constantin . . .' Her voice was friendly. 'Questions, you said. What about?'

I told her rapidly what had happened and that it was vital to get any scrap she could give me about Natalya's pager message.

'Come over straight away,' she said readily. 'I'll warn the guard sergeant downstairs to expect you.'

I drove the same route as I had driven the night before, parked in the same place and involuntarily looked down at the base of the low wall from where the old man had materialized and pointed his long dirty finger at Natalya. Jezebel, he had called her . . . I shuddered as the sergeant waved me forward and let me into the warm lobby. With a brief nod to him I passed through into the private lift. Four o'clock in the morning and the governor's away. I could see in the polished aluminium of the lift wall that he had a bumpkin's lascivious smile on his face as he leaned in to press the unmarked button.

Madame Badanova was wearing a dark blue robe. She had brushed her hair but applied no make-up. As I emerged from the lift she put her arms round me and hugged tight. 'My poor Constantin,' she said. 'This is dreadful.' She was the first person I had spoken to since Natalya's disappearance who fully accepted something was badly wrong and I found myself deeply grateful to her for that.

There was coffee on the side-table and she poured while she talked. 'What you want from me is an exact description of those few moments when Natalya received the message.'

'Any detail, however apparently obvious . . .'

'All right.' She brought coffee over for both of us, put mine down on the table beside me and sat down facing me in an ebony and gilt Alexandrine carver. 'You were in the library with my husband. Natalya had just detached herself from that fat lecher Mayor Osopov.'

'She comes across him often in meetings of the Lermontov board of directors,' I said. 'He's openly offered promotion for a weekend in Helsinki.'

'Give my husband time, Constantin, and we'll have people like Osopov out on the street.'

'Who was she talking to when she got the emergency call?'

'She had come across the room to talk to me. We hadn't really talked up to that point and I took to her immediately.'

'What did you talk about?'

'My role as the governor's wife, her job. We laughed a bit about men. What I loved about meeting her is the way she is so easy with her extraordinary good looks. Now when I was a girl, and you may find this difficult to believe, Constantin, I was an unusually attractive package . . .'

'I don't find that hard to believe at all.'

'Flatterer,' she waved her free hand. 'What I'm saying is that I was all tensed-up about men's attentions. What's so striking about Natalya is the easy way she handled even someone as reptilian as Mayor Osopov.'

'Where were you sitting?'

'Standing.' She turned. 'Just over there by the door.' She paused, frowning. 'We were laughing. We had just been offered brandy. The waiter had barely turned away when I heard a muted, very muted buzz from Natalya's handbag.'

'How did she react?'

She thought for a moment. 'Very coolly. Not with any surprise.'

I took a moment to absorb this.

Madame Badanova put down her cup. 'I don't mean she was expecting it.'

'I see . . .' I was plagued by the words of the old woman in the tent. The threat of trouble, the suggestion, if I'm honest, of another man. 'Go on, please,' I said.

'Yes . . . Thinking about it . . .' Madame Badanova got up and walked to the window. 'Thinking about it, I would say she wasn't expecting a call.' She turned and faced me. 'But I imagine, in her work, a night call-out wouldn't be infrequent.'

'Not at all.'

'I'm going to have a drink,' she said. 'A thumb of brandy?'

I thanked her. 'So she opened her bag and took out the pager?'

She nodded as she poured brandy from a silver-necked decanter.

'Did she say anything?'

She carried the two glasses across the room. 'No . . . I think she made some sort of shrug. You know, apologetic, and asked me if she could go somewhere private. I showed her into my bedroom where she made a call.'

'On your phone?'

'No, I think she had her mobile with her in her bag.'

'But she didn't get the call direct to her mobile.'

'No, it was definitely to her pager. Is that important?'

I took a deep breath. 'Natalya's pager was one of these new American things,' I said slowly. 'You could set it to page you any time up to an hour ahead.'

'A means of getting rid of an inconvenient visitor?'

'Or persuading someone it was on an official call.'

'You mean it's possible there was no call-out. It's possible Natalya was paging herself.'

I felt sick at the thought. If she'd done it, it could only have been to slip away from the party. From me. 'Jezebel!' the old tramp had called her. Jesus, what was I thinking! 'No,' I said. 'I can't see why she would have been doing that. And in any case, it still doesn't account for why she hasn't come back.'

I left Madame Badanova a few minutes later. She gave me another of her spectacular hugs, pulling my head down onto her shoulder. I think it was to disguise the fact that there were tears welling in her eyes.

6

I SAT IN MY car and the falling snow drew curtains of fear around me. *Natalya is missing.* Mere words until my imagination gave them flesh. I saw her slowly freezing to death in her iced-up Kamka. I saw her trapped, alone, helpless, injured . . .

I evoked a dozen variations on the image of Natalya being lifted into the back of an ambulance. Of her white face, utterly still. Of the paramedic slamming the doors and walking round the front. When the paramedic takes the front seat the ambulance has already become a hearse.

Yet all these fears, all this pain were in some sense a romantic agony. I didn't *believe* she was dead. But when the old fortune teller's words came back to me I stiffened with a new fear. 'A man?' She had looked up slyly from her cards and asked me, 'Do I see another man?'

And then it was not me invoking images of pale death. It was my spirit helplessly resisting images of *life,* where I saw Natalya, such is the perverse nature of my fear, in the most painful role of all – the lasciviously bucking wife beneath the gloating, thrusting lover.

Drained of energy I drove to the Lermontov. The Lermontov Infirmary is one of the few survivors of the original, Tsarist city of Murmansk. Standing before it you would say you were in Petersburg. A long stone screen inset with iron gates gives onto a cobbled courtyard. The building's flat classical planes are painted sky-blue, the dog-toothing of its great pediment is white. A searchlight slowly roams the façade.

I parked beside the bronze figure of the Russian writer Lermontov, six feet above me on a stone pedestal, one hand behind his back, the other pointing towards the future with his quill pen. *M.Y. Lermontov, (1814-1841)*, the inscription mocked me, *A Hero of our Times*.

I walked through the columned entrance to the hospital and took the long wood-floored corridor to Natalya's office. The thick, panelled door had an ancient mortise lock but the keys had long since been lost. A cheap new lock had been fitted a year or so before, vulnerable to the simple pick I kept on my key-ring.

The door swung open onto a darkened office. I crossed the room and put on the reading lamp Natalya preferred to the overhead light. I sat down at her desk. It was large, of dark oak with a frayed leather-covered top. There was an ancient date stand which had been last turned on Saturday. There was a phone and in-tray which I shuffled through quickly. Nothing unusual. A surgeon's correspondence.

I had left the burgundy leather diary in front of me untouched, as a child will keep the most delicious piece of chocolate cake till last. But when I opened it and flicked through the pages I found nothing that I had not expected, nothing that I couldn't recognize as reminders for her work. Or corroborate from our own life together. Did I *want* to find something?

There were two drawers to the right. The top one opened easily. Inside was a make-up box. A few tubes and brushes, a small mirror – and a photograph of me in a small silver frame. I pushed my hand to the back of the drawer. I had searched enough apartments to know that the most interesting items often get pushed to the back. Always get your hand right to the back of the drawer. But there was nothing.

The second drawer was locked but with one of those easy one-tongued pieces that could be opened with almost anything. My lock-pick opened it in seconds.

The green-shaded lamp tipped light over the edge of the desk and into an empty drawer. I momentarily forgot my rule. I leaned across to push it closed, and, leaning, dropped my shoulder slightly. Deep in the shadow at the back of the drawer, the sharp edge of something caught the light. I pushed my hand in and drew out a thick card about ten centimetres long. I remember the snap of my teeth as they came together. In surprise. In despair. I was holding a bubble-wrap packet of a dozen Import Durex condoms. Empty plastic eyes glowed where two of the twelve had been removed.

7

I PUT THE CONDOMS in my pocket. I closed and locked the desk
drawer. I turned off the light. I walked to the window. Below
me were the entrance gates and the statue of Lermontov. I stood
at the window as the searchlight slowly roved the hospital façade.
I flinched for the second the brightness crossed my face, then stood
in darkness and despair until the light returned. How many times,
brothers, the light crawled across my face, I've no idea. I had no
thought in my head but for those two missing rubbers.

A man, the old woman in the tent had said. A man. And if so,
who? One of the doctors at the hospital? I ran their faces through
my mind. The Mikhails, the Leonids, the Alexeis. None of them
presented as a likely candidate.

If time passed at all, it was like time in sleep. The tinnitus in
my head bubbled and hissed. It was only when I left the window
and crossed the room to let myself out that I was aware of being
returned to time and space. A cold sour draught soughed along
the dark corridor. I closed Natalya's office door behind me and
locked it.

I walked back to the reception area. The day staff were coming
on duty, cleaners, technicians, one or two of them I knew by name,
most to nod to. They nodded back quickly, apologetically. The
morning TV news would have carried Natalya's picture. I couldn't
blame people for not knowing what to say to me.

I stopped at the receptionist's desk. Again that furtive half-smile
of recognition. 'Dr Fanya Karpova,' I said. 'What time does she
come on duty?'

I could see the relief in the receptionist's expression. A simple
question. No need for condolences. 'She was on late shift, Inspector. She should be finishing about now.'

I thanked her and turned back for the surgical area. The
Lermontov is laid out with two long wings running back on
either side of the main entrance block. One is the psychiatric wing

and drunk tank. The other wing houses the operating theatres and surgical recovery wards. I knew the way well. There was a special rest room for senior surgical staff where I had often met Natalya. As I approached, Fanya was among a group of three or four surgeons coming through the swing doors ahead of me. She detached herself and came quickly across the stone floor to me, putting her arms round me and hugging with the strength of a man. She had taken off her cap and outer gown but still wore her surgical coverall, and the smell of anaesthetic in her hair was powerfully reminiscent of Natalya when she came straight from the theatre. 'We'll get a glass of tea, Costya,' she said. 'The canteen's open.'

'I wanted to ask you a few things,' I said.

'Sure.' She took charge, leading me with a hand on my arm for the first few steps until we were moving together along the corridor. In the canteen we stood together while she got the tea. 'No news?' she asked quietly.

I dug in my pockets to pay. 'Nothing at all,' I said. 'Disappeared. Into thin air.'

'No. Don't say that.' I looked at her and saw anger on her face. 'Don't say that, Costya,' she said fiercely. 'You're a policeman for God's sake. You'll find her.'

I sat down with a thump on a yellow plastic chair and she sat opposite me. She wasn't beautiful. Maybe not even good-looking, but there was a certain well-cut character to her features that people used to call aristocratic. And in fact I seem to remember she had Tsarist serf-owners somewhere in her distant family background.

'We'll find her,' I said with more confidence than I felt. The packet of condoms had knocked me sideways. The sudden revelation of the *possibility* of a Natalya I didn't know, hadn't even guessed at, had drained me of energy.

'You knew there was something wrong Sunday morning,' she said accusingly. 'Yesterday when we were at the station to interview those kids, you knew something then.'

I shook my head. 'Some sort of feeling maybe. Intuition, that's all. She'd been out all night on a call enough times before. You know that. I had nothing to go on. As the day went on I got more and more anxious. By midnight or so I reported her missing.'

'Why did you leave it so late to report her?'

The tone was accusatory again. I couldn't say I was drunkenly sleeping in front of a fifty-year-old English television series. I finished my tea, bubbling my lips at the thin, bitter taste. 'I have some things to ask you, Fanya,' I said. 'Investigations have to cover all possibilities . . .'

'What sort of things?'

'Try and think about the last couple of weeks. Was there any sense in which Natalya was different?' Did she seem different to you? Worried about something, for instance?'

'She seems to have a lot of work on recently. Apart from the surgical she's always being called off to meetings.'

'Meetings?'

'Administrative meetings of one kind or another. Natalya's a lot senior to me. She's usually the one who's called to represent Surgery if Dr Weber's off duty or unwell, as he is pretty often these days. But you know all this. That wasn't what you were asking.'

I hunched over my empty tea-glass. 'No . . . What I have to ask, Fanya, goes against the grain. But I have to ask all the same.'

I think she must have had some idea of what I was going to say because I saw her, quite distinctly, stiffen, preparing herself to defend her friend.

'Perhaps you'll think I'm asking you to be disloyal to Natalya . . . But it has to be done.'

She looked at me evenly now, watching me squirm. The words, coming from her, carried a deadly weight: 'You're asking whether Natalya was seeing someone.'

'Yes.' My voice didn't sound normal. I pursed dry lips. 'I have to recognize . . .' I said slowly. 'I have to recognize it's just possible there was a man.'

'Do you have any reason to think so?'

I hesitated. 'No. Absolutely not.'

'So . . .?'

'You worked with her most days. Was there anything, Fanya? Anything that made you think . . . Did she see a lot of any-body?'

'She saw a lot of everybody, you know that.'

'I thought if there was someone special,' I said, 'you'd have to know.'

I could not read her face. It was darkly expressionless.

'She told you about her stalker, I suppose.'

'What?' I sat up. 'She complained about a stalker?'

'Laughed about it. She didn't tell you?'

'No.'

'Well . . . you know what a worrier you are. About Natalya anyway.'

I pressed my hands flat on the table before me. 'Tell me exactly. *Exactly.*'

'Just after Christmas she said she'd become aware of someone. Hanging around the entrance to the Infirmary. Around the parking-lot.'

'Did he ever speak to her?'

'I'm not sure she ever saw his face. All muffled-up. You know what weather we've been having this winter.'

'Young or old? A tramp? An alcoholic?'

'I know nothing, Constantin,' she said with a touch of irritation I found difficult to understand.

'Did Natalya ever make a formal complaint to Lermontov Security?'

'I can't see Natalya doing that, can you?'

'When did she last see him?'

'She just stopped mentioning it. I don't know when. A month ago maybe. If I thought anything I thought he'd just transferred his attentions.'

The loudspeaker clicked and we fell silent. The call for surgical staff included Fanya's name. 'I have to go.' She stood up, hands flat on the table, leaning towards me. 'Do you really think there was a man, Costya? Not some pathetic vek who hangs around freezing car parks. A man. An affair?'

I looked up at her. 'No,' I said. 'Of course not. But, you understand, I had to ask.'

'Of course you did.' She smiled briefly and turned away.

Young women doctors with striking looks attract all sorts of unwelcome attention. For the moment I deliberately put the idea that Natalya was being stalked out of my mind. It *felt* like a red herring. It wasn't what engaged Fanya either, I could feel that too.

I watched her across the room. At the door she turned briefly and glanced back at me. She hadn't reacted at all as I had expected, the way I had wanted her to, sweeping aside the suggestion as totally impossible. Fanya was probably Natalya's closest friend. Did she know something? Was it loyalty to Natalya that had made her so edgy, almost hostile? I stood up, staring blankly at the people filing into the canteen. Thick parkas, white coats, nursing uniforms, Lermontov greens. What struck me most, what left a deep sickness in the pit of my stomach, was the fact that at no point had Fanya actually denied the possibility of another man.

I left the main entrance to the Lermontov. I was pausing to wonder whether I should cross the square to buy myself some cigarettes at one of the corner cafés when a Mercedes came to a silent halt just a few feet in front of me. I barely reacted. The hospital directors had cars like this – I probably thought it was one of them arriving. The car's glass was smoked to conceal the occupants but already a formidable-looking driver had stepped out of the front seat. I only really focused on the sequence of events when I saw he was crossing the two or three metres between us. 'Inspector,' he said amiably. 'Step this way, please.'

Now in Russia today, brothers, we step this way into black limousines no more readily than we did in Russia yesterday. The driver saw me freeze. Saw the quick motion of the eyes – left, right, looking for cover – and said quietly: 'It's an old friend to see you, Inspector.'

'An old friend.' I hesitated. I had no old friends who drove cars like this.

'Inseparable as kids, he tells me,' the driver said politely.

I felt a shiver of alarm. I stared at the smoky glass of the Mercedes as if I could penetrate it by sheer will-power. The driver gestured towards the back door. I began to step forward and he reached it before me to open it.

Inside, muffled like a Chicago gangster in black overcoat and white silk scarf, was Roy Rolkin.

'Come in out of the cold, fuck your mother,' he said in those familiar thick tones. 'I told Sergei here that you've got nerves of cotton wool.'

I clambered into the back and pulled the door shut. 'Jesus, Roy,' I said anxiously. 'If anybody knows you're in Russia, you won't see daylight again for twenty-five years.'

He whacked my chest with the back of his hand. Why should I care about this man? He was an ex-secret policeman, a thug, a new Russian businessman, without a doubt one of the *racketiry* who now run Russia, even though he was in exile. If he was dressed like a Chicago gangster it was because gangsterdom was his only role model.

'Costya.' He shuffled himself round to face me and his heavy hands took the front of my coat. He was shorter than me by a head, but I remembered from childhood the sheer strength of those hands. 'I had to come,' he said. 'I saw the newscast. I was in Finland – barely an hour's flight away. You're in trouble.'

The car had left the Lermontov and was moving slowly along Pushkin Boulvar. Here cafés and boutiques were being refurbished. Expensive women emerged from expensive shops. For a moment Roy was distracted by the colour and movement. 'Murmansk is beginning to look like a Western city,' he said. Then, as we turned off Pushkin and ran along a grim tunnel of Sixties buildings, he muttered to himself, 'Or maybe not.' He turned towards me, his odd wraparound green eyes on mine. 'What's happened, Costya? As far as you can tell?'

'As far as I can tell?' I shook my head. 'Christ, I don't know, Roy. I run in different directions every time I think about it.'

He leaned forward and pressed something to make a panel slide. There were drinks inside and he poured vodka for both of us. 'What do you want me to do?' he said.

I looked at him blankly.

'We're friends, fuck your mother. Is there another man in all this?'

I was silent.

'I'll have his balls torn out.'

I knew he meant it. I shook my head quickly. 'She's gone,' I said. 'There's not any doubt about that. But how it happened . . . of her own free will . . . or not, I just don't know.'

'I have people, Costya. Here in the city. They still take my money. When you find him, just let me know.'

'You didn't hear me, Roy. I don't know if Natalya went will-ingly.'

'What difference does that make?'

'It does to me.'

'Fucking romantic. Listen, Costya. If you need money, squawk. If you need manpower, for whatever reason, just get on the line.'

'Thanks,' I said. 'Thanks, Roy.' I finished my drink and put the glass back in the small compartment. The car had circled the block. We were moving down Pushkin again towards the Lermontov. 'I'll get out here.'

'Too bad I can't show my face,' he said. 'Too many small-minded veks here, all out to get even. What I always think about a good

54

drink in Murmansk is that there's nothing like it. There's nowhere like inside the Arctic Circle to get drunk, you know. It must be the clean, unpolluted air.'

I winced at the thought of our nickel mines and rotting nuclear submarines in Severomorsk.

'True enough,' he insisted. 'This is the only place in the world you don't wake up with a hangover.'

'The morning after we graduated,' I reminded him, 'you were so hungover you signed up as an interpreter with that American All-Girl Temperance Skiffle Band.'

'That's only because I would have killed to hump the leader.'

'Did you?'

'I can't remember,' he said. He lifted his glass. 'I was too hungover, fuck your mother.'

I gestured to the car, the rich fittings, the driver. 'I take it things continue to go well with you in Budapest.'

'Beautiful city,' he said. 'Beautiful women. Every single one's a countess, did you know that?'

I told him I didn't. 'Listen Roy, did you really fly all the way up here to see if I needed help?'

'For Christ's sake, don't get fucking maudlin, Costya. I was in Finland. If it makes you feel better to say I had business here, say I had business. Anyway,' he grunted. 'I fucked up about the Trelov nickel mine. I owe you for that one.'

I paused. He'd never been an easy man to thank. 'OK, Roy,' I said. 'Thanks for coming. It's really appreciated.'

He smiled sheepishly. Some would say rapaciously. With Roy I never really know. We were slowing down outside the Lermontov. 'Come up to the airport with me, you old sod,' he mumbled. 'My gorilla'll bring you back.'

I looked at the unmoving cropped head of the driver.

'My informants tell me you've been offered a job by Governor Badanov.'

'Pasko?'

'If you like.' He sniffed his vodka. 'This job ever involve you travelling with Badanov?'

'I turned it down. Why do you ask about the travel?'

'Our much-esteemed governor has enemies. Anyway, that's what I hear. Probably completely off the track.' Roy tipped back his thumb of vodka. 'The truth is I miss you, Costya,' he said. 'I miss all that fucking moralizing you go in for. I tell the countess, one of my girlfriends, that you're an original. I tell her that, as a referee, you weren't above awarding a penalty against your own side.'

8

I N THE APARTMENT I put on music. But even the abstractions of Miles Davis were unbearable. *No Sun in Venice* took on an intolerable significance. I sat there in the room, not large but not too cramped, and did an inventory of all Natalya had done to make the place liveable, the Khazak carpet that glowed rich and red on the wall, the lamps, the low, simple furniture and the enormous painting of the battle of Borodino that she'd brought from her apartment in Moscow.

I sat on the big sofa facing the big window and watched the snow fall. Did I mention I'd opened a half-litre? Perhaps not. But it was going to help with what came next, I knew that. So, begin, Constantin. Go to work on it. Grit your teeth. Assume there *was* another man.

Then, two possibilities. Natalya had decided, on a moment's notice, to go off with him. *Or* had refused to go away with him – and was being held or harmed by him.

Shameful as it was, each possibility scoured my mind with equal force. Natalya in ecstasy; Natalya in desperate danger – I could tolerate the idea of neither.

I started in the spare room and searched as once, long ago, I'd been trained to search. Searched as if it were someone else's apartment. Under the carpet, in the light fittings, over, under and at the back of cupboards . . . I had no idea what I was looking for.

In our bedroom I searched all the drawers in the cupboards and chest, all her underclothes, all through the notebooks and her day-to-day diary on her dressing-table.

I flipped through the diary. A slender leather-covered book, each page lined, with a thick red margin. Most of it was unused. But part of the page for Saturday, the day she disappeared, was torn out. The rest carried a reminder about collecting, from the cleaners, a dress for the governor's party for that evening.

Working through her clothes, I marvelled at the few pockets

women seem to have, and even those not designed to hold anything. I threw skirts, trousers, jeans, all empty of anything but a few shreds of Kleenex tissue, onto the bed. Just in case, I checked each pocket again, even felt the inside of the lining.

I looked round the room. Drawers hung open, clothes were piled on the bed. Now that I was coming to the end I was feeling some distaste, some shame at what I was doing. Searching Natalya's things on the excuse to myself that it would forward the investigation, but, in fact, searching at least as much in the desperate desire to know whether there had been another man.

A dark green jacket hanging over the back of a chair confronted me with an indistinct memory. Had she not worn it to work on Saturday morning? I slid my hands into the jacket pockets. A piece of paper crackled under my fingers. It was no more than a scrap, lined and with the same red margin as her torn Saturday diary page. In her writing it read: 4.30 Mandelstam.

Mandelstam Street ran off Union Square. At 4.30 on that Saturday of the party was she due to meet someone there? Wait a minute, Constantin. Think about this. Not everything has significance. She had made the note to remind her about her dress at the cleaners. Maybe Mandelstam was simply where she was to pick up her black dress for the party that night. I fitted the scrap of paper back into the diary. Like that it was clear the Mandelstam Street appointment *could* have referred to the dress being ready for collection. But equally it could have been a separate item. An appointment to meet someone.

Then a further thought struck me. By mid-afternoon Saturday the emergency at the docks was well under way. At 4.30 on Saturday Natalya had been crouched over a seaman on a burning cargo ship, amputating his trapped foot.

So perhaps she had arranged for someone else to collect the dress. If it was a dress that was being collected. Or perhaps she had been forced to cancel a meeting when the emergency siren started wailing at the docks. A meeting with whom?

Mandelstam Street I knew fairly well. It was over half a kilometre long with shops, small office buildings and low apartment blocks. Snow is the only thing that makes streets like Mandelstam tolerable. Its whole length is encased in grey cement but the snow that collects along the window-ledges, or is swept into drifts beneath the concrete piles that support the buildings, helps soften the brutality of it all. It was early afternoon when I parked my car at the Union Square end and began to work the length of the street. I knew what I was trying to do would take hours and that a call to Missing Persons would get me half a dozen men to help, but reveal to Pasko my doubts about Natalya was not something I could do.

A few cafés and hamburger places had opened up since I had last driven down the street, but I saw no cleaning and pressing shop. No dressmaker who would perhaps handle pressing for you. It was somehow as I had expected.

I turned at the far end of Mandelstam where North Boulvar crosses it and began to walk back. This time I stopped in every fifth or sixth shop and in every single block of apartments. I was looking, I told the shopkeeper or concierge, for a doctor in the street. Probably one who worked at the Lermontov.

Most people tried to be helpful. At least half misunderstood the question. People recommended doctors in other streets or as easily condemned them with lengthy stories of their own medical misfortunes. Concierges told of doctors who had stayed with friends in their blocks last year, or army doctors billeted at the end of the Civil War and now long gone.

When they had run through their stories I produced Natalya's picture and asked if she had ever visited anyone in the block. But nobody had seen her there, although one or two recognized her as the missing doctor they had seen on television.

I stopped at a café and bought some soup and a roll and started back again asking my questions, with ever-lessening confidence. Once or twice I stopped to drink coffee in a couple of the smarter cafés nearer Union Square and showed waitresses Natalya's picture. But the results were the same. Occasionally she was recognized, but only through this morning's press and television publicity. Whoever my wife had planned to meet at 4.30 in this street on Saturday afternoon, and failed to because of the emergency at the docks, was going to remain a blank to me. Perhaps for just a while – perhaps for ever.

I was leaving one of the coffee houses on Union Square itself when my station pager trilled in my pocket. Lieutenant Pinsk, the District 18 homicide officer, wanted me to call him.

I stood in Union Square, the wind blasting my face, as I called up Pinsk on my mobile. Fear more than cold made my cheeks tremble, made my lips go slack like a drunk's. 'For Christ's sake, Pinsk,' I said. 'Have you found her?'

'No.' Pinsk was a squat, round-shouldered man, unimaginative but good-hearted, impossible to hurry. 'No,' he said again. 'But we've found her hospital Kamka. Abandoned up in the North Bay area. Pasko's seen it and is on his way back. You know the old cod-drying factory on Chernenko Street?'

'I can find it.'

'I'll meet you there in twenty minutes.'

The dock area suffered more in the recent Civil War than any other part of the city. Twenty-five consecutive nights of bombing by the Anarchist air force shattered this entire section of Murmansk. Though much of the damage on the east bank of the Kola river has been cleared, and the port operates again, the whole of North Bay from Memorial Bridge to the river's right turn into the Gulf remains an area of gutted warehouses and bleak marshalling yards. The cost of restoring street lighting to streets that barely exist is considered prohibitive by the City Council. Instead North Bay is lit by eight military searchlights set up in pairs at the four corners of the roughly kilometre-square area.

The effect is bizarre. One side of a street the line of burnt-out warehouses will be in darkness; the other side will be coldly illumined, fit to pick out any movement of a river rat as it scuttles for the safety of darkness. It evokes, of course, images of a labour camp.

It is a part of the town that most people avoid. A whole life goes on here separate from the rich fittings of restaurants like the Tsar Nicholas or the Austrian pastry shop in Union Square. Even in the coldest weather, streetwalkers abound on these broken streets. Groups of two or three women share a brazier which they feed from their own stack of broken floorboards. These are not the shop-window tarts of Pushkin Boulvar, nor the confident young girls of Sin City. These are older women, shabbier, living with the knowledge that every client they take into the ruins may be their last.

There are few landmarks and no universally recognized names for the smaller streets. The locals, in derision I think, still call the main avenue the Marx-Lenin Prospekt, but the onion-domed ruin of St Andrew's (completed in the year 2000) is the dominant building here and directions are given, north, south, east or west in relation to the once impressive Millennium church.

At this time in the dark late afternoon the area south of the

Church of St Andrew is deserted except for the ageing street-walkers. I crawled forward, looking left and right at intersections, not for passing vehicles, of which there are none, but for the clutch of militiamen, smoking, stamping their feet, beating their arms across their chests, keeping warm as the temperature drops way past freezing and the chilled sea mist rolls along the walls bright with the unmoving beams of the searchlights.

At the cod-factory corner I saw them, not so very different from my expectation, six or eight men, others sitting in Kamkas with running engines. Exhaust billowed from the vehicles, obscuring everything but the outline of the Kamkas run up on the pavement. I parked and got out. Pinsk came towards me, his round neckless head enclosed in an over-large militia fur-collared overcoat.

The Lermontov Kamka had been driven into a rubble-filled alley. It stood under a light rigged by Pinsk's crime-scene team, all doors open and lifted on jacks like a demonstration model at a Western motor show. Two women in heavy fur hats and bulky fur-lined yellow overalls were taking scrapings from the tyres. One turned towards Pinsk as we passed. 'Heavy deposits of grit here, Lieutenant. Embedded in the tread.'

We stopped. 'What sort of grit?' Pinsk asked.

'Cinder, coke dust, coal dust . . . that sort of thing.'

Pinsk gave me a glance with a raised eyebrow, but grit and cinder meant nothing to me.

Against the back wall of the alley a man from the team, his back to us, *Militia* printed across his yellow overall, was arranging evidence bags on a folding table he'd set up under a blue temporary light.

It was to the table Pinsk led me, then turned, his eyes strangely cocked up to mine like a kindly Quasimodo. 'I told you Pasko's been here,' he said.

'Is that a problem?'

'Only that I didn't tell him I'd called you.' His strange eyes glared at me for a moment. Then he turned to the table. 'We've got a few items, Captain,' he said, 'for you to identify. Her shoes?' He lifted a plastic evidence bag to the light. I took it but hardly needed to examine it. A pair of black high-heeled leather evening shoes. Charles Jourdan in Petersburg. Natalya had brought them back from a surgeon's convention there, at the end of last month. I handed Pinsk back the bag. 'Hers, ninety-nine per cent certain.'

'And the coat?' He held up Natalya's black evening coat in a long plastic bag.

I nodded, tight-lipped.

'Then there's this, Captain.' He lifted a bag containing a slim black pager.

'Christ.' I took the bag. 'The message . . .'

'Three messages,' he said. He pulled off his leather glove and took a notebook from inside his bulky militia topcoat. Flipping pages, he stopped, looking up at me. 'The first was lunch-time Saturday 12.32: *Call me when you can, Constantin.*'

'OK, I remember. It was nothing important.'

'Then the afternoon. 16.02 pm: *Surgical emergency – Case Red, Lermontov dispatch.*'

'The call-out to the docks Saturday afternoon,' I said. 'Just after four o'clock.'

'Case Red just means a high-rated outside emergency. Is that right?'

'They give it when they don't know how bad things are,' I said quickly. It was the last message I was interested in. 'What about the last message that drew her out Saturday night?' Even as I asked I was bracing myself against what I might hear.

'Last message,' Pinsk lifted his head towards me. '23.59 . . .'

The minute before midnight. I nodded to him to go on.

'23.59,' he repeated. '*Need you. Call me now.*'

I think I shuddered in my shoes. *Need you* . . .

'Whose message?' I asked Pinsk and watched my breath billow through the blue militia light and disappear into the darkness beyond.

'No name given,' he said. 'I spoke to the operator. She didn't remember that particular call but her record showed no identification required.'

My head swam. I handed Pinsk back the plastic bag. 'What about the jeep? Anything?' I was putting on my professional voice. He knew it. I could see that in his over-anxious bobbing head.

'Nothing out of the ordinary,' he said. 'I take it she kept her snow boots and a Lermontov overall always ready to change into in the Kamka?'

'She kept gloves and an all-weather parka there too. No sign of them?'

'The gloves and parka are there. No sign of the snow boots or overall.'

'And her medical bags. There should be two. Drugs and bandaging in one. And surgical instruments in the other.'

'They were in the back.'

I looked across to the trestle-table. Pinsk led the way over. He nudged the crime-scene man aside. 'What do you think, Captain?'

Natalya's two black leather bags were unzipped and open under the light. Bandages and drugs were neatly arranged in one. Gleaming emergency surgical instruments were held in place by black elasticated bands in the other.

I looked from the open bags to Pinsk. 'I think the same as you do, Lieutenant,' I said slowly. 'Whatever my wife was doing on Saturday night, she wasn't attending a surgical emergency.'

I regained my car and called Missing Persons on my mobile. I was passed immediately to Captain Pasko. 'Anything new?' I said. 'Any response to Natalya's picture?'

'Where are you?' he asked instead of an answer. 'I've been trying to get you at your apartment.'

'You've got something new?'

'Listen,' he said. 'I'll meet you at your station. In fifteen minutes. You can make it.'

'If you've got something, Pasko, tell me, for God's sake.'

'Sin City. In fifteen minutes,' he said and rang off.

I started the engine and blew air at the windscreen to clear it of the river mist. In my mind's eye I could see the familiar squared-off orange letters on Natalya's pager: *Need you*, they whispered. *Call me now!*

9

ONLY THE MUSIC moves fast on the Avenue of the Pleasures of Youth. It is a broad ice boulevard through the middle of Sin City, and an unwise touch of the brakes can skid you into a café or wooden whorehouse and bring a dozen irate customers tumbling round your shoulders.

Station 18, our four linked portable office units, occupies a prime site on the Avenue of the Pleasures of Youth. I left my car in the guarded lot and entered past Sergeant Bubin in Reception. Pasko was waiting for me. With an index finger he gestured to a seat. I remained standing by the door.

Under the bright lights of the main yellow-painted interview room, Pasko stood braced back against the metal desk, slowly unbuttoning his topcoat. He seemed to be totally absorbed in what he was doing. Such an old militia trick that I was tempted to kick his legs from under him. Another old militia trick.

'I wonder,' he said, 'if you've anything to add to what you've told me so far. Any additional information?'

'I don't know what it's worth but someone was seen hanging around my wife a month or so back. I'm not sure you could call him a stalker, but Natalya mentioned it, apparently.'

'Apparently? Not to you then.'

'No, not to me. But it's maybe worth following up. Just to eliminate him . . .'

'Description?'

'No . . .'

'A snowman.' He grunted, not interested. Amused even. He pulled up a chair and slumped down in it, lifting his chin to stare at some spot high on the wall behind my head.

'For Christ's sake,' I said. 'What did you get me here for?'

He placed one boot on the table. A smile ripped his grey face. He pressed Go on a small recorder in front of him, then took out a tobacco pouch and began rolling himself a cigarette.

'Militia Officer Constantin Vadim,' he said. 'I am arresting you on suspicion of involvement in the abduction of your wife, Natalya Ivanova Vadim.' He put his other boot up onto the table. His voice dropped into a bored intonation. 'You understand that if this charge is brought against you it can, at a later date, be expanded to include the manslaughter or murder of your said wife, sufficient evidence thereunto, but not necessarily including a body, needing to be produced under section 7/5 of the Criminal Code 2015 of the Russian Republic.'

'Are you out of your mind?'

'Why should I be?'

'You had me come here to *arrest* me?'

An expansive gesture of the hand set the microbes a-flurry under his armpit. 'Where better to arrest you than in a police station, fuck your mother?' he grinned. 'Where better than in your *own* police station?'

'You're wasting my time, you sadistic bastard!' My voice was rising with every syllable. I got control with effort, fighting off the hysteria. 'Pasko, you're wasting precious time.'

'I don't think you believe that.'

'You're going to hold me here while my wife's out there somewhere . . .' My voice tailed off. It was as far as my imagination would take me. Beyond everything I knew I had to get free. While I sat in a prison cell Natalya's life could be ticking away. 'Governor Badanov . . .' I began, but Pasko cut me off with a contemptuous glare and swung his boots down to the floor. He signalled the booking sergeant. 'Inspector Vadim is under interrogation arrest. Under the Criminal Code we can hold him for twenty-four hours.' He looked at his watch. 'I'm going to get some sleep. Make sure he's well searched and his possessions logged. If we need more than twenty-four hours I'm sure we can organize some way to find it.' He switched off the recorder and shoved it in his overcoat pocket.

I pulled away as Sergeant Bubin put his hand on my arm. 'Pasko,' I said. I had lowered my voice close to pleading with him now. 'Just tell me. What's going on? Why are you doing this?'

'You know the book,' he said. 'In missing persons and related homicide, over eighty per cent of convictions are close family. The book requires me to test close family against the known circumstances.'

'The book doesn't require you to arrest close family without any evidence, you fucking oaf.'

'Without evidence?' He laughed. 'Who said anything about without evidence?'

I looked at him, frowning, trying to work out what was going through his head.

'You knew she was having an affair,' he said, smiling his smile.

'She was not having an affair.'

'Pushkin Boulvar's a good place to relax after work. Cafés open even in the middle of the night. A dance club to sweat out the tension in your loins.'

'That's enough Pasko.'

'Some handsome young doctor newly arrived at the hospital, let's say.'

'This is gutter fantasy. You're wasting time, Pasko.'

'Calm down. I think you knew she was getting it from somebody at the Lermontov.' He made a short punching movement with his fist. 'Any time they could get at it they did. The odd *duty* night at his place. But that wasn't enough for them. They snatched any opportunity they could. In her office. Across the desk. The door locked.' He walked towards the door and turned, his dull eyes on me.

'This is . . .' I could think of no other words, 'pure fabrication.'

He yawned and leaned against the door. 'This morning,' he said. 'Early. I got to Natalya's office at the Lermontov minutes before you.'

'So . . .?'

'I too have a little gadget with steel spikes.'

I half understood. 'You opened the drawer.'

His big chin moved up and down. 'Go on.'

'You opened the drawer and relocked it.'

'I did that,' he said.

'You found nothing there.'

'Oh yes.' He walked across to me and dived his hands into my overcoat pockets. As I looked down he withdrew his hands and waved the packet of condoms under my nose.

Relief ballooned inside me. 'You planted them there.'

'Too easy,' he said exultantly. 'This packet was in her desk drawer when I opened it. I have timed and dated photographs to support that fact.'

The balloon burst. Did I believe him?

'So I read it this way,' Pasko said, with a knowing grin. 'Somehow you already knew she was fucking someone at her office.'

'No . . .'

'Maybe he lives on Mandelstam Street where you've been asking questions about a doctor all afternoon. It shouldn't take long to sort that one out.'

I stared at him in despair.

'Maybe you've suspected for a few days. A week. You're mad with jealousy. But you're a cunning, calculating bastard, too. You lure her out to the Kanevka highway, where you kill her, dump the body and drop off her Kamka at North Bay. Then you go through all this rigmarole about reporting her missing.'

I couldn't speak.

'And then, sometime early this morning, it hits you. There could be something incriminating, left in her office. You go straight over to the hospital. And you're right, Vadim. There in the drawer you find a pack of our faithful friends.' He flipped the bubble card up and down on his palm. 'You know that two of them, by their absence, have already seen action. This is exactly the sort of thing you were looking for. To clear up. You take them.'

I had barely heard the last part. I found it difficult to move my lips, as if they were frozen or numbed with Novocain. A thought burst in on me that had been hanging in the air. 'The Kanevka highway, you said. Why did you say that?'

He smiled lazily.

'Tell me, fuck your mother!' I was speaking softly, without raising my voice. 'Tell me, Pasko. Have you found her? Have you found Natalya?'

He was already moving through the door. I moved after him but Sergeant Bubin reached out and blocked my path. 'I'm sorry, Inspector,' he said.

'Have you found her, Pasko?' I screamed into the corridor.

'Lock him up, Sergeant. Lock the evil bastard up,' Pasko shouted back over his shoulder and whirled away in a reek of sweat.

10

SERGEANT BUBIN OPENED the cell door and I walked in past him. I knew the procedure. I took off my jacket and tossed it to him. While he emptied the pockets I kicked off my shoes, pulled off my socks and took off my shirt and trousers. There was a small radiator in the room and I padded over and stood next to it.

'I couldn't feel worse about this, Inspector,' Bubin said. He took my keys, wallet, militia badge and placed them on the bunk. 'You're allowed three calls.' He stopped, embarrassed. 'But of course, you know that. I'll bring you a phone in.' He collected up my belongings. 'Three calls.' He shrugged. 'Who's counting?'

I stood there in my underpants in the unlocked cell, staring at the dents in the yellow-painted wall where the metal showed through. Staring. Then I began to get dressed.

I had just finished when Bubin returned, carrying a phone and a glass of tea. He gave a quick, tense smile as he put the tea down on the cement floor in the centre of the cell and plugged the phone into a socket in the corridor. 'I'm going to have to lock the door, Inspector,' he said. 'If Pasko comes back and finds it . . .' he gestured to the open door.

I nodded and squatted down to pick up the tea.

I knew he was looking down at me as I sipped the sharp lemon-flavoured liquid. 'I don't think it's right,' he said, 'to keep a man in suspense about his wife. About what's happened, I mean.'

I lifted my head but I stayed squatting on the floor.

'I was on the front desk when the call came through, Inspector. A militia snow-track was coming back from Kanevka when its headlights caught something fluttering from a highway divider. God knows why but the driver stopped. It was a scarf, blue and white, the Lermontov colours.'

'Nothing else?'

'Just the scarf.'

'And the name tab?' I got to my feet.

'Your wife's, Inspector.'

'Where was this?'

'At Intersection 33. That's about ten kilometres south of the city limits.'

I stood up. Reached out and touched him on the shoulder. 'Thanks, Bubin. I won't forget this.'

He went to the door and held up the key in apology.

'Go ahead,' I said. I had to tighten my mouth to keep my lip from trembling. 'A scarf isn't a body. I'll make a few calls and get some sleep.'

The door closed with a thud. Her scarf out on the highway. It could mean anything. Then I thought again of the old woman fortune teller. The Scorpio figure she had invoked, full of shifting lusts . . . Oh Christ. Fatigue and fear were blinding me. I stumbled about the room colliding with walls, in pain so deep I could feel nothing but the buzz-saw in my head.

I've been close to the abyss before in my life. Drink, drugs, plain everyday madness. I know what it's like to stand, staring, on the edge. Most of all I knew it would do nothing to help Natalya.

Through the thin walls of our portable station came the thud of rock music from Sin City all around us. Somehow the knowledge of that seething, dancing, gambling, copulating mass of people just a few metres beyond the walls helped to restore my mind's balance. I controlled the wild, random lurching of my body. I straightened up. I breathed in and out until my head cleared. I put one thought before another, like a blind man taking a careful step forward.

Who to call? A lawyer couldn't do much to get me out straight away. In any strict observance of the law I would be released without charge in twenty-four hours. But I knew only too well that was not the way things worked in Russia. Before time was up, Pasko would have found some very minor charge to fit me up with and I would be remanded for a week, month, six weeks, however long the investigating officer felt he needed. But a lawyer might help with that.

I called Roy Rolkin. Roy understands these problems. He exploded with fury, he who had arrested more innocent men in his career then he could remember. But Roy takes any act against a friend of his as a personal slight. 'I haven't spoken to Pasko in years. I'll crush him underfoot. Put him on.'

'Let's leave the strong-arm stuff till necessary, Roy,' I said, alarmed. 'Right now a lawyer's what I need.'

He suggested the shadowy figure of Advocate Grandov, whose reputation was the best in the region. Grandov knew how to work the system. I would need him to prevent charges against me spiralling out of control.

I put down the phone and called a Moscow number.

Homicide Inspector Ilya Dronsky is my closest friend. We worked together during my brief stay in the capital and have kept in close touch ever since. He now serves as an investigator in the Moscow Procurator's Office. A friend in the prosecution camp can't be a bad thing at moments like this. But most important of all, he knew Natalya. He had worked with her in Moscow before she and I had even met. There would be things about what had happened or not happened that I wouldn't even have to explain.

It was past ten o'clock in the evening but Dronsky had only just got home. 'You just caught me, Chief,' he said. He still calls me Chief although we're the same rank now. 'How's Natalya?'

'I'm calling about her.' I could almost feel the change on the end of the line. A straightening of the short, powerful back, a lift of the square, brush-cut head.

'Something wrong?'

'Very wrong, Ilya. She's missing. Went out on a work call – maybe a phoney work call – and disappeared.'

'Jesus. When?'

'Saturday. We were at a party.'

There was a long silence at the other end. 'Where are you now?' he asked finally.

'In my own *ston*.' I used the slang word for lock-up. 'Our Missing Persons Officer Pasko sees it as a family affair.'

He's a man of few words, Dronsky. 'I'll get something moving right away, Chief,' he said. 'Tell Missing Persons Officer Pasko to expect trouble.'

Pasko woke me at 6.30. I know it was 6.30 because I could hear the Moscow-Amerika morning jazz show beginning on the radio in the reception office. He awoke me with a toecap placed below my balls and jerked upwards. I doubled forward with the deep dull pain and he smacked me, backhanded, across the face.

Pasko's interrogation had begun.

I was answering the first questions, still thick with sleep, grunting denials. 'When did you find out she was cheating on you? Who was the man? What have you done to him? How long have you been planning it? When did you first find out she was fucking some other vek? How did you know? How did you dispose of the body?'

Cold water splashed in my face. As I gasped for air he pulled me onto my feet. I knew better than to offer resistance to an officer during interrogation. 'Bubin,' he shouted and the day duty sergeant who wasn't Bubin came to the door. 'Escort this prisoner to the interview room.' Pasko said. 'And watch him, he's violent.'

I shook my head in despair.

'And bring in a charge form,' Pasko added. 'Assaulting an officer in the execution of his duty. You can witness it.'

'I just had the prisoner's lawyer in,' the sergeant said. 'Advocate Grandov.' The sergeant was impressed. Roy, as promised, had got me the best lawyer in Murmansk.

Pasko was worried. He scowled. 'I don't care who it is. He can't see the prisoner.'

'He knows that. He said he was just here to warn me, or anybody else it may concern.'

'Warn you of what?'

'He said if I stand witness to anything I don't actually see with my own eyes, he'll make sure I lose all my housing points, set me back three years in the queue. I'm living in two rooms with three children and my wife's sister.'

'What can he do? A lawyer, fuck your mother,' Pasko said.

'Advocate Grandov is also Chairman of the Militia Housing Board.'

Pasko turned away. 'Just get the prisoner into the interview room.'

We sat opposite each other across the tin desk. 'You *will* pay for this, Pasko,' I said. 'I don't know when but you won't get away scot-free.'

'Are you threatening an officer?'

The sergeant looked at the ceiling.

'You've got it about right,' I said. 'Ask your questions.'

He punched the recorder and we began.

It took less than an hour. Madame Badanova could vouch for my time of leaving the governor's party. The Mercedes chauffeur could give evidence he had driven me home. Any garage, or anybody who had ever driven on the Murmansk–Kanevka highway could confirm that my Fiat Tolstoy could not have even reached

Intersection 33 that night. So what vehicle did I use if I had somehow trailed her after arranging for her to be paged? 'Listen to me, Pasko,' I said slowly. 'You have no case. Not the shadow of a case. Now get out there and find out what's really happened to my wife.'

He snapped off the recorder and sat back. 'The trouble with you new people,' he said slowly, 'is that you think nothing ever worked in the old Soviet Union. But you're wrong. *This* we were good at.'

My spine went cold. He pushed himself to his feet and went to the door. He was shouting for the witness to be brought in before he opened it. Pasko looked at the sergeant. 'We don't have to worry about this one,' he said. 'His name's never been near the Militia Housing List.'

The 'witness' was a man I'd never seen before. Small but broad-backed. A short overcoat and a fur cap with earmuffs. He seemed to be in his fifties, his features gaunt under a two-day grey bristle on his cheeks. But the eyes had the red-rimmed, watery look of a man twenty years older. Or of a drinker. He was everybody's idea of a nark.

Pasko activated the recorder. 'State your name, age and profession,' Pasko said, 'for the record.'

'Josef Philipovich Koslov,' the man said. 'Age fifty-six. Military officer.'

'When discharged?' I said.

'In 1998. By the Yeltsin scum.'

He had ex-Secret Police nonentity written all over him, from his mean eyes to his ancient KGB commissary boots.

'The prisoner has no right to interrogate the witness,' Pasko thundered, bringing his flat hand down so hard on the tin table that the 'military officer' stumbled back in alarm.

'Just tell us what you saw,' Pasko said, hauling the man forward until he was within a foot or two of the disc recorder.

The man drew a paper from his pocket.

'The witness has drawn a prepared statement from his pocket,' I said, leaning towards the recorder. 'It appears to be in Captain Pasko's handwriting,' I added for the hell of it.

Pasko glared at me, then prodded Koslov. 'Witness statement,' he said. 'Written, signed and dated by former officer J.P. Koslov.'

The witness began to read. This was the time for me to listen.

'On the night in question, Saturday, at approximately four

72

o'clock in the morning, I was crossing the east end of City Square in front of Gorshkov Tower. As I reached the far side, I observed two vehicles draw up about twelve metres apart outside the Gorshkov underground garage entrance. Both drivers alighted, neither was wearing fur hats and I could see clearly it was a man and a blonde woman. They walked towards each other and embraced. The man regained his vehicle and drove off. The blonde woman then walked back towards her own vehicle. In so doing, we passed each other. I greeted the woman as she was known to me as a surgeon from the emergency section of the Lermontov hospital where I have been treated for falls. She responded before getting back into her vehicle and turning into the entrance of the garage of the apartment building called Gorshkov Tower. I positively identify the blonde woman as Dr Natalya Vadim.'

I stared at Pasko and he gave a short laugh. 'So there you are. I think your Natalya faked that call-out on Saturday night.'

'Why should she do that?'

'She's desperate. She had to cancel her Saturday afternoon tryst in Mandelstam Street, remember? She can't imagine a whole weekend without him. She's crawling up the wall. Remember she'll have him anywhere, across an office desk, in the back of a parked Kamka. Anywhere at all.'

This was a torture I hadn't guessed existed. 'For Christ's sake, Pasko . . . !'

He smiled and lowered his voice. 'Anything for a few hours with him. So she waits until you're tied up with the governor. In his library, your statement said. And then she fakes her call, making sure she's out of the party before you've finished talking to his honour.'

I stood my ground but I didn't like this. It had the ring of something. Not of truth perhaps, but of an uncomfortably plausible guesswork. Always given that Natalya was seeing someone.

'Why don't you just drop it all on the table,' Pasko said. He meant confess.

'I've nothing to drop.'

'You know what former military officer Koslov's evidence does.'

I glared at Koslov. 'I know what's going to happen to former military officer Koslov if ever one of my patrols picks him up drunk.'

'What witness Koslov's evidence does,' Pasko said as smoothly as he was able, 'is to put Natalya fairly and squarely back in your apartment with you waiting to see what the fuck she's been up to for the last four hours. The rest of the picture's easy. You work yourself into a red-eyed fury – who can blame you? There she is – the smell of him still on her. You hit her. Harder than you intend. She goes down. And doesn't get up. Your problem now is where to dump the body.'

'And I drive out in my Tolstoy to Intersection 33 in a full blizzard?'

Pasko floated his hands in the air. 'The blizzard had dropped off by then. But in any case you didn't need to drive out there in your Tolstoy. Your wife had just left her Kamka in the underground car park, remember. Witness Koslov has just told us. You had the ideal vehicle.'

'Fantasy,' I said. 'Based on false evidence obtained by bribery or intimidation.'

'That's what your expensive lawyer would say. But then we look at the next eighteen hours and what do we see? We see a man making calls to the hospital, talking to his wife's friends, a man even reporting her missing. A man, in short, desperate to divert the suspicion of an experienced investigating officer like myself.' He paused. 'I'm looking for your co-operation, Vadim. Drop your trousers. A full confession. And I'll see what I can do on my side.'

Was it possible that Koslov was telling the truth? My head was spinning in slow circles. Was it possible? I jerked my head towards him. 'Where did you find him?' I asked Pasko.

'He came forward like a responsible citizen would, when he read the report that your wife was missing.'

I looked once more at the gloating smile on Koslov's face and turned my back on him. 'You low bastard,' I said to Pasko. But what else did I expect?

I I

I WAS LEFT ALONE by Pasko throughout the day. You'll take my word for it that this was worryingly strange, brothers. The time to get to me, in Pasko's dog-eared Soviet book at least, was now. When I was at my lowest, worried sick about Natalya, frightened by my inability to do anything about it.

But . . . Ah, you'll say – if Pasko knew you were worried about Natalya, he'd know you're not responsible for her disappearance. Sadly, our long and dishonourable traditions don't work like that. Pasko wants a confession – that is the only evidence that counts in our country; that is the end to which every Russian policeman works. We may bungle the forensics, we may lack trained officers – but if the judge hears the magic words *I confess*, he can destroy your life without a second's further soul-searching.

If a confession contradicts the facts – then the facts are wrong. It's simple. And if the facts are wrong – change them.

So I was more than surprised that Pasko did not follow up his advantage. When the duty sergeant brought me in soup and some extra sausage at midday, he gave me a quick wink. 'From what I hear, you'll be back at your own desk before long, Chief?'

I swung myself up from my bunk. 'What do you hear?'

'Captain Pasko's going mad out there. He's stamping around complaining about Moscow. Nothing but trouble, he says, for a devoted officer like himself.'

'So what's happening?' Dronsky was behind this, was my guess. Pulling strings in the capital.

'I don't know any more than that,' the sergeant said. 'But there's trouble from Moscow for the noble captain. Arriving soon. It can't be bad news, can it, Chief?'

Trouble from Moscow for Captain Pasko arrived late afternoon at Station 18 wearing high-heeled pumps, a well-cut dark grey skirt and jacket and a gold necklace at a slender black throat.

The desk sergeant had never seen a woman like her before, a face the colour of light mahogany, six feet tall in her heels and a look of sparkling, imperious fury in her dark eyes. He held the cell door open and *bowed*. Pasko, standing behind him, eyes popping like an advanced thyroid case, seemed incapable of movement.

'Have someone bring us in some tea, Captain,' Agent Cunningham said over her shoulder in passable Russian. 'Fresh lemon. You have fresh lemon in Murmansk?'

She didn't wait for an answer. She had already closed the cell door in Pasko's face. She turned and we shook hands.

'We've met before,' I said.

She lifted her eyebrows in acknowledgement. 'I'll skip saying I'm sorry. That stuff you don't need, right?' She looked at me gravely. 'Your wife's picture is all over the news-stands in the city. That's good. She's got a face you remember. I picked up a couple of early editions. Pasko seems to have held back on releasing details of your arrest.'

'Because he knows his case is nothing more than a fistful of air.'

She nodded. 'So first things first . . .'

'Just a moment. I have questions,' I said. 'What's an American doing here? What have you got to do with Natalya's disappearance?'

'This case has American connections, Captain.' This was a lady with a firm manner about her. 'We'll get down to that in a moment.'

'OK,' I said reluctantly. 'But just tell me this. Was it Dronsky that contacted you?'

'He flew up from Moscow with me this morning.'

'Dronsky's in Murmansk?' It was the first piece of really good news I'd had since this whole thing started.

'Dronsky had Pasko fax everything on the case to the airport lounge before we left Moscow. We read up on the plane. When we landed at Murmansk he went straight from the airport down to Intersection 33 on the Kanevka highway, where they found Natalya's scarf. He'll be back here as soon as he has anything.'

I was trying hard to keep up with what was happening. 'So Dronsky's here. That I understand. What about you?'

'I'm here with the authority of the All-Russia Procurator's Office. Captain Dronsky and myself are jointly in charge of this investigation.'

'I mean why *you*?'

'To investigate the disappearance of an American consular officer.'

My mouth opened and closed. 'Another disappearance?'

'Pasko's been keeping you in the dark. A woman was abducted from the US consular staff here in Murmansk.' She grimaced.

'Abducted?'

'It looks like it.'

'You make a connection?'

'Two attractive young professional women disappear *on the same night*. Both their cars are found abandoned in the North Bay area. I'd say there just might be a connection, Captain.'

'On the same night,' I said, my mouth open. 'Jesus Christ.'

The door opened and the desk sergeant came in. He was carrying a tray with a glass of tea and a saucer with a small mound of biscuits. 'Your tea,' the sergeant said with a look at the American woman that strangely combined alarm and unbridled lust. Pasko's shadow, I saw, was lurking out in the corridor.

Agent Cunningham shut the door after the sergeant. She opened her briefcase and drew out some papers. I saw there were two or three large photographs tucked underneath them.

'Just wait a minute,' I said. 'Did Dronsky know last night when I spoke to him that there'd been another abduction? This American consular woman.'

'My application to fly to Murmansk crossed Captain Dronsky's desk a matter of hours before you called. The moment he heard from you he called my office at the embassy and said there might be a match.'

'He said nothing to me.'

'What do you want from a friend? He dropped everything and took the next plane up here, for Christ's sake,' she said. She watched me as I leaned back against the cell wall.

'Yes,' I said, reeling under the barrage of this powerful woman. 'Of course he did.'

'Before we begin, I have a couple of questions.' Her eyes hardened. 'Did you ever meet Joan Fowler?'

'Is that the woman from the consular staff who's missing? No.'

'Ever hear your wife talk of her?'

'No.'

'Ever had any dealings with the US consulate? Visa applications, educational grants, cultural matters . . .?'

'No.'

'What about your wife?'

'Not that I can think of, no.'

'Does your wife speak English?'

'Yes.'

'As well as you?'

'No, but pretty good.'

'Never tempted to attend lectures at the consulate? American life and literature, that sort of thing?'

'My wife's more interested in Russian life and literature. I'm the Anglo-Saxon in the family.'

We stood with our eyes locked. She was only an inch or two shorter than I was, and even across the narrow cell she had no need to lift her head. I thought the hard stare of those dark hazel eyes would hold me for ever. Then she dipped her head briskly. Her tongue slipped round her upper lip; she bent down and took a glass of tea, sipped at it and set it down again on the cement floor. 'OK, here's the story.' She handed me the first photograph. A woman in her mid-thirties. Broad smile. American teeth. 'Joan Fowler. Worked at the consulate here since the Civil War ended. Good Russian. Very into Russian culture, Russian writers, painters. She ran a course of lectures on the American way . . . that sort of jazz.'

'Married?'

'Divorced.' She paused. 'When she first arrived about a year ago she ran around a little so my predecessor kept an eye on her. But she was OK, stayed within the guidelines. Nobody she was fucking seemed to have any government, Russian government that is, connections. So we lifted the surveillance to intermittent.'

'And missed him.'

'We suspended surveillance over six months ago.' She bit on her bottom lip, not a lady who found a concession easy to make. 'Her boss,' she said, 'the US consul up here, Miles Bridger, said there had been more recent reports of some sort of stalker hanging around.'

'A stalker?'

'Ring a bell?'

'There were similar reports of a man hanging around Natalya some time after Christmas.'

'Description?'

'In winter people muffle up in Murmansk.'

78

'Spring too,' she said. 'Summer for all I know, if they've any goddam sense.'

'The story,' I said, handing back the photograph.

'Joan Fowler had two dates Sunday morning. One to meet her boss Miles Bridger to go over some accounting anomalies.'

'Anomalies? You mean the books didn't add up?'

'We have the accountant checking it out now. It may be nothing.'

'How much are we talking about?'

Abby Cunningham turned down her full lower lip.

'I'm in this too, remember.'

Her tongue flicked across her teeth. 'Fifty thousand dollars,' she said.

'That's nothing?'

'It's not certain it's missing yet, Captain.'

'Over how long?'

'A couple of months, maybe. Miles Bridger is confident it'll turn up.'

'Good for Miles,' I said. 'This could only happen in Russia, uh?'

She glared at me. 'Sunday morning,' she said heavily, 'Joan failed to turn up at her meeting with Miles. Nor did she make the Sportika Club where she had arranged to meet a friend for lunch. By afternoon the consul had sent someone round to her apartment. Nothing. No sign of Joan. Further enquiries, and by Sunday evening we start getting a story about a man she'd been seeing.'

'A new friend?'

'She told her girlfriend she'd met a Russian guy at her lectures. He hung around her. A sort of sheepdog type.'

'So we have a description?'

'Joan's girlfriend saw him once only. He came in and sat at the back. As soon as she saw him, Joan called a coffee break and slipped out for a few minutes with him.'

'You're sure he *was* Russian?'

'The girlfriend heard him speak. Limited English with a Russian accent.'

'What about a description?'

'Unhelpful. Quite tall, fairly young . . .'

'That's all?'

'Edgy. Agitated. Tense. Super-stressed-out. That was the body language, according to the girlfriend. She's a lifestyle adviser to the American business community here. Super-stressed. Negative body language. She talks like that.'

'You've tried a video-fit? '

'Nothing usable.' She paused to drink some tea. 'According to her, Joan and this man had been seeing each other for about a month.'

'Screwing?'

'From Joan's record it could be safely enough inferred.'

I was struggling to absorb all this. 'When was Joan Fowler last seen?'

'We have a witness who can place her in her apartment early Saturday evening. Joan turned down a dinner invitation – from the Lifestylist. Joan said she was busy – didn't say who with.'

'So she disappeared sometime Saturday evening. Like Natalya?'

'Looks like it.'

I dropped my head, baffled. 'Anything else?'

She looked away, then back at me. 'Something else. But strange.' There was something in her dark eyes, but I couldn't work out whether it was sympathy or indifference. 'You'd better prepare yourself.'

'Prepare myself?'

'For something pretty weird. A trade mark.'

I gagged at the idea. Murderers leave trade marks, rapists very rarely. Abductors . . . I just didn't know. 'A trade mark. What is it?'

'Joan's car was found abandoned, as I said.' She consulted her papers. 'The North Bay area.' She looked up at me. 'Two or three hundred yards from where your wife's Kamka was found.'

'A trade mark.' I moved to face her. 'There was something in the car?'

'Yes.' She looked at me evenly and passed me another photograph. Colour. It was of a medium-size Audi, dark blue or black, stationary against a background of the ruined buildings of North Bay. But at the window of the car was an outline of someone sitting in the driver's seat . . . more than an outline. A face. 'I thought you said there was no-one in the car. Who's this?'

'*What* is this?' she corrected me. 'It's an effigy, Captain. A doll. Life-size.'

I stared at her, speechless. 'A sex doll?' was all I could think of saying.

'Not obviously. Latex. Reddish hair like Joan's. Fur coat. American underwear, Joan Fowler's.'

'Jesus Christ,' I said. I was standing still but my mind was reeling. Maybe Agent Cunningham saw this, and wanted to give me time to recover. I couldn't guess.

For whatever reason she went into a formal description that she might have been reading from a catalogue. 'My estimate is that its original manufactured purpose was a model intended for high-quality window dressing. Legs, arms and neck articulated. There's certain evidence of repaired damage, but, new, a thing like that could cost over five hundred bucks.' She handed me the last picture. An astonishingly, shockingly realistic face. Pale, deliberately whitened, even. The eyes painted closed, as in death.

I stared at it, my heart thumping. 'What sort of a man . . .?'

'As of now we know nothing,' she said in a hard voice. 'We have to work on it.'

I took a deep breath. It fluttered uncertainly into my lungs. 'OK . . . this, but no sign of a body.'

'Not so far.'

'You mean a matter of time?'

'I don't know. We don't know what we're dealing with yet.' She picked up her glass of tea and handed it to me. 'Drink.'

I took it and drank. 'Do you have a cigarette?'

'I shouldn't admit to it.'

'I'll keep your secret.'

She gave me a cigarette and lit it. She didn't take one herself.

'What about the forensic on this model?'

'I'd say the model was carefully cleaned before painting. Free of hair and fibre. The nail polish matched Joan's own make. American Max Factor Black Rose. Probably from Joan's purse. The paint is a common water-base emulsion. The most useful information is about the latex itself. Work's continuing on it. It could provide us with a lead to the manufacturer. And with luck from there to a supplier and from supplier to our man.'

'You got all this from *our* forensic?' I couldn't believe it.

She grimaced. 'We sent samples to Helsinki. We got it all moving before I left Moscow.'

I inhaled. 'Did the car have anything to tell us?'

'*That* we couldn't ship,' she said. 'Lots of fingerprints which Station 5 Homicide tells me will take the best part of a month to check out.'

'Anything else?'

'There was some frozen vomit on the side of the car. Bread and alcohol. Our abductor was under strain.'

I could see him there, the car parked, the job done. And then the terrible relief, the urge to vomit as he stood with one gloved hand resting on the roof of the Audi.

'You OK?' she said.

'No. I'm very far from OK. I'm locked in a police cell while my wife is, in all probability, in the hands of a sex lunatic.'

'Sit down.' She reached up and pressed hard on my shoulder. She indicated the cigarette. 'Inhale.'

I drew deeply on the cigarette. It hit my head like a warm, cotton-filled sock. 'It's weed,' I said.

'So?'

'So nothing. I have to get out.'

'Is Pasko's witness going to be a problem? If he can be squared away Advocate Grandov says he'll have you out of here by morning.'

'Pasko's witness could be bought for a litre of shampoo vodka. But there's something else,' I said. 'Pasko's line is that Natalya was fooling around. I'm down as the jealous husband . . .'

I could see she was waiting. I inhaled deeply. My head swam with the weed. But the smoke dulled, comforted. Thinking was like a march in slow circles. 'I went to Natalya's office . . .' I said. 'You know that.'

'I read Pasko's report.'

'The packet of condoms . . . it was a plant.'

'He says no.'

'What else would he say, for Christ's sake.'

'OK – a *possible* plant.'

'By Pasko, or by someone else,' I said desperately. 'I don't know.'

She looked up. 'I have to ask you, Inspector . . .' Her eyes were troubled. 'There's no doubt? I'm asking, do we have a man who takes a woman out a couple of times to gain their confidence, then . . . then abducts them? Do we have a situation like that?'

I kept control. 'Why would a vek like that take two women on the same night?'

'OK, we have two men. They get their kicks by working together. It's rare but not unknown. In Los Angeles in 1999 two cousins . . .'

I held up my hands to stop her.

'Presumably your wife had ample *opportunity* to fool around – odd work schedules, call-outs at all hours . . .'

'Dronsky must have told you about Natalya, for Christ's sake,' I said fiercely.

Nothing moved in her face.

'It's a thing a man always knows,' I said. 'If Natalya had been running something on the side . . .' I stopped and pulled in a sharp breath. 'She couldn't have been as she was. You understand me?'

She finished her tea and stood up. 'A thing a man always knows, uh? Well, maybe.'

I felt a flare of anger. 'You know what I'm saying.'

She stood her ground. 'I'm not digging around in your life, Captain. At least not just for the hell of it. But take it from someone who's been there. This is *not* a thing a man always knows.' She turned away. 'I'll be back before morning.' She crossed to the door and hammered on it, then turned back to me as she waited while the sergeant's keys rattled in the lock. I think she wanted to change the tone as she left, to ease the moment. 'Uh . . . I forgot to pass it on,' she said as the door opened. 'Dronsky made a point of saying V.I. Lenin sends his best wishes.' Her eyebrows shot up.

I looked at her. V.I. Lenin is a cat. Dronsky's office cat in Moscow. Dark marmalade, with a sort of weird tuft on his chin which makes his name apposite enough, but no more agreeable to contemplate across the desk. He has one party trick which is to raise his paw in greeting or farewell, and this has endeared him to Dronsky. Not to me. I am not seduced by his feline charms, brothers. I'm happy for V.I. Lenin to stay in Moscow. Or accept a posting as office cat to some weather-bound station in Norilsk. Maybe Agent Cunningham doesn't realize. I try and let her down gently. 'V.I. Lenin,' I tell her, 'is a *cat*. Dronsky's office cat.'

'We met in Moscow.' She nodded approval. 'Real cute.' She lifted her hand and opened her fingers in a V.I. Lenin salute. 'Take care.'

Agent Cunningham passed through into the corridor and the sergeant swung the door closed behind her. I stood and stretched my arms. With my fingertips I could touch both walls, even touch the names and dates deeply scratched into the painted metal.

You wouldn't think a small cell with a chair, bunk and basin and a biggish man standing alone in the middle could be an empty place. But it is.

None emptier, brothers.

AN HOUR LATER, I was in chains. On Pasko's insistence. A heavy overcoat, a militia fur hat and thick gloves protected me from the ice in the wind. The raucous music, the shrieks of women, the raised angry voices of drunk men – all the sounds and smells of Sin City came floating in invisibly around me. But I was in chains as they bundled me across the inner courtyard formed by the portable huts, and into the first of two waiting riot vans. Ilya Dronsky was sitting in the back seat.

It was three months since I'd seen him. 'Dronsky . . .' Chains clinking, I put out my hand to shake his. With a grunt he pulled me forward in an enveloping hug. Dronsky is a man of few words. He released me and sat back, his hands resting on my shoulders. 'We'll get you out of this, Chief,' he said. 'We'll find her.'

I tried a wry smile. But it didn't work. My lips had gone rubbery. I was finding it hard to keep control of my mouth. I swallowed hard and quickly looked across to where Pasko was crossing the yard and making for the van. 'Before he gets here,' I said urgently. 'What's happening now?'

'We're going out to the highway. Intersection 33.'

'Where her scarf was found?'

'I was out there straight from the airport. There's more work to do there. Maybe something else to find. I reminded Pasko it's a possible scene of crime. He was failing in his duty to keep a couple of men posted out there.'

'And what now?'

'I'm insisting we take some men back and check over both sides of the road. I said you had to be there. We couldn't miss the opportunity of an on-site confession.'

This time I raised a smile. On-site confessions are dear to Russian murder inquiries. The emotion of revisiting the scene of the crime is supposed to trigger an overwhelming desire to tell all.

Pasko was in a black mood, cursing that he had not had a decent night's sleep since I called him out in the early hours of Monday morning. He swung himself into the passenger seat and grunted a go-ahead to the driver. Slowly we pulled out onto the gaudy main street of Sin City, the driver glancing in his mirror to make sure the other van was following us.

The blizzard was down to little more than a few short ferocious tugs of wind, with, every now and again, a swirl of powdered snow rising in the headlights in a pale twister like a Disney ghost. At Intersection 33 the two vans drew cautiously onto the roadside and the ten militiamen with picks and shovels climbed out of the vehicle behind us. I was escorted by our driver, armed with an ancient Kalashnikov AK 47 against the wholly unlikely event I made a wild dash in my chains for the endless snowfields on either side of the road.

Dronsky took control of the men. 'The scarf was found fluttering from that post on the central reservation,' he said. 'We're here on the assumption there was some sort of accident. Maybe real, maybe staged. I want you to clear the fresh snow from each side of the road thirty metres forward and back.'

'The scarf could have blown miles in the blizzard we had on Saturday night,' Pasko said.

Dronsky nodded. 'But I don't think it did. It had a silver clip attached to it.'

I shuddered. I had given her the clip when she got her appointment to the Lermontov.

The men had been clearing snow less than ten minutes when a shout from one of them brought Pasko and Dronsky over to where he was working. I followed up behind them. When I got there I saw that several small trees had been snapped off back a few metres from the roadside. Two men with birch-twig brooms were brushing at the loose snow between the broken trees and the road.

As we watched, tyre marks were revealed, the rubber having bitten into the ice below. A vehicle had run off the road and crashed through the trees. As the militiamen brought up more lights I could see broken pieces of orange plastic indicator lights scattered in the snow.

Dronsky turned from Pasko and came back slowly towards me, a squat figure in a bundled parka and rubber boots. He took out cigarettes and offered one to me. I shook my head. 'What do you make of it?'

'A truck,' he said. 'Not enormous. Maybe even a van. Wearing chains on a good new set of tyres. Even so, it's going fast enough to skid off the road.'

'When?'

He shrugged inside his heavy-weather parka. 'It has to be Saturday night. The tyre marks are fresh enough. And a crash next to the place Natalya's scarf was found . . .? I'd say it was Saturday night for certain, Chief.'

He walked back to the section of roadside where six or seven militiamen were working, sweeping snow in wide strokes of their birch brooms. With every two or three strokes they rested the handles of their brooms against their chests and banged their gloved hands together. Pasko had gone to sit in the van. He had turned the radio on and I could hear some soupy music from fifty years ago. The Nostalgia Channel. Not the Beatles or Rolling Stones. Certainly not Duke Ellington. Marisa singing soupy hits from the Soviet era: *'Oh bring me a love-gift, dear Stork, my feathered friend.'*

As the men swept snow, the picture emerged. In order to provide some grip for the tyres when the driver reversed back onto the road, packing had been placed behind the wheels. Splintered branches of fir, a foot, two feet long, crushed and snapped by the weight of the vehicle, were embedded in the snow. Dronsky picked up a few of the bigger pieces.

'So there was an accident,' he said. 'Something had run off the road, maybe somebody hurt. Natalya was called to it. How? We don't exactly know beyond the fact it was a call to her pager. Who called her? A blank. So was it a real accident – or a staged accident?'

'An accident was *staged*?' The cold and a pressing apprehension seemed to be clogging my thought processes.

'Maybe, Chief. Remember we don't have any evidence of injured admitted to any city hospitals.'

Alarm surged through me: 'Staged. To get Natalya called out there? Lure her out there, you mean?'

He was looking down at his snow-encrusted boots. Or maybe at the pieces of splintered fir in his hands. 'Perhaps it was just a straight accident. But an accident that for some reason hasn't been reported. Now say someone passing, perhaps on the other side of the crash barrier, saw it and called for help.'

'And Natalya took the call?' I shook my head. 'It won't play,

Ilya. The call would have been routed to one of the hospital emergency departments. I checked. It wasn't.'

'Unless this was someone who knew her and decided to make the call straight to her.'

'Why would anyone do that? They'd call the Lermontov, surely. Or some other hospital on this side of town.'

'OK,' he said slowly. 'But they didn't, did they, Chief? Signs of a recent crash within a few metres of the place Natalya's scarf was found say they didn't. *Why?*'

The wind cut through our coats and sent swirling snow whistling and dancing across the blank slopes around us. I watched the men brushing and digging. In this inhuman climate it looked like newsreel film I had once seen of a group of Stalin's zeks working under bright lights in the inhuman cold of Siberia's Magadan camps.

'Captain,' Pasko's militia sergeant came over. 'You should see this.'

We turned to where two of the men were brushing carefully, removing snow from dozens of trampled footprints underneath. 'A lot of footprints,' Dronsky said almost to himself. 'A light army truck. Or a minibus even?'

I looked down at the footmarks. 'The passengers got down and pushed.'

Dronsky was frowning. He pointed with the long branch of wood in his hand, touching the heel and toe of one footprint after another. It took me far too long to see what he meant.

'The size,' I said. 'They're too small for adults. Children . . .?'

He nodded. 'The passengers were all children.'

'A busload of children? At that hour? It was midnight or more.'

'That's what all those footprints tell us, Chief.'

'OK,' I said reluctantly. 'We'll think about the children later. So one of them was hurt. Someone on the bus knew Natalya's pager number and called her as the quickest way of getting help out here. They'd know Natalya wouldn't stand on red tape if a child was in pain.'

'Keep going, Chief.'

'So she comes out. Treats the child. And maybe a couple of others. Nothing serious, as it turns out. So they get the vehicle back on the road, heading God knows where. It's left the scene as Natalya gathers her things together and heads back to her Kamka ... Or she's standing alone watching the bus drive off.'

'And?'

I take a deep, freezing breath. My head is clearing. I think of the old lady in the tent. 'No. If she was abducted here, her Kamka would have been left here.'

Dronsky frowns into the wind. 'Then what about this? A passing car has stopped to offer help. The children's van is back on the road but it's Natalya who has driven off first. The vek who stopped now follows her. Closer to the city he pulls alongside and cuts her into the side.'

'Could be . . .'

'Then this is not a lover, remember that. This is a stranger. A man looking for a woman, Chief. Any woman.'

But it wasn't any woman. It was Natalya.

I was standing staring at the smooth white of the snowfield on this side of the road, wondering how Joan Fowler's abduction fitted into all this, when the square shape of a building materialized from the whiteness. I pulled Dronsky by the arm and pointed. For a moment he stared before he saw it too. A long factory-like building, not sixty metres away, in a dip which had received heavy drifts of snow. Its access would have been from the road which crossed the highway to make Intersection 33.

Pasko was no longer afraid we would make off into the snow. We took one of the militia vans and drove the few metres off the highway which brought us to the entrance to a factory yard. Dronsky turned in through the gap and parked the van on the side away from the snowdrifts that reached to the roof of the building.

We got down into the stinging wind. The factory was long abandoned, the doors hanging off. From the lines of overhead wires I'd guess it had once been one of the many fish-drying plants that were located just beyond the outskirts of the city.

The wind had driven a wide swathe of snow across the entrance to the shop floor. Dronsky moved his flashlight beam into the building. We could see clearly, under a light covering of snow, the tracks of a vehicle which had been driven and stopped there. A set of tracks returning towards the door suggested the vehicle had been driven out again, probably, to judge from the snow cover here, some hours later. We examined the tracks. The driving wind had broken up any tyre patterns we might have identi-fied.

'So if these tracks are Natalya's Kamka,' Dronsky said, 'then I was wrong about her being followed back to the city.'

'Which means any abduction must have taken place here on Intersection 33,' I said.

For a moment neither of us spoke, both, I suppose, conjuring his own version of the scene out there on the highway during Saturday night's blizzard.

For another half-hour we searched the factory and found no evidence that anybody had penetrated further than the front doors where the vehicle had been left. Ten bitterly complaining militiamen raked the snow in the yard outside, driven mercilessly by Dronsky. But the search there produced nothing.

So Natalya's Kamka had simply been left here for collection later and disposal in the wastelands of North Bay. But why do that? Why take the risk of coming back to collect the Kamka? Why not just abandon it here?

13

I WAS BACK ALONE in my cell. Police cells, even temporary cells, have their own noise routine. The desk sergeant's footsteps along the corridor, a snatch of tuneless whistling. The clatter of soup bowls. The rattle of keys against a metal door; the squeak of hinges. And the shouts of protest.

Even the special shows don't differ a lot from gaol to gaol. I could swear I'd heard a hundred times before the voices of the two drunks next door, rendering, with the same bathos, the first chorus of *Your eyes as blue as cornflowers on the steppe* or, in fighting mood, a rousing denunciation of tyranny from the *Internationale*.

I sat on my bunk with the Communist *Internationale* ringing in my ears. It was less than six months now to the centenary of the Communist Revolution of 1917. For a moment my mind drifted over all those things Natalya and I had talked about. She had been passionate in her belief that 1917 was the single greatest disaster that had ever struck a nation. And yet there had still been no word of apology or regret, no national denunciation of the racism and anti-Semitism and sheer blood lust that had carried away so many innocent millions of the citizens of the Soviet Union. Facing reality is something nobody does easily, Russians least of all. It's been a Russian problem since long before the façades of model villages were being built by Potemkin, the Tsarina's chief minister, to create a false sense of affluence for gullible foreigners – and, of course, a comforting sense of superiority for Russians. We more than half believe our own deceptions, you see.

I cannot avoid wondering if this is true for me too. Have I deceived myself about Natalya? Is *my* Natalya no more than a woman I have shaped and sculpted from my own needs? Is the *real* Natalya somebody quite different? Is it possible the old fortune teller at Sin City was trying to tell me exactly that? And had I, like a good Russian, looked away?

* * *

At eleven o'clock the burring of the electric bell meant the shift was changing and the night duty officers were coming on. Ten minutes later Sergeant Bubin unlocked my cell and came in with a plate of good sausage and a half-litre of Hero City vodka. He waggled the bottle. 'The best I could do, Chief,' he said.

'It's very welcome.'

He put the plate and bottle on the floor and took two glasses from his pocket. 'Don't mind if I join you? It's a quiet night as nights go in Sin City.'

'Bubin, it's a pleasure.' I gestured for him to sit on the bunk. A broad-beamed man like desk sergeants anywhere, he winced as the springs groaned under him.

'Now when's this nonsense going to be over, Chief?'

'It can't be soon enough for me, Bubin.'

'This American woman from Moscow's giving Pasko the run-around.' He poured two glasses of vodka and began to cut off slices of sausage. 'Will she make him release you?'

'I'm sure of it.' I was reassuring him.

We chewed sausage and downed the vodka together. 'You heard the news about the governor, I suppose?' he said, between dangerously picking at his teeth with the point of the knife.

'Governor Badanov? No. What's happened?'

'A helicopter accident last night. Faulty fuel gauge. He was coming back from Petersburg. The report says they never cleared Lake Lagoda.'

'They crashed in the lake?'

'Seven killed.' Bubin cut some more sausage. 'For the city it's a disaster. There'll be no visit from the American Mission now.'

I thought of Mariya Badanova. I wanted to see her. To tell her how sorry I was. 'Listen, Bubin,' I said. 'I need to send a message tonight, to Madame Badanova. Will you fax it for me?'

He went off to get writing-paper and I sat in the cell, the door open, sipping the vodka so that it rolled across my tongue. If it's good vodka, it's worth doing. Even with bad vodka like this it gets you drunk more slowly.

I lifted my glass. What would we do without it? An echo there, somewhere? Of the tenth-century prince Vladimir who decreed Russia should be Christian rather than Islamic on the good grounds that Russians would never give up alcohol. So Russians were already mad for release even before hard liquor appeared on the scene. From Western merchants, of course, in

1386. The English, or maybe the Scots, obviously recognized the potential of the market because within no time the naturalized word *Drinki* was the Russian call for a thumb of vodka. Since then, we haven't looked back. Two bottles a week is now the Russian male *average*.

You'll understand, brothers, that these ramblings served to keep my fears at bay. If not at bay, at fingertip distance at least. It was seventy-two hours since Natalya disappeared. Seventy-two hours since she drove into a snow blizzard on the Kanevka road and, for whatever reason, stopped at Intersection 33.

Abby Cunningham came back just after midnight. When she peeled off what appeared to be a cashmere topcoat, she was wearing jeans, a blue V-neck sweater and a white shirt. She threw a pack of newspapers down on the bunk. 'Thought you might want to catch up with the other news,' she said.

I could see Governor Badanov's death in the helicopter crash was the *Kola Pravda* headline. I didn't bother to look at the other papers. I pushed myself off the wall. 'Listen to me, Agent Cunningham,' I said. 'We have to talk.'

Her eyes lifted and rested on my face.

'How close am I to getting out of here?'

'Very close. Your lawyer, Grandov, packs a big punch. He's blocked off every single attempt by Pasko's office to mount further charges.'

'But I'm losing ground here.'

'You're losing no ground, Inspector. Dronsky's doing everything you would have been doing yourself. The guy's a bulldog.' She paused. 'A bulldog and a hell of a good friend.'

'Listen to me, I need to be out, working this. I need to be on the street looking for this man, for Christ's sake.'

'Right now you can do more here than you can out on the street,' she said. She dropped a pencil and militia notepad on the bed. 'I want you to write me a full account of Natalya's life in the last three weeks. All the detail that doesn't usually rate a mention.'

'I've already done that.'

'Sit, Constantin,' she said fiercely. 'Think like you never thought before. Two abductions. Connected only at this moment by the identity of the perp.'

'What's that?'

'Jargon. Not pretty. The perpetrator. What do you call him?'

'The vek. Just means the guy. The guy who did it.'

'The vek,' she said. 'I like it.'

'So what are we looking for?'

'Connections. They're there somewhere. A whole network. At the end of every case I say it to myself, every single time: *we could have known earlier*. We *should* have known earlier. You're probably the only one who can do it.'

'Make the connection between Natalya and Joan Fowler? You don't know they're connected.'

'I know they are,' she said.

'He took them both the same night. That's the connection.'

'No. There's one step beyond that. Believe it,' she said. 'They used the same hairdresser. Or the same gas station. Maybe the same sauna masseuse. Or they both played badminton, painted in oils, played the fucking violin. Any detail could lead us to the vek who took them.' From her jacket she drew several sheets of paper and put them down in front of me.

'What's this?'

'Lists,' she said. 'Made by Joan's boss, the consul. Made by her colleagues, her friends. Joan Fowler's life is in those lists.'

'What do you want me to do with them?'

'Read them. Something might jump out at you. If nothing does, start drawing up a similar list for Natalya. Something, somewhere will match.'

I think I believed her. I wanted to believe her. I wanted to believe I could contribute something. I watched her sit down and take out a packet of plain wrapper cigarettes. She waved the pack at me.

'Not now.' I wasn't going anywhere but the weed would dull the acuity of the moment. If I was to make the connection she said I was capable of making, I would need to be more sharp-thinking than the weed would leave me.

'Go ahead, write,' she said. 'I'll just sit in with you a while.'

She straddled the chair, took a cigarette from her pocket and like a card-sharp rolled and twisted it across her fingers.

'You're better than Dronsky.'

'You grow up in South Boston,' she said, making the cigarette stand on the manicured nail of her index finger, 'as a kid you need *something*. Later you learn to wiggle ass to get what you want.' She flicked the cigarette to me and I caught it. 'For later when you can write no more.'

I sat on the bunk, pulling my feet up. Like a child frightening himself in the dark I let the most appalling thoughts steal through the tunnels of my mind. I started to write. I listed every detail of Natalya's life in the last weeks. So many. I scribbled like a madman, making list on list. After ten or fifteen minutes, she got up quietly and left without speaking. I worked on. I was sweating, writing and concentrating as I've never written or concentrated in my life. I was lost in the passage of time.

It was a bad night. But the anguish of dreams is nothing like as bad as the anguish of waking reality. Four or five times I woke in the night, running in sweat and relief that the nightmare was over – that it was just a dream, that Natalya was not really missing. Only to reach out for her across the prison cot and be shocked awake and do what? Moan, cry out . . .? All I know it was enough to get a voice next door yelling. 'Quiet, fuck your mother. A man's got a right to sleep at least!'

And I would turn over and lie there thinking of Natalya in the days before Saturday night until I drifted back to sleep.

I awoke the next morning to the sound of singing in the next cell, a younger occupant, a new melody, a free adaptation of an American song: *In the wee small hours of the morning.* 'A tribute to the late Frank Sinatra,' the new man announced.

I rolled into a sitting position and got up, not at all inclined to shout for the tuneless singing to stop. Resting my hot forehead against the cold steel door, I even concentrated on the shockingly bad translations of a set of old Frank Sinatra songs that followed. I had this strange feeling that the anguish of the night had wrung me dry of pain for a while at least. Missing her, being fearful for her, had been like this from the beginning, reaching peaks of awfulness before subsiding to something almost tolerable.

I sat back on my bunk. I had to get a shower. I shivered in the sticky gaol temperatures. Along the corridor I heard the footsteps, the whistling, the keys, the clatter of the morning soup bowls. Another day.

The papers Abby Cunningham had brought in were lying on the floor. I picked up the *Pravda* and read the story on the governor's death. He had taken off from Petersburg in a big all-weather helicopter and had gone down on Lake Lagoda, crashing through the ice some fifty kilometres from land. The rescue teams had found the wreckage fifteen metres down, hanging by the rotors from the ice shelf. Any man who was not killed on impact was drowned in the freezing water.

I thought of Madame Badanova again as I turned the pages. There she was in a photograph with her husband when he was elected governor on an anti-corruption platform.

I flicked through some of the other papers. The stories were much the same. There were a few suggestions that the fuel gauge on the helicopter had been tampered with – but there always were these suggestions in the press. Nothing was allowed any longer to be a simple accident due to forgetfulness and incompetence. And, God knows, vodka made sure there had always been enough of both in Russia. But I had to think of Roy's hint. Maybe the papers were right.

Yet already Anton Badanov was yesterday's news. By sometime next month we would have a new governor. I was sorry. I was sad for Madame Badanova. But my own worries preoccupied me.

I fretted through one of those endless prison mornings. I refused the soup and accepted an apple the turnkey slipped to me. Then I went through a few old Navy exercises which only succeeded in pulling muscles I'd forgotten about. I had slumped back onto the bunk to read the papers from page to page and was dozing through the messy divorce of unsuccessful architect Boris someone and his wife, successful health-shop owner Irina, when I heard Pasko's voice in the corridor. He did not sound pleased with life.

I got up and stood stretching, rubbing my eyes as he entered, bringing his own particular odour into the cell as he heeled closed the door. He glared at me and kicked at the newspapers on the floor. 'Sergeant,' he yelled for the day-man. 'Prisoners for interrogation have no right to newspapers unless the interrogating officer . . .'

'Agent Cunningham brought them in.'

Pasko stopped in mid-shout.

'She required me to read them as part of *her* investigation,' I said.

Pasko's shoulders slumped. He pushed his peaked cap back from his forehead. It was difficult to gauge his mood. He took out his tobacco and began to roll a cigarette. 'How can anyone be expected to conduct a proper investigation these days?' he said suddenly. His lip thrust gloomily.

Was he looking for sympathy? 'Things aren't what they were when you were young,' I said.

'That's true enough.' He handed me his tobacco pouch. 'Listen, Vadim. We do our best, uh?'

'What?'

'Sometimes things are not exactly what we think. Help yourself to a smoke. That's an everyday fact of life for the investigating militia. We've all been through it. And an honest mistake, freely admitted . . .'

'What's happened?' I said.

'How do you afford a lawyer like Grandov?'

'I have friends.'

He scowled. 'He's got together with the black bitch. They've been examining my witness.'

'The drunk you paid to say he saw my wife go into our apartment early Sunday morning? What happened, he caved in?'

He stretched his long neck. 'At the end of an hour, my witness formally withdrew his statement.'

'I'm astonished.' I pushed the tobacco pouch back into his pocket. 'The condoms in the desk drawer, you planted them too.'

'No.'

'You're lying.'

'No,' he said. 'Nor did I plant Lydia Vavilova.'

My stomach dropped. 'Vavilova?'

'She's a cleaner at the Lermontov. She has your wife behaving very strange the day before she disappeared.'

'How's that?'

'Locked herself in her room.'

'Natalya did?'

'According to the cleaner. You should speak to her.'

'When I get out of here, I will.'

Pasko urged his big mouth into a smile. 'Listen, my case against you is now shot full of holes. I've had a word with the major commanding Missing Persons. We talked it through this morning. We're pretty much in agreement. We see your arrest as an error in good faith.'

'In good faith?'

'Exactly that.'

'You mean I'm free to go?'

'Any time, Captain.' He stretched out a hand. 'No hard feelings.'

'Plenty,' I said as I walked past him out into the corridor.

14

I COLLECTED MY TOPCOAT, badge-wallet and keys from the day sergeant and walked down the aluminium steps into the cold dark air of morning. Sin City looks bad any time. Early morning it looks like the encampment of a medieval army. The last skeins of smoke from cooking fires drift, desultory, through the alleys of coloured tents. The tramp of feet has turned the surface of the ice to a refrozen brown slush. The rickety wooden structures look more gaudy, more dangerously perched than ever. Men in rabbit-fur hats stumble about, yawning, beating their hands across their chests or lifting vodka bottles to their mouths as they move about their business.

To my astonishment there were, I saw, a few election posters up in the colours of several no-hopers. Or rather up and already defaced. People like environmentalists can't expect a look-in on the Kola Peninsula. But by far the boldest display, and noticeably untouched by the defacers, was in colours with a sinister background for us all. The deep red banner was all too familiar from the Soviet era. The white circle in the lower left-hand corner was filled with a simple cross in the form of an X. It was far too close an evocation of a combined Communist and Nazi banner for comfort. There was, I noticed, no candidate's name given.

I hitched a lift on a cruiser going into the city and, from where I was dropped off, caught a trolley-car to the Lermontov just six stops away. It was still early, before the main day staff began to arrive. I walked past Mikhail Lermontov and his accusatory quill pen, up the steps of the columned portico and through Reception. The security man knew me by sight.

'Where can I find Lydia Vavilova, the cleaner?'

'She was on her way to Surgical when I passed her five minutes ago,' he said.

I thanked him and hurried down the still mostly empty corridors. A few departing night-staff wandered past me, a face or two I recognized. I took the stone stairs and, at the wide landing under the glass dome, turned under the sign pointing to the surgical department wing. The long corridor was empty but for the green overalled figure, almost immediately ahead of me, of Lydia Vavilova. With her bucket and mop she was backing her wide rump into the swing doors of an operating theatre. She stopped, seeing me, and let the doors swing against her back. 'Inspector,' she came forward. 'Any fresh word about Dr Vadim?'

I walked heavily across to a wooden bench under a vast red Aids vaccination poster and sat down. 'Nothing that makes sense.'

Leaning on the mop, squirting soapy water over the lip of the bucket, Lydia looked at me, chewing her lip and staring emptily at the poster above my head.

'When did you last see her, Lydia?' I didn't mention that I knew she'd already told her story to the police. 'Did you see her Saturday?'

With one soapy hand, she lifted strands of grey hair and wove them back into her bun. Her eyes almost disappeared in her round face. 'Saturday, the day she disappeared, there was a call at the docks. A ship on fire. No. The last time I saw her was sometime during the week.'

So what was it Pasko was onto? I looked at Vavilova and she avoided my eye. 'What is it, Lydia?' I said. My heart was pumping hard.

She shrugged. 'On the Friday, some time early afternoon I tried to clean her office but the door was locked.' She hesitated.

'What was unusual about that?'

'The doctor was . . . inside.'

She had something else to say. You have a weighty second sense about such things after you've been a policeman for a few years. Habit set me searching my pockets for a cigarette. Lydia rested her mop and took cigarettes and lighter from her Lermontov overall. She waddled over to sit beside me on the bench, offering a brown paper cigarette.

'The door was locked, you said.'

She lit my cigarette, and nodded as she gestured with her own. 'The door was locked but Dr Vadim was inside with some-one.'

A chill snaked through me. 'You heard voices?'

'Just the one, Dr Vadim's.'

'So she was alone in there on the phone, perhaps?'

She shook her head. 'There's no carpet near the window. I could hear someone else pacing on that side of the room.'

'You're sure of that?'

'There were two of them,' she said firmly. 'I heard Dr Vadim's voice just as I was about to try the door. I heard the other one's footsteps as I was gathering up my cleaning things outside.'

As she was listening at the keyhole, she meant. I had to ask her. 'A man or woman?'

'A heavy tread.'

'You heard nothing that was said?'

She lit her cigarette and took a draw which caused the glowing tip to crackle and spark. 'No . . .' she said. 'Not really.'

'What did my wife's voice sound like?'

She looked at me blankly.

'Calm, worried? Angry, cheerful?'

'She was laughing a lot.'

'You must have caught something. A word or two at the very least.'

Lydia's lips pursed and then flattened across her teeth. 'Two or three times she said: *"No, not here."* Something like that,' Lydia said, her face expressionless. 'But laughing. I didn't tell the other inspector that.'

Somebody turned into the long corridor at the far end. Lydia was on her feet, the burning end of her cigarette flicked by her thumbnail into the pail of water. A quick hiss as it touched the surface. 'My supervisor,' she muttered.

I stood up as the footsteps approached. 'The man . . . did you hear him say anything?'

Lydia kept her head down. 'Just the footsteps, Inspector, I swear to you. Nothing else.'

She picked up her pail and barged her way backwards through the operating theatre doors before the supervisor drew level.

I dropped my head to avoid talking to him. As his footsteps passed, my mind was on that locked door. On the packet of condoms in Natalya's drawer. On her voice, laughing, *'No, not here.'*

Not here, of course, means something. Something I just couldn't push away. *No, not here* means: *Somewhere else, yes!*

I walked slowly down the long stone-floored passage towards the entrance. I managed a nod to some familiar faces but couldn't remember them seconds after they passed. At Reception there were already more people about, staff coming on duty mostly, a sense of bustle and greetings being exchanged. I knew this was one of the things Natalya loved about working in a big hospital.

People flowed around me. The young man in the white coat, turning away from the newspaper stand with a copy of *Murmansk Pravda* in his hand, nearly struck me with his shoulder. 'Constantin,' he said.

I stopped. 'Mikhail . . .' I didn't really know Dr Mikhail Karpov that well. As the husband of Natalya's friend, Fanya, he had been at the same parties a few times. I knew he worked on Natalya's team with Fanya. But we were not friends as Fanya and Natalya were friends.

He stood there awkwardly. 'It's easy to say I'm sorry about Natalya,' he said. He was a tired-eyed, darkly good-looking young man of about thirty. 'But saying I'm sorry doesn't anything like cover it.' He pressed his lips together, waiting for me to answer, to say something, anything.

'Thank you Mikhail.' I paused, part of my mind still floating back to that locked office. 'Nothing you can think of casts any light . . .?'

He shook his head. 'Nothing I can think of.'

'However small.' Policemen always say that.

'That American FBI woman,' he said. 'Agent Cunningham, she called over to see Fanya and me last night. Fanya told her about the car incident. There was nothing else.'

'The car incident? What car incident?'

He looked wary. 'The American woman, she didn't mention it to you?'

I took his arm and drew him away from the flow of the crowd. 'What car incident?'

He looked uncomfortable.

'Let's have it.'

'It's nothing. Crossing the parking-lot in front of the hospital, Fanya saw Natalya sitting in a Kamka, talking to someone, that's all.'

'A man?'

'She thought so.'

'When?'

'Friday. Around lunch-time.'

'So? What's significant about that?'

He shuffled himself about. 'Sometime later – I think maybe half an hour she said – she needed some instructions from Natalya about a medical matter and went looking for her. Apparently Natalya was still in the Kamka, still talking.'

'She was sure it was Natalya.'

'Yes.'

'Did she go over?'

'No . . . no, she decided it could wait, whatever she wanted to ask about.'

'She didn't see the man with her?'

'No. Just a shadow. The car was parked in the corner of the lot behind the statue. There's not much light there.'

'Wait a minute, when exactly was this?'

'Friday afternoon. About two o'clock.'

Which made it immediately before she locked herself in her office with someone. With the same man?

Mikhail Karpov slapped his folded newspaper against the palm of his hand. 'That's all. Look, I must be going,' he said apologetically. 'I'm on duty in five minutes.'

'Sure . . .' I reached out to shake his hand but he was already moving away.

I left the Lermontov and walked slowly through the morning tide of hospital workers. Try it again, Constantin. Why had Natalya locked herself in her room? Unthinkingly. A reflex. You close the door behind you. You lock it. But the new lock was almost at shoulder height. You wouldn't lock *that* unthinkingly, would you? Or – she wanted to be sure of a few moments' privacy. To make a phone call. Because that's what she was doing, talking on the phone. Surely. Even though there was someone else pacing about in the room. And her laughing refusal, *No, not here*, was quite innocent of the meaning I had forced on it.

Wasn't it?

Or look at it the other way. Assume the worst. Assume a lover. The man talking to Natalya in the Kamka. The man who followed her afterwards to her room. Now how does this fit with Natalya's disappearance the following night? How does it fit with the scarf, the tyre marks beside the highway at Intersection 33? Unless he went with her to Intersection 33. *Unless he was himself a doctor.*

I walked on, shaking my head. I knew that the whole element of doubt had been raised by Pasko with his planting of the condoms. And I was sure he'd planted them, despite his denial. Apart from that, what was there? People barged into Natalya's room a dozen times a day. If she was about to examine a patient – a woman patient in at least equal probability – she might well have locked the door . . . And sitting in a car for half an hour? She could have been with anybody. Discussing a hospital matter. In a car you have some privacy.

So, there you go, Constantin. These dark flashes of suspicion don't become you. Worse than that, they take your eye off the ball. What's important – do you need reminding? – is that Natalya is missing. Don't get distracted. For Christ's sake, Costya, don't get distracted. You're playing his game. Playing the vek's game. Yes. I nodded vigorously to myself like a tennis-player who has just pulled off a point-winning shot.

At a bar on the corner I bought a thumb of vodka and the use of the phone to call Madame Badanova. A sense of guilt had been growing in me since I first heard of her husband's death. I caught her mobile as she was driving towards the city centre.

'I've got your note,' she said. 'The fax from Sergeant Bubin. I was very touched, Constantin, that you remembered in the midst of everything that was happening to you.'

'If I had taken the job your husband offered me . . .'

'You would probably have died too,' she said. 'In the same helicopter.'

'Is there any suggestion that it wasn't an accident?'

'Only from me,' she said, a harsh ring in her voice. 'These things are serviced by boys who haven't eaten a square meal for a month. Haven't been paid for much longer. What do you expect – NATO standards?' Then her tone changed. 'Do you have ten minutes?'

'I'll make it.'

'Meet me at the Austrian coffee house on Union Square, Constantin,' she said. 'I'm five minutes away.'

I was unshaven and distinctly unwashed and the head waiter was not anxious to let me enter the plush red interior of the Emperor Franz Josef Coffee House. I couldn't blame him. Only Madame Badanova's arrival prevented me being escorted out into the snow. I stood up and walked towards the entrance.

She was not alone. A young blonde woman in her late twenties, dressed expensively against the cold, had got out of the Badanova Mercedes. They exchanged a few last words just inside the entrance of the coffee house before Madame Badanova came towards me and the girl left to go back to the waiting car. An American, I would have said at a guess, from the clothes but also from the manner. Moscow and Petersburg, of course, are full of young American advisers, mostly on politics and public relations, communications as we call it nowadays. A few of the more intrepid have even penetrated places like Murmansk. Politicians have them, the Church even. The *racketiry*, of course.

'That was Jay Dellerman,' Madame Badanova said. 'Used to work for my husband . . . She's helping me clear up the odds and ends.' She paused, with a swallow that held back the tears in her throat. 'Anton left a lot of odds and ends, Constantin.' She squeezed my hand. 'Come and sit down.' She led me to a corner table discreetly lit with a cluster of gold-tasselled ruby shades. From where we stood she followed my glance around the panelled room. 'You're not happy with the contrast between this and the life of Murmansk you see out on the streets?'

'Who could be?'

'There's something I want you to remember, Constantin, in the days to come. My husband, Anton, was not happy about it either.'

I knew too little about politics to argue. I had been away in Moscow during the election. All I knew was that some people were making huge amounts of money while others were begging on the streets. Little Governor Badanov had seemed happy enough in his huge official apartment in City Hall.

'Perhaps,' she said, 'he was a little too complacent. There. I've said it. Now I don't want that to go any further.'

'It won't,' I said. I understood she had made an important admission.

'Is there any more news?' she asked as I helped her off with her long sable coat and settled her in the Louis XV chair.

'They've sent an American woman up from Moscow. A policewoman. From the FBI. She's investigating the disappearance of a member of the US consular staff here, Joan Fowler. She disappeared the same night as Natalya.'

'I saw it on television,' she said, shaking her head. 'They found her car. Out on North Bay. And a sex doll with the face painted dead.'

'Not exactly a sex doll. A shop-window model.' It seemed important to make the point.

'But do the Americans see some connection with Natalya's disappearance?'

'They think there could be.'

'The same man?' She reached forward and squeezed my hand. The gesture brought tears to my eyes. I was brushing them away as the waiter came.

We ordered coffee and Black Forest cake. The bill for two would have paid an army master-sergeant's salary for a month – if anybody was bothering to pay the Army this month. Madame Badanova saw me flinch.

'We live in mad times, Constantin.' She paused. 'My husband was a wealthy man. Not *new boyar*, you understand me, not filthy rich. But well-off. An air-force general doesn't make a fortune. But after that he prospered.'

'The famous Texas-Badanov jeans.'

She smiled deprecatingly. 'Well-known throughout Murmansk, if not very far beyond. But they aren't bad jeans. And they made Anton enough money to go into politics.' She paused while a waiter in a short red jacket brought us coffee and cake. 'I admitted to you that he could be too complacent about things. Things that weren't directly in front of him,' she said. 'I felt it my duty to make sure some things were pushed right under his nose. Together we made far-reaching plans.'

'And now?'

'And now those plans are to be buried with him. You only have to look around you to see that the opposition has the money and the muscle.'

'The red banners with the black X?'

She inclined her head sombrely. 'We have a candidate X running for the Kola governorship. Can you believe? A Candidate X is a hoodlum by definition.'

I sat back in my seat. Candidate X is a purely Russian phenomenon. Since Yeltsin's day a degree of legal immunity has been extended to elected politicians and even political candidates during the election period, immunity which in practice now obtains throughout the period of office. 'Do you know who he is?'

'Our Candidate X? I hear Valentin Fortunin feels he's spent enough time behind bars.'

Fortunin was well-known as a man who ran a group of contract killers in Moscow before Anton Badanov arranged his arrest on a visit to his old mother in Murmansk.

'Will he win?'

'Against the environmentalists?'

'No part of Europe needs them more.'

'True, Constantin.' She looked down. 'But take my word for it, for Candidate X, it'll be a walkover.' Her eyes came up slowly to meet mine. 'Unless . . .'

'Unless?'

'Unless I stand myself.'

Seventy years of spurious Soviet gender equality had done nothing to enhance the status of women in the eyes of Russian men. I struggled with the notion of a woman governor. Possible, I suppose. Or, at least, not crazily impossible. And she was Anton Badanov's wife. She was gutsy and eccentric enough to be sitting in the Austrian coffee house with a man who stank like a convict. And she was a woman, I instinctively knew, who would do all she could to help me unravel the mystery of what had happened to Natalya. 'The job was made for you,' I said.

She grasped both my hands. 'We are friends, Constantin. Anton's death and Natalya's disappearance bind us together. I shall call on you for help. And I expect you to call on me in the same way.'

I reach the apartment, still feeling positive. Still feeling that the idea of a lover, the idea of Natalya having been abducted by a lover just doesn't fit. Joan Fowler was abducted on the same day, for Christ's sake. No, this vek is a crazy. A psycho. I stop dead as I close the apartment door behind me. I am overwhelmed by a deep feeling of shame. Fuck your mother, Constantin, you're drawing comfort from the fact that Natalya is in the hands of a *psycho*.

There are times I hate men, times I hate what love does to men. What love does to me. I leaned my back against the closed door.

When the entry buzzer went off next to my ear I jumped like a scalded cat. I walked quickly through the hall to the front door and lifted the door-phone to grunt into it.

'It's Dr Karpov. Mikhail Karpov,' a voice squawked.

I pressed the button and went into the kitchen to start making coffee. The kettle was just about to boil as the doorbell rang.

Mikhail Karpov stood at the door in a grey parka. He looked as if he desperately lacked sleep but then young doctors are exploited the world over, I'm told. So are policemen, come to that. Of any age. I told him to go through to the living-room and followed him a couple of minutes later with two cups of instant coffee.

'I hope you didn't mind me calling in,' he said.

I placed his coffee on a low table in front of him. 'I thought you were on duty.'

'No . . .' He sipped his coffee, burnt his lip and stared wincing down at the cup. Then he lifted his dark-rimmed eyes to me. 'The roster was over-subscribed. They didn't need me.'

'You look as though you should be heading home for a few hours' sleep.'

'I thought I'd call in. It's on the way.'

I waited.

'To see if there was any further news.'

'In the last hour?'

'No . . .' He put the coffee down. 'I got to thinking there might have been some sort of news that you hadn't told me when we met in the Lermontov.'

'Why should there be something I haven't told you?'

He didn't answer. I sipped my coffee without speaking. There was something almost eerie about the way Mikhail Karpov kept glancing up at me, then quickly down again. This was a young man on the edge of a confession. I had seen enough of them to be able to trust my instinct. What I couldn't guess was what he was about to confess. Sometimes you have to ease it out of a witness. Sometimes it's like drawing teeth. 'That story you told me this morning about Fanya,' I said. 'I'm not sure it sits too comfortably with me.'

He made a tiny movement of his head. What he didn't want to do was to ask why.

'Aren't you curious?'

'Of course.' He ducked his head. 'Yes.'

'It's a good walk from Surgical to the front car park. A good few minutes.'

'Yes.'

'Now what did you tell me? Fanya knows that's where Natalya was half an hour earlier, in the car park. She needs some instructions so she decides that Natalya might still be there, talking to the stranger. A half-hour or more later.'

'Yes.'

'Wouldn't you say that was an unusual assumption? A more reasonable assumption was that Natalya had gone to her office, or was visiting a patient in Surgical Recovery.'

'But she wasn't,' he said. 'She was still in the car.'

'And when Fanya finds her there, having come all the way from Surgical to receive her instructions, what does Fanya do?'

He was silent.

'Does she go straight over and ask her question? No. She turns back and re-enters the hospital. What does that suggest to you, Mikhail?'

'I don't know,' he said, awkwardly. 'I hadn't thought about it like that.'

'It suggests to me, Mikhail, that the purpose of Fanya going out front was less to find Natalya than to check whether she was still talking to her stranger.'

He lifted the coffee-cup to his lips and this time managed to drink a mouthful – and to avoid my eyes.

'I think what was worrying Fanya Friday afternoon was *who* was in the Kamka with Natalya,' I said.

It was coming to me. Slowly, because I've learnt to accept that I'm not that quick. I don't have the instinct of a Dronsky or the bite of a Roy Rolkin. I held the silence for a second or two longer. I could almost *feel* Mikhail's discomfort. Slowly he found himself forced to raise his head.

He tried to shrug but managed only a twitch that spilt coffee on the table. He glanced down at it, rubbed at it with his sleeve and looked up at me again, the dark eyes wide.

'What was worrying Fanya,' I said, 'was that she thought it was *you*.'

'Fanya's off her head,' he banged down his coffee so hard it slopped across the table. This time he left it.

'That's what was worrying her. Am I right?'

'It's a fixation. Everybody at the Lermontov admires Natalya. Obviously so. But I happen to work with her.'

'*Was* it you in the car with her?'

He hesitated. 'No. Of course not. I would have said.'

'Perhaps you left the Kamka and went with Natalya straight to her office?'

'I told you. It wasn't me in the Kamka with her.'

'Where were you Friday afternoon?'

He stood up. 'Listen, Constantin. Not you too? I've had enough of this from Fanya.'

'I'm asking as a detective, not a husband,' I pretended. 'Friday afternoon, where were you? At the Lermontov?'

'OK.' He pushed his hands into the pockets of his jeans, bunching his padded anorak. 'I was sleeping. I'd come in early to get some sleep in the doctors' rest room. I'd had a skinful the night before and I was on duty Friday. Late afternoon shift.'

'You don't do your sleeping at home?'

'I do when I know Fanya won't be coming back. Things are difficult at the moment. She's onto me all the time.'

'She thinks you're having an affair with Natalya.'

His shoulders jerked in a convulsive affirmative. 'Look, I'm sorry to have troubled you. I was passing and I thought I'd just see if there'd been any developments. You know . . . something perhaps you hadn't mentioned at the Lermontov.'

I walked with him to the door. 'Give my love to Fanya,' I said.

'Of course. And you didn't mind me calling in?'

'Not at all.'

We shook hands. The magazines talk of smouldering eyes, smouldering passions. This young man was smouldering in all his carefully casual movements. As he turned away I reached out and grabbed him by the shoulder of his anorak and jerked him back into the apartment. My other elbow was tight against his chest, just below his throat, pinning him to the wall. At any increase of my weight on the elbow, he would begin to choke. 'Why did you come?'

'Christ, you're hurting me. I came to ask about Natalya . . .'

I increased the weight until he began to gag. Tears streamed from his eyes. 'All right . . .'

I released him. 'Now tell me,' I said. I walked ahead of him back into the living-room.

He stood in the doorway holding his throat. 'I'm not ashamed of it,' he said, but his head was hanging. 'I'm not ashamed of it.'

It was as if a vacuum cleaner had sucked at my stomach. 'Of what?'

'Working with her for a year it was almost inevitable.' He looked up at me. 'Given the woman she was.'

'*Was?*'

'The sort of woman she is,' he stuttered. 'I fell in love with her, Constantin. Surely you of all people can understand that.'

'And?'

There was a long silence.

'*And?* And nothing. She told me it was an infatuation. She treated me as if she were the older woman. She told me to go home and work at what I had with Fanya. Go home to my wife.' He took a deep breath. 'It was humiliating.'

'She told you this in the car on Friday?'

'I wasn't in the car with her on Friday, fuck your mother! If

Natalya spent an hour talking to a man in her car, it wasn't to me,' he said bitterly, turning for the door.

This time I let him go.

I checked the messages on my phone.

Roy Rolkin called from Helsinki to congratulate me on my release. The lawyer Grandov had kept him informed. His own football team, Janus Budapest, was meeting Murmansk Dynamo in the Euro-cities League next week. Roy's message said he would be staying in Helsinki for a few days to oversee training.

The second call said Abby Cunningham had established offices at the American consulate. I should get over there as soon as I had cleaned up. I took a quick shower and changed my three-day-old clothes. In less than half an hour I was driving past the Lermontov to No 1 Pushkin Boulvar.

I had never been to the US consulate before but I'd been many times to the old building that housed it. One of the few buildings in the city (apart from the Lermontov) to be constructed of anything but cracking concrete, to Murmanskers it was known as the Old Nunnery. It had been first a convent under the Tsars, then the head-quarters of Stalin's secret police and of all their evil successors until political police organizations had been declared illegal last year. More beatings had been given, more false confessions extracted, more lives threatened and destroyed in the basement cells of the Old Nunnery, than in any building in Murmansk.

Yet in itself it looked harmless enough, a yellow stone building with iron-grilled gothic windows and swallow-tailed battlements. At the far end a good-sized, brick-vaulted arch was set into the frontage, over which an American eagle and a sign reading *US Consular Office* now modestly advertised last year's dramatic change of use.

I passed under the arched entrance. Ahead of me a lane ran down the side of the building past what had once been the Nunnery's well-kept vegetable gardens. Parts of the long wall had by now collapsed and the Amercans had not yet got around to repairing it, possibly even had no intention of repairing it. Their stay in the Old Nunnery was strictly temporary while a new, modern building was being erected near the port. I was let into the familiar refectory hall by a uniformed security man. I don't know what changes I had expected but the blue and gold paint was still peeling from the fan vaulting above me, the flagstones underfoot were still cracked and worn by the passage of countless pairs of boots. There were the same partitioned sections, the same preoccupied clerks and ringing phones. On the rickety wooden benches they might have been the same waiting supplicants. But a large American flag now hung from a white pole attached to the far wall, the stars and stripes undulating reassuringly in the currents of warm air given out by a powerful new heating system.

Abby Cunningham met me. I was struck by how comfortable, how much in charge she seemed. She wore a pale pink shirt and a black pleated skirt which allowed her to walk with both hands in the pockets. She withdrew a hand to point an index finger to the floor above. 'We've been assigned some crumbling old rooms at the back,' she said. 'Apparently at one time, this building . . .' My gesture cut her short. 'But obviously you know all that.'

We took the main staircase.

'You said *we've* been assigned. Is Dronsky staying?'

She led me along a narrow corridor into a part of the building rarely used in Roy Rolkin's days here. 'Dronsky's staying until the Procurator's Office calls him back to Moscow.' She opened a door onto a shabby grey-painted room furnished with good modern office furniture. 'There was no time to get a paint job done before I moved in. I work from here. You and Dronsky are across the hall.'

We stood together in the corridor. She picked up on my frown. 'I've arranged with your station commander for your secondment to this case, OK?'

'I couldn't work on anything else right now.'

'So I figured.' She hesitated and called through an open door to an office I couldn't see into. 'Anna . . . Anna, come and meet Inspector Vadim.' And to me: 'Anna is going to handle documentation for us.'

I knew before Anna appeared in the doorway who she was. The blinding mix of camphor and Mother Russia toilet water was unique. Anna Danilova was the Records secretary at Station 18, a fifty-year-old battle-axe of a woman (shapely if she had lost a foot all over), broad-shouldered and convinced she had never made a mistake in her life. Russian women are seldom prim – but Anna's religious beliefs were derived from an obscure puritanical group in Bognor Regis, England. Working together, she treated me with the sort of respectful disdain that Russians keep for foreigners.

Appearing in the doorway, filling the doorway, she shook me

firmly by the hand as if we had not worked together almost daily for the last two years. 'Welcome aboard,' she said in deep-throated English. She leaned over and opened the door opposite.

It was a smallish room with a stone floor and a tattered red Turkish carpet. The furniture was American with a PC on the desk.

'There's another office through there,' Abby said. 'It has a cot and a wash-basin. Dronsky said he'll take it. He's going to bunk down in there.'

I frowned. 'I thought he'd be staying with me. At my apartment.'

She coughed. 'Ah ... Apparently that wouldn't work out. According to Dronsky.'

'Why not?'

She made her eyes huge.

Beyond the glazed door I heard a faint sound and saw a blur of movement. Vague, unworthy suspicions coalesced. I walked across and threw open the door.

With a screech of alarm a shape flew across the room. As it landed on a filing cabinet I leapt backwards, knocking over a side-table and shattering a glass ashtray on the stone floor. The marmalade cat stood on the cabinet, head up, tail lashing, staring at me with concentrated feline disdain.

You've heard of V.I. Lenin, brothers.

Agent Cunningham moved into the doorway. 'Anything wrong?'

'Nothing he'd ever be prepared to admit,' I said, looking from the cat to the smashed ashtray.

'Dronsky brought him along,' she said. 'Sort of a lucky mascot.' She was trying to suppress a smile. The cat leapt down from the cabinet. 'Dronsky says you pretend all sorts of hostility to V.I. Lenin, and vice versa. But that's just the complex nature of your relationship.'

'Mysterious but somehow wonderful? Is that it?'

'If you say so. What do you think of the office?'

'Barely room to swing a cat,' I said. I faced V.I. Lenin with a stare as unblinking as his own. His hiss was low-key. His goatee maybe trembled. I walked across to the window and looked out into a dank courtyard. It was a good drop. When I turned back into the room the cat had advanced into the middle of the carpet.

'As long as you're sharing an office,' Abby said, 'maybe you two could make an effort to get along.'

I scowled at her.

Cats are never slow to acknowledge a victory. V.I. Lenin sat back centre stage and raised, magnanimously, a paw.

Abby Cunningham's hand covered her mouth.

15

THREE POLICE CARS raced towards the hospital, sirens howl-
ing, ripple lights flashing. In the leading car I concentrated
everything on the driving, accelerating down the central lane of
Pushkin Boulvar. As the pale blue Lermontov rose before me I
crossed the square at an angle and passed through the iron gates
into the cobbled courtyard. Skidding the car to a halt that nearly
broadsided the statue of Lermontov, I jumped out and ran for the
main doors. Abby Cunningham was out of the passenger seat a
few steps behind me.

Among the crowd of people waiting, looking for directions,
trying to catch the attention of the receptionists, I saw Dronsky
in the opening of the corridor leading to Surgical. His chin lifted
as he saw us.

'This way, Chief,' he said over the top of several heads. He turned
immediately and set off down the crowded corridor before I was
able to reach him. Behind me I could hear the click of the American
woman's heels.

Then suddenly people were no longer moving, going somewhere.
Cleaners, patients, white-jacketed interns were standing, staring. Two
militiamen were holding them back. Dronsky was still forging his
way forward. I was catching up with him as he turned a corner into
a corridor with a hanging Accident and Emergency board above
our heads. There were militiamen standing by all around us now.
Dronsky came to an abrupt halt before a wall of medical screens that
closed off the mouth of the corridor. 'What's going on, Dronsky?' I
pushed my way between two militiamen to reach him. 'What is it?'

He threw me a tense look. 'You have to see this for yourself, Chief.'

Fear swept over me. 'It's not Natalya? You haven't found
Natalya?'

'Not Natalya . . .'

The uniformed officer at the entrance to the screened-off section was Lieutenant Pinsk. Not Pasko – Pinsk, a Homicide officer. I looked at Dronsky in mindless alarm. With a faint movement of his hand he signalled Pinsk to lead the way.

We passed in single file between the gap in the screens. Ten paces ahead the vaulted, white-tiled corridor was sectioned off with blue and white incident tape. I looked past the tape to a door where a militia sergeant stood guard beneath a chandelier from a different age.

'Someone tell me, for God's sake. What's going on?'

'The door,' Dronsky said. He held down the blue and white tape as I stepped over it. 'It's all right, Chief,' he said. 'It's not Natalya.'

Dronsky led the way through the service door into a small courtyard, a light well. Frosted glass windows looked down onto an area no more than ten by ten metres. A spotlight had been rigged up to shine down onto the darkest corner. Onto a woman's body, face down, arms extended, blonde hair flowing left across her face.

I stepped forward. The woman was wearing green hospital coveralls. I could read the word Lermontov across her shoulders. I knew what it was, of course, before I saw the printed tape across the upper arm: Dr Natalya Vadim.

My blood was racing but I couldn't speak. It was Natalya, but it wasn't Natalya. I leaned forward, kneeling, and lifted the fall of hair from her eyes. A pale face of moulded latex was turned towards me, the eyes closed, the cheeks painted the pallor of death.

I rocked back, dumb with shock at the realism. Stupid with bewilderment. Having no idea of what it signified, it seemed infinitely sinister in its power to possess me, in its power to suggest a message. I turned and looked from Dronsky to the American woman. Her lips were pressed together, her eyes unmoving.

'What in God's name does it mean?' I asked them. But I could read no answer in either face.

16

D RONSKY HAD BROUGHT the model into an examination room, leaving the crime-scene men to see if they could get anything from the light well. He was touchingly shy about opening the Lermontov overalls. 'Maybe you should do this, Chief,' he said.

I looked at Abby Cunningham where she stood, her back resting against the wall, arms folded against her breast. She nodded. The thing lay on its side on a trolley. But it was more than a thing. It carried an iconic quality that caused me to speak in a low voice, that made Dronsky avert his eyes from the legs exposed to the thigh. 'It's a rubber doll, for Christ's sake,' I muttered but I stepped forward.

There was a large, rusty-red bloodstain on the breast of the green overall. Perhaps the size of a football. 'It's not Natalya's group,' Abby said. 'It's not Joan's. That much we know for certain.'

Using gloves, I unbuttoned the overall. Beneath it was a black bra. I stood away from the trolley, my mouth suddenly and completely dry. The eeriness of the whole thing was making me shake. I had to remind myself that it wasn't Natalya's body I was examining.

And yet again, in some sense, it was.

Dronsky pulled a flask from his back pocket and handed it to me. I took it from him and drank. The stinging liquid burnt its way down and suppressed the reflexes in my stomach. I took a deep breath and another pull at the flask. I was at my wits' end, suddenly unable to engage any thought processes. It was perhaps like a stroke or an epileptic seizure. For Christ's sake, it was a latex model, the sort of thing you'd find in a very expensive Moscow or Petersburg shop. How could it have this impact on me? I turned to the American woman. 'Do you know what it means?' I asked her. 'Could it mean she's still alive? Or does it mean he's already killed her?' It was an appeal in utter desperation. 'Do you have *any* idea what it really means?'

Abby Cunningham came off the wall. 'The model of Joan Fowler was found three days ago. We still have no sign of a body. We can't just make guesses about this. We need a forensic psychologist to help us through the maze.'

'Then we'll have to get someone up from Moscow,' Dronsky said. 'It could take days to get him attached.'

'Right now,' Abby said, 'we just need a first-flash opinion. Doesn't this hospital have a psychiatric department?'

'A separate Psychiatric *Clinic*,' I said. 'Dr Potanin. Gabriel Potanin.'

'Do you know him?'

'I've met him a couple of times. He stinks like a goat. He serves on the senior departmental committee with Natalya. He studied in America,' I added. Interest flickered on Abby's face. 'Natalya's always thought he's crazier than the people he's supposed to be treating.'

The Lermontov Infirmary has a shabby, comforting grandeur about it, even in its most cluttered corners, but the Psychiatric Wing at the west end of the building conveys immediately a different impression, of hopelessness and grim restraint.

We were hurried by a heavily-built white-coated assistant across the hallway and up two flights of stairs to the office floor. Gabriel Potanin's room was plastered with pages torn from books and newspaper cuttings of Russian murderers back to Tsarist days. There were court accusations against Rasputin, details and tinted photographs of Malakov the Dismemberer. There were clippings on Ted Bundy in the US and the Yorkshire Ripper in England and full front pages of newspapers on Andrei Chikatilo's butchery of fifty-two people in Rostov in the nineteen eighties. And arranged round these major figures were half a dozen lesser serial murderers who had only seen the light in Soviet days through ill-typed militia reports, facsimiles of which papered the walls. I saw that Abby Cunningham, overwhelmed by the squalor of a room that looked more like an abandoned antique shop, had noticed that the first press reports on the finding of Joan Fowler's car were already up there – and next to them, a colour newspaper blow-up of Natalya.

Potanin himself was drunk as Abby brought him up to date with the finding of the hospital doll, but then I doubt that, in the last five years, he had ever been entirely sober. He looked Abby up and down with his small, pale eyes. 'So the famous FBI have come to Gabriel Potanin for advice?' He laughed explosively. 'You'll excuse my merriment, Miss Cunningham. On several occasions in the past I have offered my theories to your Quantico headquarters.'

'I'm sure they considered them.'

'If they did it was without the slightest acknowledgement. What could a man living on the roof of the world, and a Russian to boot, know about a crime being committed in Columbia, South Carolina? In fact my analysis of the Shari Faye Smith abduction was one hundred per cent accurate. And fuller than your FBI profile.'

'We're here to ask your advice on Joan Fowler and Natalya Vadim,' Abby said diplomatically. She pointed to the walls. 'I see you have an interest in such matters.'

'A consuming interest.' Potanin eyed her, saliva sparkling at the corners of his mouth. 'You'll take a thumb of vodka with me.' He was already on his feet, a thin frame on which hung malodorous tweeds, but tall, tall enough to make Abby look up at him. He held a large, near-empty bottle in one hand and two shot glasses in the fingers of the other.

She nodded acceptance and he poured for both of us, not even looking for my assent.

It was not easy to guess his age. He had a bald crown fringed by long straight reddish-grey hair, his face creased and pale, his eyes pink-rimmed. He had long ago destroyed his body with drink; but from what I'd heard, his mind functioned erratically but mostly unaffected by his huge daily intake. He dismissed abduction with a few gestures of his long arms. 'There's no reason to believe the American consular woman and your wife, Inspector, are dead. But we would deceive ourselves if we refused to accept that all the signs are that they are in the hands of a serial murderer. And on average your serial murderer does not keep his victims alive for more than three days. True, Agent Cunningham?'

Abby's face set in her refusal to answer. But I thought I knew what the answer would have been. My stomach tensed.

Gabriel Potanin looked at me over his half-lens glasses, a silly apologetic smile on his face. 'We must talk freely or not at all.'

'Say what you have to say, Professor. I'm here as a *syschik*, an investigating officer. Not as a husband.'

'A serial murderer?' Abby said. She was looking at Potanin with a peculiarly penetrating stare. 'Do the *broader* circumstances really suggest that?'

'Even so, yes,' he said. He shuffled within his stained tweed jacket like a tattered bird arranging his feathers. He had already sidelined any special concern I might have in the case. Before this young American woman, and in her own language, he was about to perform. 'Serial murder . . .' he said. 'That's what we should be talking about. Even now. Long before we've found the first body.' His dark eyes glowed with interest. He turned towards the bottle-lined mantelshelf behind him. 'The way I look at things,' he said, 'all such murders are like works of art.'

I saw Abby's eyes turn upwards. So did Potanin, in the mirror above the mantelpiece. 'You doubt me, Miss Cunningham? Making murder is like making art in the sense that it's a complex statement.' His jacket parted and he pulled down the thick green polo-neck sweater to reveal holes scattered across the belly through which tufts of grey hair escaped. 'Murder, I believe, is both a personal and a public statement. An affirmation to oneself and a declaration to others. But in the end, like the artist, with the same crude intensity, the murderer is simply satisfying himself.'

Abby watched him with pursed lips. 'That's all there is to it, uh? The pursuit of satisfaction?'

'Too simple for you, Miss Cunningham? Well of course it doesn't remain simple. When does it possess a man, this urge to kill? Does it creep up slowly? Does it arrive unbidden? Or has it always been there?' He paused. 'I don't know, of course. Perhaps we all have it – all the time. Perhaps what we should be trying to understand is not that throbbing urge, but why suddenly, apparently without warning, it is converted by the sight of a girl out walking, the glimpse of a woman's secret lustful smile . . . Converted by *something,* so that the idea of killing suddenly represents an irresistible source of satisfaction.'

'Satisfaction seems a pretty feeble motive for killing,' Abby said.

'If you face facts you'll see we're incapable of acting for any other reason. The serial killer and the philanthropist are both pursuing their own satisfaction. Satisfaction is no feeble term. Its pursuit can involve all passion or bestialities known to mankind.'

'Wait a minute, Professor,' I said. 'We don't always do what we want. People make sacrifices. There's such a thing as abstinence.'

He smirked. 'A refusal to succumb to desire sometimes provides its own satisfaction. If that's so, the man or woman abstains. It'd be foolish, unscientific to think there's anything morally superior about abstaining. It's simply doing what you want.'

I can tell you now, brothers, I'm not happy with this talk. I don't have the ready tongue to argue against it, but it seems to me to reduce a lot of good people, a lot of good acts, to some level of pointlessness I don't accept. If we can't believe in God we ought at least to believe in people.

He poked me in the chest. 'You see, Vadim, I am the most rigorous thinker in this field. Too rigorous I fear for Agent Cunningham's FBI directors. But let us move on to the central point. Profiling is not about describing that need for satisfaction. That's a fact. Profiling is about striving to understand what is being satisfied by the act in front of us.'

I admired Abby's coolness in front of this didactic, posturing provincial. 'OK, Professor,' she said. 'It would take us a long way down the road if you could give us your ideas on that.'

'We enter forbidden territory, Miss Cunningham. We must lift veils. In my clinic I have people pursuing the most bizarre satisfactions. People whose need is so great they have no shame. Men who parade in baby clothes. Men who do nothing but flagellate themselves all day. Women who live their lives as Joan of Arc or Catherine of Medici.'

'But they don't kill, Professor,' Abby said evenly. Her perfectly balanced face showed nothing. 'The dolls,' she steered the subject easily. 'What do they tell us?'

Potanin strode restlessly, a thin, malodorous stick of a man, exuding energy. 'I don't know,' he said at last.

'You can't help us?' She was challenging him.

'I said I don't know. I don't know yet. They're shop models, not sex dolls.'

'Is that important?'

'Perhaps.' He wagged his head from side to side. He hunched his shoulders. 'The superficial characteristic of a latex shop mannequin is obvious.'

'Not to me,' I said.

'No sexual organs.'

'Could that really be significant?'

'I'm not a Freudian. Who does follow the old fraud these days? But he said so much, a few truths might have slipped in. So your mannequins, are they perhaps female castrati. We could think about that. And the faces were painted? Deathly, one report said. Ghostly, another, perhaps a more accurate press description.'

'Ghostly?' Abby said.

'Why not? Ghosts are castrati too, are they not? Do ghosts fuck? Do they reproduce? No. Ghosts are safely asexual. They can be, male ghost or female ghost, troubled by love or loss . . . but never by rank, crude, necessitous demands for *sex*.'

We stared at him, both, I'm sure, feeling the totally theatrical nature of his performance – but neither of us quite sure he was a total charlatan.

'What do *you* think, Agent Cunningham? You've no doubt attended the famed Behavioural Science courses at Quantico. What do you think? Is he taunting you with the dolls?'

She shook her head. 'He's taking risks, especially with this last Natalya doll. I don't think he's the type to taunt. I think he's using the dolls as some bizarre form of *apology*.'

I looked at her in astonishment. Apology was as bizarre as Potanin's talk about ghosts and castrati. 'Apology?' I said. 'For abducting them? Are you serious?'

A no-nonsense quick nod of confirmation. 'Quite serious. I think we're dealing with an effigy, a substitute for the abducted person. A crude attempt by a dangerously muddled mind to somehow provide a replacement. To me that spells out an *apology* for what's he's done.'

Potanin smiled. A superior smile from his superior height. He dismissed her theory with a quick shake of the head. 'We can guess this personality is all about control. He abducts to dominate. Murder is the ultimate act of domination. This personality does not apologize, Agent Cunningham. With the placing of these dolls he is *exulting* in the act. He *taunts*. Without being aware of it you've probably had messages from him already. Check back, Miss Cunningham. Check that you've missed nothing.' He waved his hands dismissively. 'I'll do what I can with your profile,' he said. 'Now you must excuse me.' He turned towards an unopened two-litre bottle of vodka and shook it like a madman. 'I have a great deal of catching up to do.'

We left Gabriel Potanin's private rooms and took the iron balustraded staircase down to the entrance. Wards, if that's what they were, opened on either side of each landing. No doors prevented us looking in at the long lines of crumpled beds and the dancing, shouting, salivating patients. Television sets flickered in profusion and each seemed to gather its own following. Each doorless doorway offered up new wafts of cooking cabbage, sweat and the sickly sweetness that might be lice but is always present with the unkempt, the unwashed, the unregarded in any society.

'This is some place,' Abby said in disbelief. People came out on the landing to stare at us. There were men and women, young and old. And no-one who was identifiably a member of staff. 'The patients,' the American woman said as we reached the ground floor, 'have taken over the asylum.' She cast her eyes up towards Gabriel Potanin's living quarters. 'I include the Chief Patient.'

'You think it was all a waste of time,' I said, stung. After all, a psychologist was her suggestion.

We came out of the Clinic and crossed towards the parking-lot. 'Ghosts?' she said. 'Women castrates . . . I suppose it's possible. But I'm out of my depth, toots. Is our abductor behaving like a serial killer? Serial killers take trophies. They don't *give* them. The question we need answering is what is our vek doing. OK, he's seeking some form of weird satisfaction when he sticks up a doll of Joan or Natalya. But is our philosopher-shrink right that he's taunting us, exulting in what he's done? Or is there anything in my gut feeling that somehow this man is apologizing? That Joan and Natalya are themselves the trophies.'

'Does it make a difference?'

'It could do.'

'A difference between Natalya and Joan Fowler at this moment being alive or dead?'

'Yes.'

'And Dr Potanin thinks they're already dead.'

She looked up at me from under heavy lashes. 'He does.'

'And you?'

She took a deep breath. 'I think the presence of those dolls is an apology.'

'Why? Why apologize?'

'I don't know. I'm not psychic for God's sake. I've never come across anything like this. But think how they were presented, carefully dressed and made-up . . .'

'If you're right we won't be getting taunting phone calls.'

'No. This man will stay away from us. He's not proud of what he's done.'

I was at sea, uncomfortable with all this theorizing. Did it really matter if the dolls were an apology or a taunt? I wanted solid evidence to bite on. The name of the factory where the models were made. A session with the sales director. A list of purchasers to work through. Places to search where Natalya and Joan Fowler might be hidden.

We got into my blue Fiat. I sat for a moment without starting the engine. Anger, frustration, was rising in me. 'I've got a problem,' I said.

'Let's have it.'

'We've compared the lists that I made on Natalya with the Joan Fowler lists. Pinsk has checked everything down to did they buy their toothpaste in the same shop. And we can find nothing.'

'So we're not looking hard enough.'

'I think we're riding the wrong road looking for a connection between Joan Fowler and Natalya. I think chance connects them. I think our vek just stumbled on two different women on the same night.'

A touch of stubbornness drew faint lines on either side of her mouth. 'We should still keep looking. There must be a connection. Take it from me – OK?'

'Why?' I said. 'How about you take it from me – if there had been a connection I would have known about it.'

'Jesus, you're stubborn,' she said, the words hissing angrily from her lips. 'However casual, there's a connection between them. What we need is the identity of the man who knew about it before you did.'

'It's down to pure chance, can't you see that? A man with a special lust for women sees Joan Fowler at the consulate lectures one day. She fits his fantasies. She stirs his loins as only he could be stirred.'

'And Natalya? When did he see her?'

'I don't know, for God's sake. In the street. In the hospital. How does it help to know that?'

'He took them both on the same night,' she said deliberately. '*That* is what we have to explain. Did he bring them together for his purpose?'

'You can't have it both ways,' I insisted. 'You can't have the idea of somebody who organized this, carefully brought two women together for the purpose of abducting them ... And at the same time, somebody who's a pure crazy bouncing on the end of a string – landing here or there as chance takes him.'

'Let's hold it open.'

'I don't have time for that,' I said desperately. 'I don't have time for considered opinions. My wife is being held by a sexual lunatic. I have to do something. *I have to act.*'

17

WE WERE STILL talking when the throb of a drumbeat came from somewhere on the left side of Lermontov Square, a signal for a blast of trumpets from the other side. Within moments two columns had entered the broad open space from different ends. From the left marched the head of a loose column of students, mothers with babies and a spattering of young priests. Their boards and banners proclaimed their support for an active Green programme and Mariya Badanova for governor. Her campaign colours (the same as her husband's I recall) were green and yellow.

The head of the column entering the square on the other side offered an entirely different aspect. Young men, dressed preponderantly in black leather or bare-armed in sleeveless furs, marched eight abreast beneath the white banners and black eagles of Nationalist Russia. But the double-headed eagles were mixed with other flags too: a sudden, shocking reminder of the European past unfurling red with a white circle on which a heavy black X was stamped.

I looked at Abby. She was staring shocked at the waving banners. 'The X stands for Candidate X,' I told her. 'An undeclared contestant. That's the way it works in Russian politics.'

'I don't have to know a thing about Russian politics to know that *that* X is for neo-Nazi,' she said. 'Let's get out of here.'

I put my hand on her arm. 'We can't move yet,' I said. 'We're stuck with a grandstand view.'

She took a deep breath and sat back. 'OK,' she said carefully. 'Just as long as we stay in the grandstand.' She nodded out towards the marching columns. 'Badanova I know. What's Candidate X all about?'

'These days there's a Candidate X in almost every election. High elected office gives legal immunity to the holder from a whole raft of charges, even temporary release from jail for the period of office.'

'So the hoodlums move onto the hustings.'

'Right. To the *racketiry*, elections have become a legal means of springing their leaders.'

'What about this one? This Candidate X?'

'Almost certainly a man named Valentin Fortunin. He was a major gang boss in Moscow and was lured back home to Murmansk. Apparently Governor Badanov got him six years for banditry last year. He's not happy in gaol.'

'Jesus,' she said.

'You mean Jesus – what a country!'

'No . . .' she said thoughtfully. 'I know there are good people like Natalya and Dronsky and Mariya Badanova all the way across Russia – but your laws give the others a pretty free hand.'

'Laws?' I said. 'There are only two laws that have *ever* been universally recognized in Russia.'

'What are they?'

'The one for the rich and the other for the poor.'

Out on the square, the two columns marched towards each other. The stewards for the Badanova column had run to the front and were heading the standard-bearers off towards a road on the far side of the square. Some young marchers refused to be diverted and stood their ground in the middle of the square, facing the steady tramp of the opposing column. I think at that moment the first orange flare came arcing out of the Candidate X side. Seconds later, stones, bottles and petrol bombs followed the flare. Orange smoke bombs added to the confusion as the leather jackets hurled themselves forward, arms linked like an old Germanic phalanx. The screams of girls and men's shouts of pain now rose from every hidden part of the dense orange smoke of the battlefield; the heavy drumbeat, somehow maintained by one side or the other, was punctuated by sudden hysterical notes from the bugles.

We were no more than thirty metres away from the drift of orange smoke. Abby sat by my side in shocked silence. That dark marble, controlled quality of her features had gone. She looked, not frightened, but younger, more uncertain. She watched young students pursued across the square by leather-jacketed supporters of Candidate X, watched them dragged, men or girls, to the ground and kicked unconscious. All around us the spurt of petrol explosions and the sharp stink in the nostrils of the orange smoke added a further Dantean dimension to the fighting.

The first cars to burn were those parked on the far side of the square outside the Lermontov Infirmary railings. When the petrol bombs hit them they flared blue like a flamed pudding, then flew apart as their petrol tanks ignited in a blaze of yellow fire. If there was anybody still inside they stood no chance.

I was calculating as hard as I could now. Within minutes the first cars were going up on our side of the square. Behind us, in the mirror, I saw groups of leather jackets trashing cars not thirty metres behind us.

'Let's get out and run for it,' Abby said.

'Run where?' There was no time for discussion. Her brown face would call down the thugs the moment she was seen. There was no other way out than the Marshal Zhukov Boulvar on the far side. I fired the engine and started the car moving.

'You'll get us both killed,' Abby said quietly. But she leaned forward and pressed the door lock.

I drove deep into the orange fog with headlights blazing. There were men here wielding sticks and batons, men punching and kicking, men rolling across the blacktop. Flags were burning, patches of asphalt bubbled and flickered where petrol bombs had exploded, car tyres gave off thick black smoke. I was counting on the confusion.

Abby had pulled up her coat collar until only her eyes were visible – they widened, I saw at a glance, with every baton that thundered on the car roof, every man who wrenched at the handles or kicked vainly at the door panels.

I pushed forward ruthlessly, swerving right then left to avoid struggling bodies, bouncing leather-jackets out of the way and every moment aware a petrol bomb might smash against the windscreen and immerse us in a sudden, inescapable blaze. Somewhere in the middle of the square we were forced to stop by the sheer mass of people around us. Men with batons began to beat at the side windows, one lighting a flare ready to force it into the car. As the window shattered I knew this could be the end. Putting my foot down steadily, I pushed the car through a whole group of struggling people. The man with the flare was running beside us. As he leaned down to Abby's shattered window she reached out and hit him under the chin with the heel of her hand. He reeled back, dropping the flare. Orange smoke billowed around me as I realized it was in the car, then seconds later the smoke began to clear as she picked it up and hurled it back into the crowd.

When we burst out of the orange gloom I could make no guess about what the outside of the Fiat looked like. The glass beside Abby's head was shattered. The windscreen and rear window were badly cracked and the interior was almost as dense with smoke as outside – but we had crossed the square and the Zhukov Boulvar was clear before us.

Minutes later we sat in a bar drinking coffee. Abby's face was smudged with smoke and any trace of make-up gone from her lips. Relief made her features softer and somehow rounder. She lifted her cup of coffee towards me. 'Thanks,' she said wryly. 'You kept your head when all around were losing theirs. Including me.'

'Jesus, it was *sauve qui peut*,' I told her. 'If I'd been able to get out and run for it, I would have left you flat.'

She smiled.

Militia units were arriving as we left the bar, driving down towards Lermontov Square. We stood on the sidewalk. The Fiat was scratched and dented, the front fender almost ripped off, but the acrid interior nevertheless held a powerful memory of our survivors' triumph. 'Let's roll,' Abby said.

'Where to?'

She got into the car. 'Joan Fowler's apartment. I haven't seen it yet. I asked Miles Bridger, the consul, to attend any police examination of it and to seal it up as soon as the militia was through.'

'What's the address?'

'Hold it a moment . . .' She fumbled in her briefcase. 'The street's named after a poet . . . Arrested and tortured, if I remember.'

'In Russia that's like saying a poet who wrote poetry.'

She shuffled through a fistful of papers. 'Under Khrushchev they wrote his wife to say sorry, kicking him to death was a mistake. Mandelstam, that's the man. Here it is: 24 Mandelstam Street.'

I felt my whole body react.

'What is it?' she said.

I puffed my cheeks. 'The connection I said didn't exist. Natalya was going to meet Joan Fowler on the day she disappeared.'

18

I HAD CALLED UP Dronsky to meet us at Mandelstam Street. In the afternoon twilight we stood together looking down from the sitting-room of Joan Fowler's apartment in the three-storey cement-block building. We had searched for over an hour and found nothing. Nothing, certainly, that threw any light on why Natalya had arranged to meet Joan. The signs of Pasko's visit were all over the place, boot marks on the light carpets, drawers hanging open, the bed stripped.

On a side-table was a folder with a yellow sticker marked American Orphanage. I picked it up and flicked through it. Dronsky watched me. 'Natalya was one of the directors of the Orphanage,' I told him.

He nodded as I turned over pages. The last, some sort of financial statement, carried two signatures:

Honorary director: N. I. Vadim. Honorary treasurer: Joan P. Fowler.

Abby took the folder and glanced through it. 'So we know how they met,' she said.

'They met as volunteer officials of the American Orphanage.' I felt angry at all the time wasted making lists. 'There was no need to see a man as the connecting link. Natalya met Joan at work. Some time, Joan introduced Natalya to the man.'

'I was wrong,' Abby said briefly. She didn't say she was sorry. She turned away and continued her search through the apartment.

Almost from the beginning I'd been doubtful we'd find much here in the apartment. It had been too heavily vandalized by Pasko and his team. Now when Abby talked of getting a crime-scene squad over to collect up any possible hair samples the vek might have left in the bedroom, I told her I wouldn't wait. She looked at me, lips pursed. 'OK,' she said after a moment. 'What are you going to be doing?'

'I'll leave you to meet the crime-scene people,' I said. 'I'm going to talk to some old friends of Natalya's. Who knows, one of them may have been with her when they ran into Joan and her vek.'

'You want me with you, Chief?' Dronsky volunteered.

'No . . .' I said. 'No. I'll just go down to the hospital to talk to a couple of people. I'll take one of the Kamkas.'

'Okay,' Abby said. 'We'll meet back at the Nunnery.'

I didn't like lying to them like this, but what alternative do I have? The steady progress of an investigation is unbearable to me. I think of Natalya and her plight stings physically, like psoriasis on my skin. I am tormented by the possibility that she is still alive. A trophy, Abby said. So it's possible. It's possible to save her if I can act in time. But even if I find her now, I know that, however quickly I have moved, whatever dark spirits I've called to my assistance, whatever chance or luck has favoured me, it is already too late to save her from whatever she is going through at this minute.

Downstairs I get into the Kamka. Starting the engine, I pull away down Mandelstam Street to Union Square, heading for the new Millennium Bridge and the road that warns that the Norwegian border is only eighty kilometres distant.

I dare not tell Abby Cunningham why I am going to Sin City, perhaps Dronsky even less. But so far I have only been *acting* like a sane man, talking the easy talk of sanity. In truth, I am prepared to do anything. Anything. To get Natalya back I will forgo pride and reason and, if necessary, humanity. I am against black forces – I will use black forces. I pull the flask from my inside pocket and unscrew the cap with my teeth. I drink a good thumb. It's comforting. This way I can claim to myself that it's the drink that makes me mad.

It is no longer snowing. My four-wheel-drive police Kamka moves slowly to the crest of the hill. I can hear music as I stop. Below me, snowfields roll away into the afternoon darkness and there, in a ring of light on the huge flat lake, is the encampment, the tents of striped canvas, round, bell-shaped, topped by fluttering pennants. A piled bonfire burns on a raised metal plate in a circle of trampled snow and other, smaller fires flicker among the tents. A lazy drift of grey smoke trails away towards the north.

For a moment I sit here and see below me the forward encampment of a Russian medieval host. It is a recurring image. Perhaps

Boris Godunov's or Prince Dimitri's. Then I recognize the music. It's the English Beatles, *When I'm sixty-four*. And at that moment the lights come on over the wooden gateway, garishly, in red and green and yellow to announce another night in this great, sprawling, vicious funfair on the lake.

I get out of the Kamka and slide and slip down towards the encampment. Once through the wooden gateway I am among dozens of tents of all sizes. Already hundreds of people wander along the main avenue. Teenagers in small tribes, chanting their provocations, American visitors with their minders, whores in high-heeled boots and face-masks of Marilyn Monroe, Bergman, Elizabeth Taylor . . .

The alleys off the main street are thronged with Sin City workers. Pure Breughel this, men in strange garb carrying boards and pieces of rolled canvas, signboards that invite you to see the singing bear or talking dog, to play games of roll the rouble, test your shooting skills with rifle and crossbow, to achieve peace through hypnosis or to take the boxing-ring for three rounds with Max, ageing former middleweight champion of General Lebed's old 14th Army.

Her tent shows two shadows, herself and a customer. I wait in the shadows of a diesel truck, fighting to keep my mind from images of Natalya. What sort of man . . . ? I ask myself a dozen times . . . and then anger, fury explodes. I sweat with the lust to hold a dagger at the corner of his eye . . . to force him to tell me where he's hiding her.

Underfoot, snow crunched. I stood back in the shadow until the man left the tent, then stepped forward quickly, lifting the flap and letting it drop behind me.

The old lady recognized me. I saw her shoulders go back, her rubbery lips press together. The fingers of her right hand were making endless circles on the chenille cloth that covered the table. Her black eyes sparkled in the candlelight.

I put two ten-rouble notes on the table. 'You said you saw a man.'

She shrugged almost skittishly. 'The inspector with the doctor wife,' she lisped. 'I knew you'd come back.'

'You were right,' I said.

'Wives disappear all the time, you know that. They find something, richer, younger, stronger . . .'

I shook my head. 'You know it wasn't like that.'

Her head went back and her mouth opened in a soundless laugh.

'You have to laugh,' she said. 'Men are such creatures. A few days ago I was just some catchpenny gypsy. Now I'm your only chance of getting her back. If I asked for a hundred roubles you'd slap it on the table without another thought.'

My hand moved to my pocket but she shook her head. 'Just sit down. Let's see what the cards say about all this.'

She took a stained and dog-eared pack of cards from the pocket of her flowing dress and shuffled and dealt three hands of three cards each. One she pushed towards me. 'Yours.' One hand she pushed to the far corner of the table. 'That's the Scorpio's. *His*,' she said. She invested the word with a compacted malevolence. 'The vek who's got your doctor wife.'

The third hand she picked up. 'This one's your wife's hand. What's her name? Nadia, was it?'

'Natalya.'

'Good. Natalya. I like it. Describe her to me.'

'She's a doctor, you know that. Young, seven or eight years younger than me. Tall, fair.'

'You tell me nothing. Is she a survivor? Will she fight?'

'She's a fighter,' I said. 'That's for certain.'

'Good. That's what I want to know.' The old woman studied her three cards – Natalya's cards – her lips working. 'You must arrange your cards in your hand, Inspector. Any order. Highest to lowest . . . lowest to highest . . . low-high-low. At random. But whatever order you choose, you must stick to.'

I arranged my cards. I was sweating, ashamed at what I was doing, terrified of wasting time, even more terrified of wasting an opportunity.

'His cards,' she jerked her head towards the hand she had pushed to the corner of the table, 'his cards remain in the order they fell. We offer him no additional advantages. He has the advantage over us already.' She looked up at me. 'It's a battle of wills, Inspector. Concentrate. Fight to get her back.'

Desperation ballooned through me. I threw the cards down. 'You're talking as if she's run off with someone. She's disappeared, you old fool. She's been abducted.' I was halfway to my feet. 'By a murderer!'

'I know,' she said calmly. Our eyes locked and I sat back down again on the stool. 'She is being held. I feel the strain, the struggle. As raw as fraying ropes on the skin.'

'You can see that?'

She shook her head impatiently. 'I read the newspapers, Inspector.'

'If all you know is what the newspapers tell you, why am I here?'

'Because just sometimes, not often I freely admit, but just sometimes there's, added to what I know, something I feel. And sometimes that feeling translates itself into an image.' Her fingertips began to make circles on the chenille. 'Perhaps it's a cave. It's deep – but not cold. And then why do I feel that vibration, hear that faint throb and rattle of a passing train?'

'Can you see Natalya?'

She closed her eyes.

'Or the other woman, the American?'

'The other woman ... is dead, Inspector,' she said almost casually. 'I get nothing from her, no warmth, no body warmth. She's dead.'

The certainty of her tone shocked me. I stared at her. 'But Natalya?'

The old woman opened her eyes. 'I can feel heat there, tension . . . She struggles, Inspector. Natalya struggles . . .'

'She's alive?'

'Alive and fierce. Fierce in her determination to live. She will not give up easily, your blonde Natalya.' She stopped abruptly.

I shook my head dumbly. No, Natalya would never give up without a fight.

The old woman relit her roach from the candle. Smoke and the soft odour of weed wreathed around her. 'There's another,' she said, staring into space.

'Another abduction?' Joan Fowler.

'And beyond that another . . .'

I stared at her, not speaking. I could not afford to think she was a charlatan.

'The cards now,' the old woman said, crushing out her cigarette. She turned the top card in front of her. Natalya's hand. 'A seven. Not good. Your card now, Inspector. Quick, quick.'

I turned over an eight.

'Not bad, not bad . . .' She reached for the top card of the third hand and threw it down. A dog-eared ten of spades. She spat angrily at the card. 'He wins the first round. Another, quickly.'

I could feel the ferocity of her engagement, see it in her narrowed, angry dark eyes. 'And you, go now. Go first this time!'

I turned a five and heard her contemptuous hiss. 'You must force a better card. It's an act of will. A better card is an act of will. There!'

For Natalya she had turned a nine of hearts. I looked towards the third hand. It was already *his* hand. She reached for it, turned a card. It was a six of clubs.

'She's fighting back, you see. A nine to his six.' The old woman stared past my head. 'It's as I said. A road perhaps, a roadside. Something lies there . . . something flutters like a bird's wing.'

'Something?'

'A kingfisher's wing. Greenish-blue.'

'A scarf?' I said.

'Perhaps. To lead you to her. Your Natalya's chances lie equally balanced now. This is the outcome, Inspector. Everything now rests on this last turn of the cards.'

I stared transfixed as her hand moved. The bony knuckles shone white against the brown skin. With a flourish, she turned over her last card, Natalya's last card, a queen of diamonds. The slow grimace of triumph drew her lips back to show her gums. 'She'll break loose. A strong woman, this Natalya . . . I can feel her energy now. She'll break out. I swear it.'

Completely caught up in the struggle, in the battle of the cards, my fingers reached out.

'Turn your card.' She nodded sharply to me, eyes on my last card like a stoat on a rabbit. I turned a knave of clubs.

She growled low in her throat. 'Not much help to her, Inspector. But she's done enough. I swear it.' She paused and slowly reached for the last card at the edge of the table. His card. 'Unless, of course, this last card is a king.' Her fingertips rested on the patterned obverse of the card. 'This one will tell us. This card holds her fate.'

'For Christ's sake,' I urged her. 'Turn it!'

She lifted it, glanced at it and her face contorted as she threw it down in disgust. A leering wolf's head in cap and bells.

The joker.

Panic seized me. 'What does it mean? What does it mean, for Christ's sake?'

'It means the game is far from over.'

'Game?'

'I speak of cards. Your man is clever, lustful, devious, resourceful . . . cursed with a hatred of women.' She paused. 'One who has learnt at the feet of a master. But he has not won yet. She holds him at bay, your Natalya.' The old woman's hands were up like claws. She was almost shrieking with excitement. 'In the struggle for her life, somehow, somehow your Natalya holds this man at bay!'

Adrenalin surged back and forth through me, surging hope and deep exhaustion just seconds apart. 'Can you see him, fuck your mother? Can you see his *face*?'

'A dark outline. An outline of a man's face.' She shook her head frantically.

'Try, for God's sake.' I leaned across the table and grabbed her shoulders. 'Try! Is he tall, short, what age is he?'

'You think he's a stranger. But he's no stranger. You've seen his face. When? How long ago? I can't tell you.'

'A description, *any* description.'

'He's a shape. No more.' Spit bubbled on her lip. 'Don't force me.'

'His face,' I screamed at her, shaking her until her head rocked on her shoulders. 'Is he Russian, Chechen, Siberian? Describe his face.'

'I see a shape, that's all. Understand for pity's sake! We're in a world of ghosts. Shadowlands.' She shook her head wildly. 'There are figures circling round him, floating . . .'

'Women. You see women? Other women he has killed?'

Her head jerked up and down. 'One, two, three . . . four. No, dozens . . . dozens . . . Floating . . . like ghosts . . .'

'Dead?' I screamed at her like a maniac. 'The women are dead?'

'Paralysed,' she said.

The dolls! I shook her until she fell forward onto the table.

'I see nothing more, your honour. I see nothing, nothing, nothing.' She lifted her head and took a deep breath. And then another. I could see her eyes were watering. 'Over there,' she gasped. 'Quickly.'

I let her go and turned. An old leather bag hung on a hook. She had fallen back into her chair. I handed her the leather bag as she fought for breath. Her dirty brown arm plunged into it and brought out an inhaler.

I watched while she squirted ventalin into her throat.

'Chief . . .' I heard the voice behind me but I continued to watch the old woman. When I was sure she was all right, I turned to leave. As I stretched a hand for it, the tent flap lifted.

I saw the shape outlined garishly against yellow neon behind him.

Dronsky, standing in the entrance, one arm holding up the flap, reached forward and led me from the tent.

19

I STOOD, BESIDE MY Kamka, shaking my head. 'Jesus, you had no right, Ilya,' I said. I'd never been angry with Dronsky before. 'Was this your idea? Or Abby Cunningham's?'

In his old rabbit-lined blue militia parka with the Moscow city badge, he shuffled his shoulders until the hood fell back. 'Both of us, Chief.' He rubbed his hand across his brush cut. 'We meant no harm. With this happening to Natalya, you're under the knout. She didn't think you should be left on your own.'

'*She* didn't.'

'She's worried about you, Chief. We both are.'

I took a deep breath, the cold searing my throat. I didn't like the idea that I needed looking after. Yet even so the idea of the cool FBI operative being worried about me was not displeasing to the vanity. That's just the muddled sort of individual I am. Be angry about it, Constantin, for Christ's sake. Or be pleased. Make up your mind.

I looked at Dronsky suffering my displeasure for the act of a friend. 'Listen,' I said. 'Thanks for the thought.'

His face lightened.

'But say nothing about this,' I gestured towards the lights. 'Say nothing about this to her. We're Russians. We know our lives don't run like a trolley-car on straight lines.'

He looked at me, frowning. 'Does that mean you believe in all this, Chief?'

Did I? Christ, I don't know. 'It means what I said. That we're *Russians*. We both know deep down that these things sometimes have a part to play. Abby Cunningham comes from a different world.'

I saw the familiar doubtful look on Dronsky's face. Normally it made me love the man. But not today. 'What did the old woman say?' he asked.

'She says she's sure Natalya is still alive.' I hesitated. 'That's hope. If it's nothing else, it's hope. You wouldn't ask me to ignore that?'

'No . . .' He hesitated. 'No.'

I grabbed him by the shoulder as he turned to open the door to his Kamka. 'Just tell me, Dronsky. You believe she's still alive, don't you?'

He reached up, half turning, and put his gloved hand over mine. 'I want to, Chief. As much as you do. But I'm not sure about all that . . .' he gestured to the fair below. 'Cards, charts . . . I'm not sure it tells us much either way.'

'We've got nothing else.'

He faced me. It's not often Dronsky makes his own special point but when he does, you know it. 'You're wrong there, Chief. We've got the *fact*, the solid fact, that so far this is an abduction. Two abductions. Nothing more. And despite what your professor of psychology had to say, we have not one scrap of evidence that the man we're dealing with is capable of killing.'

I swallowed the idea whole. I needed the nourishment it gave me. 'That's right, of course,' I said. 'There's no evidence that he's any more than some disgusting kook.'

'So we're dealing with two abductions. Just stick with that, Chief.'

I could have hugged him. Sometimes I need that solid common sense as much as I need the old woman's intuition.

Or perhaps my problem is that I really need both.

I slept a ridiculous, troubled night, tormented by dreams. In what seemed a half-dozen different enactments Natalya and the old fortune teller merged and I enjoyed her cackling favours before I woke, shocked, then deeply miserable. In the middle of the night I was up, working the phone to San Diego. It was midday there, sunny, optimistic. I could hear nurses from the Scripps Memorial Hospital laughing in the background. 'I'm checking the details of a Dr Potanin who once ran therapy courses at the Scripps,' I said.

It was a long wait, even with a couple of thumbs of vodka to see me through it, but it turned out pretty much as I'd guessed. There were no therapy courses. And there was no UCLA doctorate. Potanin's stay in the United States had been less successful than depicted. It didn't really change the situation but it did, at least, reveal Potanin's bleak view of Natalya's chances of being alive as so much amateur guesswork.

By five o'clock I was in the shower, strangely refreshed by my night of lust and mistaken identity, suddenly, improbably certain that today I would find her.

Energy thrummed through to my nerve ends. By just after six I was banging on Dronsky's inner office, a Styrofoam of coffee in one hand, a hamburger and, God forgive me, a fishburger in the other. 'Get up Dronsky – throw that beast off your bed – better still, throw him out of the window,' I yelled through the door. And stood back to Dronsky in pyjamas, unsteadily opening the door – with V.I. Lenin cowering behind him as if the barbarians were at the gate.

I left them to their breakfast and went in search of Pinsk who was handling nights. Abby was in her office on the phone. Pinsk was standing looking down at her. She looked up and nodded to him.

'What is it?' I asked him.

I could detect the excitement in Pinsk's Quasimodo shuffle to where I stood. He kept his voice low. 'It could be a crazy, Chief, and God knows we've had enough of them tonight. But he doesn't sound it.'

'Who is he?'

'Some factory-owner.'

'What's he saying?' The optimism was roaring through my blood. I knew this was the day.

'He claims to identify the models we broadcast on television last night.'

'He knows where they're made?'

His head rolled on his rounded shoulders. 'He makes them.'

'We'll be there,' Abby was saying, the phone to her ear. 'We're leaving right away.'

Sasha Roop was smooth. You see more smooth Russians these days, of course. They emerged from the Yeltsin era with rough haircuts and shedding dollar bills like flakes of dandruff. But it wasn't long before the suits got better, the gold jewellery got more discreet and even the bodyguards wore French cologne. Roop was, he told us as he met the two police Kamkas in the parking-lot, a self-made man. At twenty-two years of age he had rented the big rambling helicopter-repair hangar no longer used by the military. Placed near the northern highway, it was ideal for his manufactory. Its Soviet occupants were remembered in the faded painting above the door of a huge attack helicopter, angled for action, rockets firing the inscription in six-foot-high letters, 351st Assault Helicopter Regiment.

Black-haired, black-eyed, with a Mexican-bandit moustache, Sasha Roop wore a dark three-piece chalk-striped suit with a scarlet lining and a cream silk handkerchief tucked into his breast pocket. If he had started at the age of twenty-two that could not have been more than four or five years ago. But it was the name that intrigued me. Roop is not by any means a common Russian family name. 'When I was at school,' I said, 'No. 36 Primary here in Murmansk, there was a boy named Roop in my class. Lukas . . . Lukas Roop.'

Sasha smiled. 'Dysfunctional big brother Lukas. He works for me.'

We were trailing across the old cement helicopter apron towards the entrance, Roop and myself slightly ahead, Dronsky and Abby bringing up the rear.

'My good fortune was to escape the family web at an early age, Inspector. My mother drank her fill of vodka for the last time a few years after I was born. Lukas was already at work – he's fourteen years older than me.'

'What happened to you?'

'I was sent into care. That's what they call it. The *Internat*, the care house.'

'And Lukas?'

'As soon as he could he got me out. In his way he brought me up. Don't think I'm putting my brother down. Lukas is a noble soul, Inspector. A sensitive spirit. Give him a chance to do something for the common good and he'll snatch it with both hands.'

'You'd do the same yourself,' I said, hoping I'd be forgiven.

'I got in touch with you, didn't I?' He grinned. 'My principle is . . . be helpful if you need help yourself.'

'You need help?'

We had reached the main entrance, a doorway cut into the original massive hangar doors. 'I need a degree of understanding, Inspector. The reason you couldn't trace a manufacturer of the models is because I'm not registered as being in that business. A manufactory pays taxes. An educational establishment does not.'

'So that's what you are, an educational establishment?'

Abby and Dronsky caught up with us at the door.

'We're the Murmansk Ballet School. We prepare pupils for entry to Western ballet companies.'

'Does the tax authority believe that?'

He grinned again, his wide easy grin. 'They need regular persuasion, of course . . .' he rubbed his thumb and forefinger together. 'But they're prepared to be reasonable. They're willing to accept the model-making is just subsidiary – that we use the models as aids to teaching dance.' He turned to Abby and led her forward. 'Listen, it's freezing in here at the moment. The heating's given up. With help from brother Lukas. But my office is on a separate system. I can promise you a comfortable twenty-five degrees. You'll be able to . . .' he grinned down the length of Abby's body, 'divest yourself?'

He opened the inset in the hangar's giant doors and we stepped inside into a remarkable building. At the highest, nearly twenty metres high, its arched roof curved down to floor level. From the topmost metal spars faded silk military banners hung. Three levels of galleries looked down into the centre, the top two lined with bald naked women standing in elegantly silent poses. As I turned my head they seemed to be revolving about me. I suppressed an intake of breath as the fortune teller's vision of ghostly figures of women came tumbling back into my mind. Excitement surged through me. I wanted to turn to Abby and tell her . . . Only at the last moment I stopped myself. What was I talking about? An old woman's vision, nothing more.

I brought my eyes down. The lowest gallery was equally populated. But there the figures were clothed and outfitted with wigs. They leaned on the balcony rail, cigarettes held to their painted mouths, or stood, heads thrown back, as if haughtily assessing each other. The overwhelming sense was of silence in this seemingly crowded building.

'How many people do you have working for you?' I asked him.

He pointed to two portable office sections parked at the far end of the hangar and a ten-metre-long gun-metal machine crouching beside them. 'The Patzweisser Latex Press was brought in by sea from Norway – that takes four operatives. Packing and distribution take six more. A couple of pretty girls in the office and that's it. A dozen altogether. It's a lean, fit operation.'

'What does your brother do for you?'

'Ask him.' He turned and shouted up into the roof of the

hangar. 'Lukas. Lukas! Get your ass down here. An old friend's come to visit.'

Dronsky had wandered off to look at the models in ballet sweats posed realistically against an exercise rail.

Abby opened her briefcase and handed a ring-bound folder to Sasha Roop. 'Take a look at these, Mr Roop. Would you say they're yours?'

Sasha took the folder from her and opened it. Inside were front and rear photographs of the models of Joan Fowler and Natalya. Their wigs and make-up had been removed and they stood stark and pale against a black background. Abby glanced over Sasha's shoulder at them, then frowned up at the galleries above our heads. When Sasha closed the folder with a snap, her eyes came back to his face. 'Well?'

He turned to her. 'Everything about them says they're ours. Height, vital statistics, even expression. They're all variations on an original sculpted by brother Lukas.'

'Definitely yours.'

'No doubt at all.'

Abby flared her nostrils in satisfaction. It was, I suppose, our first big step forward in the investigation. It was, I knew, going to be my day.

'What we're interested in, of course,' Abby said, 'is anybody who could have gotten hold of a model.'

'We call them dolls. You don't want to look around, see the range we have on offer?'

Abby shook her head. 'Let's talk about your customers. Who are they mostly?'

Sasha counted up on his fingers. 'We sell a few to the smarter clothes shops in Petersburg or Novgorod. One planeload even went to Moscow, the new Paris-Paris store. But mostly we sell to the West. We run them across the frontier to Norway. That way we undercut Western prices by fifty per cent or more.'

'You smuggle them out to the West?'

He raised a finger. 'I thought we had a gentleman's agreement.'

'We do,' Abby said firmly.

'OK. So with the Norwegian border only eighty kilometres west of here, we're well placed for export.'

'What about a domestic market, here in Murmansk?'

'Very varied. You'd be surprised at the range of uses. We even sell to the militia, Inspector, for training purposes.'

'Look at the pictures again, Sasha,' I said.

He opened the folder. With my index finger I traced two deep lines, one across the back of one model, the other down the thigh. 'You sell them to your high-class Western customers like that?'

'No. That's what we call machine grazing. It often happens when we start up a new batch.'

'When they come out like that, do you throw them away?'

He smoothed his already gleaming black hair. 'It's not really an important part of our business. But we sell them locally to artists, photographers and God knows what sort of kooks. Damaged goods.'

'How are they sold?'

'Separately. Usually unpackaged. Brother Lukas looks after the shop.' He jerked his head up and scanned the galleries. 'Where is he, by the way? Skulking about like a frightened fox.' His voice rose to a shout. 'Lukas, you great big ugly girl! Get down here.'

A sound of heels on the gallery above us drew our eyes to a group of dolls in swimsuits, lounging excessively. A real girl appeared among them and leaned a blonde head over the balcony rail. 'Lukas has skipped outside, Sasha. You want me to get him?'

'No,' Sasha shook his head irritably. 'We'll catch up with him later.' He turned to Abby. 'It's you,' he said with a big, meaningful grin. 'He's shit shy of beautiful women. He'll be hiding in the shop.'

Abby's face remained a dark marble. 'We're still going to have to talk to him,' she said.

'I'll do it.' I started moving away. 'Renew our acquaintance.'

'Was he always like this?' Sasha said. 'When he was at school, I mean.'

I stopped. I wanted to be diplomatic. 'I don't remember him too well. He joined late. A year or two after the rest of us.'

'He would have. The family, what was left of it, was out of luck in Rostov. They came back home to Murmansk just before I was born.'

I nodded slowly, my eyes on him. I found this younger brother uniquely unlikeable. I must have been staring hard.

He opened both hands, palms towards me. A wide grin. 'I mentioned it . . .' He bubbled laughter. 'That's all.'

I pushed open the door of the long low hut, once used to house a squad of helicopter-borne infantry soldiers. Inside it was dark and smelt heavily of paint. There were shadowy figures on either side, standing in fixed awkward positions. A desk light at the end of the long room illumined the head and hands of a man painting a latex face propped in front of him. For a moment I stood absorbed: he was painting with both hands at once. I felt for the light-switch. 'I'm going to turn on the light,' I called. I pressed the switch and neon flickered in the ceiling before bursting an ugly brightness onto the models' nakedness. Beyond the light, walls in deep shadow were lined with shelves stacked with books and paint-pots and bottles of brushes, hands, arms, feet and the occasional head and shoulders in pale latex.

'Lukas Roop,' I said. 'You remember me?'

The head turned, greyish, kinked hair above a young face. 'I remember Primary 36,' he said. He stood up, taller than average, thin, with large hands, each of which held a delicate Chinese brush. 'Come in.' He turned and spent a moment putting the brushes into a jar on the desk as I walked towards him. I could see this was a man who dealt in long silences. 'I can call you Constantin, can I?' he asked over his shoulder.

'Of course.' I looked around me. 'You paint with both hands at the same time.'

'The best Chinese porcelain painters were said to be ambidextrous.'

'You work in a strange place. What is this, a repair shop?'

He turned to face me. 'And where I live.' He pointed to a bunk near a big iron stove in a book-cluttered corner. A double-barrelled shotgun sat in hooks above the bed.

'A lupara?' I said. An Italian wolf-gun. 'You're a hunter?'

He pointed to a wolf's head mounted high on the wall. 'I hunt but it's not sport,' he said. 'Wolves prey on the forest game. I hunt the gamekeeper's way by trailing a piece of reindeer meat.'

'Leave the meat in a clearing and hide up until the wolves arrive?'

'I get a hundred roubles a wolf's head from the Hunters' Co-operative. It helps out what I earn on the broken dolls.'

He came forward, wiping his hands on a cloth. Under the neon light, I saw that what I had thought of as grey hair was in fact more blond than grey and his features, though still youthful, seemed stretched and tense as he produced a shy half-smile. 'I used to think of you as a god,' he said, extending a hard, knobbly hand. 'And your friend, that foul little bully Roy Rolkin, as king of the underworld.'

'That's more or less what he still is,' I said. 'Except happily it's the Budapest underworld he lords it over.'

'I hated him. I was afraid of him too. I was never afraid of you. You were big, but you were never a bully. Do you ever hear from Rolkin?'

'Not by choice.' What else is there to say about Roy? Certainly I had no wish to admit I had spoken to him within the last few days. 'I have to talk to you, Lukas. You know why?'

Again he held a long silence. 'Yes,' he said eventually. 'Of course I know why.'

'I mean you know why I want to talk about the dolls.'

'Yes. Sasha told me he'd been in touch with the police. I saw you and the dark-skinned woman from the balcony.'

'Sasha's identified the two models found as coming from this factory.'

'No-one else makes them.'

'In all probability they were acquired through sales made from this shop.'

He nodded very slowly. 'You mean it's my fault, selling them to someone who did this awful thing?' His eyes were flinching, like a wolf in captivity.

'That's not the issue, Lukas.' The retiring, nervous child of nearly thirty years ago came back to me forcibly. The boy who hung back, unwilling to join the circle of boys Roy was teaching to masturbate. 'What I want to know is whether or not you have any sort of sales record?'

He was already shaking his head. 'Sasha wouldn't want any record kept. He's told me I must sell for cash.'

'Who buys them?'

'People who own small shops, painters or sculptors sometimes . . .'

'Mostly local people?'

'People who drive up from the city. They buy parts or sometimes complete damaged dolls. I paint and repair the least damaged.'

'How many have you sold, complete dolls, over the last year?'

'Through the shop? Two, three dozen perhaps. If that. Sasha allows me to keep the money. It's the way he pays me.'

'Two or three dozen?' I lifted my head. 'So you know most of your customers.'

'Most of them? Yes, I suppose I do.'

'Good. I want you to start writing.'

'Now?'

'Now, Lukas. I want as full a list as you can make. Anybody who's bought in the last few months.'

'Parts as well?'

'Parts as well, if they could add up to a complete doll.'

'It'll take time.'

'I don't have time, Lukas. You know why.'

He stared at me, too embarrassed to speak. 'Your wife . . . your second wife,' he said finally.

'Yes.' I'd forgotten, of course. He'd have known my first wife, Julia, as a child at Primary 36. 'Start writing, Lukas. Now.'

He backed towards his desk, nearly knocked over his lamp, just caught it in time and sat down, awkwardly.

'Last Saturday,' I said. 'Do you remember what you were doing?'

'Here I suppose. Yes here.'

'Saturday evening. Night.'

'Hunting? Yes, I would have been out in the forest.'

'Did you take a wolf that night?'

'I haven't taken a wolf for over a fortnight.'

'And you were alone of course, Saturday?'

'Always. I hunt alone, Constantin. I do everything alone.'

I nodded. 'I'll be back in ten minutes for the list,' I said. 'Go through your memory like a mother searching a child's head for lice.'

'I will . . .' He put a note-pad on the desk and began to write.

I turned for the door. I'd walked no more than a step or two when this strange electric tingle moved up my back. I reached the door and switched off the neon. Lukas was still at his desk, the lamp shining full into his face – but he was staring at me.

'Something Sasha mentioned,' I said. 'What made your family move from Rostov?'

'You know how families move. Reasons that seem important at the time. I can't remember now. There's always more work up here. People don't relish the cold.'

That wasn't all of it. That wasn't the way the family ran out of luck in Rostov. 'And the rest, Lukas,' I said.

His head turned away, towards the bright light no more than a foot from his eyes. I walked slowly towards him, my hands in the pockets of my topcoat, and stopped ten paces away from where he sat. Still his head did not turn in my direction. 'Why was it, Lukas? Why did you come to Murmansk?'

He turned to me, blinking with that owlish innocence I now remembered so well. But owls aren't innocent, are they? They're savage predators.

'A family tragedy,' he said. 'We left Rostov soon after my sister died. My mother brought me here to Murmansk where she had one or two relatives.'

'And Sasha was born here.'

'He never knew his father.' He twisted his lips. 'But then I don't think my mother did either. Not for certain. She died soon after Sasha was born.'

I nodded to the list. 'Just as soon as you can. As full as you can make it. Don't fail me, Lukas.'

Sasha's office was a long way from the crowded nest Lukas had created for himself. It took up most of one of the well-heated portable buildings he had shown us and was furnished in New Russian style. Every item of furniture was from Norway or Finland. Rosewood, stainless steel and black leather were the chosen materials.

A girl named Nessa placed a tray of coffee on Sasha's desk and he paused to watch as she clicked in her high heels back across the birchwood parquet flooring. When the door closed behind her he began to hand out coffee.

'Alibis, you said?' He passed Abby a cup. 'For everybody who works here!'

She took the coffee from him and shook her head to milk and sugar. 'That's it, Mr Roop. We'll have a team out here this afternoon. Twelve employees won't take up much time.'

Sasha Roop stuck his tongue in his cheek, mock thoughtfully. 'I have to tell you that my lean, fit operation includes about twenty young men from the air force barracks you passed down the road.'

'What do they do for you, Sasha?'

'You know how it is, Inspector. The Ministry of Defence can't pay the generals, the generals can't pay the Ivans. So this is a public service. They used to run this helicopter-repair site. Now they cut wood for me to heat the hangar. They unload the raw granules we import from Finland. They do the heavy work.'

'Would any of these soldiers have access to the dolls?'

'I couldn't see how. In any case I run a rigid stock control. Brother Lukas's operation is the only possible leak.'

When the secretary came in to give me Lukas Roop's list I looked quickly through the names. None of them meant anything to me until I turned to the second sheet. There was only one name on it. *Lermontov Infirmary . . . 17, reconditioned.* 14 November, 2016.

While Sasha perched himself on the arm of Abby's chair, I phoned over the top sheet of the list to Pinsk at the Nunnery. 'Bring every one of them in,' I told him.

'I could doorstep them first?'

'We don't have time. Bring them in – we'll talk to them at the Nunnery.'

'Where will I put them, Chief? Twenty-five names.'

'Get someone to check out the basement.' I thought back to the days when the Nunnery had been occupied by Major Roy Rolkin's secret police unit. 'If my memory serves me there's room for twice that number.'

Abby and Dronsky had stood up as I rang off. I finished my coffee quickly and followed them out through the hangar. Sasha had hung back and again I found myself walking with him out to the car.

'So Inspector, do you have suspects?' He tugged at my arm. 'Is my brother Lukas a suspect? He's strange enough. But harmless.'

'Everybody who had access to those dolls is suspect. You don't need me to tell you that.'

'Even me, the one who called you out here?'

'Even you. Where were you, Sasha, Saturday evening for instance?'

'The American woman already asked me that. I told her I was getting my leg over.'

'Who with?'

'An unknown beauty . . .' He held the pause, his black eyes sparkling. 'In Petersburg. The Nicholas II Hotel. I told Agent Cunningham to give them a call. They'll remember me. I tipped a fortune and took the Tsar's suite.'

'She'll check it.' I looked at him but his glance was already back on Abby.

'She's something, your American colleague,' he said admiringly. 'I'd like to get a leg across her.'

'I have an idea,' I said deliberately, 'that you might very well lose the leg.'

He grimaced uncertainly.

I took the list Lukas had given me and turned to the second page. 'What about this?'

He glanced at it casually. 'The Lermontov takes some of our damaged goods, I'd forgotten that. Knock-down prices. The man in charge of the crazy house, Dr Potanin. They use the dolls for group therapy sessions, he tells me. Makes your blood run cold to think of all these crazies confessing to dolls who can't speak back.'

'Any other department at the Lermontov?'

He turned down his mouth. 'Accident and Emergency training uses them . . . And Nursing School on the top floor. I deliver there myself.' He grinned his wide grin. 'It's a public service.'

I turned towards the Kamka. Dronsky was sitting next to the driver. I said goodbye to Sasha and began to climb into the back seat next to Abby. My eye caught Lukas, at the door of his paint shop, that familiar worried little boy look on his face.

20

WE WERE TO drop Abby at the Continental Hotel where she had taken a suite.

Seconds before we pulled up outside the hotel I saw Dronsky purse his lips. From my position in the back I could see nothing, but Abby's head was turned towards her side window. 'Jesus Christ,' she said.

I ducked my head to be able to see where she was looking. The entrance of the two-year-old hotel, part of the Murmansk Shopping Mall, glittered with light and warm welcome. Then I saw the flags arranged in clutches higher up the walls. Red with a single white circle in the middle in which was stamped a black cross. High above the entrance a horizontal banner read: Campaign headquarters for Candidate X.

'I'm moving. I'm not staying at a hotel that supports the neo-Fascists, for God's sake.'

'You'll be out of luck,' I said. 'During an election, all the main hotels will be full. All three of them. Any second-class hotels, you wouldn't be keen to stay in.'

She thought. 'Then I'll move in with you,' she said. 'You've got a spare room?'

I opened and closed my mouth. 'Sure,' I said.

'I'll get Miles Bridger to drop me off with my bags.'

'Sure,' I said again.

'Do you have keys?'

I fumbled in my pockets and took out a key-ring.

'Won't you be there? You look beat.'

I need something to drink, is what I need, I told myself. To Abby, I said: 'I'll call in at the Lermontov first. There's a couple of questions I want to ask Potanin.'

Potanin was watching television when I was shown into his office. To his embarrassment, a Tom and Jerry cartoon. 'Good stuff,'

I said. 'Just like life itself. The villain never fails to get his comeuppance.' And, as he scowled at me, 'Relaxing anyway.'

He switched off the set and stood staring at me, his moment of embarrassment behind him. I was struck again by the arrogance of the man. 'Tell me about your degrees,' I said.

His mouth dropped slightly.

'Go on, Doctor. Give me the full CV.'

'If you want my co-operation in this unfortunate business . . .'

'Unfortunate business? Is that what you call it?'

'A phrase. That's all.' He looked at me. 'What is it you want to know.'

'You never took any sort of degree at UCLA.'

'I took my first degree at Moscow University. My second degree was taken in California.'

'UCLA?'

'I went to California to complete my studies.'

'A Californian university but not UCLA. Ruskin Holmes College,' I said.

'There are stiff entry qualifications for students.'

'From what I learn they net them in off the streets.'

'Are you here to insult me?'

'And there was no professorship at Scripps Memorial, was there? My informant tells me you worked the cleaning detail at Scripps for two years, 2008 and 2009. Rose to maintenance superintendent, maternity and surgical recovery.'

'I was studying in my spare time. There are many routes to excellence in California. You don't necessarily need a formal degree.'

'Why didn't you tell us you used Sasha Roop's latex models in your therapy classes?'

His eyes slewed, looking for a bottle. 'Didn't think to. I hadn't seen them here for months, years even.'

'But you ordered them.'

'No. The Lermontov, as you may know, still uses the old Soviet system of central buying. These were bought a year or two back before I was Director here.'

'Who ordered them?'

'God knows. Central buying was invented to remove every trace of responsibility, you know that. There'll be an order form somewhere. But signed by a committee, if at all.'

'How do we check if there are any missing?'

He laughed. 'In the Lermontov, if it isn't bolted down it's missing. You must know that.'

'Have you ever used them?'

'No. Some of my junior colleagues no doubt still use them. I don't.'

I glared at him, frustrated.

'Just accept, Inspector. When we were talking about latex dolls, I'd seen them in many other contexts. Fashion shops, even art galleries. Here, in the Psychiatric Wing, I hadn't seen one for months. So they simply didn't come to mind.'

'We were discussing abductions where latex dolls have been left dressed in the victims' clothes, and you're saying the fact that you had the same brand of models here, *in a hospital for the criminally insane*, didn't come to mind?'

'Are you in charge of this investigation?'

'In all but name, Agent Cunningham is in charge. Why do you ask?'

'Tell your American woman she's wasting her time if she's looking here. I maintain a special list of inmates. These are people who remain under surveillance twenty-four hours a day. Nobody on the list is free to leave the Psychiatric Wing for any reason whatsoever. She should be scouring lists of those who passed through these doors before I became Director. During the Civil War years the Psychiatric Wing was closed down and its patients dismissed, did you know that?'

'They were recruited for the defence of the city.'

'And freed when the war ended. There are dozens of men loose in the streets today who are a threat to every woman in Murmansk.'

'Those lists exist? The names of the men who were released?'

He wriggled his shoulders. 'I sent over a partial list. It's the best I can do.' He rummaged through papers on his desk and drew out a single sheet. 'But this is the man you should be looking for,' he said.

I took the paper. It contained three short paragraphs.

The killer is a man of between twenty and thirty, Russian, once married but with a string of unsuccessful relationships behind him. Highly organized, possibly a member of the military or recently ex-military. He will be clean-shaven, neat in his appearance, interested in clothes and fashion.

His most developed characteristic is his confidence in himself and his contempt for the militia investigation. This will lead him to insert himself into the inquiry if he is not already central to it, as a militiaman for instance. His most likely course is to call in to the incident room taunting the militia for its inefficiency. He might also pose as someone trying to make helpful suggestions. These suggestions or the provision of information may well prove genuine but the advance in understanding for the investigators will be less real than apparent.

I looked at Potanin. This wasn't a bad description of Sasha Roop's part in the investigation. I read on.

The crime has all the hallmarks of a crime of opportunity. The dolls are part of a later staging operation to confuse the investigation and can, as a contribution to the understanding of the mind and motivations of the killer, be ignored. In profiling we look for the signature of the killer. The dolls are not his signature. The true signature has not yet emerged.

'Well?' he said.

'Pretty astute. Some things fit.'

'Everything will fit in the end.'

'You are completely ruling out the dolls as an important element in revealing what this man is about.'

'I am. As I've recorded there, the dolls are what profilers call staging. A false lead in other words. Ignore them.'

'And you describe the abduction as a crime of opportunity.'

'Yes.'

'There's something you weren't told.'

He raised his eyebrows.

'There was a stalker,' I said.

He shook his head. 'A crime of opportunity. This man was suddenly presented with circumstances which left him no choice.'

'And Joan Fowler and my wife Natalya were completely unknown to him?'

He seemed to hesitate. 'Take my word for it.'

'Like the appointment board did when you applied for the job here?' I handed him the paper back. 'No. I just don't know, Professor, how far I can go along with that. With any of it,' I added.

I ducked into the brick archway and rang for entrance at the studded door. A security guard let me in. The consular offices were long closed, but up in our wing there were reassuring lights and footsteps and the sound of phones ringing and keyboards being tapped. I put my head round the corner of Anna Danilova's office and saw she now controlled a team: a girl and a young militiaman were seated at desks with earphones and recording equipment before them. Two more girls were keying in transcripts.

I was backing out when she called to me. 'Inspector Vadim. I'd like you to hear this.'

I came forward.

Danilova crossed to a desk and slipped a disk into a player. We both stood staring at the black box and I was aware that other activities in the room had ceased. Danilova turned and, at a sign from her, the others got up and quietly left the room.

'This came through at four forty this afternoon,' Danilova said, leaning her weight on one hand splayed on the desk. She pressed a button and I heard a ringing tone. It immediately had a particularly mesmeric quality. The call was picked up and Danilova's voice answered with the formula I guessed had been worked out with Dronsky: 'Inquiry centre. Joint Russian Procurator's Office and American Federal Bureau of Investigation. Can I help you?'

'Much more likely I can help you. You've got two women missing and you're getting nowhere. Am I right?' The voice sounded angry rather than taunting.

'As you say, perhaps you can help us there.'

'You're floundering around with no idea where to look.' A few seconds' silence preceded a wet breathy laugh. Angry? Nervous? Just plain drunk?

'Where should we be looking?'

'It's far too early to disclose that.'

'Then why did you call if you weren't going to help?' Danilova said, the voice of sweet reason in the maniac's ear.

'I called to tell you that you were on the wrong track.'

'Are we? Then you must tell us how to get onto the right one,' Danilova said. She was good. Calm, neutral.

'Why should I do that?'

'It's what you've called for, isn't it? What's your name, now. Tell me what I should call you.'

'You'd like to know that.'

'I'd like something else much more.' I was astounded at the touch of provocation this middle-aged Baptist allowed into her voice.

'And what would that be? I'll have to see if I can oblige.'

'I think you can. I'd like you to tell me something that lets me know for sure that you're involved in this matter. We get so many time-wasters, you see,' she said reasonably. 'Inadequates looking for a cheap thrill. I mean if you can tell me something, one small thing perhaps, about this matter that the rest of the world doesn't know . . .?'

'Wait a minute.' The voice was strange, partly because I could hear the excitement in it, the tension. Partly because the words were distorted, as if he were speaking though a thin cloth or perhaps a metal grille. It was impossible to guess at his age.

The pause hung on. 'The two women,' the voice said. 'They knew each other.'

'We just released that fact to the press,' Danilova said coolly.

'You didn't just release *why* they knew each other.'

'No. Why did they know each other?'

The voice dropped low. 'They knew each other because they were lovers.' Then the sudden breathy laugh. 'Because they met to have sex together.'

The line went dead and I was left staring at Danilova. 'I'm sorry, Captain,' she said. 'But I felt you should hear it straight away.'

21

I FOLLOWED PINSK ACROSS the hall to the oak door that led down to the basement. I was thinking of Natalya. Of Natalya and Joan Fowler. Did it make any sense to be so disturbed by a voice on the phone? I had heard so many crazies before, sobbing, whispering, taunting. So this one got off on the idea of two beautiful women together. This one liked the idea of talking about it. Potanin had said our man would. Did that mean Potanin, the fraudster, the man who might well not have any medical knowledge at all, was right? And Abby with her FBI trained view that our vek was apologizing by offering models of his victims – did that mean she was wrong?

I put the idea from my mind and watched Pinsk's round, neckless head bob on his broad shoulders as we walked in single file through the narrow stone corridors. Every time we passed under a light his shaven head gleamed. 'We've pulled in twelve on the list of Roop's customers you phoned over, Chief,' he said over his shoulder. 'Three others being picked up now. Four women buyers we've asked to make a statement, but for the moment we're leaving it at that.'

'And the men, what reason do they give for buying the models?'

'A ragbag of reasons, Chief. Most of them genuine enough, I've no doubt. In any case it's not illegal to buy a damaged shop-window model.'

'Do any of them have priors?'

'Captain Dronsky came in while you were listening to the tape. He's downstairs now. I gave him the record on two of them. The rest are clean for the Murmansk area. We'll be getting dossiers from the rest of the country over the next week.'

'Week?'

'Since it's an emergency. Otherwise most provinces wouldn't guarantee better than a month. The Siberian regions turned us down flat.'

We started down the twisting flight of steps to the basement. The old frightening smell of carbolic still lingered. Men had been beaten here. Forced to confess. The fact that Roy Rolkin was in charge in those days is just one of the reasons Natalya has always refused to speak to him.

The cells were a double row of small rooms with heavy wooden doors, cells of a different kind, I imagine, in the days when the nuns were still here. Through the grille I could see that the men were, for the most part, sitting head in hands, or staring into space, stunned at the speed of events that had brought them to this dank, evil-smelling place. Two militiamen from Pinsk's detail patrolled the narrow corridor making sure no-one spoke. Dronsky sat at the small guardroom table studying the dossiers on the two men with priors. He looked up as I came in with Pinsk.

'What do we have?' I gestured to the papers in front of him.

'Arlevsky, Vladimir, 65. Drunk and disorderly. Fourteen arrests, fourteen convictions . . . Assault on a woman in a bar, 1991.'

I shook my head. 'Too old.'

'Sovolev, Arcady, 34. A doctor. One arrest for propositioning an under-age female. One arrest and conviction – three years labour camp – for indecent assault on a female fellow doctor.'

'A doctor? Where?'

'Up at one of the nickel mines.'

'We should talk to him.'

Dronsky pointed through the open door to where a neatly bearded young man, dressed in a crumpled grey suit, sat in the cell across the corridor, staring into space. I was already walking towards him when Pinsk touched my arm. 'He's alibied,' the lieutenant said.

'And checked out?'

Pinsk rolled his head so that his right eye cocked towards me. 'He's got the best alibi of the lot, Chief. He crashed his car and spent the Saturday night of your wife's disappearance in the drunk tank at Station 7. He was there from eleven p.m. until the following midday.'

I was reluctant to let it go. Dr Sovolev was shifty yet sure of himself. The sort of combination that makes policemen's fingers tingle. 'Stand up,' I said. Perhaps the abduction of Natalya and Joan had taken place much later than I had imagined. What if the voice on the phone were right? What if Natalya and Joan did meet for sex? They could have spent Saturday night together at Joan's apartment and someone – Dr Arcady Sovolev perhaps – might have abducted them sometime during Sunday morning.

He got to his feet.

'When you were released at midday, where did you go?'

'Straight into a fight.'

'What?'

'My wife and her brother were waiting outside the militia station. She was screaming at me for crashing the car. He tore into me as I came down the steps. I spent the rest of Sunday giving evidence against him for assault. I left at six o'clock Sunday evening. It can be checked.'

We spent the next hour questioning the most likely detainees, looking for anything odd or out of the way in the manner they presented to us. Most importantly, we asked if they could produce the models they had bought from Lukas Roop.

One or two claims needed confirming, but all detainees insisted they still possessed the models they had bought. They were at home, stuffed under their beds, in their shop windows, posed in their backyard ateliers.

Dispirited, the anxiety boiling within me, I climbed the stairs from the basement with Dronsky. 'You'll run yourself into the ground if you don't take a few hours to sleep,' he said, as we stood under the flaking paint in the entrance hall. 'You can't do it all yourself, Chief.'

'If only I could. I'm certain they're still alive, Ilya. Certain Natalya's still alive,' I said more honestly. I didn't say where my certainty came from, but by the way Dronsky's eyebrows jiggled I had a feeling he knew.

'Work's going on. Agent Cunningham's taking a tip from Sasha Roop. She's hired a two-hundred-man army unit on US embassy funds. They'll be deployed over on North Bay tonight. A twenty-four-hour search of the ruins, the cellars, the basements, the whole rotting area.'

We shook hands. 'You'll let me know if anything comes up. Anything at all. Any time of the night.'

'It's a promise, Chief. Get some sleep.'

Of course I didn't go home. Instead I drove straight back to the Lermontov. At the reception desk I asked for Fanya and found she had finished her surgical shift moments ago. If I hurried I'd catch her in the rear car park.

I ran through near-empty corridors and burst out into the back of the building. Here the enclosed parking-lot was assailed, from one side, by the stale odours of boiling laundry and from the kitchen side by the smell of boiling cabbage. The effect was not much different from the stink of Anastasia, that lowering cloud of pollution over the southern suburbs of the city.

Fanya was just getting into her car. The lights flicked on as I walked, breathing heavily, into their brightness. She switched off. When I recovered my sight she was climbing out of the car. 'Constantin . . .'

I came up and gave her a quick hug. My breath was still billowing misty clouds around our heads. 'They told me I'd catch you.'

She smiled. But not really the old friendly Fanya smile. 'I heard you were being held by Missing Persons.'

'The man's a lunatic,' I said.

'Pasko? He questioned me about your manner on the Sunday morning after Natalya disappeared.'

I thought back. 'When we were interviewing the two kids.'

'You were,' she said. 'They'd bolted by the time I arrived, remember?'

'What did you tell him?'

'I said you were distracted.'

'Distracted?'

'Preoccupied, if you like. Didn't really want to talk to an old friend about Natalya's disappearance.'

'Thanks a lot, Fanya. Those kind words probably got me banged up.'

'Well,' she stood her ground. 'You didn't want to talk about it that morning, did you?'

'I didn't know she was missing at that point, for Christ's sake! I was going home to cook her breakfast – remember that?'

'I remember that's what you said.'

I stared at her. A tall, strong woman, hatless, despite the chill.

'You're wrong, Fanya,' I said, keeping my voice down. 'You could not be more wrong. You think I might have had something to do with Natalya's disappearance? It's grotesque.'

She shrugged uncertainly. 'What did you want me for?'

'Believe me, for God's sake, Fanya,' I said. 'You can't think I have anything to do with what's happened.'

She eyed me. Not in a friendly way. 'OK,' she said. She allowed the slightest beat. 'What was it? What did you want to speak to me about?'

It was as far as I was going to get with her. I hesitated. 'In a case like this,' I said, 'we get a lot of calls. Hoax calls mainly. Poor creatures who get their moment of attention breathing down a line. But they all have to be screened.'

'And there's something someone said that I can help you with?'

'Yes . . . It's just closing down lines of inquiry. It's just . . .'

'What is it?'

I stood, one gloved hand on the top of her car. 'You're Natalya's closest friend.'

She made a quick, awkward nodding movement. Then: 'If you're asking that same question, the answer's no. You were the only man . . . *are* the only man in Natalya's life.' She threw the words at me, irritably. 'You must know that.'

'Four days ago, I thought I knew a lot of things,' I said. 'But if you're so convinced I'm the only man in Natalya's life, Fanya, let me ask why you were so concerned about what your husband Mikhail might have to talk to her about for nearly an hour in her Kamka on Friday last.'

She stared at me for a moment, not a friendly look. 'It wasn't Mikhail.'

'You thought it was. You thought Natalya was having an affair with Mikhail? Is that it?'

'Well, for God's sake, it's not impossible, is it? We all work in each other's pockets.'

'Crazy hours . . .'

She nodded, then looked up at me and scowled. 'If it's any help to you, I don't think she was. What do you want to know, Constantin?'

'Did you ever meet Joan Fowler?'

'The American woman? No.'

I took a deep breath. 'Is it possible . . . that Natalya and Joan were having an affair?'

She looked at me with flaring nostrils.

'We have certain information . . .'

'I guessed something was going on,' Fanya said, her face flushing a sudden red. 'The bitch.'

I looked at her, shocked back into my shoes. 'Natalya?'

She bit on her lip. 'Is this what you've been told?'

'We get all sorts of crazies on the line . . .'

A silence bound us like light. Fanya's face was hard. 'You'll have to know sometime.'

I didn't want to know. I wanted to walk away from this foul-smelling car park and *never* know. 'Know what?' I said.

'About Natalya and me.'

I leaned more heavily on the car. It was what I had been protecting myself against. It wasn't Mikhail and Natalya that Fanya was worried about. It was Natalya and *anybody*. 'Tell me,' I said.

'Last Christmas . . .' She looked at me. I don't know what she saw in front of her eyes, but it must have been hangdog and pathetic enough for her to gesture to the car. 'Why don't you get in?'

I walked round to the passenger side. Snow, I noticed, was melting underfoot. I opened the door and got in. 'Last Christmas . . .' I said.

'There was a party here. Surgeons and surgical only.'

'I remember.'

'It got pretty wild, as these things do sometimes. I can't remember how it happened but Natalya and I ended up alone in Surgical One. The men don't like to dance. They like to drink. We were dancing, Natalya and me. Just the two of us. Slow, smoochy music.' She paused. 'So I kissed her.'

'I don't think I want the details.'

'I need to tell someone for God's sake,' she said angrily, 'or I'll explode.'

She took a pack of cigarettes from the glove compartment, gave me one and lit it for me.

I didn't want to smoke. I didn't want not to. 'Had you ever . . . before . . . had you ever had an affair with a woman?' I asked her, more I think to gain time than anything. I didn't care if she'd been through the whole of the island of Lesbos at that point.

She drew on her cigarette and waggled her head. 'I've always known I was attracted. Two or three little incidents when I was at school. Then a full-blown affair at university which blew up in flames just before I met Mikhail.'

It wasn't difficult to know what she was telling me about Mikhail. She had met and married him on the rebound.

'But Natalya was something different,' she said deliberately. 'Oh, for Christ's sake, you must know half the fucking Lermontov was in love with her! And not just the men.'

Smoke flared from my mouth. 'I knew I was, that's all. And still am. So what happened next?'

'The last weeks before Christmas we had become very close. I could *feel* it. I could feel us coming together. As a couple.'

'Please . . .' I said, exasperated. 'Spare me.'

'All right. That night in Surgical I told her we should have an affair. Of course, I knew Natalya wasn't in love with me as I was with her. But I was sure, at the very least, she wanted what I had – a woman's body. Exotica. She had love and sex with you – but there was something in her make-up that sometimes wanted something more.'

'Did she find it with you? Did she say she wanted to try?'

She laughed. Not a friendly laugh. 'No Constantin. We stood in Surgical, not two inches between her mouth and mine and she told me, coolly, you know how cool Natalya can be, that it was an interesting idea. An interesting idea!'

I sat silently trying to crush my cigarette out in the hopelessly small, overflowing ashtray.

'She told me that she had had some experience with a woman in the distant past, in Moscow I think, but it had not been a success. She had no doubts you were the focus of her life and always would be.' Fanya put her hands to her face. 'I cried my eyes out. Now I discover she was just putting me off to move over to some American woman.'

'I have no evidence of that,' I said. 'I've a phone call, that's all.'

'It fits,' she said bitterly. 'I can see it's why she pushed me aside.'

'It could have been a hoax call. Some men like to get mixed up in an investigation. They get a lift . . .'

'A hoax,' she said. 'Or someone who saw something? Saw them together?'

I got out of the car. Can you believe it, brothers – I'm feeling sorry for her, although she's never once, in all this, shown concern for anybody but herself. I have to recognize that I'm not a man who finds it easy to get his emotions in order. So somehow I'm *angry* that I'm feeling sorry for her.

I had gone a step or two from the car when I turned back. She buzzed down her window and looked up at me, damp-eyed. I came close. 'You said as far as men are concerned I was the focus of her life.'

She pursed her lips cautiously, waiting.

'In her office drawer, locked, I found a set of condoms. Two of them used.'

'Condoms?' She burst out laughing. 'You found condoms locked in your surgeon wife's drawer?' She threw her head back and laughed louder, like a child pretending amusement.

'For Christ's sake,' I said. 'It's Natalya I'm talking about.'

For a moment she sat staring ahead, debating, I thought afterwards, whether to tell me. Then she turned her head slowly towards me. 'Constantin,' she said. 'Every accident surgeon in the Lermontov carries a packet of condoms.'

'What?'

'There's a chronic shortage of surgical bags. At the accident site we use rubbers to seal in a torn-off finger. A splinter of bone, half an ear . . .' She fumbled in her pocket and pulled out a pack of bubble-wrapped Import Durex. She waved them at me. 'And it's a long time since I fucked a man,' she said.

'Ah.' I stood there for a long moment. Relief, there at least. I realized we were staring at each other. Somehow I needed to say it. 'All the talking about her, Fanya,' I said, 'and you haven't once asked about her chances. Did you realize?'

She shrugged heavily and switched on the engine. 'Not so surprisingly. For you it's different. She's still yours to lose or find. I've lost her anyway. Worse – I never had her.'

Tears were rolling down her cheeks but whether for herself or Natalya, I couldn't guess.

Buttoning up my leather coat, I walk through the Lermontov without, luckily, seeing anybody I know. I'm not sure I would notice them anyway. It's this sense of relief I can't understand. Since Fanya pulled that bubble card of rubbers from her pocket, the relief has been growing. *There was no man.* There was no man spreading her on her office table. All and every one of the hideous images I've had to contend with there have dissolved. OK, sisters, tell me it's pathetic. Tell me it's discriminatory in the most essential way a man can be. I have to tell you I don't give a damn. So sometimes she lusted after a woman . . . Perhaps, even, Joan Fowler . . . Perhaps it was Joan Fowler sitting in her car and later in her office that day. Well . . . somehow I can live with that. Somehow that isn't half as threatening to me.

Maybe because I feel what Fanya insists on: I am still the focus of Natalya's life.

I get into the car. The murk has cleared. I have one problem now, a terrifying problem, but at least it's singular: to find Natalya, to bring her home safe.

And, of course, I have taken one step forward. What Fanya has just told me confirms it. The man who made that call to Danilova was no hoaxer. He knew something that not even I knew. He was the man who abducted Natalya. And he feels the need, whether in arrogance or uncertainty, to talk to us about it.

Potanin was right. He will be back.

22

GET SOME SLEEP, Constantin, I tell myself. Get it into your head there's nothing more you can do – and believe it. Be ready to start tomorrow with the next lead. But I was reluctant to end this day. This morning I'd had so many hopes. So much belief that today would produce an answer.

I stand at the window looking down at the port. The snow falls lightly past the pane. North Bay, out across there on the other bank of the river, is dark and silent. Sin City, maybe ten kilometres away across the lake, is alive with sparkling lights, the cloud above it reflecting a red haze.

I turn away. First a shower. First, even before a drink. I don't have to justify to myself taking a shower. And I know it's these small everyday decisions that are holding me together. I strip off my clothes and hang my gun. Warm water is a balm in itself. It induces surrender in even the most busy mind.

I am in the shower when I hear movement in the flat. I wrap a towel round me and move quickly from the shower to where my gun hangs. We're all like this in Russia today.

I push open the living-room door and Abby is standing there, two suitcases on the floor next to her, a couple of coats over her arm. She smiles. 'This is a classic Cary Grant situation,' she says. 'You manage to look a little goofy but quite charming at the same time. Put your gun away and dry your hair.'

I do as I'm told. How in God's name does she know about Cary Grant?

Three minutes later I was back, in a bathrobe and without a gun.

'You don't mind me dropping these things off?' she said, her FBI manner returning. 'I tried your buzzer but got no answer.'

'The spare bedroom's through there,' I said. I picked up her cases and carried them through. 'It's not opulently furnished.'

'As long as it's not hung with latter-day swastikas,' she said, following me.

'Be assured,' I said. 'Would you like a drink?'

She dropped her spare coats on the bed. 'No thanks. Miles Bridger is waiting for me downstairs. Maybe later if you're not fast asleep.' She paused. 'I appreciate you letting me stay.'

I let her out and came back into the kitchen for a beer. A white sheet of paper lay on the kitchen table, paperweighted with a bottle of Scotch whisky. Scrawled on the page were the words: *The black chick says thanks a million.*

I made a sandwich of damp bread and sausage. I took a can of beer and, on second thoughts, the bottle of whisky and a shot glass. I went into the living-room and put everything down on the coffee-table in front of the sofa. For a moment I stood there.

Have you ever noticed that all the great detectives of Western fiction have twenty-twenty memories? *Where had he seen him, her, it, before? Ah yes . . . the dark-haired girl staring from a picture of the graduation ceremony at Oxford University . . . the tall young man staring from the group of young people round the barbecue at Martha's Vineyard . . . the scarred face staring from that page of LAPD mug shots. Always staring . . .* For these Western detectives something may obscure the memory for a moment or two, but it's not long before it all comes galloping back in total recall. That's the way life is in the West.

I sat down on the sofa.

The truth is different. The human memory may be more subtly selective than any computer program yet written, but there's a downside. Information can sit in separate storerooms of the mind for years and we still don't know the nature of the spark of current that suddenly links them. The other way of putting it is that some minds are just slow to catch on, and extremely lucky when they do. Mine.

I got up and checked for messages. There were two. Roy was asking me to call him at some hotel in Helsinki. And Madame Badanova asking if there'd been any developments. I erased Roy without another thought. Madame Badanova, I felt I should have called, but I lacked the will or the energy.

I slumped on the sofa. As an idea which seemed to me to be close to inspiration, I took Abby's whisky and threw back three thumbs one after another. It was the only way I was going to see sleep tonight.

But as I hooked my finger on the ring-pull of the can of Foster's Import, I was back on the mind and its mysteries. One of those mysterious electric sparks leapt in an arc from one compartment of my brain to another. A connection was made.

Roop. It had tied up with something for a microsecond there. I put down the can of Foster's. I tried to force my mind back in time, back three, four seconds. The arc had crackled brightly for a moment, before the connection failed.

I took a few bites of the sandwich but it was too soggy for enjoyment. The whisky was slowly taking the edge off my world. I took a taste of the beer and another quick whisky. In front of a blank television set sipping my beer, I tried to elbow my way back. *Roop*. I had seen something there for a fraction of a second but my magpie mind had lost it. I was off now on a wandering survey across the electrical currents of the brief two years I'd had with Natalya. Right up to that very last glimpse of her on Saturday night, when I had glanced over as the governor had called me into his library and I had seen Natalya give me a quick lift of the eyebrows. So intimate, so suggestive, so reassuring. No, she could not have been planning to run out on me ten minutes later, not for Joan Fowler or anybody else. Never.

As I sit here, drinking beer on a sofa, I can't conceive how this will end ... Two hundred soldiers are searching North Bay, a fully manned twenty-four-hour incident room is on duty in the Old Nunnery. Ilya Dronsky, I suppose the man I trust most in the world, has come from Moscow. He and a senior FBI agent are in charge of the hunt for Natalya. Is there really any possibility of me doing anything that they can't?

When my mobile rang I was in a semi-dazed state. It was Dronsky. 'Chief. I've just been talking to Records for this region, the Kola Province.'

I grunted. 'I could have saved you the trouble, Dronsky. We lost the Records Building in the last air raid of the Civil War. The crimes and misdemeanours of the city are all under ten thousand tonnes of best quality Soviet crumble-concrete. We'll dig them out one day.'

'No need, Chief. I was checking on your friend Lukas. Brother Sasha mentioned he'd once been a teacher so I thought maybe Education Ministry records in Moscow might tell us what happened to bring his career to a stop.'

I was alert now, rubbing my eyes. 'And?'

'Lukas Roop taught in a girls' high school here – the Maxim Gorky. He was dismissed in 2009 for an assault on a seventeen-year-old.'

'A sexual assault?'

'Not too obviously. He hit her with a table-tennis bat. He stuck to the ass and thighs. The records speak of a paroxysm of anger.'

'What provoked the attack?'

'The details are sparse. Given the climate of the time I think he would have got away with it if he'd just claimed she was insolent. But instead he said he was punishing her for the life she was leading.'

'What did he mean by that?'

'He accused the girl of having a disorderly sex life.'

'What?'

'You remember the old Soviet days,' he said. 'That was the phrase for a girl on the streets. She was said to have a disorderly sex life.'

'Opinion polls tell us becoming a hooker is the number one career choice for Russian high-school girls. This girl was probably just honing up her skills. So he got off?'

'Not entirely. He was dismissed without charge. But the incident was recorded. And he lost his job. What do you think, Chief?'

I drank some beer. I wasn't really convinced it meant much. 'Anything else?'

'No. Nothing I can find. Very good colleagues' reports. The principal thought highly of him.' He paused. 'Listen Chief,' he said. 'I don't know that it takes us anywhere . . .'

'You've got something else?'

'Maybe part of the jigsaw somehow. I was sitting here with V.I. Lenin, thinking about the Roop brothers. No, more than that, I was thinking about the name *Roop*. Wondering where I'd heard it before.'

'And?' I said, thinking of those Western detectives.

'Not at all a common name, I was thinking, when suddenly something popped into my head. Rostov-on-Don. Andrei Chikatilo.'

'Yes?'

'The Wasteland Murderer. Remember?'

'Who doesn't? Biggest serial killer of all time. But what's the connection with Roop?'

'That name Roop. It's driving me crazy. Somebody who worked on the case, maybe. Or a witness. You got any reference material there, Chief?'

'Some.'

'Look up the Wasteland Murders, 1982 to 1990. There's a big red light flashing somewhere in the back of my brain.'

I hung up. For thirty years Roop had been the name of a tall weedy boy I knew at Primary 36. But suddenly Dronsky had ignited a charge from another compartment. The system was working. Suddenly I was aware that Roop was also the name of a young girl. Nadia? Maria? No . . . *Yelena Roop.*

Yelena Roop. The name of one of more than fifty victims of Russia's most notorious serial killer. The Wasteland Killer, as he became known, is an important part of Russian criminal history. He is probably the most carefully documented street murderer of the Soviet period. We studied his case in Militia Training College.

The spark fizzed and sputtered freely now. Down in the Cossack towns around Rostov-on-Don, from 1982 until the last days of the Soviet Union when he was finally arrested after nine years of horror, Andrei Chikatilo had murdered at the very least fifty-two young people, choosing girls, young women and finally boys indiscriminately. I could probably call to mind not more than one or two other victims among the terrible toll of Irinas and Veras and Svetlanas. But for some reason I remembered a child named Yelena Roop – most probably because at one time I'd known a boy at Primary 36 with the same name.

I sat feeling strangely breathless. Images from the story of Andrei Chikatilo, the Wasteland Murderer, flooded my mind. Misty outlines of the lost teenage girls he preyed on for nearly ten murderous years, at bus stations and on the *Electrika,* the suburban train lines that ran out of Rostov. The Russian nation, and indeed the rest of the world, had watched him on television during the summer of 1992, snarling and screaming like a wild animal in his cage in Rostov courtroom, hurling obscenities at the prosecution witnesses, inviting the judge to have sex with him.

I put down my beer and got up. I kept a few casebooks for reference. I took down from the shelves a compendium of Russian homicides. Andrei Chikatilo's case occupied over a hundred pages, nearly one quarter of the book. I spent the next hour taking in as much of it as I could. I studied pictures of the man, a tall, slightly bent fifty-year-old, a one-time teacher. In some poses, an almost kind face. A quiet, kindly neighbour whose advice was sought-after, whose presence was reassuring. Less so when, head shaved for prison, he was demonstrating how he cut up his victims or when, from behind the bars of his courtroom cage, he held up pictures of nudes and openly drooled and salivated and screamed his lust at the women present in court.

At the end of the section were two pages of photographs, mostly children ten to fourteen years old, with perhaps a half dozen young women in their early twenties. Yelena Roop was a small-faced, blonde child, closer to Lukas in appearance than the dark-haired Sasha, just slightly cross-eyed with concentration before the camera.

I sat on the sofa and thumbed the book. Yelena Roop had left home to spend the evening with a schoolfriend. She had never returned. Somewhere between the station at Novocherkassk where she lived and the nearby metropolis of Rostov-on-Don, where she was heading, she had been *abducted*.

Her body was never discovered. But she had been added to the list of Chikatilo's victims for a good and sufficient reason: *the Roop family, the victim's mother, Yelena herself and younger brother Lukas, had lived in the downstairs apartment from Andrei Chikatilo and his wife!*

The idea hit me in the stomach like an aimed boot. Lukas Roop had lived in the same apartment building as Chikatilo. He had been about ten or eleven years of age. He had experienced all this, the anguish of an abducted sister . . . the pain of finally accepting that she had been violently murdered.

I let the thought seep in. He had *known* Chikatilo. Yet he had never told us at Primary 36. He had never boasted of knowing a murderer. He had never exploited the fact, as children will, that he had been at the centre of an extraordinary national event. And even today, talking about his move from Rostov to Murmansk, he had talked only of a family tragedy, the death, not the *abduction*, not the *murder* of his sister, Yelena.

I tried to steady myself. So what did it mean? Certainly it didn't necessarily point the finger of guilt at Roop in this present case. Yet I was finding my own reaction impossible to gauge. That Lukas Roop had known, had lived on the same staircase as a man who was a serial murderer on a scale probably unequalled anywhere in the world, churned my stomach in a way I could neither identify nor resolve. Chills moved like iced fingers travelling my spine. I felt uncertain and deeply disturbed, perhaps because almost all of us, even policemen, live in a world where that extra leap into the unspeakable is always so *extra*, so profoundly difficult to imagine that it is easier to keep it at a distance, to depersonalize it.

But with Lukas Roop this was impossible. At Primary 36, I had known the child who, just months before he came to Murmansk, had been forced to face that something in human beings, unspeakable and extra, face it in the form of a tall kindly neighbour, who said 'Good morning, Lukas,' on the stairs or asked about the football scores on Saturday night.

Perhaps that was the reason I felt churned as I did. Was it that, or was it, in truth, the fact that I could not rid myself of the idea of Lukas Roop's guilt by association?

When the phone rang I dropped the book to the floor. It was Abby Cunningham. 'The Lermontov Morgue as soon as you can,' she said. 'They've found the body of Joan Fowler.'

I came down the stairs into the basement mortuary under the Lermontov and stopped dead. The smell of these places is a warm soft blanket of corruption that surrounds you and clings lovingly. It's true enough we have trouble with maintenance of the equipment. The ventilators don't work every day so you could easily be suffering an assault from yesterday's body. And the refrigerated drawers don't fit too well any longer. I was once here on a day green putrescence began to ooze and drip from them.

All of this makes the morgue here one of my favourite places ever. Most of the staff, I'm convinced, are crazy. Lenny with the rolling eyes is the chief supervisor. He has a nice trick with grieving relatives who are nevertheless anxious about the jewellery left on the fingers of the deceased. He lifts the podgy hands of a mother or favourite aunt and tells the family that the rings *could* be removed if they truly insist. His eyes roll at the very thought. His teeth come together with the click of a cleaver on a chopping-board and the mourners are left in no doubt. Poor or sentimental as his listeners may be, Leonid Yureivich has made his point.

Hardly has the family left and the door closed behind them, when Lenny lifts his cleaver. The podgy fingers spin across the chopping-board. He retrieves the one he wants and strips off the rings. A gold band for the investigating officer. Something simpler for the sergeant. And the diamond for Lenny. Leonid Yureivich has a dacha in Finland. Some say he also has a young foreign wife and a Finnish passport for his retirement.

If you were looking for an axe murderer you wouldn't have to look much further than Lenny. Tonight he looked madder than ever. He stood and flashed me a crazy smirk, his hand on the steel table where that unmistakable shape of death lay under a stained green cloth. I tried not to look directly at it. Inconsequentially my eye caught the laundry tab on the corner trailing the floor.

Dronsky and Abby Cunningham, talking quietly in a corner, looked up and walked across the long basement room towards me.

Abby stopped in front of me. 'I'm sorry, Constantin,' she said.

I nodded, finding it difficult to speak. Dronsky put his hand on my shoulder. We both knew what she meant. This was no longer an abduction case.

'Gabriel Potanin was right, then,' I said.

'Not about everything.'

'About this. We're looking at murder. Where was she found?'

'On some waste ground in North Bay,' Dronsky said. 'The army unit searching the area heard the sound of a vehicle revving outside one of the factories. It drove off without lights so there's no description. Their officer ordered a search of the wasteland where they'd heard the vehicle. They found the body lying beside a low wall. A very crude attempt had been made to cover her with bricks and small pieces of concrete.'

'Had the body just been dumped?'

'Almost certainly. We'll get a closer idea from the medical examiner,' Abby said, 'but she was probably only an hour from dead when they found her.'

'After that, they searched the whole area?' I had a terrifying image of Natalya lying out, alone in that wilderness.

'Pinsk was in charge,' Dronsky said firmly. 'He kept the army men in the area of the factory for another two hours. There was only one body, Chief.'

I pulled him closer. 'Dronsky,' I said. 'Lukas Roop was the brother of one of Chikatilo's victims.'

'Christ . . .'

'Wait. There's more. The Roop family lived in the same house as Chikatilo. He and his wife had the apartment upstairs. Lukas Roop is a man who has *lived* with a killer. Admired him maybe . . .'

'Hold it, Chief.' Dronsky's face showed alarm. He glanced over towards Abby Cunningham collecting a green overall on the other side of the room. 'Lukas Roop was a child at the time.'

'That's when we absorb influences, for Christ's sake.'

I know when Dronsky's worried – and he was worried now. 'Listen to me, Chief,' he said. 'I know where you're going. I can see why. But it's the wrong road.'

'How can you be so sure?'

'I'm not sure, but if Lukas Roop is our man we're going to have to have a stronger case than that against him.'

Frustration flared in me. 'I'm not building a case, fuck your mother,' I hissed at him. 'I'm trying to get to Natalya before she ends up . . .' I pointed to the cadaver on the table . . . 'like *that*.'

The medical examiner came in before Dronsky could say more. She was a short, blocky woman with a big bosom which fused with a distended stomach. 'Dr Zoya Samatova,' she said briskly. She nodded to Lenny and he whipped off the green cloth with a quick dance movement and a 'Dah-daaah'.

'For Christ sake, Lenny.' I glared at him then dropped my eyes to the body. Oh, I don't pretend to be one of those men who are indifferent to the presence of death, brothers. In Russia death is blindfolded. A band of towelling cloth with the victim's name printed in felt-tip covered the eyes but did nothing to cover the swollen, blue-grey face, the tightly pulled-back reddish hair, the puffy arms and legs. Nausea swept over me. What sort of man, I kept thinking, but I could only relate this horror in front of me to Lukas Roop. He had access to the models, he roughly fitted the description of the man at Joan Fowler's lectures. He was a womanless loner from puberty – and he had had experience of abduction and murder. First-hand experience with Russia's most notorious serial murderer. I put my hand to my face. For Natalya's sake, I dared not wait for a *case* to be built.

Abby had come forward. She leaned close. 'You could wait outside,' she whispered, 'if you're not feeling too good?'

'Million dollars,' I assured her. I swallowed bile. 'I'll just stay for the prelim.'

The medical examiner came forward with her red and white striped pointer and her voice took on that peculiar professional drone. 'The corpse presents as a young woman in her early thirties. One metre sixty-five in height and . . .' she stopped and looked at me bleakly, 'a life weight of approximately fifty-six kilos. Cause of death to be determined later. But almost certainly . . .' she jabbed with her pointer at the throat, 'strangulation by ligature.'

The purple marks of a cord ligature encircled her neck, the face puffed up above it. I forced myself to stand there, but images of Lukas Roop ballooned in my mind.

Dr Samatova changed position, standing with her pointer held under her chin. 'A particularly striking aspect of this case is that the body was washed down, hosed outside . . . and in. We are doing tests now but I think you can probably rule out any hope of DNA material. Any sperm present was almost certainly washed away by the action of the hose.'

'How many times have you dealt with a body washed out like this, Dr Samatova?' Abby asked her.

'Never. But this hasn't been entirely successful. Both the mouth and nostrils, for instance, retained a black dust which is easily identifiable as coke dust. There are traces of the same dust under the left armpit.'

'Is coal or coke still used for heating, Constantin?' Abby said.

It was a relief to have an excuse to turn towards her, away from the table. 'Very little now. Oil or gas are pretty much universal.'

'So where would we find coke?'

'An old-fashioned boiler. Thirty, forty years old or more. Or a ship, of course. Any very ancient small steamer might still be using coke. But only just.'

I closed my eyes for a moment as the droning voice continued. 'There is trace evidence of use of a sedative, probably Propteknol but we shall be able to confirm that later. Despite the the sedative, there are several indications of restraint – bruising to the skin of the wrists and ankles.' As I opened my eyes again Samatova touched the appropriate parts with her pointer. 'There are matching abrasions to the knees . . .' Tap, tap went the pointer. 'Suggesting the victim had been forced to kneel for some time. Extensive bruising to the vaginal area' (a vague wave of the pointer across the abdomen and a discreet tap on the reddish pubic hair) 'suggests violent penetration by objects with the hardness of wood, metal or rigid plastic. There is no semen trace present for reasons given.'

Violent penetration with objects with the hardness of wood, metal . . . Nothing in the medical examiner's voice to suggest how much Joan Fowler had really suffered, how often the beast had used her. *Violent penetration* . . . But all that was for us to imagine, not Samatova.

'If we turn the cadaver . . .' She waited until Lenny and the mortuary assistant had turned Joan Fowler's body to lie face down.

'If we turn the cadaver we see lateral and diagonal scarring which is almost certainly the marks of a whip, leather probably, the thongs perhaps even metal-tipped. The whipping was inflicted on several different occasions.'

I watch while they turn the body onto its back. To me, she is still a human being. Not to Lenny and his assistant. Not to the medical examiner. To me, she is still a woman, a friend of Natalya's, a woman who has been savagely beaten, raped, murdered . . . And, at this very moment, Natalya is in the hands of the same man.

The medical examiner signalled to Lenny to plug in her electrical cutters which stood on a side-table. I turned for the door. Behind me I heard the medical examiner's voice. 'The body was free of almost all foreign matter. There was however something that might be useful.'

I stopped and turned. Dronsky and Abby were getting into their gowns.

'There were small quantities of caked blood on both knees, residues from larger quantities which had been washed away. But there was something more.'

We waited.

She held the red and white pointer upright. 'On the right knee, two hairs lodged in coagulated blood.'

'Not hers?' Abby said, looking up from the strings of the gown she was tying.

'Nor his,' the medical examiner said. She relished the brief moment. 'Not human at all, in fact.'

'What?' Abby said.

'Animal.' Dr Samatova let this sink in. 'Short, straight, coarse hair. Grey. A dog perhaps . . .'

'Or a wolf,' I blurted.

I had the impression of the group round the table looking at me, frowning. I left it hanging in the air.

'Perhaps.' Samatova shrugged. 'A dog – or wolf, why not?' She nodded to Lenny to switch on the current to her power tool. 'Let's get to work,' she said.

I was already heading for the door as I heard it whine. But for once disgust at what was happening to another human being there on the table, or what had once been a human being, was not uppermost in my mind. As I blundered up the steps one idea swamped me, obliterating everything else. 'Dog or wolf,' Samatova had said. 'Why not?'

23

I HAD ALREADY TURNED off the headlights. I slowed the Fiat about two hundred yards from the helicopter hangar and turned off the road onto a track which took me through the woods. Within minutes I had reached a point just above the huge squatting building. Moonlight created deep steps of shadow on the hillside, and rendered the huge barrel vault of the hangar an even stranger shape than it appeared in daylight.

I got out of the car and stood among the fir trees, the wet snow shifting and falling from the branches above my head. I was deeply uncertain how to proceed. If his victim had been any other woman but Natalya I would not have been standing here. The blue ripple lights of police cars would now be surrounding the place. It would be handled by the book. And then what?

Lukas Roop would deny everything. Yes, he had suffered an extraordinary trauma in childhood. Yes, he had lived for much of his young life in the same house as a multiple killer, known him, joked with him on the stairs. Yes, he hunted wolf for profit. Yes, his van, no doubt, was smeared with wolf's blood and hairs. But living with a murderer did not make him a murderer. And many others hunted wolves. The semi-rural poor from the fringes of Murmansk had hunted the wolf since the founding of the city.

Which left me with the fortune teller's wolf's-head joker. I couldn't admit to anyone that somehow that leering animal head, in red fool's cap and bells, was the single most potent pointer to me of Roop's guilt. How could I admit *that* to Dronsky or, even worse, to my unsmiling FBI colleague? In Abby Cunningham's world of DNA and trace analysis, how could I tell her of the faith a Russian could put in the turn of the cards of an old woman?

I was standing with my back against a tree. Perhaps I had needed these few extra seconds for my eyes to become accustomed to the sharp patterns of black and white that the moonlight threw among the fir trees around me. Before me the white van emerged as a shape, slowly distinguishing itself from the jagged patterns around it. A few steps through the crackling undergrowth brought me beside it. It was old, a VW, badly dented. But its tyres were new, snow tyres of the best quality to be found in Murmansk. My jaw clamped so tight I could feel my pulse beat. Tyres of the same pattern we had found in the snow at Intersection 33.

I circled the van, careless of the twigs crackling underfoot. As I came to the back of the van I stopped. A peculiar thrill of triumph passed through me. The offside indicator light was broken. Pieces of orange plastic were missing, exposing a bare bulb. The memory of those shards of orange plastic we had found at 33 jumped before my eyes.

I stood for a moment staring down. Then turned away. I had found the van – but it was the driver I needed now.

I moved quickly down the slope, using the moonlight to keep my torch switched off. Through the trees I could see faint lights coming from the long hut on the far side of the hangar in which Roop lived and worked. There were six or seven small windows on the side from which I was approaching, and as I came closer I saw they were all covered with a crude insulation of newspaper stuck to the panes. From my time in the hut I had remembered the darkness rather than the cause of it.

Close to, I could see that the newspaper was far from a perfect fit. Light gleamed more strongly from splits along the side of some panes. At two or three metres I could hear music. Not Western or modern Russian music. Instead the unfamiliar rise and fall of something that might have been Asian, played on instruments I could barely guess at, gourds perhaps and bamboo-sounding sticks. Reaching the side of the wooden hut below the most promising window, I lifted my head level with the lowest pane and peered past the torn flap of newsprint into the long room.

Stripped to the waist, his face rouged and lipsticked, Lukas Roop was dancing.

What first struck me was how muscular he was. The arms were long but powerful, the chest-cage was naturally narrow but the musculation rippled with development. The movements of the dance were bizarre, but not erratic, crudely balletic even. His path seemed set by the change in pace of the music. Up and down the centre space of his hut he moved like a lithe animal, arms outstretched, offering ... receiving ... God knows what, brothers, but certainly performing a dance that sent a shiver down my spine.

I stood there at the window, immobile. There was little or no chance that he would see me. His face was set expressionless, unsmiling, the head twisting this way and that to music I had only thought to be Asiatic because it was so totally unfamiliar to my ear. I now realized it was more folkic, Slav, not dissimilar to strains I had heard rendered by peasant players out on the peninsula.

Then, watching him, the hair rose on the back of my neck as I realized there were other things to see in the hut, things I'd missed by the intensity of my concentration on this strange, androgynous dancer.

He was, I now saw, dancing within a circle of figures. Latex dolls, naked and sometimes headless or armless, had been moved out from the shadows at the back of the hut to surround him. And, in central position in this pale ring of unmoving spectators, propped on a table, with blood streaming from the neck, was a shaggy grey wolf's head.

I fell back from the window breathless with panic, with shock. I moved slowly across the snow, which had become crisper with nightfall, towards the door of the hut. I had no plan. Don't even ask me about my state of mind at this moment. Not far, I'd say, from that of a killer himself, still thinking rationally but totally, utterly concentrated on that one single object of my intent.

I hammered on the door.

24

INSIDE THE MUSIC stopped. I heard a voice, tentative and unsure, it seemed, until I thought of that muscular frame. 'Who is it? Who is it calling at this time?'

I left him a long anxious moment. 'It's Constantin Vadim,' I said. 'Open up.'

There were two or three minutes of shuffling inside. I had hammered again, twice, before bolts were drawn and a rhomboid of yellow light hit the snow beside me. Roop, dressed in jeans and dark sweater now, the make-up hurriedly cleaned from his face, stood in a door opened not more than a foot or two. Even so I could see the bleeding wolf's head on the table. 'It's late,' he said, more tentative than aggressive. 'What is it you want, Constantin?'

'It's your van,' I said, thumbing over my shoulder to the white Volkswagen van standing between the main hangar and Lukas Roop's hut. 'There's something in the back.'

I saw his frown. 'Something? What?'

'You got the keys?' I watched him bring them out of his back pocket and I took them from his hand. 'Let's go and see,' I said.

'I'll get my coat.'

'Don't bother,' I said. 'It'll only take a minute.'

We walked towards the white van. 'I shot a wolf tonight,' he said in explanation of what I might have seen through the half open door. 'The Hunters' Co-operative only require me to deliver the head for payment.'

I nodded and we headed for the back of the van. 'You didn't tell me, Lukas,' I said conversationally, 'about Rostov.'

He blinked.

'Tell me now.'

He was shivering without a topcoat. 'Rostov? What is there to tell?'

'Tell me about when you were living in Novocherkassk, Lukas. Tell me about Yelena.'

He hesitated a pace then continued walking, looking down now. 'That was a long time ago.' His voice had dropped to a mumble. 'My mother was working in the champagne factory. Before Sasha was born.'

'I want to hear about Yelena,' I said.

'My sister, Yelena . . . She died there, in Novocherkassk.'

'She was murdered.'

He stopped walking. 'We don't know.' His face was creasing, breaking up. 'Perhaps she ran away. Perhaps she was taken away. We never really knew.'

'Abducted,' I said, brutally. 'By your neighbour, Andrei Chikatilo.'

He looked at me, his eyes blinking, his mouth moving.

'Chikatilo who killed more than fifty people,' I pressed. 'Mainly girls of Yelena's age.'

'Yes.'

'After your sister disappeared,' I said. 'After he killed her. How long did you live in the same apartment with Chikatilo upstairs?'

I had hit some nerve, I could feel it. He drew air through his teeth. 'Almost a year,' he said.

'You saw him every day?'

'We knew nothing about him then.' He looked at me, reluctant to talk but knowing he had no choice. 'He was kind. He came down and sat with us. He listened while my mother talked about Yelena.' Lukas lifted his shoulders and shivered. 'Sometimes he brought small cakes for us. Or tobacco for my mother. To comfort her.' There was a long silence.

I was sure there was guilt somewhere. Why else would he have disguised it all those years? 'Did you like Chikatilo? Was he kind to you too?'

He began to breathe heavily, as if he had just run a race. 'Yes. He was kind.'

'Did he give you presents?'

The air was hissing between his teeth now. 'What is this?' He stopped, his lips pursed. 'What are you doing?' He looked towards the van. 'What is it?' His eyes blinked with fear. 'You said there was something in the van.'

I used the keys to open the back door. He was shivering now in big uncontrollable tremors, his black roll-neck sweater no proof against the night cold.

'See for yourself,' I said, opening the rear doors.

He leaned forward to peer into the darkness. At the furthest moment of balance I kneed him hard, jackknifing him forward into the back of the van.

I heard his shout of alarm, caught a glimpse of his head turning towards me, then, as he rolled across the metal flooring, I slammed closed the doors.

For a moment I stood still. I knew full well what sort of a divide I was crossing. I took from my pocket Abby's whisky I had brought with me, unscrewed the cap and gulped a good mouthful. With his fists he was hammering on the metal sides of the van. From where I stood, his shouts were muffled. I walked slowly to the front and got into the driving seat and started the engine. If I turned my head I could see him through a metal grille, see at least the dark outline of his face.

'What are you doing, Constantin?' His voice came through the grille as an anguished whisper. 'What are you doing to me?'

I was back in that moment of time when Lenny had ripped the green covering from Joan Fowler's body with his obscenely inappropriate dance and his snatch of song. I faced Roop through the grille. 'We're going skating,' I hissed at him. 'You're going to skate till your blood and bones can't hold together any longer. You're going to skate until you tell me what you've done with my wife.'

I dropped the van in gear. I could hear him scrabbling like an animal to get closer to the grille. 'Believe me, Constantin . . .You must believe me . . .'

I turned away and took my foot off the clutch. The van jerked forward, hurling him back, away from the grille, thudding against the rear doors.

I braked and he came sliding back. Wrenching my neck round I could see his pale face appear like a prisoner at the grille. And a prisoner he was, of course. My prisoner. And he had to know it, learn it.

'Where is she? Where are you holding her?'

His voice dropped to a whisper through the grille. 'Listen to me, please . . . You must listen to me. I swear to you, Constantin, I had nothing to do with their disappearance.'

'They were in this van,' I shouted through the grille into his face. 'There was wolf's hair embedded in Joan Fowler's knee, you unspeakable creature!'

'I swear . . .' he was saying when I pressed hard on the accelerator.

I paid no attention now to the mewling cries from the back of the van. With spurting snow beneath the tyres I drove . . .

The lake is a natural marvel. It fills the scooped-out top of a hill and in summer can often seem in danger of overspilling. But now as we came up the twisting road and over the brow, the frozen lake lay matt and white in the moonlight, watched over by the silent *Alyosha*, the gigantic stone memorial statue of a World War II Soviet infantry soldier. In the back of the van, Lukas Roop, throughout the journey, had alternated periods of silence with shouts of defiance and protestations of innocence. Only when we drove off the made-up road and bumped across the uneven stony ground that fringed the lake did his voice change. 'What's happening?' His voice rose in alarm. 'Where are you taking me?'

I put my foot down. Downhill, the old van made seventy, eighty kilometres an hour and we hit the ice at close to a hundred. A few lights shone in the Panorama Hotel up on the lake shore to my left. When I braked, the tyres screamed and the tail swung away violently. A turn of the wheel brought us round in a huge complete circle and another touch on the brake swung the van in a sickening tight triple spin across the ice.

From behind me I could hear the rush and thud of Roop's body as he was thrown against the sides, shot forward or jerked back to crash against the rear doors, each movement producing grunts or shouts of fear and screams of pain as we spun in a mad waltz across the great flat, frozen expanse of the lake.

As the moon passed behind grey-streaked cloud, it began to snow. To an outsider, I could hardly guess what sense of madness the scene projected, the white van racing forward, braking, spinning wildly across the ice. Then slowing almost to a stop, to pick up speed again to leap through the falling snow, the headlights cutting tunnels from the darkness. As for me, I drove like a man possessed, as indeed I was, clutching the wheel as we spun, seeing little more than the changing, unchanging face of the snow flying past the windscreen as if the flaring headlights could barely keep up with the whirling vehicle.

It was minutes, five or six perhaps, before I became aware that the thud of Roop's body against the metal sides was no longer accompanied by groans or cries of pain. I gave the van one last burst of acceleration, braked and let go the wheel. We were sliding backwards at fifteen, twenty kilometres an hour when we bounced off a section of high bank, spun again for a last time and slithered to a halt.

What I dragged out from the back of the VW was difficult at first to recognize as Lukas Roop. He was no more than half conscious. His nose was split and blood was bubbling from his mouth. He was groaning, mumbling words and phrases I could not understand. I took him by the front of his sweater and dragged him upright so that he sat slumped on the tailboard of the van. My face was inches from his. 'Don't speak, just listen. Can you hear what I'm saying?'

His head nodded forward.

'One single question, Lukas. Where is she? Where have you got her?'

His head rocked back. He lifted a hand and rubbed it across his bloody mouth. His blinking eyes reflected fear and, I think, hate in about equal measure. 'I made a mistake.' Blood drooled from the side of his mouth. 'There's as much of the bully hidden in you,' he said, 'as there was in your friend Rolkin.'

At this moment I could not afford to care if he was right. Did not dare even to think it. I knew he was playing on those hang-back scruples he had seen in me in childhood. In defence, I put Natalya in the front of my mind. I laid her out on a metal table with dented blood gutters and covered her with a green shroud. Then I took Lukas Roop and shook him until his head jumped from side to side, crashing against the half open door. 'You knew them,' I said. 'You knew Joan Fowler. You knew Natalya . . .'

'Yes.'

Strength poured through me. I threw him to the ground. I could have thrown him clear across the ice.

'Stop for God's sake . . .' he was pleading through battered lips. 'Stop! I'll tell you.' I stood back and looked down at him. He was sobbing now and vomiting onto the snow. Very slowly he brought his head up. He forced his eyes open, blinked them clear until they stared straight into mine. 'You're wrong, Constantin.'

I moved to take him by the throat. He reared back, his hands in front of him. 'I wouldn't harm your wife,' he said, in as steady a voice as he could. 'I swear to you I wouldn't harm Dr Vadim.'

'You knew her,' I accused him.

'Of course I knew her. I *worked* for her.' His head fell forward.

It was, I suppose, brothers, my first terrifying moment of doubt. I was looking down at the black blood matted in his hair, the split and bruised forehead. Had I really done this to an innocent man? I stared at him, even at this moment teetering on the edge of a apology. Instead I threw good roubles after bad. I bent forward and took the blood-soaked front of his sweater in both hands. It was fear now, fear of being wrong, that gave me strength. 'Tell me,' I shouted in his face.

'I met your wife, Dr Vadim, through Joan Fowler,' he said. 'They employed me.'

'Employed you? To do what?' I was still holding him but I was conscious that my grip had loosened with my certainty.

'I drove the van.'

Confidence ran from me as if it were lifeblood itself. 'What in God's name did they want a van for?'

'For the children,' he said. 'To carry the children.'

The cold air was stinging my eyes. 'What children?'

He looked at me flinchingly. Why should he make it easy for me? 'The children they were kidnapping,' he said.

'*Kidnapping!*' I stared at him. I don't know for how long I looked into his battered face. I only know it felt as if I had a Catherine wheel whirling in my head.

I pulled him to his feet and slammed closed the doors. He leaned against the side of the van, his head back, his mouth open. Dark bruises were already forming around his temples, blood bubbling from one nostril. Everything now told me that I was going to have to make the most abject apology of my life. But I wasn't prepared to make it yet.

'Get in the van,' I said. 'In the front.'

Fear straightened him. He felt his way along the side of the van. He reached for the door and hung onto the handle for a moment.

'Get in,' I said, avoiding his eyes.

He had difficulty making it and I took one arm to help him up into the passenger seat. Rounding the van I climbed in beside him. He was slumped forward, breathing heavily. 'My ribs,' he said.

Feelings churned through me, so mixed, so confused I could not extract one single thread. What did a few cracked ribs matter now? 'I want every detail, fuck your mother,' I said. I started the engine. 'Talk, Lukas. You're talking for your life.'

25

IT HAD STOPPED snowing and the moon was out again, shining through broken cloud, outlining the huge, lonely statue of *Alyosha* overlooking the lake. I drove slowly, partly from exhaustion and the emotions that tore at me, partly not to miss a word of what Roop said over the whine of the engine.

'I first met Joan Fowler just after Christmas this year. I had seen a poster advertising talks and seminars on American life. At the consulate, the Old Nunnery. I had a great desire to know more about the West so I began to attend the lectures.'

The effort to speak even these sentences was almost too much for him and he wiped his bleeding nose on his sleeve and hugged his ribs again before he continued.

'After the second or third lecture, I can't remember which now, but it was about children in the United States, Joan Fowler asked me to stay behind for coffee. She was interested in the questions I asked at the end of the lecture. There's a coffee machine in the reception hall.'

'Is that the first time you'd ever been alone with her?'

'Yes, of course,' he groaned.

'Before you attended the lectures had you ever seen Joan Fowler?'

'What are you talking about?'

The stalker was what I was talking about. Had it been Roop following Joan Fowler, then Natalya? 'Did you know who was going to give these lectures?'

'I knew it was an American woman named Joan Fowler. I knew no more than that.'

'You never knew where she lived. The apartment in Mandelstam Street.'

'Later, yes. But at that time I knew nothing about her, Constantin. Why should I have known? She was a name on a poster. That's all Joan Fowler meant to me.'

I was breathing as heavily as he was. 'OK,' I said. 'You had coffee after one of the lectures.'

'She was a sincere woman, Constantin.'

'Sincere?'

'Sincerely felt emotions. She cared about children. In her lecture, she had talked about many black children in virtual ghettos in the great cities of America as well as the millions of privileged children who lived over there. She presented an honest picture, I felt. That's what I meant by sincere.'

I glanced at him and then back at the narrow road ahead. Moment by moment he was sounding less and less like my idea of a killer. A knot of something – not regret, because I was moving closer to learning what had happened – but shame, I suppose, at the method I had used, rose into my throat. 'All right,' I said, more harshly than I felt. 'Get on with it. When was the next time you saw her?'

'Wait . . .' He raised a hand. The blood running down the knuckles made me wince. 'This is important. Things I said during the discussion about children obviously had an effect on her.'

'What sort of things?'

'I had a bad childhood, Constantin. I don't have to say more than that. It was not just the death . . . the murder of my sister. Anyway, enough of that. I spoke to Joan Fowler from the heart. She asked me about myself and I told her where I worked, that I drove a van for my brother. I knew she was interested in me.'

'Interested – in what way?'

'At first I didn't understand. One evening, after the lecture, she invited me to a café. We talked for a long time, drinking tea together. Then she asked if I would undertake some driving work. Not for the consulate, but for her personally. Herself and Dr Vadim.'

'She didn't explain what you would be doing?'

'She warned me it might be dangerous. But she promised to pay well.'

'My wife was part of this?'

'If anything she was the leader. The first job I did for them was to pick up Dr Vadim and six children at South Beach and drive them to the Norwegian frontier.'

I gaped at him. At the nearest point the Norwegian border was a hundred and fifty kilometres there and back from Murmansk. If Lukas was telling the truth, this must have been on one of those nights Natalya had told me she was on call-out.

'How many nights did you drive for them?'

'Only that first night with Dr Vadim and the Saturday when . . . last Saturday.'

'What happened there, when you arrived at the border?'

'We were met by a group of men.'

'Russians?'

'Norwegians I believe. Their cold-weather clothes were of the best quality. I was in the van, too far away to hear them speak. They took the children, transferred them to a horse-drawn sled and drove away into the woods, across the border into Norway.'

'The children, where did they come from?'

'I never knew. I only know somebody was paid well for them.'

'They were paid for?' I said. 'Bought, you mean? Who from?'

'Some ex-soldiers. Deserters maybe or Anarchists. Their leader was a man called Venya.' His head came up. 'I only know that money changed hands. Dr Vadim, or the American last time, carried a billfold packed with US hundred-dollar bills.'

I found myself unable to speak. Natalya had lived a life I knew nothing of. I could not even begin to guess at her purpose. All I knew was that the pain of exclusion now joined with the pain and fear of loss.

The great hangar of the former 351st Helicopter Regiment loomed on our right. I pulled into the forecourt, drove past the hangar and stopped outside Lukas's hut.

We sat in his hut, a foot or two between us. Lamplight lit the eerie figures of unmoving latex women. The wolf's head was covered in a black cloth. My eyes ran along the shelves of books behind his bunk.

He had washed his face but bruises were beginning to swell under his eyes. 'I used to be a teacher,' he said as he followed my glance towards the wolf's head. 'I taught the history of Russia and the old Slav myths long before Christianity arrived.'

I nodded to the table. 'And what does the wolf mean in the old myths?'

He shrugged. 'The wolf is the leader. He holds the balance between good and evil.'

It was an echo of the old woman's words which sent a shiver up my spine. But I had to recognize that it didn't make Lukas Roop a killer. 'Do you believe in all that stuff?'

'I draw comfort from it,' he said.

'Comfort?'

'Yes. I don't have friends like you, Constantin. I am the same boy you knew at Primary 36. I have built a life in the imagination. In the old Slav myths and dances I find freedom. In the imagination, I am safe.'

Except from me, I thought. 'Tell me about last Saturday night.'

'I lied,' he said.

'I know that.'

'I was sworn to tell no-one about what they were doing. Whatever happened, Dr Vadim said. More than that, I was afraid. I knew what we were doing was not legal.'

'Tell me now.'

'On Saturday afternoon I went by arrangement to Joan Fowler's apartment.'

'At what time?'

'The meeting was at four-thirty but Dr Vadim was unable to be there.'

'No . . .'

'She got a message to Joan Fowler. A medical emergency at the docks.'

'But you went ahead with your meeting with Joan Fowler.'

'Yes. We discussed the operation. Dr Vadim was, in any case, unable to take part that night. She was attending a private party at City Hall.'

All this was undeniably the truth. 'So what happened then?'

'Joan Fowler and I left in my van at about six.'

'For South Beach?'

'You know the hulks?'

Every Murmansk schoolboy has heard the story of the Luftwaffe bombing of the port in the Great Patriotic War. And of the sinking merchantmen that were towed and beached down river. 'I know the hulks,' I said. 'I've heard of them.'

'The ships there are empty, rusting . . . Dozens of them.' He paused to draw a painful, deep breath. 'There was a big fire blazing in the middle of one of the holds. I could see the reflection through holes torn in the decking. I stayed in the van. Joan Fowler took the purse and went alone into the ship. Within a few moments she returned leading a group of children.' He paused. 'The procedure seemed well-established. The American woman, and your wife, had done it many times.'

'Alone?'

'The two of them, yes.'

'Why did they decide they needed you?'

'It was becoming difficult . . .' His eyes flicked towards me. 'Becoming difficult for your wife to get away at night.'

Without me discovering it was not hospital business. I tipped the whisky bottle to my mouth. The thought rushed back to me that Natalya had done all these things while I slept or dozed before a television programme. Without thinking, without caring, I passed Lukas Roop the bottle.

'That night,' he said, 'I waited in the driver's seat while Joan Fowler seated the children with blankets inside. There were the same as before, six or seven of them.'

'These children, were they boys, girls?'

'They were very young. The boys all with close-shaven heads.'

'The girls?'

'The girls with very short hair.'

'As if recently shaven? From a children's labour camp, perhaps?' I thought immediately of the green tattooed K on the arms of the dead children in the United States.

'They told me they were helping the children. That's all I know.'

I was silent, baffled. 'Shaven heads. There are enough child gulags in the area . . .' I was talking almost to myself.

'Some people call Kola the Children's Gulag,' he acknowledged.

I shook my head. 'My wife would have told me.'

He looked at me, a half smile on his bruised lips. 'That she was engaged in the kidnap of children from government labour camps?'

'You don't know that for sure.'

'I heard enough talk in the back of the van. Whatever the purpose of it, the operation was illegal. How could Dr Vadim confide in an inspector of police?'

I wanted to argue the case. I wanted to tell him that between Natalya and myself there were no secrets. But I knew now that there were. Joan Fowler herself was a secret. 'Go back to Saturday night,' I said.

'The children were always frightened, sometimes crying. For that reason, the American stayed in the back of the van with them for the journey to the Norwegian border.'

'So what happened that Saturday? Something went wrong.'

'It was the night of the blizzard, remember. Conditions on the Kanevka highway were bad.'

'I remember.'

'I had snow tyres but it was not enough. Somewhere near Crossing 33 I went off the road. A bad skid. The children mostly escaped harm. Joan Fowler got slightly hurt holding them upright. But they were lucky. A couple of bad nosebleeds, nothing more.'

'How was she hurt?' An idea was forming.

'Nothing serious. Scraped hands and knees.'

'Hands and knees.' A tear in the knee of her grey sweats. A scrape of flesh across the metal flooring where any number of dead wolves had been thrown. 'Go on,' I said.

'We waited an hour in the hope of a passing truck that could pull us out. Joan didn't want to call your wife from the party. But, in the end, there was nothing else for it. Joan called Dr Vadim's pager as if it were a Lermontov emergency.'

'And Natalya came out.'

'She arrived in her Kamka. They're well-equipped for this sort of emergency. I packed branches under the wheels of the van and the Kamka hauled it back on the road.'

'What time was this?'

'Close to three in the morning.'

'Did you go on to the Norwegian border that night?'

'I wasn't sure the van would make it. The offside front tyre had blown and I only had a standard tyre to replace it. I couldn't have made the journey up to the border like that.'

'So what happened?' I was urging him on now.

'It was decided to pack all the children into the Kamka – and for the American and Dr Vadim to take them on while I turned back.'

'And that . . .' I said, 'was the last you saw of them. Driving off towards the border.'

'The last I saw of Joan and Dr Vadim, this I swear to you Constantin, was in my wing mirror as I pulled away, heading back to the city. They were standing in the snow by the Kamka. They waved to wish me a safe journey.'

The lamplight fell on Lukas's battered face, on his knuckles black with congealed blood. I passed the whisky to him, this time in conscious apology. I tried to form sentences, phrases, even words which would somehow match what I had done. But all I managed was the simplest form of all. I said: 'I'm sorry, Lukas. Very sorry.'

He looked at me for a long moment, then his head moved up and down in the lamplight, not in acceptance of my sparse apology, I'm sure, but somehow, I thought . . . I hoped . . . recognizing from the depths of his own past suffering how it was possible that I had acted as I had.

26

I RECOVERED MY OWN vehicle and drove back to the Nunnery.
I needed to talk to Dronsky. I knew what I had done. I knew I
should not have done it. But Lukas Roop had his own part to play
in all this. When we had first talked he had not admitted knowing
Natalya. He had curled up in that tight ball and hoped the storm
would pass. As I stood in the arched entrance of the Nunnery and
rang the bell I pulled a sharp draught of air through my teeth.

But I knew that even Dronsky would not be able to go the last
part with me. I felt totally alone as I walked past the security
guard and through the empty reception hall. My footsteps seemed
to follow me across the flagstones as I climbed the steps towards
the second floor. It was in this place, through this hall and down
those chipped iron stairs, that so many innocent victims of the
Soviet political police and the Nationalist Cheka of the last few
years had been dragged to be beaten senseless in the basements
below. On no stronger grounds, I was forced to admit, than those
that had made Lukas Roop *my* victim.

The corridors of our own wing of the Nunnery were empty.
The day staff had long gone home. Behind Danilova's closed
door I heard the murmur of voices, but I saw no sign of life
until I rounded the bend where the statuette of the Virgin had
been replaced at some time since the Americans took over the
building. I took another mouthful of the whisky, registered it
was the last and tossed the bottle into a trash bin mounted on
the wall.

Here the lighting was dim, a blue lamp in the ceiling and the
shadows deep. At first I saw no more than a movement, then the
tawny eyes of V.I. Lenin winked at me as he hugged the wall
low down by the skirting. Perhaps he was looking for his own
innocent victims as they scurried behind the wainscot, perhaps
he intuited some shameful connection between us. At any rate, he
stopped and sat, his eyes unblinking now, locked on mine. Then

with that movement that you at first think of as a gesture towards an invisible ball of string, he lifted his paw in greeting.

Never in my life, brothers, did I think to be accepting sympathy from a cat. But this was a truly low ebb. I glanced along the corridor. All office doors were closed; even the murmur of voices from the main office was barely audible. I looked down at the cat. Keeping my hand at no more than about waist level, I opened the palm in response.

With what might have been, equally, a smile of triumph or complicity, V.I. Lenin passed on his way.

Dronsky and Abby Cunningham were in her office, drinking coffee. He stood, in his blue boating shoes and khaki suit, leaning his back against a wall. She sat in an armchair beside her desk, her rounded knees crossed, swinging a black leather high heel which she balanced on the toes of one stockinged foot. I had thought it was going to be overwhelmingly difficult. But strangely I found that all those apologies I had been unable to make to Lukas Roop, I could now, in my confession of what I had done, direct to these two people before me.

'For Christ's sake, how is he?' Abby said when I had recounted every shameful detail of the white van wildly skidding under the wall-eyed stare of the *Alyosha* statue.

I took a deep breath. 'Bruised. Nothing broken, I'd say. A cracked rib maybe. I was lucky.' I hesitated. I wanted to say all there was to say, to put the whole thing behind me. 'I might have killed him,' I said. 'In the back of the van there I might easily have broken his neck.'

I sat down and stared at the blank wall behind Abby's head. Dronsky poured me coffee and put a cup on the low table next to me. Neither of them asked how much whisky I had drunk this evening; neither of them said much at all.

I could feel anger growing in me. Surely they understood. Dronsky at least. But still neither spoke. Perhaps it was only seconds. Looking back I'm sure it was no more. But to me the silence seemed to drag out for ever. I looked from Dronsky to Abby Cunningham. 'Don't tell me . . . I know what I should have done. Brought him in, questioned him . . . But I don't have that sort of time. Natalya doesn't,' I said savagely.

They said nothing.

'Look, for Christ's sake. I thought I had him. The man who was holding her. How could I guess that they were all working together? And he's a crazy, there's no doubt about that. A sort of controlled reasonable crazy, maybe. But still . . . odd . . . eccentric. He's into painting his face and Slavic myths and . . .' I was staring at their blank faces, not unfriendly, not unsympathetic even, just blank. 'Every minute counted,' I said, my voice harsher as my defence became less tenable. I turned to Dronsky. 'You must see that, fuck your mother!'

'But he's not your man.' Abby took a cigarette from her purse and lit it.

I shook my head. 'In the end, his story explained everything. Even down to the blood on Joan's knee and the wolf's hair. She was in the accident that Natalya was called to. She was in the back of the van with the children.'

Abby leaned sideways and put her cup on her desk. 'These children that Joan and Natalya were shipping, did Lukas know where they came from?'

'No. Joan and Natalya preferred to keep it that way. Lukas thinks maybe for his own safety. All he knows is whoever the children were, the deserters, Anarchists, whoever, were well paid for them in American dollars.'

Abby nodded to herself. 'That, at least, makes American sense.'

American sense? Is that different from Russian sense? 'I don't understand.'

'I just talked turkey to Miles Bridger, the consul,' she said. 'He says he's been over Joan's books. In the last two months there's been more than fifty thousand dollars "diverted" to cash from three social funds Joan was running.'

'The pay-offs.'

'Looks like it,' Abby said. She looked from me to Dronsky. 'So where do we stand now?'

He sucked hard on his lip. 'First thing, we have to consider the possibility of a completely different working sequence.' He went to the board on the wall and started rubbing out and rewriting the known events under the heading *Lukas Roop's evidence*. 'It now seems as if our abductor was returning to Murmansk at two, three in the morning. It was a bad night. Anybody out was likely to be professional . . .' He selected a piece of red chalk. Against the time and place *0300 hrs – Crossing 33*, he placed a huge red question mark. 'A truck driver maybe . . .'

'And by the roadside,' I took it up, 'by the roadside, he sees two women, waving goodbye to a disappearing tail-light.'

I looked from one to the other. Slowly Abby nodded. 'Time for you to get some sleep, Constantin.'

'I couldn't sleep.'

'Take a couple of knock-out pills. You need the sleep.'

As I shook my head, I saw her flick her eyes towards Dronsky. He put away the pack of cigarettes he had been about to open and mumbled something about going to his office.

Abby Cunningham waited until he had left. 'You think,' she said slowly, 'you had every excuse.'

'Only if I'd been right,' I said.

'But you were wrong.'

'Yes.'

She stood slowly, but her eyes were wide with anger. 'Goddam Russians,' she said quietly. 'You can't get it out of your blood.'

'Such a thing has never happened with an American cop?'

'Not one that worked for me.'

'I may be working for you – but just remember I'm also searching for my wife.'

'And if you want to stay working for me, remember we work as a *team*. Is that understood?'

'What does Dronsky say?'

'You want to ask him?'

I stood without answering. 'No,' I said at length. I made to leave, to find Dronsky.

'Wait,' she said. The voice brought me up short. 'There's another aspect to all this that your actions tonight have buried.'

I leaned back on the door-frame, exhausted. Her eyes, much smaller and darker than I had ever seen, buttoned onto me.

'The children,' she said.

I waited.

'If Lukas is right and Natalya and Joan were abducted on the roadside at Intersection 33 – and that's what Natalya's scarf suggests – what happened to the children?'

'I don't know.'

'Perhaps the children were removed, perhaps recovered by who-ever had lost them? They were worth something, we know that. Joan Fowler was embezzling consular funds to buy them. Why?'

'I don't *know*.'

'No. Nor do I.' Her voice remained on a normal conversational level. Did this woman ever get rattled? 'But I'm challenging your assumptions,' she said. 'You believe we're dealing with a crazy?'

'Don't you?'

'Let me finish, for Christ's sake. Yes, maybe we're dealing with a crazy. The dolls obviously point that way. But the children slot into this too. We should be looking to find out *how* they slot in. Before we take up Lukas's idea that the two women were just standing there when the maniac drove up.'

'You're saying you don't accept Lukas's story?'

'I'm not saying that. It sounds OK. In any case, we'll get him in to go over it. What I'm saying is however airtight his story, we don't need his *suggestions* about what happened.'

The door opened behind me and Dronsky came into the office. He looked up at me. 'Ready, Chief?' He held car keys in his hand.

'No,' I said. 'I've things to finish here.'

He shuffled awkwardly and ran his hand across his short cropped head. 'Would you mind if I had a quick word with Abby? I'm sorry Chief.'

'You mean alone?' Of course he meant alone.

'Would you just wait outside a moment?' Abby said.

I stepped out of the office and closed the door. I'd asked for all this, I suppose. I waited with my back against the wall, as if waiting outside the head teacher's office in Primary 36 while my case was considered behind closed doors.

It seemed only a minute or two before the door opened. 'Come on, Chief,' Dronsky said. 'I'll drive you.'

Glances moved between Abby and the man I thought of as my best friend. 'You've had a hell of a night,' he said.

Perhaps it should have struck me earlier. Perhaps it would have been obvious to someone less anxious to justify himself. To someone less disturbed by Abby Cunningham's insinuations. But it was obvious enough now. *They were holding something from me.* I started to say something and stopped.

'Come on, Chief,' Dronsky said. 'Let's get you home.'

I looked at Abby. Her dark features barely moved in a nod of agreement.

'I can drive myself,' I said. I turned away. Dronsky stood aside.

I knew what was happening, and the pain of it burnt into me. We were investigating the abduction, perhaps even the murder, of my own wife. But after what had happened tonight, after what they had learnt tonight, Ilya Dronsky and Abby Cunningham had come to a decision in those two minutes they had conferred in her office, a simple and devastating conclusion: I was not to be trusted.

27

W ELL, I WASN'T going to take it, fuck your mother! I was not
going to let myself be pushed off onto the sidelines while
there was the slightest chance Natalya was still alive. I walked
through the reception area and past the security guard. I owed it
to Natalya. I owed it to her not to give up. OK, I'm not one of the
country's great homicide detectives. Not even one of Murmansk's
great homicide detectives. But I still owed it to Natalya.

I had left the Fiat in the lane beside the Nunnery. Just past it I
knew I would come to the old wall which once enclosed the nuns'
garden. A small grille door set in the wall enabled me to see up to
the wing where Abby had her office. There was activity up there.
Dronsky wearing his blue police parka was holding open the door.
I stood for a moment watching Abby put on her fur-lined leather
parka, then seconds later the light went out.

I ran back to the Tolstoy and got in. From where I sat I could
see Dronsky and Abby emerge from the main consulate door and
get into an American car which had pulled to a halt at the mouth
of the brick arch.

There were few cars on the street. I followed the American car at
a distance along the main boulvar. Black and red election banners
were now stretched across the road from side to side at intervals
of no more than a few dozen metres, giving the wide avenue a
falsely festive air. A few clubs were turning out, and among the
men milling on the sidewalks I saw the black and red of Candidate
X rosettes in buttonholes and fluttering as pennants on the waiting
limousines. Perhaps there were many fewer Badanova rosettes and
posters but they were not, I was glad to see, completely absent from
the well-dressed crowds seeking out their Mercedes and BMWs.

At Union Square the car ahead turned right and continued up
Pushkin. It took another moment before I realized we were heading
for the Lermontov. But not the front courtyard. The consulate car
drove on past the main gates and took the side street that would

bring us to the separate entrance to Potanin's Psychiatric Clinic. I followed and pulled up behind them as Dronsky and Abby Cunningham got out.

Dronsky looked at me uncomfortably. 'Got a call just as you left, Chief,' he said.

'What is it?'

Dronsky raised his Groucho eyebrows. 'Let's see what Dr Potanin has to show us.'

I turned to Abby Cunningham. Whatever Dronsky's nominal position, I knew she was in charge. She felt no need for excuses or even further explanations. 'You can come up,' she said, 'if you're prepared to hold yourself in. Is this a deal?'

I could have throttled her. Instead I nodded and followed as she climbed the steps and leaned heavily on the night bell.

Potanin himself came to the door. He was wearing ancient pyjamas and a robe as unsavoury as the sweater beneath it. The lights behind him were low in the corridor but there were no longer the unsettling cries and sounds of ubiquitous shuffling feet that I already associated with the place.

We went straight up to Potanin's office. He flicked the lights on as we entered and I stopped. I stared at the gold necklace on his desk. I had no need to examine the hallmark. I knew it would be Irish – Dublin, hallmarked 1883. I had bought the nineteenth-century watch-chain for Natalya's wedding present. Near the clasp there was a tiny engraved initialling.

'N.V.,' Potanin said. 'Natalya Vadim unless I'm mistaken.'

The smugness I seemed to hear in his voice was intolerable. I swung around to face him. 'Where did you find it?'

Without answering, he went to the door and called down the corridor. The shuffle of an inmate preceded the appearance in the doorway of an overweight but young woman, perhaps twenty- to twenty-five years old, her dark hair curled inexpertly and with make-up that travelled freely across her plump, pretty face. She wore a thin floral dress and a heavy belted green cardigan. Newspapers, for additional warmth, were visible, packed below her neckline. 'This is Zoya,' Potanin said. 'She's housed in E Wing. Hit her mother with a brick when she was twelve,' he added as if she weren't there. 'Buried her in the back yard.' He stopped. Zoya was staring, much more absorbed by Abby than any crudely spelt-out details of her early life. She lifted a finger to point and began to giggle. 'Zoya,' Potanin said sharply. 'Listen to me. We want to know where you got the necklace.'

Zoya stared at Abby, transfixed, not giggling now.

Abby stepped forward and took the girl's hand. Very gently she ran Zoya's fingertips down the side of her own brown cheek. 'There . . . that's what you wanted, Zoya, wasn't it? My name is Abby,' the American said softly. She walked across to the desk and reached over to lift the necklace by the hook of the clasp, holding it up to the light. 'Pretty, isn't it, Zoya?'

The Russian girl said nothing, watching the swinging necklace as if mesmerized. But no more mesmerized than I was myself. How, in the name of God, had it got into this bleak place? Fatigue and drink and longing conjured images of other days . . . the necklace around Natalya's neck glistening with steam-drops as she stepped from the bath, the necklace rich and warm around her neck as she lay in bed next to me. Through these visions, like a camera device, the gold links dissolved back into terrifying reality. When Abby spoke again, I started.

'Were you given it, Zoya? Was it a present?'

The girl put her hand to her neck as if realizing for the first time the necklace was no longer there. 'The doctor gave it to me.' She turned to Potanin.

The tall figure straightened his back. 'You're lying again, Zoya,' he said in a resigned voice. 'Tell them what you told me.'

Abby stepped forward, between Potanin and the girl. 'Did someone give it to you, Zoya? Is that what happened?'

The girl shot a quick look at Potanin. 'I found it,' she said dully.

I could hardly restrain myself from pressing questions on her. But I knew better. Just this once I knew better.

'Listen carefully, Zoya,' Abby said. 'I want you to show me where you found it. Can you remember where?'

'In the garden,' Zoya said brightly and without the slightest conviction.

'Can you show me?'

'In the boiler-room,' the girl said, unaware that she had changed her story.

'Did you find it? Or did someone give it to you?'

'The boilerman gave it to me,' she said.

Potanin frowned. 'We don't have a boilerman. We changed from coke to gas three months ago – under the American Hospital

Refurbishment Program. In any case the boiler-room is securely locked.'

'The boilerman . . . The boilerman . . .' Zoya sang.

'Tell me, Zoya. Truly. Where did you get the necklace?'

'The boilerman gave it to me,' Zoya said, at home now with the strange faces around her. 'He wanted bom-bom.'

'She's a pretty enough girl,' Potanin said as we descended the stairs towards the boiler-room. 'And younger than most I have here. The men are onto her whenever they have free association. They give her small presents, tobacco mainly, smuggled alcohol sometimes. She takes it all in good part.'

'I bet,' Abby said.

He shrugged. 'She's been sterilized, of course, against any serious developments.'

'Well, that's a relief,' Abby said coldly.

At the bottom of the stairwell, Potanin stopped. 'The door's open,' he said.

We went forward into a long, low room. There were lights set into the ceiling. All around us we heard the scrape of shovels and could see the outline of men in yellow overalls. Heavy clouds of coke dust restricted visibility. Abby put a handkerchief to her mouth. 'Jesus Christ,' she said. 'If this is a crime scene these goons are making sure there's going to be nothing left to find.'

Emerging from the gloom, Pasko, carrying a heavy torch, crunched his way across to us.

'What the hell are you doing here?' I said.

'I'm here with my crime-scene team. The doctor here . . .' he thumbed towards Potanin, 'called Militia Central and they routed it to me naturally. The maintenance manager gave me the key. One half of this is still a Missing Persons case, let me remind you.'

I looked towards Potanin. 'I thought Militia Central would be the quickest way of reaching Agent Cunningham,' he said.

Pasko wiped his blackened lips. 'No point in a turf war between us,' he said. 'My boys have turned the whole place over. Waste of time,' he said. 'There's nothing here.'

'How would you know?' Abby said furiously. She stared through the clouds of dust. 'How would anybody know?'

I turned away and walked across the boiler-room, coke and coke dust crunching under my feet. Coke dust, I remembered the medical examiner saying, lodged in Joan Fowler's nostrils. I was trying to get my bearings, reminding myself we were still in the Lermontov complex. The low barrel-vaulted brick roof of the boiler-room helped me orient myself. The Central Mortuary has a similar roof. It was, I guessed, only a few metres away on the other side of the wall. I was, I guessed, facing towards the garden at the back of the Psychiatric Wing. The high iron doors at the far end of the boiler-room must open onto some sort of ramp which enabled the horse-drawn coke carts of the past to be brought in for unloading.

I stood for a moment in the heavy, warm, dusty atmosphere, reminded, despite myself, by the low ceiling and the ancient green art deco iron boilers, of the cargo ships I'd done my National Service training on: Second World War rust-buckets whose engine-rooms leaked carbon monoxide from the boiler flues and sprinkled men and machinery with a fine-ground coke dust. In those days we worked with bare chests, running with coke-sweat, and wore a red kerchief round our mouths. To me, becoming a commissioned officer in dangerously unstable submarines for a further two years had been an escape. But the coke furnaces were no longer operating down here. Two large white metal boxes at the end of the room, still new enough to carry a Stars and Stripes sticker, had silently and cleanly taken over the task.

Standing there, I was conscious that I was swaying and light in the head. Pasko's team had turned over huge piles of coke that remained from the old system. I stood there looking and not looking. Terrified that at any moment they were going to uncover a pale dusty arm. Terrified, as I listened to the scrape and draw of shovelling, expecting every moment that dull, almost soundless thud of shovel on flesh.

I knew this was the place. I closed my eyes and felt that Natalya had been here. Perhaps was still here. 'You sure you don't want me to get someone to take you home, Chief?' It was Dronsky beside me.

I shook my head.

'You can't go on taking this hammering,' he said. 'Nobody can.'

'Coke dust, Ilya,' I said. 'You remember the medical officer's report?'

'Of course.' He nodded. 'I still think you should leave this to me,' he said.

'You're saying there's nothing here?'

'I'm saying I don't think so. Pasko's team are blundering farmboys. But they've turned over tonnes of coke. They could have missed almost anything – but they couldn't have missed Natalya, Chief. She isn't here.'

'I just feel it,' I said. 'I feel it, Dronsky.'

'We'll get a better look around when the coke dust settles. All we have up to now is the word of a poor creature who doesn't seem clear about what happened.'

'The one certain thing, Ilya, is the necklace. *That* was not invented.'

He looked across to where three men, in a thick cloud of black dust, were digging into the last mound of coke. 'You're right, Chief,' he said.

We turned towards the door as Abby returned with Potanin. 'I've been talking to Zoya,' she said. 'She now says the boilerman, the stoker, gave the necklace to her in the garden.'

'Do you believe that?'

She puffed her cheeks. 'Except there hasn't been a boilerman since the new gas-fired boilers arrived.'

'Do you think she found it in the garden?'

'Maybe. Or someone gave it to her in return for a bom-bom session. If so, his secret's safe with her.'

'We have a necklace,' I said. 'That's real.' I felt I had to keep repeating the fact, hang onto it.

She nodded. 'That's real,' she said. And I understood that she was promising me that she would not just turn away from the fact.

The crime-scene team had stopped work. They stood, leaning on their shovels, wiping their mouths. 'There's nothing to be found here, Captain,' the sergeant in charge of the team said to Pasko. 'What do you want us to do now?'

'I want you to wait until we can see our hands in front of our faces. Then I want you to go back over and sift through every kilo as if it were gold dust,' Abby intervened. 'We're not finished yet.'

Their black-rimmed eyes opened wide.

'I'm in command of these men,' Pasko said. He turned to the sergeant. 'No use hanging around here. The job's done. Pack up and let's go.'

Abby's eyes tightened. She turned away.

Pasko hesitated, then grinned acknowledgement of his victory, licked coke grit from his lips and spat. The saliva exploded in dusty globules on the cement floor.

As the dust fell slowly through the yellow light we began our own search of the boiler-room. It took barely minutes to find the line of metal rings at shoulder height along one wall. Whatever their original purpose, they had certainly been used to secure Joan and Natalya. From one a length of bloodstained rope trailed to the ground. The brickwork beneath it was heavily splattered with blood.

Further along, in a second ring, a thick tuft of long blonde hair had been caught in the metal ring bracket. I had no doubt at all that it was Natalya's hair. But there was no rope, no blood. Desperate as I was, it gave me hope.

28

W HILE PINSK'S OWN crime-scene team had been sent for to
see if anything could be salvaged from the wreckage left by
Pasko's men, dogs had been brought in from Station 20, three
black German shepherds, to search the garden.

What was sustaining me now was the idea that Natalya had
somehow escaped. What I needed to know was that she had got
further than being cut down in the inmates' garden.

We stood in a group, Abby, Dronsky, Potanin, now in fur
hat and topcoat over his pyjamas, and myself, and watched
the dog-handlers divide up the overgrown area. Security lights
shone from the forbidding brick walls of the clinic, creating deep
shadow beyond clumps of the snow-laden pines which, with a few
evergreen bushes, were the remnants of a planned garden. Narrow
walks, brushed or trudged clear of snow, criss-crossed the white
space. A high chain-link fence, rusty and sagging in parts, ran
around the perimeter, enclosing an area about sixty metres long
and roughly the same depth. A rear double gate, ill-secured by a
padlock, hung on its hinges.

Dronsky stayed close to me as we watched the dogs pulling
at their leads, and yelping and stopping and pulling again. Their
militia handlers spoke to them unceasingly, a sort of baby-talk
of encouragement, urging them into this dark corner, under that
low bush.

At every outbreak of barking my balls tightened in a spasm of
fear which ended in a throat full of bitter bile. But the handler
would shout back that it was a rat, a dead bird, an abandoned
hamburger package, and the panting scrabbling of the dogs sawing
against their collars would continue.

In places the snow was still thick. Each twig was circled in a
band of ice. The sudden spring thaw had struck twice already
only to refreeze again, and anything beneath the snow might as
easily rest below an ice-cap. For this reason the handlers prodded

with their sticks at every low mound and held the dogs on a tight chain as they scrabbled and scuffled around the heaped snow.

We stood in Potanin's office, Abby Cunningham and myself.

'Access to the boiler-room,' I said. 'Who has it?'

'Officially only the maintenance manager. Used to be the boiler-room staff when the furnaces were coked up.'

'Who is he? Who's the manager?'

'A woman, Sonia Maklova. She took an injured leg in the Anarchist bombing in the late war. She's been maintenance manager here ever since she started walking again.'

'We need to see her straight away,' Abby said.

'She has a small apartment on the top floor. Enough for herself and her small son. Goes with the job. I've warned her you might want to talk to her.' He lifted his phone and punched two numbers. 'Sonia. You're wanted down here. My office. Immediately.'

Joan and Natalya had been attached to those iron rings in the boiler-room. Natalya's necklace had been found either in the boiler-room or the garden. Either way it positioned the investigation squarely in Potanin's Psychiatric Wing. But how to proceed from here? I was looking at Abby, waiting for her, I realized, to cut through the fog surrounding me.

'We could be talking about a patient here who knew the boiler-room years ago. We could be talking about someone who was not even a patient here. The truck driver who delivered coke in the old days, his assistant. Our man's knowledge of the boiler-room could go back years. But not his access to it. Not since the new locks were fitted to protect the new gas boilers.'

'So we concentrate on the question of access?' I said.

'We do. In the meantime we ask Dr Potanin to draw up a list of his most violent patients, from say three years back to current. If our vek is one of your residents, or recent residents, you can narrow it down for us.'

'The FBI needs my help?' Potanin said slyly. He was looking at me.

'If what you give us is good, you'll be well paid,' I said. I was thinking of his fake medical credentials. So was he.

Abby looked up. 'What are you saying?'

'An old Russian joke,' I said.

'Or an old Russian deal,' she muttered. She hesitated, decided against pressing further and swung round towards Potanin. 'Before you go, tell us who gets to use the garden.'

Potanin bent to take a wad of more modern-looking files from the filing cabinet. On the way to his desk his free hand reached out and captured a vodka bottle. He took three glasses from a shelf and talked as he poured. 'The Psychiatric Wing and garden is completely separate from the main Lermontov hospital building,' he said. He gestured to the window. 'We've been assigned what was the old hospital physic garden. This is where herbs were grown for treating the sick. Today it's a recreational area for non-violent patients. You can see from up here that the physic garden is fenced off from the main area of the Lermontov.'

I walked to the window and glanced down. My stomach pulled as I saw the lights and searching dogs below. Dronsky stood on the main path out to the back gate directing the operation.

Potanin gave me a glass. I took it without turning from the window. I raised it to my lips and stopped. Across the chain-link fence of the garden was the Lermontov staff parking-lot. If I raised my eyes two floors, I was looking at a row of long elegant windows, mostly dark, but one or two belonging to the long curtainless wards. If I moved my eyes fifteen or twenty metres to the right, I was looking directly into Natalya's darkened office window.

From the garden below I could hear the yelp of dogs and even imagined I could hear the scrape of men digging.

At a knock on the door we all looked up. The woman who entered wore a black trouser suit that effectively covered any damage to her leg.

'Come in, Mrs Maklova,' Abby said. 'Dr Potanin has told you we need to ask you some questions.'

She was quite young, in her late thirties, blonde hair pulled back behind her ears, a once attractive face that was now drawn and sallow. She came into the room, nodded to Potanin and faced Abby. 'What questions?' she said.

'We have good reason to believe there's a connection between the crime Inspector Vadim and myself are investigating and the clinic here. Or to be more precise the furnace-room downstairs and perhaps the physic garden.'

'The garden's not part of my responsibility,' Maklova said defensively.

'But the boiler-room is.'

'Yes.'

'Tell us about the change-over,' I said. 'The change from coke to the new American gas boilers.'

'It put four men out of work. That's what these American advances do.'

'Sometimes,' Abby conceded. 'How often does anyone have to go into the boiler-room now?'

'It's all automatic. Controlled by the computer in my office. I haven't been down there for a month or more. These days I have no need.'

'And the time before that?'

'Same. A month. Six weeks. Last time I was laying rat poison. Nothing to do with the new boilers.'

'And no-one else has a reason to go down there?'

'Not that I know.' She looked towards Potanin and he tipped back his vodka before shaking his head. 'The boiler-room is more or less as it was when the American gas boilers were installed last year. I haven't even got anyone to cart away the coke.'

'Who were these four men who worked down there?'

She took a sheet of paper from inside her overall and passed it to me. There were four names on the sheet – Rybkin, Semlovsky, Assarian and Partenko. A brief life history accompanied each name: school, military service, marital status and reason for committal to the clinic. None of them was being treated for violent crimes. Persistent theft, depression, alcoholism. The one case of arson came closest to the sort of criminal background we might be looking for. Igor Semlovsky.

'Are all workers in the clinic also inmates, in one sense or another?' I asked Potanin, giving Abby the list.

'Where else would we find cheap labour?' he said. 'There are no funds for hiring at market prices, so we exploit the sick, Inspector. What else would you suggest?'

I looked up at his raised eyebrow. Potanin, with his abrasive candour, was not an easy man to fathom, on the side of the angels one moment – very much elsewhere, the next.

'What happened to these men – Igor Semlovsky, for instance?' Abby asked, looking at him. 'The arsonist.'

'Semlovsky's back in a long-stay secure ward. Dr Potanin has discharged the other three on medical parole.'

'Think carefully,' I said to Maklova. 'Could any of these four have come away with a key to the boiler-room?'

'The old keys wouldn't have done anybody any good,' Sonia

Maklova said. 'When the new boilers were installed the Refurbishment Fund demanded the boiler-room be fitted with new locks. New gas boilers have been dismantled before now and carted away.'

'And who has keys now?' Abby asked her. 'Yourself . . .'

'I handed my keys over to Captain Pasko's militia team earlier. One key to the back doors is kept in the boiler-room in case we ever needed to bring anything big in.'

'That key's been recovered by the crime-scene team,' Abby said. 'They're testing it for prints. Any others?'

'Apart from that, Dr Potanin keeps a set in his safe. And that's it.'

When Maklova left Abby turned back to Potanin. 'I'm elbowing my way into your deal,' she said. 'The one you have with Constantin.'

She had picked up quickly on the fact I had something over Potanin.

'I want an answer that matches the facts.'

'Answer to what?' Potanin asked cautiously.

'I want to know how good your security is here. If every one of your violent prisoners were safely under lock and key last weekend, we'd be wasting our time even looking at them. Right?'

I've never seen a man look so shifty. He picked at his decaying sweater. 'Security isn't always as reliable as it should be. I have to admit that right away.'

'Tell us,' I said from my place by the window.

'We had an escape.'

'When?'

'At the end of last week. Friday night. Early Saturday perhaps. With our staff shortages it's difficult to be certain.'

'Jesus . . .' Abby covered her eyes. 'You didn't even mention it.'

'At that time we had nothing to connect the abductions to my unit,' Potanin protested.

'We do now, fuck your mother.' I was trembling with anger.

'OK,' Abby looked at him dubiously. Then at me. 'Hold off, Constantin.'

'An escape,' I said. 'Who was it?'

'A man named Borchuk. Borya Borchuk. A Ukrainian. Moved up here to the north about four years ago to take a job as pork butcher in the factory there . . .'

'Convictions for sexual violence? Murder?'

'Yes. His wife and sixteen-year-old daughter. Both sexually assaulted and cut to pieces.'

'Is he still at large?' Abby interrupted him.

'No. He's back in his cell on the fifth floor. He was found unconscious drunk just inside the back gate this afternoon.'

'Inside?' I said. 'You mean he came back after being away since the weekend? And when he came back he had a key to the back gate?'

Potanin lifted his shoulders in a hopeless gesture. 'We know back-gate keys are on sale in the clinic. We do our best to track them down. Without more staff there's nothing we can do . . .'

Keys on sale to known sex murderers . . . 'Isn't it possible that keys to the boiler-room were also on sale?' I asked him.

'No, Inspector. They were new locks, new keys. Apart from the single key kept *inside* the boiler-room, Sonya Maklova and myself were the only ones with a set.'

'Did you report the escape to the militia?'

His eyes dropped shiftily. 'He's escaped before. He always comes back.'

Furious, I gestured at him. Perhaps the gesture had more the shape of an aimed blow. He pulled back and the vodka leapt from my glass and splashed over him. He looked quickly at Abby for support.

But her eyes had narrowed. 'Borchuk was found this afternoon, you said. About the time Zoya acquired the necklace, then?'

'More or less,' Potanin said.

'And the models, the dolls that you use for training, had Borchuk used them?'

'He doesn't fit the profile.'

Without thinking, I moved towards him. Abby's hand shot out and held hard onto my wrist. 'Had Borchuk used the dolls, Potanin?' Her voice was steely. She slowly released her grasp.

'I understand so.' Potanin puffed his grizzled cheeks. 'One of the younger teams had been using the dolls to get him to therapeutically reconstruct the murder of his wife and daughter.'

I was moving towards the door. 'If Borchuk's here, let's see him.' I took Potanin by the arm and pushed him in front of me. 'Now.'

Boris Borchuk, Borya to the staff, was a short broad-shouldered man of about forty-five, fat but powerfully built all the same. He had very thin black hair and one of those trimmed beards without a moustache, dirty teeth and a leering, empty confidence. God knows, there was not much to him. A paper-thin personality supported the bull-like structure of his body. He stood up, rattling the chain that was secured round his waist, when he saw Abby enter the cells behind me, and I pushed him back onto his bunk. 'What about him?' I said to Potanin who stood in the doorway. 'Let's have the story in detail.'

'Perhaps we should talk outside,' Potanin started back into the corridor.

'Just tell us,' Abby said. 'We're not worried about hurt feelings.'

'Innumerable arrests for brawling. Mostly women involved,' Potanin said. 'Last August they found his wife and daughter buried beneath some paving he'd been laying for the City Council. Both of them had been sexually attacked and dismembered. He was convicted a month ago and remanded for my report. I haven't got round to it yet.'

Borchuk laughed.

'Where did he live before he was arrested?' Abby asked.

'Kanevka,' Potanin told her. 'It's on the road south of the city.'

'Would you pass Intersection 33 on your way there?'

'Yes,' I said shortly. I turned to Potanin behind me. 'Get the girl, Zoya, down here,' I said. He hesitated, about to stand on his dignity, then thought better of it and turned angrily away.

Borya was rocking back and forth on his bunk. A great fat carcass with an infant's mind. Saliva drooled at the corner of his mouth.

'Where did you go,' I said, 'when you got out?'

He looked blank.

'Did you go home, to Kanevka? Did you steal a car, a van?'

He tried to jump at me but the chain held him back.

'Don't let him get his hands on you, Constantin,' Abby said, but the truth is I would have welcomed it.

'Where did you go, Borya?' I asked him again. 'Were you driving home to Kanevka?'

He made driving movements and his flabby lips imitated the sound of a vehicle. I suppose he meant yes.

'Did you see the two women by the roadside? The two women at Intersection 33?'

He cocked his head. Did he know what I was talking about?

'The American woman,' I said, 'and the doctor.' When he made no answer I walked over to him and dragged him to his feet.

'Be careful,' Abby warned, but Borchuk hunched his shoulders and loosened his knees, resisting passively like a boy being hauled out by a schoolteacher.

I shoved him against the window bars and pointed downwards. 'The doctor who lives there,' I said. I pointed to Natalya's darkened office window. 'You know who I mean?'

He seemed to shuffle out some affirmative. I let him go.

'Where is she? Where's the other woman? The woman that escaped,' I said.

Behind me Potanin led Zoya into the cell. She was staring at Borchuk. A giggle shook her cheeks.

'Do you know Borya?' Abby said.

Her whole body quivered.

'Is this the man, Zoya, who gave you the necklace?' Abby asked.

I looked towards Borchuk. He had fallen back on his bunk and now, half lying against the wall, he was jerking his pelvis out towards Zoya.

The giggle exploded in merriment. She pointed down at him. 'He wants bom-bom,' she squealed with pleasure. 'Borya wants bom-bom.'

I turned away from Borchuk's glazed eyes and wet lips. Among all the other emotions, disgust stirred powerfully. I knew that something in me needed more than this. If Natalya had to die, it had to be by the hand of someone or something more than a pathetic creature like Borchuk. I had come across this feeling in my work before, when parents of young people killed in accidents couldn't accept it was the simple fact of a rope frayed, or a tile slipped from a roof. It's the basis of all those student conspiracy theories. We need our icons or our loved ones to die a death of some significance.

But no. I had to understand I was not going to get even that consolation. I was left with Borchuk, the pork butcher. I had to accept it as a strong possibility that by his scarred, thick-fingered hands Natalya had been taken from me.

The call came half an hour later. I was standing in the garden surrounded by trampled snow. It was a dog's yelp, a handler's excited exclamation.

Not five metres from where I was standing, the militiaman was holding the dog clear, lifting it by the chain as its front feet scrabbled the air. I ran between two fir trees and felt the frozen snow sprinkle my shoulders. On the edge of the path, the handler had now pulled the dog back from a white mound. I stopped, staring, unable to move. The wet crumpled piece of black material lay with snow in its creases. I knelt down. The pattern at the neck was unmistakable. This wet black rag was Natalya's dress, the one that had attracted so much comment at Governor Badanov's party.

I was aware that Abby and Dronsky were by my side. The American woman turned to me, wordlessly, her eyebrows rising.

I could hardly speak. My chin fell onto my chest. 'It's Natalya's,' I said, my voice little more than a low murmur. A hollow certainty was engulfing me. 'It's Natalya's,' I said again. 'She's here somewhere. Here in the garden or still in there – hidden somewhere in the boiler-room.'

29

S HE WAS.
We lifted her down and laid her naked body on Dronsky's parka beside the new American gas boilers. I covered her to the shoulders with my jacket. Her face looked extraordinarily serene and her blonde hair barely dirtied.

We knew now, more or less, what Joan Fowler had been through. But what had happened to Natalya? As Dronsky drove me back home I made a last effort to piece it together. I thought it through, sitting, unspeaking, in the passenger seat of my own car as we sped through the seedy concrete blocks of the city. This night of horror had begun for her in the blizzard on the Kanevka highway as Lukas had driven away.

I could almost see her, standing in the driving snow, her Lermontov overall bloodstained from the nosebleed of the injured child she had treated.

For a second or two she seemed to stare after the departing van before shrugging snow from her shoulders and turning to climb up behind the wheel of the Kamka.

Was this the moment headlights had come up from behind her? Was this the moment Borchuk had stopped, smiling?

It was certainly the moment she had thrown the blue and white Lermontov scarf out onto the roadside at Intersection 33. So that was her first intimation of danger. It was all chance, of course, as murder so often is. He was passing that way in his stolen car. Passing that way *en route* home to Kanevka at just that moment, a fugitive from Potanin's Psychiatric Clinic.

Who knew what demons pursued Borya Borchuk, pork butcher? All I knew was that on Saturday 3rd April 2017, at midnight or just past, these demons no longer pursued him. Once again they had inhabited his body, they were directing his mind.

What then? They had arrived at the unused back entrance of the Lermontov Psychiatric Wing. She had thrown her necklace.

She had seen the chances of that being found in the snow were too low. The black dress she had changed out of when she set out was beside her in the Kamka. Somehow, as the killer forced them from the vehicle down into the boiler-room, she had let fall the dress by the side of the path.

Dronsky gave me a cigarette and lit it without speaking.

'She didn't give up, Ilya. She was fighting right to the end.'

'You'd expect nothing else,' he said.

I slumped back in the seat. At some moment in the boiler-room, Natalya had broken free. To judge by the desperation of what she did next, Joan had already been tortured and murdered. In all probability while Natalya watched. So her own death was now only a matter of time, of hours, perhaps even minutes.

She had somehow sawn through the cords around her wrists. And then climbed, high above the newly installed American boilers into the inspection chamber of the gleaming zinc flue that carried waste gases above the Lermontov rooftops. I could almost read her mind working. Chained to the wall, she would die as Joan Fowler had just died, violated, and savaged by an expert. In the narrow inspection chamber, she was safe until the boiler automatically relit. At that point she could not survive five minutes of the warm, colourless, carbon monoxide gases which would flow up past her. She would die – but the killer would have been cheated of his prey.

I think I smiled, brothers.

But it was the last time for many weeks.

30

O UT HERE IN the wilds it's the cold whiteness that soothes. The whiteness and the distance from almost anywhere. Not perhaps so many miles from the city but still a place where I can stand on the edge of the lake and watch the white Arctic foxes becoming darker every day with the approach of summer, or the distant mass of a bear fishing out on the spit of land that separates lake and sea.

Butane gas heats and lights the small cabin in the belly of the boat. With two of the bunks folded there is room for a table. There is a cupboard full of tinned food and cooking oil and jars of soya flour; one shelf holds about twenty litres of vodka. A few books are to be found under blankets or pushed into corners. Outside, a fishing hole, cut in the lake ice, supplies me with water.

So I have all I need to maintain life. Except I can see no point . . . I lack equally the will to live and the will to die. All my life I have put off the simplest of decisions. I suppose that is what I am doing on the lake.

I've mentioned perhaps that my father was, like myself, a navy man. But, unlike myself, he was a seaman too. A man who loved the sea, loved its risks, felt its menacing enchantment. Before he died, he built a boat. I can see him now, in the long winters, the greying beard beaded with ice, as he hammered and sawed and riveted and welded in a makeshift boatyard up river from the city. Not a big boat, there were no materials for anything truly impressive in size or finish, but a sturdy six-metre fishing-craft, a summer boat as others in milder climates might have a dacha. When it was finished he had proposed naming it *Nadia* after my mother, but her barely articulated refusal contained such scorn that the boat had remained without a name.

The summer before he died he obtained permission to sail up river and east along the coast of the Kola Peninsula. He was a solitary; it was no surprise to my mother or myself when he took off. A week or two later he had returned, somewhat mysteriously I remember, from this expedition, not by boat but on foot, leading a baggage reindeer which he had bought from some hunters he had met out in the land of a thousand lakes.

The night of his return we had sat up together, in a too rare show of adolescent affection on my part, and attacked a bottle of good Polish vodka. But before we got too drunk he had made me promise that if anything should happen to him I would go out, each spring, to repaint and repair the boat on the nameless lake where he had hidden her.

Of course, after the first few springs I had lapsed badly and it was probably now four or five years since I had been out to the lake. Even so, the boat had seemed sound enough.

The night he had first told me about it, I remember shaking my head in befuddled surprise. On board, he said, were provisions for a whole winter. A man and his family could escape even Russian history up there for a few perhaps crucial months.

He had, you see, some sort of premonition. The Soviet Union was falling apart around us. My father believed that the Yeltsin years could not end without some sort of violence. As many others had believed, before the turn of the century.

When he had tried to put this to my mother she had, of course, turned down her lips. By this stage in their marriage it was all she needed to do. Her quiet contempt had long ago eroded almost all his belief in himself. Though I'm bound to say that had she listened with less scorn she might have been alive now. When Russia's Civil War finally arrived, she might have spent that winter of the Anarchist air attacks on the city safe on my father's nameless craft out on a nameless lake.

'Go away somewhere,' Abby had said the night we found Natalya. 'Buy yourself a flight somewhere. Paris or London or New York, even.' She had put her arms around me and hugged me, her brown cheek smooth against my unshaven chin. 'Leave all this to Dronsky and me. We'll tie up the ends . . . Just go – get out of this city.'

Before I left Murmansk that night I had not thought about my father's boat for years, yet curiously no other place to go had even entered my head. Driving east in my collapsing Fiat until I ran out of road, I abandoned the vehicle at a point which I knew was several days' trek from the lake. I was heavily laden but I had all the time in the world. I trudged, flat-foot in my snowshoes, through the pine trees stripped bare by acid rain, before turning along the Teriberka river line in the direction of the northern ocean.

Perhaps I blundered on for the best part of a week. It was an area I knew well enough from teenage summer expeditions with Roy Rolkin. This much earlier in the year, with summer two months away, the weather is still bad but to pass a night or two outside is not necessarily suicidal. And even if it had been I would not really have cared. To make a journey you have to have an end. I suppose, in a sense, to reach the boat was my end. But it was an end I could have sacrificed a hundred times, in those few days, to exhaustion or vodka or just the sudden insurmountable misery of the idea that Natalya was dead.

I had a hunting rifle on my shoulder and the thought moved in and out of my mind that I might choose to use it as my own inelegant version of a bare bodkin. And why didn't I, as I tramped through the snow towards the low rise of white mountains before me? When I look back on it I think it was, paradoxically, because I lacked the energy. It was easier to keep on walking. In those first few days I made a mild, less than epiphanic discovery. It takes a certain amount of energy for a man to decide to kill himself, even to let himself die.

On the third or fourth day I came to the lake. On my map there are uncountable patches of frozen water here, small and large, broad and narrow, many linked by narrow waterways to the not far distant North Polar Sea. Ten thousand freshwater lakes. But the co-ordinates do not lie. I found again, without difficulty, *this* lake, trumpet-shaped, frozen and surrounded by sloping pine hills. My father's landing-place.

Still there, the boat was locked by ice into the narrow creek which might be seen as the mouthpiece of the trumpet. To prevent it being washed out into the lake when the spring thaws came, my father had secured it with steel wires attached to chocks hammered into the sides of the creek. Though time had rotted his own covering of pine branches, the winds had bent young trees across its deck. Up here, north of the acid-rain belt, the broad black-green needles hold frost and snow well into spring. Climbing onto the deck I found myself enclosed in a translucent ice cavern.

I keep no count of the days. Time flows past me. When I think about it I notice the serried ranks of vodka bottles are markedly thinned. A routine of sorts has quickly imposed itself. I rise late and drink tea and a few thumbs of vodka to ease the spirit throughout the morning. Before midday I have usually circled the lake three or four times. I fish in lengthening afternoons and sometimes I hunt a hare. In the evening I cook my one meal, I drink a half-litre of spirit and lie on my bunk reading until I pass out.

A volume of Russian history is my favourite. It had been written in the early days of the twentieth century by an English merchant traveller, John Hardy. The man, I'm afraid, knew something about us. He describes the Russian as savage and servile in almost equal parts, which the next seventy years under Communism would fulsomely confirm. But he describes too a brilliant, talented people in the arts and sciences, individuals of great charm and liveliness – yet still, he believes, a dangerous people. Dangerous in their resentment, their ever-present sense of inferiority, in their desire to be not so much respected as *feared*.

Now this is a Westerner writing in 1900. He is not talking of nuclear weapons and ramshackle power stations. This English merchant has seen the problem with commercial clarity. The danger we Russians present is always first and foremost to ourselves.

So if I try hard enough I can sustain these thoughts about my beloved country until the book falls from my hand. Like this, I urge on the passage of time.

Listen, brothers, I could talk about the gulf, the abyss, the emptiness of being without her. But what good would it do? If you've experienced it, I can't tell you anything new – if you haven't known it, you'll never begin to imagine what it's like. It's a presence, you see, and, at one and the same time, an absence. That's what makes it so hard to take.

So my routines, my vodka, my reading are all devices, of course. When the last provisions are eaten, the last thumb of vodka downed, I shall have a decision to make. In a week or so now. No longer.

Tonight I lie in my bunk reading the English merchant-historian. I neck the bottle because it's easier than drinking from a glass. My head swims agreeably. Spring is almost upon us. For the past few nights bright patches of the northern lights have flared across the sky. By day I see vast swathes of forest appearing from under the snow. Birds are arriving in their thousands.

The grip of winter is, I know, loosening round the hull of the boat and once or twice I've felt some movement beneath me as the narrow river flows faster below the ice. Spring in the Arctic comes and goes. A thaw can refreeze overnight. Not that I pay any attention to these shifts in the hull. And I only notice the creaking of the chocks when I am in my bunk, far too drunk to get up and investigate.

The first rush of flood water came while I slept. The retaining chocks my father had driven into the bank were giving way as I struggled to separate dream from waking. The boat was already moving forward, rocking violently from side to side. Thunderous batterings struck the hull. I was thrown from the bunk and lifted, dumped like a sack on the far wall which was, strangely, now beneath me. Bottles, tins, boots were falling in what seemed all directions. Gravity had gone mad.

In a sudden moment of stillness I found myself lying on my back, staring up at my bunk which hung down, trailing blankets from its diamond-wire frame. For a moment the past chased out the present. Confused by vodka and the speed of the disaster, I was back in an emergency in our K-class submarine when it had rolled onto its side, moments after surfacing in a storm. Our captain had righted her by an emergency dive which threw men and metal at each other until we levelled off a few metres above the sea bed.

When my sense of the present returned, I realized that my boat, the *Nadia* that might have been, was floating on its side, rammed every few seconds by the lake's shelf of melting ice, splintering, splitting timbers all around me. When the cabin port burst open the water rose from under me like a geyser. In the confusion of green mist and floating objects I struggled for my life.

No doubts now, brothers, no easy equivalence of life and death. As the water roared and bubbled past my face I fought like a maniac, beating off the blankets that swirled around me, grasping for the bunk above. Hauling myself up, streaming water, terrified, I rolled onto the wire mesh of the upside-down bunk. There I lay watching the water rise towards me, flinching at the cracking of timbers as the ice closed around the upturned boat, crushing the life out of it.

And then silence. Or rather silence, but for the gentle lapping of water less than a metre below where I lay on the reverse side of the bunk. The gentle lap of water and the clink of floating vodka bottles.

I LAY THERE IN terror. The boat was somehow wedged between the sheets of ice. There was no more cracking of timber, no more groaning or splintering sounds. Perhaps my first real perception was that I was not in total blackness. It had been my practice to turn off the butane lamp and read by a waterproof rubber flashlight. This, still on when I fell asleep, had miraculously lodged itself in the diamond-pattern wiring of the bunk.

When terror abates, a certain chuckling nervousness holds stage. I lay back in my bunk and switched off the torch. My breathing was returning to normal. I was, I supposed, in some sort of airlock. How many cubic metres of air does a human being breathe a day? How many cubic metres did I have? Six or eight? And above me, twenty metres of lake? The irrepressible chuckling seized me when I thought I had once been a submarine officer. I had been trained on the Russian Navy's most up-to-date escape apparatus. Inherited from the Soviet Union of course, but like much defence equipment (though nothing else), on a par with the most sophisticated the West deployed.

The chuckling shook the wire bunk under me. So sophisticated was the escape apparatus I had trained on that I was not capable of diving free of a wreck twenty metres down in a still lake. I could not exist under water for more than five seconds without an Issue 759 breathing-mask. The truth was I couldn't even swim. Dilemmas don't come tighter than this.

I switched on the flashlight and checked my assets. A blanket had somehow attached itself to a deck fixing and now hung from above my head, dry until the last few centimetres were lapped by the water. I retrieved it.

The floating vodka bottles contained each of them a few centimetres of spirit. It was not going to be enough. I lowered myself in the water and found I could just about stand. Forcing myself to keep my eyes open, I dropped below water level. When I rose it was with a tin of vegetable soup, a Swiss army knife attached to a belt and a two-litre bottle of Hero City.

I was too weak or drunk to count the hours. I've no doubt days passed, perhaps two or three. Once or twice I dived again for a vodka bottle or a tin of soup. Inexplicably the air supply seemed inexhaustible.

In clearer moments I was grateful the decision had been taken from me. Each time I drifted into sleep I thought it would be endless. Each time I awoke it was with surprise.

I thought of Natalya a great deal. I dreamed wild dreams of my lost son Mischa, lost long before I had ever met Natalya, in the wild confusion of civil war. Many nights or days I found him again. He was a fifteen-year-old honours student at Moscow University, a cadet officer on a submarine, an American basketball player, an English spy with bowler hat and umbrella.

When I first heard the buzzing in my ears I thought it an unwelcome return of my tinnitus. But this was a droning buzz. More the sound of a hornet than a wasp. A circling hornet.

I had only just woken up and I lay in the darkness listening. A finely tuned resignation to fate is doubtless an aspect of the Russian spirit – but when the unseasonable droning of a hornet suddenly turns into the sound of a helicopter we react no differently from anyone else. With the weight of a full vodka bottle I began hammering on the upside of the boat, shouting abjectly for deliverance.

For what seemed hours my hopes veered between headlong advance and full-flight retreat. The helicopter came closer, maybe even circled overhead, then faded again until the engine noise disappeared. The boat rocked, presumably on the bed of the lake. Would it stay? Or would it right itself with a gigantic gurgle and engulf me in a rush of water? This was perhaps my worst moment on the lake.

But slowly my heart rate settled. The helicopter pilots might not have seen me, deep in Davy Jones's Locker as English sailors once called it. But they would have seen floating deck wreckage and, I was certain, gone for help. I lay back in the fading light of my torch and treated myself to a sip or two of spirit. Curiously, the very presence of salvation, the very possibility, changed there and then my mode of thinking. I began to think about Natalya

– about Joan Fowler – about what they were doing that Saturday night.

Mesmerically the floating vodka bottles touched and separated as the weak eddies of water washed them back and forth. In the light of my flashlight I watched four or five bottles, below the bare wire of my upturned bunk, floating together and dancing away from each other in a delicate gavotte. It was as if it had suddenly been given to me, like a good fortune teller's gift of perception, to read the secret of the dance. The soft chink of the bottles acted as a mantra, formed a pattern that lulled me, soothed me. I turned off the flashlight and lay in darkness. Perhaps I had a second in which I registered that my altered mental state might be ascribable simply to the thinning of the air in what remained of the cabin. But whatever the cause, a new sort of clarity had been given to me.

Borya Borchuk, the Ukrainian pork butcher, filled my senses like a slowly expanding Michelin man and, below me, the bottles clinked mocking laughter. There was meaning here if I could force it free.

The water, disturbed by a movement of the hull, now brought another half-dozen bottles together below the cross-wires of the bunk, clinking merrily in praise of folly. Because by then, of course, I knew it was folly. The fat, ambling Borya Borchuk was not our man. My seventh sense had rejected the idea from the moment I had found Natalya dead, but now I *knew*.

Somewhere out there, there was another man, inspired to the horrors he had committed not by simple blundering lust like Borya. A somehow smoother, less obvious man, a true Scorpio.

It was the only possibility. Natalya and Joan were illegally transporting children to the Norwegian border the night they were taken. It was inconceivable that Natalya's secret activity that night was unconnected with her death. So what had happened to the children? Why had we not found them frozen at Intersection 33? An accomplice had driven them away. In Natalya's Kamka. And the Ukrainian pork butcher was certainly not a man capable of arranging all that in twenty-four hours. *Ergo* . . . the abductor was not Borya Borchuk.

A lurch of the hull caused a quick wave to pass below me. The vodka bottles fled from each other across the ripples then raced together again with a single, bright explosive clink. Shattered, the pieces of glass dropped slowly through the water to the dark bottom of the boat. Now, suddenly, the raging desire to get out of here, to get back to the city, was intolerable.

What had the helicopter pilot seen? Wreckage, surely. But could he make out the shape of the boat ten, twenty metres down? Or had he passed over the lake as he had just passed over so many dozens of others?

I waited. An hour passed and then another with no hornet drone above me. I had fallen, not asleep but into a world of hazy daydreams: I saw myself hauled to safety by a pair of Navy divers from Severomorsk. I was wrapped in warm red blankets and flown back to a hospital where nurses whispered to each other in admiration and astonishment that I had survived.

My daydreams had faded with my hopes when I heard a new drone above me. I waited and this time it seemed to be here to stay. So low that I could even hear the chopping of its blades. Then the boat began to rock, causing the water in the cabin to slosh from side to side. Seconds later the high whine of a drill bit into the timber somewhere above my head. I turned the flashlight on the area of the drilling. The cabin wall (as it had been when we were upright) had been lined by my father with thin tongue-and-groove pine planking. The drill whined to a pitch of excitement. Sawdust, caught in the torchlight, filtered down. I reached up a hand to catch some. It was my first tangible contact with the outside world.

The drill stopped. A hammer blow rang out on metal, on the head of a chisel perhaps. The pine tongue-and-groove split in two. No water poured in. Instead a chisel blade widened the split and a shaft of daylight blinded me. I cried out in alarm. And, I have to admit, wonder. The hand grasping the chisel was beringed and manicured; the fingers slender and distinctly brown.

32

I HELD ONTO HER hand and wouldn't let go. From my place on the bunk I could not see straight up to her face. But that hand and wrist and the long slender arm, I was not going to lose. This was a moment of salvation. A moment for resolution. I thought for a few seconds. Let it be resolved, I said to the slender brown hand I was holding, that Constantin Vadim will never drink alcohol again.

I heard her voice. 'Constantin,' she said. 'Can you hear me?'

I croaked.

'Are you OK? Nothing broken?'

'Nothing broken.'

'This is what's happening,' she said. 'The boat's on its side and over half-submerged in the water. Dronsky's coming down from the helicopter with a chain-saw.'

I stroked her hand and on up her arm where the loose-sleeved parka had been pushed back.

'When the helicopter comes down lower, the blades will start churning the water. There's a lot of ice about. Chunks like small icebergs floating all round us. We don't want one of them to upturn the boat.'

Americans are so prosaic. I pulled on her arm. 'Come closer,' I said.

'This is as close as I get. I'm lying flat on the boat now. I've got my cheek pressed next to the hole. What have you been doing down there, for Christ's sake, trying to pickle yourself in vodka?'

'I'd given myself up for dead,' I whispered. I couldn't let my rescue pass without them knowing. 'Did you hear that,' I repeated. 'I'd given myself up for dead.'

'Luckily for you, Dronsky didn't,' she said flatly. 'He knew you had a boat somewhere out here among the lakes. Finding the abandoned Fiat gave us a pointer to the direction.'

'I must tell you,' I said. 'Borchuk, the pork butcher, is not our man. I have detected a gap in our thinking.'

'Forget Borchuk,' the voice above me said. 'We have. There never *was* a chance it was him. We're continuing the inquiry.'

I had no real time to absorb what Abby had said. I could hear the helicopter above the boat. Even hear Dronsky's voice as he was winched down. But the boat was rocking crazily, pieces of ice were floating against it with a dull thudding sound. With great reluctance I let go of Abby's hand.

I could hear the chain-saw now, hear the splitting and tearing of timber as Dronsky worked. The boat was rolling badly so that I worried about him keeping his balance. In the cabin, water rose from beneath the bunk, almost immersing me from below. Then what must have been a huge slab of ice rolled against the side of the boat. I knew it was bigger by far than the others by the way it dragged along the hull. I could hear Dronsky's voice, shouting up for the helicopter to back off. Then another, much heavier, thud made the ketch shudder. The angle of everything about me altered frighteningly. I was now clinging on the criss-cross wire of the bunk to stop myself sliding down into the water. Beneath the noise of blades and engine I thought I heard a cry of alarm. A man's hoarse shout. Then the clatter of the blades faded as the helicopter lifted away and Abby's hand slid back through the split timbers to grasp mine.

Only when I was settled in a private room in the Lermontov did Abby tell me what had happened. Dronsky had slipped as a massive piece of floating ice had struck the boat. Falling into the water he had been caught between the ice and the keel before the helicopter had been able to lift him clear. He was in Surgical now, Abby told me, undergoing investigation. Broken legs seemed certain. But it could have been very much worse.

33

A T THE LERMONTOV, I was checked over and given injections and allowed to sleep. When I awoke sunlight angled across the green linoleum floor. It was midday and a nurse delivered to me a razor and a cup of coffee.

Abby had left a change of clothes from the apartment. But she seemed not to have noticed it was a lightweight summer suit. As I got dressed, conversations in the helicopter flight to Murmansk came back to me. Dronsky had been sedated and lay bound in a stretcher. I lay in another stretcher with Abby sitting in a jump seat between us. I could hear Abby's American voice: the Ukrainian pork butcher was never our man. She and Dronsky had eliminated him within hours of finding Natalya. 'We're dealing, Constantin, with a much subtler mind than Borchuk's. Just as twisted. Just as sadistic, but much cleverer.'

I couldn't fight away the image of the Scorpio.

'One single fact alone rules out someone like Borchuk. Natalya, also, was found to have been injected with a heavy sedative . . .'

I flinched away from thinking about how that had been established.

'. . . A sedative that had been selected from her own surgical bag. This was not our Ukrainian pork butcher. No, Constantin. We're still looking for our man.'

I had arrived at the same conclusion by different means. 'I didn't want it to be Borchuk anyway,' I said. 'How could I accept that a halfwit like that was responsible for her death?'

In the winking red and blue lights of the helicopter, Abby's face had carried a frown. 'You don't get to choose, Constantin,' she said. 'You have to take whoever you get, whoever the evidence points to. Remember what happened last time.'

I remembered. I remembered my certainty that it was Lukas Roop, I remembered even my satisfaction at the idea. He fitted so much better than the pathetic Ukrainian pork butcher. But I also remembered the shame I felt afterwards.

*   *   *

When I had finished dressing I stood, shaky but undamaged, and made my way to Dronsky's room at the end of the corridor.

Both legs suspended in splints fifty centimetres above the bed, he grinned sheepishly and ran his hand across his brush cut. Medical examination had revealed no more than cracked bones. He had escaped the icy embrace without other damage. My relief was immense. He didn't want to talk about it.

I sat on the side of the bed. 'I have vague memories of you being something of a hero,' I said.

He nodded sombrely. 'It's not a matter of choice, Chief. It's printed there in the genes. I. S. Dronsky. Hero.'

I pointed at the splints. 'At least those legs'll keep you off further deeds of daring for a while. When are they flying you back to Moscow?'

A ripple passed along his thick eyebrows. 'I'm staying on the case, Chief. I'm getting in a phone and fax and a couple of helpers to process material. You can report findings to me nightly.'

'Wait a minute. You have Irina and the kids in Moscow,' I said. 'I don't understand. In a few hours you could be in the Pasternak Hospital, right round the corner from them.'

'Irina agrees I'm fine here for the moment, Chief,' he said.

When that firmness comes into Dronsky's voice, you know his mind's made up. We talked a few moments, not really about Natalya's death, circling the subject. I drew comfort from the fact that it had hit him badly. It brought us even closer. He had made all the arrangements I had been unable even to contemplate before I left, that night, for the lake. You won't be surprised I couldn't bear the thought of a post-mortem, of mad-eyed Lenny . . . I couldn't bear the thought of a funeral. I had said my own goodbyes to her in the Lermontov boiler-room. And left for the lake.

'You'll want to know . . .' Dronsky said. 'I took the ashes, Chief. And scattered them.'

I steadied myself with a deep breath. 'Where?'

He paused for a long moment, a frown wrinkling his brow high into his cropped hairline. 'Just scattered, Chief. Over the river. No place in particular.'

I thought about that. The whole thing seemed unreal beyond acceptance or refusal. But I trusted Dronsky to do the right thing for me. I said what came into my mind first. 'You did the right thing, Ilya,' I said. 'That's best.'

*   *   *

Lermontov Square is unrecognizable. Election posters cover every blank space. In the cold winds that caress them, coloured banners and streamers flutter and pirouette. One of the candidates has adopted the Sinatra song *My Way* as his theme tune and it is repeated endlessly from wall-mounted loudspeakers. The election has at least brought a little colour to our grey sprawling city.

As I came down the hospital steps, Abby was sitting behind the wheel of a car in the Lermontov senior-staff lot. I got into the passenger seat.

She looked out through the windscreen, then turned slowly to look at me. 'How are you feeling?'

I bobbed my head in evasion of an answer.

'You want to talk about Natalya?' she said.

'No . . .'

She pursed her lips. 'The received wisdom is we shouldn't bottle these things up.'

'Is that what you think?'

'It's what I *think*, Constantin. But I *act* the same as you. When my husband died, I hammered a cork in the neck of the bottle.'

I nod, I hope sympathetically. This is the first time she has mentioned a man, but at the moment I can't think about this woman's husband. About her distant loss halfway round the world in some American city I shall never visit. I'd like to think about it, feel for what she suffered, but here in the Lermontov forecourt I don't have that much heart. 'I have a lot of catching-up to do,' I said.

'Why not take some time off first?'

'No.'

'OK.' She turned in her seat. 'You think you're ready to be briefed.'

'Do I look ready?'

She smiled. 'In that linen suit, Constantin, you look something out of a rerun of *LA Law*,' she said. 'I should have brought a camera crew before you freeze to death.'

I shook my head. 'You chose the right suit. It's time to put winter behind us.'

She looked at me a moment, then glanced out at the packed, blackened snow in the gutters and raised her eyebrows slowly when she saw I was serious. Starting the engine, she drove out into Lermontov Square and took the road to the Nunnery.

'We followed up the leads from Lukas's story. Pinsk took a squad up to the hulks to see if he could locate the deserters Lukas talked about, but nobody's talking up there. The problem is we don't have anything to crack them with. Lukas stayed in the van. He's unable to identify any of them.'

I nodded. It was what I had expected.

We sat in silence for a moment. I knew I had to return to it. 'Your husband?' I half turned in the seat. 'What happened?'

'You're allowed one question only.'

'OK,' I said slowly. 'That's it. What happened?'

She breathed deeply. When she spoke it was quite rapidly. 'He worked the Drug Squad in Cleveland, Ohio. One Sunday morning he took our boy to a library meeting. It's where the kids talk about the books they just read.' She was quiet for a moment. 'You understand this is strictly the way things don't happen. There's a sort of agreement that a cop's family is not in play. Maybe even they didn't see Jackie in the car.'

'Go on.' My stomach was sinking. Why had I asked her to tell me this?

'The car was raked as my husband drove from the house. Heavy-calibre – one-in-five tracer. The Volvo exploded.' She stopped. 'Jackie was thrown clear. Twenty feet away. The elves or fairies must have caught him as he came down. There. That's all questions answered.'

I felt stunned as if struck. 'Your son . . . he's OK.'

'Thank God.'

'How old is he?'

'Five,' she said, 'and he's raised by his grandmother. That's the end of question time, Constantin.'

'Just one more.' It seemed important to know, to be able to visualize . . . 'Your husband . . .' I said. 'Was he a white man?'

She sat up straight. 'What the hell difference does it make?' she said, turning on me.

'I don't know,' I muttered, pulling back from her anger. 'I don't even know why I asked. Maybe we're all racists at heart, *all* Russians.'

For a moment we sat with a glass wall between us. Then she reached out and held my forearm for a moment, tight, as she had done when we escaped the election demonstration in Union Square. 'Forget it,' she said. 'Crazy things jump into people's heads. Sometimes they even say them.'

34

WE ENTERED THE Nunnery and crossed the busy lobby. The consul, Miles Bridger, was coming down the stairs. With his English wife, Isobel. They reached the hall and came towards me. I could see by the way they were both shaping up that they were going to say something about Natalya's death. And I knew I wouldn't be able to shrug them off as I had Abby.

They stopped in front of me. Isobel gave that special smile, lips pressed, eyes crinkling. She stretched out her arms and drew me to her. 'My poor lamb,' she whispered. She's English, remember. You have to understand she's not nearly as insincere as she seems. Not insincere at all, in fact.

When Isobel stepped away, Miles Bridger put his arm on my shoulder. 'It's no use saying I'm sorry,' he said.

'No.'

'Rely on Abby. She'll find the man. She has a hell of a reputation.'

I knew it was well-meant and I tried to respond. But there was a cool centre to this tall well-dressed couple that made even spontaneous, friendly gestures, like the arm on the shoulder, seem diplomatic or *practised*. As they left us Abby gave a small apologetic shrug before she turned for the stairs.

'One thing,' I said, 'before we get to the office. While I was away, did you take a statement from Lukas Roop?'

'I brought him in for a formal statement the day you left for the lake.'

It was a question I was afraid to ask. 'Is he OK?'

'No bones broken. Amazingly he's not planning to sue for assault – but maybe things don't go like that in Russia anyway.'

'What did you think of him?'

She stopped for a moment on the staircase. 'He answered my questions directly, no hesitations. Basically the same account he gave you. If you read him as a shy, reclusive guy then the picture fits. If you think he's holding out on us . . . then he's a suspect. He has to be.'

'We don't want to make the same mistake twice,' I said.

Her look held me for a moment. 'You mean *you* don't want to make the same mistake twice. Lukas was involved with Natalya and Joan. He was with them on the night they disappeared. He didn't speak up until you beat it out of him. OK, he knew that whatever they were engaged in, it wasn't legal. He was scared. But until we find our man, he stays on my list.'

In silence we continued on up the stairs. As we reached the top, Abby seemed to have come to a decision. 'There's been an important development while you were at the lake,' she said. 'I asked for an Interpol broad scan on child murders in Western countries over the last four years. It came up with three more cases of children or young teenagers carrying the K tattoo. In London, Hamburg and a third child, male this time, discovered a month ago just outside Paris.'

'Signs of sadistic abuse?'

'In all cases. Every one just slightly different.'

'But no leads on any of them.'

'In each case the bodies had been dumped, probably miles from where they were murdered.'

'You said an important development.'

'It is,' Abby said. We had stopped at the top of the staircase. For a moment we leaned on the banister rail looking down into the busy hallway below, then she turned towards me. 'The French autopsy measured the strontium-90 reading in the victim's bones. It was astonishingly high. They passed this on to the FBI who ran the same tests, then checked atmospheric radiation levels in all those areas of children's penal colonies where a K tattoo might have been used. The Kola region is the only one that could have given a reading that high. There's no doubt now that the green shoulder tattoo of all these children stands for KOLA.'

'So how did they get to the West?'

She inclined her head. 'It's the big question.'

'One thing we know,' I said. 'We know they weren't children taken across the border by Natalya and Joan Fowler. That'd put Natalya in Murmansk four or five years before she ever laid eyes on the city. Joan too. So who are they? Kids that have escaped from penal colonies over the last five years or more? Kids who have somehow smuggled themselves to the West and fallen into the wrong hands?'

She shook her head. 'Escaped? Fell into the wrong hands? No, Constantin. If that's the way it was, six children found dead in the West must represent hundreds, even thousands, who made the journey. Your escape would have had to have been a mass break-out.'

'So what are we talking about?'

'Figure it out,' she said.

I already had. At least I now knew what Natalya was fighting. 'In these numbers we're talking about a business.'

'No. In these numbers we're talking about a *trade*.'

We were both silent.

'We're talking,' she said slowly, 'about an organized slave trade in Russian children to the West.'

I needed a moment to look down at the queues of visa applicants below. When I turned to Abby I was swallowing air. I had had a son who'd disappeared. Of course hundreds of thousands of other children had been lost or disappeared in the mists of civil war, gone their own ways, fallen on their feet or not. I dragged my mind back to the present. 'So at what point were these children rounded up and shipped West. We now know they were once children from Kola penal colonies. We have a solid point of departure.'

'While you were at the lake I checked with a Colonel S. R. Fetisova, overall commandant of the children's camps in Kola. You know her?'

'Pure poison,' I said. 'I've had more than enough official dealings with her.'

'She's a brute. But completely unworried when I confronted her with the idea that these were children from her camps.'

'She denies it? Despite the tattoo?'

'She claims flatly there are no children missing. There have been a few escapes over the years but all escapees have been recovered. She checked the records. According to her, every camp reports all detainees present and correct. As for the tattoo, she still insists that it comes from Krasnoyarsk or Kursk or some other place.'

'She's lying. It is second nature to Fetisova.'

'She's made her mark with you, I see.'

'She was a couple of years above me at the university here. President of the Students' Union. Everybody could see she was destined for no good. It was no surprise when she took up camp work.'

For a few moments we stood looking down in silence as the daily work of the consulate continued below us.

'I understand,' Abby said carefully, 'that for you, this will always be first and foremost an investigation into Natalya's abduction. For Dronsky and myself, it's suddenly widened. However it works, these children found in the US and France come from Kola. Natalya and Joan were also doing something with children. Were they camp children too? We don't know. There's plenty we don't know. But I think we can work both investigations at the same time because they're essentially one. Can you go along with that?'

'I can go along with that.'

'It means treading carefully.' Abby's eyes flickered towards me. 'I'm saying I think there are big toes we could step on, Constantin. High officials.'

'You're giving me advice?'

'Yes,' she said flatly. 'I am. I don't want this investigation closed down before it's finished. Nor do you.'

Like all Russians, I'm quick to recognize a threat when I hear one: if I didn't play it by the rules, she was saying, I was off the investigation. 'No . . .' I said. 'I don't.'

She inclined her head slowly. Then she started along the corridor towards her office. We had made, I felt, a new alliance.

'You have me marked down for anything right away?' I asked her.

She shook her head. 'Just make your peace with V. I. Lenin again and take the day to settle in.'

'Good, then I've got time.'

She turned at her office door. 'For what?'

'I have to see Lukas Roop.'

Her back straightened in alarm.

'I have an apology to deliver.'

She hesitated. 'Sure.' She opened her door and turned to face me. 'Go ahead, Constantin.'

I got out of the car to find Lukas Roop waiting for me at the open door of his hut. He wore jeans and a dark blue sweater and looked almost relaxed as he came forward cautiously and shook my hand.

I was looking at the fading bruises on his face. 'I'm not sure I deserve that,' I said.

He looked at me for several seconds. 'We must put all that's happened behind us,' he said.

'That's generous,' I said.

'We'll speak no more of it.'

'OK.' I looked around at the closed hangar. 'You close on the weekend, of course.'

'Sasha must seek his pleasures,' Lukas said wryly. 'Murmansk can't supply the quality he claims he needs. At the weekend he flies to Petersburg or even Tromsö in Norway. Girls are different there, he tells me.'

'More expensive for sure.'

He made a gesture meaning either that Sasha didn't count the cost or had more than enough to pay anyway. 'Did you want to see Sasha too? He's leaving in a few minutes for the airport.'

'No . . . Just you.'

'What is it you wanted to ask me?'

'Shall we go in?' I said.

He looked up at the sky. 'It's a fine evening. Summer's almost here.'

I looked round at the banks of snow piled along the roadside. Certainly it was blackening and smoothed by the constant thawing and refreezing, but it didn't really have a summer look yet.

'In Rostov,' he said, 'by this time of year the beaches are crowded with people.'

In real life I had never seen a beach. Not a crowded, sunny beach.

'We lived in Novocherkassk but a train trip to Rostov on the *Electrika* was free if you dodged the conductor. Each week we made three or four trips to the beach.'

'We?'

'My sister Yelena and my aunt Valya.'

'I know about Yelena . . .'

'Valya was a lot younger than my mother. Not much older than Yelena. She's only in her fifties now.'

'You don't keep in touch.'

'No. I heard she comes back here sometimes, in the winter I suppose.'

'Why the winter?'

'She works in Sin City. It's what she does. As far as I know she's never done anything else. But she's getting old for that now. What was it you wanted to see me about, Constantin?'

234

he said with that sudden formality I had come to associate with him.

I listened for a moment to the rustle of melting snow dropping from the fir trees on the side of the hill.

'I've come to say that I should be disgusted at what I did to you.'

'Should be?'

'It's only the memory of my desperation to find Natalya alive that makes me even consider the idea of pleading some justification.'

He smiled. 'Is that an apology, Constantin?'

'I'm trying to be honest with you, Lukas. I'm trying to say that in the same circumstances I would certainly find myself doing the same thing. And in the same circumstances I should certainly regret it as much as I do now.'

He looked at me as only he did, smiling and flinching at the same time. 'I accept your apology, Constantin. Can I offer you a drink? I don't drink much myself. But I've a good lemon vodka buried behind the hut.'

'I appreciate the offer,' I said. He was a man who *imposed* a certain formality on relations with him. 'In the circumstances, I particularly appreciate it,' I added. 'But I have to get back to the city. Thanks, Lukas.' I paused. 'Perhaps there *is* something I wanted to ask you. Did Natalya or Joan talk about any further operation, something they'd planned after that Saturday?'

'I think something was said about an operation some three weeks ahead. I'm not sure when.'

'Three weeks would make it about now.'

He shrugged. 'Yes.'

'I've been thinking about Natalya's absences from home,' I said. 'I think these operations took place either on Saturdays or midweek, Wednesday.'

'It could be. The first I took part in with Dr Vadim was on a Wednesday. The last one was a Saturday of course.'

'So the next could have been planned for this Wednesday.' I said.

'Perhaps. But I don't see it makes any difference now.'

We both turned as a white Mercedes took the corner of the hangar at too great a speed, turned recklessly on the concrete apron, powered towards us and came to a controlled stop, the Mercedes grille not a pace from where we were standing.

The door flew open. Sasha was dressed for a night out on the town, silk shirt, gold medallion and tan leather jacket. His face, I noticed, was flushed. With drink was my first impression. I was wrong.

He jumped out of the car and came straight at me, his finger prodding the air. 'I want a word with you, fuck your mother.'

It was only then I noticed that in his left hand he carried a heavy automatic pistol, held down, against his leg.

'It's all forgotten, Sasha.' Lukas tried to push his way between us but was thrust aside by his younger brother.

'You see this,' Sasha said, raising the big pistol and waving it in my face. 'I'll shoot your fucking teeth out if you lay a hand on my brother again.' The low sun sparked off the bright barrel of the gun.

'Back off, Sasha,' I said. Now, brothers, this I admit was pure American cop-show bravado. I didn't think he was going to shoot me but the waving gunsight mounted on the barrel could alone have torn my lip apart.

I reached forward and eased him back with the flat of my hand but he reacted immediately, snapping the pistol across my forearm. The pain shot up almost to my elbow and he grabbed the front of my jacket. 'I'm not afraid of the militia, Vadim. I pay your bosses too fucking much a quarter to need to worry about people like you.'

'I've made my apologies to Lukas,' I said, the pistol barrel digging under my ear. 'It's between us. Now take this thing out of my face and I'll go.' Even *in extremis* we try to force concessions.

He pushed my head with the flat of his free hand. 'Go,' he said. 'Now. And don't come back. You understand me.'

I reeled a step or two backwards. Removed from the gun I felt braver. However much he was paying some senior militia officers, he would have been a maniac to have used it. 'I'll come back if I have to,' I said.

The thunder of the three shots, loosed skywards, reverberated off the hillside. I nodded to Lukas and walked, not too quickly I think, a little stiffly perhaps, to my car.

35

THAT AFTERNOON I stood in the boiler-room at the Lermontov Clinic, thinking of what Natalya had suffered here. Suffered as she watched Joan Fowler's even more immediate suffering at the hands of her killer.

What twisted my stomach was the idea that I knew so little about the man who had abducted Natalya. Abducted Natalya and murdered Joan Fowler. Was he tall, short, dark, fair . . .? Married perhaps, as Andrei Chikatilo had been married, to an unsuspecting wife?

Hands deep in my pockets, I walked the length of the low room. From time to time I kicked at the piles of crumbling coke which would now never be used again and watched the dust rise in ghostly shapes through the yellow light.

He had walked this cavernous, barrel-vaulted space, too. Stalked back and forth in front of his two victims roped to the wall. Jeered and insulted and lasciviously humiliated them. Yet I could still draw some comfort – *some* – from the fact that Natalya had cheated him in the end.

Near the open mouths of the old cast-iron furnaces, their upper lips hooked back, I sat on a green slat bench. Cast into the front of each of the four iron monsters was the name Shakley Bros, Boilermakers, Sheffield, England. In front of them, the pokers and slag-rakes were of rolled iron bar, three centimetres thick and over three metres long. In my imagination I could almost see the angry red of the boilermen's faces as they broke up the thick crust of glowing slag and raked it out onto the cement floor beneath.

Why had I really come here? I had not told Abby where I was going. Was I here because in the figure of the demonic boilerman I could come closest to the shape of Natalya's killer? But however satisfying to my imagination the figure of the boilerman seemed to be, I knew it didn't work in practice. Those four former boilermen, and anyone who held the job before, no longer had a key to the boiler-room. Only Maklova and Dr Gabriel Potanin had possessed keys to the new American locks.

I was unaware of hearing anything, but something caused me to look up. Potanin was standing in the doorway. Not everybody's idea of Murmansk's most distinguished psychiatrist, he wore his old tweed suit and an open-necked check shirt. More or less shaven. Hanging from his hand was a bottle he held by the neck. 'I heard you were down here,' he said. 'I thought you might . ...' He raised the half-litre.

I felt the dust coating my lip. 'Why not?'

He crunched across the coke and sat on the bench. What was I to make of this man, this jumble of posturing resentments and fears? His interest in the deaths of Joan and Natalya *could* be professional. On the other hand, it could be just that desire to be involved in the crime that he described as a characteristic of serial killers. I glanced at him, not disguising my doubts.

'You don't much approve of me, Inspector, do you?' he said.

'An incompetent doctor can do a lot more damage than an incompetent militia inspector.'

'You think I'm incompetent?'

'You faked your degrees.'

He pointed upstairs with the bottle. 'See who else you'd get to run that place. Of course, it shouldn't be me. I lack the academic qualifications.' He laughed. 'But I haven't lost sight of the fact that they're human beings locked up in there. That's why, for instance, I allow Zoya her beloved bom-bom, much to the disapproval of your American colleague. Bom-bom is all Zoya has to give. She's intensely proud of being wanted.'

'I won't argue with you on that,' I said.

He placed the bottle on the floor between his knees. 'I might not be able to offer much help to the exalted FBI, but I'm sure I could help you, Inspector.'

'How?' I licked my dusty lips again, my eye on the bottle now. The coke dust felt gritty in my throat but that was tolerable compared with the nausea I was suffering. Every time I glanced up at the shiny metal ducting of the new gas boilers my stomach turned over.

'You're presented with a classical locked-door mystery.' He picked up the bottle and pointed with its base. 'Main door from Clinic – new American lock.' He swung the bottle to point to the iron doors at the far end of the boiler-room. 'New locks replace the rusting nineteenth-century bolts and mortises on the rear door.'

'Conclusion – whoever was using this boiler-room to hold his victims must have possessed one of the new keys,' I said.

He unscrewed the cap on the bottle and handed it me. 'Further conclusion,' he said. 'Either Sonia Maklova . . .'

'The maintenance manager.'

'Or myself.'

I tipped the bottle and drank a good thumb. It was the first edge of recovery time. This bottle would either clear my fortnight's hangover away or bring it back full strength.

'You should know,' Potanin said, 'that Sonia Maklova and myself have conducted a relationship for the last two years or more.'

I handed him back the bottle. 'What does that tell me?'

'At the very least it tells you I am not morbidly desperate for the company of women.'

'You came down here to share that with me?'

'No.' He stood up, shaking the bottle as a lure which I must follow. 'I came to solve your locked-door mystery.'

'And thus get yourself off the hook.'

'It puzzled me as much, perhaps even more than it puzzled you and your colleagues. You see I *knew* all keys were safely in the hands of Maklova or myself. But you only had our word for it. So what did I do? While you were away I began questioning Igor Semlovsky. You remember, one of the four last boilermen we had here. He has regressed this last six months to a sort of sullen autism. It wasn't easy.'

'Did he have any answers to give?'

'Finally, yes. *The* answer.'

I stood up. 'Let's hear it.'

'Easier to show you,' he said. He took a good mouthful from the bottle. 'Over here, in the corner.' He waved the bottle towards a row of brick arches just short of two metres high and of about the same depth and width. Each arch fronted an area which was recessed in the wall as extra storage space, probably for the finer-quality lighting coke – the fuel used to light the furnaces from cold.

We walked towards the row of arches. On the way Potanin handed me the bottle and picked up a shovel that had been left by Pasko's team on a pile of coke.

When we reached the far wall he swung into action. There was no other verb for the way he attacked the coke piled like a black snowdrift against the wall. What was remarkable was the fluency of his movements, his control of the heavy shovel, the powerful slide and thrust generated by his broad, thin shoulders. In seconds the air was full of dust, rising like river fog towards the overhead lights.

'There . . .' he said, straightening up. 'Igor was right.'

I looked down and saw nothing.

'Give it a moment,' he said and pulled me by the sleeve clear of the dust cloud. His eyes were rimmed like some Himalayan monkeys I had once seen pictures of. His thin hair was bouffant with sweat and dust. I passed him the bottle and he drank, swilled vodka in his mouth and spat it out onto the coke heap.

'What is it?' I leaned forward into the miniature dust-storm. As it settled I saw the outline of a doorway set low into the back of the arch.

'A way in,' Potanin said.

'Not if you already have to be on the inside to shovel a half-tonne of coke dust out your way.'

'The coke was piled like that by Captain Pasko's militiamen. Given the conditions perhaps you can't blame them, but they didn't do quite the job your American boss would have liked.'

'We're colleagues,' I corrected him. I was staring at the low door. 'Where does it lead? Out to the physic garden?'

'Igor doesn't know. It was just an old door.' He almost jumped across the pile of coke he had made and ducked low into the recess. Reaching out for the handle he wrenched on the iron door. With a squeal of metal across the floor the door opened easily.

A damp cold draught slapped my face.

We descended a long ramp into a brick-floored tunnel. There was enough borrowed light from the boiler-room to see that one or two ancient gas brackets still hung on the wall, one with a broken globe.

'We need a flashlight,' Potanin said. 'Give me two minutes.' He ran back without waiting. I could hear his crunching footsteps across the boiler-room floor and the door open and close.

There was not much for me to see. A few metres of brick tunnel closed in total blackness. I picked up a piece of broken brick and threw it as hard as I could into the darkness. It seemed like an arrow fired at night until a faint rattle announced its fall to the floor thirty or more paces ahead.

Was this the way Natalya's killer had come? At least the way he had come to take the key which would allow him to drive the kidnap vehicle from the physic garden?

I was bursting to move further down the tunnel. And incapable of moving through the pitch blackness before me. Like a schoolboy, I reached up and turned on and off one of the green brass gas taps on the neck of the broken lamp.

To my surprise I could smell gas.

It was many years since gas had been used to light the city. Back perhaps to the days of its founding in 1916 by the fated Tsar Nicholas. But I supposed it was quite possible that some gas still lurked where old pipes remained and perhaps gathered, particularly below ground level.

I turned the tap again, heard a faint hissing sound and flicked my lighter at the setting where once a delicate mantle would have burned. The gas popped and spluttered. A tongue of flame a hand's width high leapt up and burned yellow and blue.

Using the faint light I walked a little way along the tunnel. When the next gas bracket was just a bare outline I turned the tap and lit the flare. There were broken pieces of mantle in some of the lamps and the light then hissed and glowed an intense yellow, much as it had a hundred years ago.

In an underground brick tunnel, lit by ancient gas lamps which might fail any moment, a tunnel whose purpose or outlet I could not even guess at, the atmosphere was tensely evocative. A man had passed this way. Probably several times. And ahead of me now at the top of a slight incline of the brick floor, I could see the faintest outline of a rectangle, a door lit from the other side.

I had come thirty or forty metres. Not more. But I was disorientated by being underground, by the flickering gaslights and the dripping darkness above my head.

I came up to the doorway. I stood for a moment with my hand on the iron handle. I had no idea what I might see on the other side.

Carefully I turned the handle. I could feel the tongue of the lock retract, easily as if oiled. I pushed the door a few centimetres and an edge of light flooded my face.

I could hear footsteps, some sort of grunting mutter. I threw open the door and found it hard not to vomit.

I was staring down at an eviscerated corpse. The man with the knife in his hand was green-robed and mad-eyed.

'Fuck your mother,' Lenny shrieked, dropping his scalpel to the floor with a clatter. 'Where did you spring from, Inspector?'

I reached out and steadied myself against the door. There were at least three other bodies stretched out on mortuary trolleys. In shock and disgust I was close to fainting.

'Come over to the rest area,' Lenny said, peeling off his red rubber gloves. 'You look like a man who could down a half-litre.'

I walked with him to the small room off the main mortuary used by people who had come to identify relatives. A samovar was boiling.

'Listen, Lenny. I'll take tea.' I sat down hard on the black leatherette sofa. 'And a cigarette if you have one.'

He gave me a cigarette and busied himself making tea. 'Now tell me, Inspector,' he said, his back to me. 'What were you doing down in the tunnel?'

'You know where it leads?'

'Of course. But that door's normally kept locked now.'

'Have you ever used the tunnel?'

'Many times. In the old days when they had real furnaces, we used to trolley a binful of unwanted entrails a day through the tunnel to the clinic boilerman. Simple, hygienic. Did they think of that when they installed these new American boilers?'

He gave me the tea and I sipped it hot. Within seconds it had settled my stomach. It's one of the very few things we Russians have in common with the English. We both believe passionately in the restorative effects of *chai*.

Distantly I could hear Potanin shouting through the tunnel.

Lenny's head came up. His eyes glittered. 'Who in God's name is that?' he said, his voice low.

I got up, carrying my tea. 'It's Dr Potanin,' I said. 'From the Clinic. Just tell me, Lenny, you said that door was normally kept locked.'

'Management orders.'

'Where's the key now?'

'God knows, Inspector. Used to hang beside the door.'

'And how many people knew that? Knew where the tunnel led?'

'As many as I've had mortuary assistants, Inspector.'

'Do you have a list?'

He laughed.

'You must have some sort of a list.'

He rolled his eyes.

'One of them could have been the killer of my wife.'

His face composed marginally, but I think death had become so everyday to him that he was almost inured to the suffering of the living.

'Take the last two or three years, how many men have you had working here? How many men knew where that door led?'

He shrugged. 'The last two or three years? Listen, Inspector, work down here is given as community punishment for minor offences. Two weeks. A month. It saves sending them to jail. In the last two or three years I've been through more mortuary assistants than you could count on the fingers of every hand here.'

He was gesturing to the boxes set into the wall.

When Potanin emerged from the tunnel, bemused, alarmed and waving his flashlight, he stopped and looked slowly around him. I watched. In shock myself, I couldn't make up my mind. Was his air of bemusement real surprise? Or was it no more than a carefully calculated act?

36

ONCE THE ICE begins to melt, Sin City looks the way I imagine the wreckage left by the sinking of a great liner. A few lights from still-working generators shine across the cluttered water. The prevailing wind drives empty boxes and broken timber rafts, plastic bottles and piles of unrecordable floating garbage along the shoreline. Most of the tents, the clapboard huts and the stalls have been rolled and packed and hauled by horses or ancient, coughing lorries onto the steep bank. They are being loaded up to be carted south to a summer site in one of the small towns on the river below Murmansk. Only the permanent structures, with the trapped garbage bobbing between them, remain in the lake – the dance floors, the onion-dome whorehouse churches, some of the high walkways, all resting solidly on timber posts or anchored rafts until the ice and the customers come back again in October.

Militia Station 18 had been dismantled with the rest of the city. Its officers, now operating from rubber boats powered with an outboard motor, were supervising the vast heaving deconstruction. A mile or two further on, if you take the airport road, the lakes become uncountable at the base of each low line of hills. There are a few lights from small electric booster stations and the houses of their solitary guardians, but they quickly disappear in the low undulations of the hills. From time to time, a flicker of light in the northern sky illuminates the whole landscape, momentarily obliterating even the cluster of house lights a kilometre or two along the valley to which I was heading.

Twenty-five years ago kids like Roy Rolkin and myself used to call this building the Admirals' Palace. We all suffered then from a desperate need for relief from the verbal functionalism which produced the description, Soviet Naval Building 6.

The palace is in fact a well-built stone and wooden structure, with a bell tower and a general shape, an English travel journalist had written, vaguely reminiscent of the old Royal Navy head-quarters at Greenwich, England.

As the Russian naval establishment declined in the Yeltsin years, the admirals moved away and their palace no longer served a purpose. It had been sold off and the private buyer, Madame Badanova had told me on the phone, had leased it to her for a peppercorn rent as her campaign headquarters – close enough to the city centre, far enough from the strong-arm gangs of Candidate X.

As I arrived that night, she was out on the forecourt to greet me, arms out, hugging me. We both, I'm sure, felt strongly the similarities in what had happened. Her husband dead in a helicopter accident, if indeed it was an accident, and Natalya dead at the hands of a lunatic.

'We have a duty to life,' she said, 'you and me. A duty to go on living in the face of all that's happened. We're very different people, Constantin, but I sense we've important things in common. It's not just that, in our different ways, we're both survivors. I think you and I, Constantin, have something to *give*.'

I didn't tell her that I'd been floating in alcohol in a capsized sailing-boat for the last week. I didn't tell her that it was only through the perseverance of Dronsky and Abby Cunningham that I was here tonight. But what she said rang a bell, a deep-throated, sonorous bell. I was going to rise above defeat. And I was going to find the man. I was going to avenge the death of Natalya.

We stood together at one of the tall sash windows and looked out towards the city.

'I want us to fight together,' Madame Badanova said. 'I believe we're both ready to fight for an older, nobler Russia than the murderous dross we've seen in this past century. We both believe *our Russia* can be resurrected.'

She could, I felt, have been speaking for me. I too believe in something quintessentially Russian. Under Communism I had not been educated to God, but I feel strongly there are invisible connections between people and events, connections that go back to the past, and yes, reach forward into the future. Often enough, I believe it's only a bizarre figure like the old woman at Sin City who can interpret these invisible connections for us. Why that should be I don't know. But I do know there is a great compulsion in me to believe that only through an understanding of these ethereal bonds linking past and future can Russia's present be looked upon with sympathy.

Madame Badanova had lit a black Russian cigarette and the rich tobacco smoke stung my nostrils as it drifted with the wind. 'I see us as natural allies, you and me, Constantin. I think you share my feelings.'

Now I'm not really used to this openness. My first wife used to say that there were aspects of the Vadim personality that were more English than Russian. But then she always regarded the Vadim personality with less than awe.

Madame Badanova had turned towards me. 'Constantin. I want you with us, when we start this journey.'

'Journey?'

'Tomorrow night is Declaration Night. The night when the candidates in this election officially declare themselves. The beginning of our journey.'

'It's a foregone conclusion,' I said. 'As soon as the people of Murmansk know your opponent is a vicious criminal serving time, they'll turn out for you in their tens of thousands.'

'Don't be so very sure, Constantin. Come with me.' She continued talking as we entered the house, passing through the busy, poster-covered hall into the main salon. It was a large square room, low-ceilinged. A huge relief map covered the world's oceans from Murmansk three-quarters of the way round the globe to Vladivostok. In this room, presumably, the old Soviet admirals played out their war games. A round table with at least a dozen chairs occupied one corner. Several large sofas were grouped before a wood fire at the end of the room.

'On election night, Constantin, we'll hold the party to end all parties here.' Then, as if speaking to thin air, she said: 'Put the Fortunin tape on, will you, Jay.'

From one of the high-backed armchairs, a girl rose. She was in her mid-twenties, dressed in black jeans and sweater. She said nothing – just smiled her wide-mouthed smile in acknowledgement. Her blonde hair undulated as she walked across to the TV in the corner. She was, I remembered, the adviser I had pegged as American at the Austrian coffee house the day Pasko released me from custody.

'Constantin . . . you've never met Jay, of course. She was my husband's public relations consultant. Jay Dellerman . . . Constantin Vadim.'

The girl came slowly back across the room.

'Jay's American. Russian mother. United Nations upbringing. She appears to speak every language in the Western world.'

Jay reached out her hand and shook mine, green eyes on mine. 'Constantin Vadim,' she said. She clearly felt no need to add to the greeting. I thought she was the most strangely self-contained woman I had ever met.

'Now let's look at Valentin Fortunin,' Madame Badanova said, pleased, I thought, with the impression her adviser had made. Jay turned back and knelt by the cupboard beside the television screen.

A sudden succession of images burst from the centre of the wall-screen and slowed to what was probably the news show, *Kola Round-up*. A man, escorted by four uniformed militiamen, was climbing the steps of the Lermontov. He was broad-shouldered, wore his hair cropped, dark glasses and a black overcoat draped across his shoulders.

'Valentin Fortunin,' Madame Badanova said. 'Released from prison on compassionate leave.'

The commentator took up the story as Madame Badanova, Jay and myself watched Fortunin as he passed along the familiar corridors of the Lermontov, turning left at Coronary Care: 'Tonight as Valentin Fortunin's mother Olga fights for her life, the man who could well put himself forward on Sunday as the next governor of the city has been granted leave to visit her.'

Valentin Fortunin disappeared in to an intensive-care cubicle and the commentator returned. 'Arrested during the tenure of office of Governor Anton Badanov, Valentin Fortunin was convicted and sentenced to ten years' imprisonment as head of Polar Cities group of hitmen operating in Moscow and Petersburg. If he can present, at the ceremony on Sunday night, the signatures of ten city councillors, we may well have the solution to the identity of the mysterious Candidate X who is clearly spending freely in the pre-election process.'

The camera, which had been focused on a scratched hospital-cream door, closed in and Fortunin emerged. His thin upper, and jutting lower lip gave him a petulant air. In answer to questions about his mother's health he was, however, barely controlled. 'She is hardly conscious,' he said, tears welling in his eyes. 'She's fighting for her life. We can only pray.'

He began to walk forward, with his militia escort, slowly so that the camera could stay with him. In answer to all questions about the declaration, he jutted his lower lip and said only: 'We shall have to wait and see, won't we?'

'A hundred thousand dollars' worth of free publicity,' Jay said, snapping off the set. 'I wouldn't be surprised if the old lady wasn't in the best of health.'

Madame Badanova smiled. 'What I like about Jay,' she said to me, 'is that she never even pretends to be fair to the opposition. Now leave it, darling,' she said to the American girl. 'I know you can't take your eyes off him but the next few minutes are for Constantin's and my ears alone.'

Jay's eyes flicked towards me and I stood as she walked, unhurried and even stately, from the room.

Madame Badanova smiled again. 'I have something to ask you,' she said.

She put her plump hands together and for a moment studied the rings on her fingers. I thought how much Lenny at the Lermontov morgue would like to get a chance at them then stopped myself . . . What in God's name was I thinking of?

'You've probably not noticed it yourself, Constantin,' she said slowly, 'but because of all that's happened, the disappearance of Natalya, your arrest, your discovering her . . . because of all these things you attracted a great deal of favourable publicity in the press and television. Did you know that?'

'All this when I was up at the lake trying to drink myself to death?'

She nodded. Her chins, I noticed, all came together as she did so. 'Wrongfully arrested, maliciously accused, justified in the tragic manner . . . you became, in the last weeks, quite a heroic figure.'

I sat down in astonishment. Open-mouthed, I dare say.

She smiled. 'You had no idea?'

'Is this all really true?'

'A little exaggerated perhaps, as I'm inclined to. But basically true.'

'So what do you want from the tortured hero of Murmansk?'

'I think,' she said, 'we're about to enter one of the dirtiest election campaigns in the all too short history of Russian democracy.'

'One look at Valentin Fortunin is enough to make me think you're probably right.'

'I'm going to ask you to act, not for me alone, but for the sake of a fair election, as one of an electoral troika.'

'What's that exactly?'

'Three commissioners are to supervise the coming election. One is appointed from Moscow, and one each by the two leading candidates. That means one by Candidate X and one by me. The actual duties of the troika are mostly to put a gloss of democracy on all that happens. But they are empowered, on a majority vote, to validate or reject the election process.'

'This is one of those honours . . .'

' . . . that may not be entirely welcome? I can see that, Constantin. And I know you're in the middle of a vital investigation. But I need you. I think Murmansk and the whole of Kola does.'

'Can I think about it?'

'Not for long.'

'Let me take a turn outside. Fifteen minutes.'

She took my hand, turned it up and planted a heavily lipsticked kiss in the palm. 'I'm putting weight on you, Constantin,' she said. 'Believe me, I wouldn't do it unless it were vitally necessary.'

I passed the silent security men and walked into the gardens. The lights of Murmansk were over on my right and I could see the stadium floods blazing in the distance.

Leaning on a stone balustrade I tried to think about the offer. I have political views along the lines of Madame Badanova's but I'm not a political animal. Yet I already knew I was going to accept. It's people that sway me I suppose in the end, not ideas.

A waft of wind-borne cigarette smoke made me wrinkle my nose and turn. Jay Dellerman was leaning her back against the balustrade. She wore a black pea-jacket against the spring chill. 'Do you use these?' She held a packet of Red Leb in her hand.

'I've given up on giving up,' I said. I crossed to where she was standing and she flipped the top of the pack with her thumbnail and offered it to me. We went through the minor ceremony in silence.

'Were you struggling with the Angel of the Lord when I interrupted you?' she said. 'Or some other angel altogether?'

I looked towards the lights of Murmansk. 'I was thinking how much work needs to go into this city to reach just a decent everyday degree of corruption, like Boston or Glasgow or Nice.'

She inhaled deeply on her cigarette, and blew smoke in rings that floated out across the snow-covered lawn. 'I like the city,' she said. 'It's a frontier town. It makes me think of the Klondyke in the 1890s. It's exuberant, it bubbles with life. Koka-Kola's a great name for the region.'

'How long have you been here?'

'Six months. A little more perhaps. I came up from Petersburg with a job in the US consulate here.'

'You worked at the Old Nunnery?'

'I was assistant to Joan Fowler in Petersburg. She asked me to come up with her when she got her appointment.'

'So you knew her really well?'

'Of course.'

'Did you ever meet Natalya, my wife?'

'No,' she said. 'Never.'

'What sort of woman was Joan Fowler?'

'She did her job. She liked guys, but I guess it wasn't impossible to know she could swing both ways. Is all this significant?'

'Some way. At just this moment I can't work out how. What made you move on?' I said. 'What made you leave the service?'

'The consul and I never really saw eye to eye.'

'Miles Bridger?'

'You know him?' she asked.

'I've met him a few times. What happened?'

'He likes girls.'

'So do most men.'

She smiled and flicked her cigarette into the water. 'I'd met Governor Badanov a number of times at commercial functions. He had already hinted there was a job waiting for me at City Hall. So when Bridger got too heavy at the Nunnery, I moved over.'

'And Madame Badanova asked you to stay on.'

'I like what Madame B does, Constantin. I like the way she does it. This city is going to disappear into a black hole if she's not elected.'

'Russians have a way of hanging on,' I said. 'A way of surviving. I think even with Valentin Fortunin as our next governor, there'd still be a Murmansk in five years' time.'

'And the kids?'

I looked at her. 'The kids?'

'Aren't they the ones you care about? The street kids that run like mice over this city. What will Valentin Fortunin do for them?'

'Not a lot. Despite the breast-beating, no-one ever really has. Way back before the turn of the century, Mrs Yeltsin announced she would head a presidential commission on the welfare of Russia's children.'

'What happened?'

'The moment the old autocrat had won his election, there was never another mention of it.'

'They're a central part of Madame Badanova's programme, Constantin,' she said. 'Improving the conditions in the children's penal colonies, too. Which is why you can't stand aside. You have to commit. You have a part to play in this. Madame B intends to get things done, Constantin. She means it.'

'She means it. But can she deliver?'

'Listen, you know Madame B. You know you can trust her. Valentin Fortunin is well-placed among the *racketiry*. An electoral commission can be fixed in five minutes. She needs someone who can't be bought on this commission. Otherwise she's dead in the water.'

I gave it two more seconds' thought. In Russia it's more important to have power than justice on your side. I was thinking of the trade in children. 'I'll go down and tell Madame Badanova she's got an electoral commissioner,' I said. 'I'll tell her you sold me.'

'It's my job after all,' Jay Dellerman said with a lift of the eyebrows.

37

I WAS BACK IN the apartment for the first time in two weeks. First I'd spent ten minutes coughing concrete dust in the basement where each tenancy is allocated a wire-caged cubicle. From our cage, I brought out a pack of six collapsible cardboard cartons. I tucked the pack under one arm and climbed the cement steps to the lobby and took the lift to the tenth floor. As I let myself in it seemed impossible that Natalya wasn't going to walk in from the kitchen, or call me from the bath.

I poured myself a thumb of vodka and took my six-pack into the bedroom. I opened cupboards, drawers, and began some of the grimmest work I've known. If I knew one thing it was not to stop, not to dwell, not to remember, not to wonder. Natalya's clothes and shoes went into four cartons. Books, handbags and a whole host of miscellaneous stuff filled another. Photographs, her medical certificates, some paintings we'd bought on a trip to Petersburg, a few trinkets of no value any more, all went into the last carton. I was stacking them in the narrow hall when I looked up to hear the key turning in the lock.

For some reason, it had not occurred to me that Abby was still living in the apartment.

She came in and closed the door behind her and her eyes rested on the stack of cartons as I straightened up.

'I've been packing up,' I said. 'Natalya's things.'

She stood just inside the door, making no attempt to take off her black sheepskin coat. 'You want me to go? I could take over Dronsky's bed at the Nunnery – maybe it would be best.'

'I don't know . . .' I let out a long breath. 'I don't know anything much anymore. Except that somehow I'm going to find him. I'm going to catch him if I have to work on here long after you and Dronsky have gone back to Moscow. Catching this lunatic, that's all I think about.'

'So do you want me to go?'

'No,' I said. I leaned back against the wall. 'It might surprise you, but I'd prefer you to stay.'

'I hoped you'd say that.'

I grimaced.

'Don't think I'm feeling flattered,' she said. 'At times people settle for any kind of company.'

'That's about it,' I agreed.

'I know how you feel,' she said. 'You want to get drunk with me?'

'Why not? Drunken people tell each other secrets.'

'I'll risk that,' she said. 'Tonight at least.'

I woke in darkness. I was lying on my back. Not pitch darkness because looking up I could see the underside of a table. Information feeds through slowly. My right hand is holding something. Experience, and indeed likelihood, tell me that it's the neck of a bottle.

Now here's something interesting, brothers. My left hand is holding something too. Something small and rather flat. With thin leather straps attached. I lift my hand and hold the object of mystery before my eyes. A woman's watch.

I roll over onto my right shoulder, being careful to keep the bottle upright. This proves unnecessary. The bottle is empty. The label reads *Jack Daniels* and lower down, *Sour Mash* and that describes pretty well what my mouth feels like.

Getting up on my knees, abandoning the bottle, I crawl from under the table. Abby Cunningham is emerging from her room fully dressed. She wears a cream shirt and dark green suit which I think I've seen before. Black pumps instead of her usual leather knee-boots reveal very shapely legs. She asks me if I would like coffee, pauses for a moment and feels it necessary to add: 'It's morning.'

I mumble something she rightly takes for yes to the coffee. I use the sofa to help myself to my feet. Abby has gone from the room. A black wave of guilt sweeps over me. I remember nothing of last night. Or do I? I sit on the sofa and think.

Abby comes back and pulls open the curtains. All men know that this first drawing of the curtains can be an act of aggression in a woman – but Abby is smiling her wide-mouthed smile. 'You couldn't look worse,' she says amiably. 'Coffee is coming.'

Perhaps I fell asleep again. When I opened my eyes she was standing in the middle of the room.

'About last night.' I forced myself to my feet.

'You're going to apologize,' she said, walking back to stand at the window. 'I can feel it coming on.'

My head reeled in panic. 'Do I have anything to apologize for?'

She turned slowly. 'No more than I have.'

I blinked my eyes at her. 'Please . . .'

'Take it easy, Constantin,' she said. 'Nothing happened. And if it had, it would have ended in farce.'

'Farce.' I sat down heavily.

She pulled her lips into a wry smile. 'Your efforts to disrobe me, if that's what they were, never got further than removing my watch.'

I stared at her in shock. 'I tried to do that? Disrobe you. To *undress* you?'

'Don't worry, there was nothing personal in it. You were on automatic pilot. I could tell by your eyes.'

I pushed myself back onto my feet. Two unsteady paces across the room and I let the watch tumble into her outstretched hand. I felt terrible. Guilt swamped me. 'Was that all there was to it?'

'Plus a lot of drink and a fair amount of musing on the condition of man.'

'Yes, I've been told before. When I have a drink I get concerned about my fellow creatures. You don't hold that against me?'

'I don't hold anything against you.'

'What angle did I take – on the condition of man?'

'You were very anxious to talk about slavery.'

'Slavery?'

'You made the point several times that slavery in one form or another has been part of Russian life for centuries.'

'To Russians it comes naturally.'

'Russian serfs and American slaves, you reminded me, were freed in the same decade, the 1860s. You made a big point of that.'

I scratched my head. 'Did I say why?'

'I think you might have but by then I was asleep.'

'Where did you sleep?'

She pointed to the sofa. They say you can never look at a woman the same way once you've slept with her. Making that adjustment isn't too much of a problem to me. You either feel very good about it or very bad – or somewhere in between. But what if you're not sure? I can tell you it's an unhappy experience to be left to mull over, brothers.

I tried to ease away from the possibility. I made a casual flick of the hand which nearly unbalanced me. 'Before you went to sleep, you must have talked, you must have talked about yourself.'

'I guess.'

'So what did you tell me? Any secrets?'

She spread her hands. 'All I have.'

And I don't remember a thing. 'You really talked, did you?'

'Much, much more than I intended. I was pretty drunk too.'

Had she really told me more than she intended? Much more? I looked around the room. 'Let's have another drink,' I said. 'It might set my memory going.'

Her hands came up, in prohibition this time, and I noticed how pale the palms were. 'No more drinks,' she said.

'Jog my memory about last night at least. About what you told me. Do you realize I have absolutely no idea what kind of a woman you are?'

'Remarkably like others, I'd say. On last night's performance.'

Performance. 'Did something really happen between us?'

She looked at me for a long time, eyebrows raised. 'No.'

'Look, I'm sorry, Abby, more than sorry. I'm devastated I don't remember.'

'I told you, Constantin. There was nothing worth remembering. That's it – all of it. Finished. OK?'

I was silent, totally chastened. 'And did we really talk about your past?'

'In some detail.'

I searched for the word. *Schmuck*. What a schmuck I am! What an insult to offer a woman like this. To offer any woman. 'Just remind me of one thing then,' I said in a desperate attempt to trip the levers of memory. 'One thing about your past.'

'How far back do you want to go?'

'I don't care. Far as you like.'

'OK. One fact. I told you that my great-grandmother had been a slave in North Carolina and that at home in the US I had her $325 bill of sale to a Mr Augustus Cunningham, a goodly proportion of whose genes I no doubt have.' She looked towards the kitchen. 'Coffee's ready. Get yourself a shower. We have to be on the road.'

38

SUNDAY AND THE Nunnery was empty of consular staff, the entrance hall looking more than ever as it did in the days of its occupation by Roy Rolkin and his secret police unit.

We climbed the broad stone stairway in silence. Perhaps she was still thinking of last night. For myself I was trying to wrestle with the contradictory facts we were presented with. I liked to call a spade a spade: the man responsible for the deaths of Natalya and Joan was sexually insane. Whether Potanin was right that the dolls were taunting us, or Abby was closer with her bizarre idea of an apology, our killer was insane. So why had Natalya and Joan been abducted? Because they were two women that he had happened to come across, alone on a deserted blizzard road? Or for some reason connected with what they had been doing, transporting children to the safety of the Norwegian border? Was our killer inspired, in other words, by opportunity or calculation? It seemed it had to be one or the other. There was no possible way I could conceive that it was *both*.

We had reached the corridor that led to our offices. 'I could use some more coffee,' I said. 'How about you?'

Abby nodded heavily. I was pleased to see she wasn't entirely immune to the effects of last night.

'I'll make a pot and bring it along to your office.' I pushed open the door to the small kitchen where we made tea and coffee. V.I. Lenin was crouched on the shelf below the store cupboard. A carton of long-life milk lay on its side, ripped open with considerable ferocity. V.I. Lenin's right front paw rested on the carton, rocking it backwards and forwards to increase the flow of milk.

In flagrante! I thought to myself. At last I've caught the beast red-handed, so to speak. I expected, I'm bound to admit, a powerful reaction on the cat's part. A quick lift of the milk-soaked chops, a guilty screech as he leapt from the shelf.

To my astonishment he did nothing of the kind. For a second our eyes locked. Then, quite casually, V.I. Lenin looked down at the torn carton, rocked it again with his paw, achieved an adequate flow of milk onto the shelf and calmly began to lap at it as if I were not there.

My reaction was to shout or stamp or clap my hands. But I did nothing. There was an intimidation in his feline indifference that I had not yet got the measure of.

I put on the coffee, deciding against trying to direct some of the spilt milk into a jug or catch the trickle which fell from the edge of the shelf to the floor. Near subliminal flashes of last night teased the hollow recesses of my hungover mind. Was it possible that Abby and I really had had sex together? Did she believe me when I claimed not to remember – or did she take that as a cowardly evasive device to avoid confronting my guilt when I thought of Natalya? But I didn't feel guilt towards Natalya. I felt guilty because I was unable to remember what happened. I felt guilty because Abby would never believe that. I suppose that meant I felt guilty about Abby.

Western drinkers tend to doubt the degree of amnesia a healthy Russian can achieve in a single session. But it's all true, brothers. After such sessions – try as I might to summon up remembrance of things past – I usually draw a complete and humiliating *blank*.

I made the coffee in speed and silence. With the coffee and cups on a tray I backed out of the kitchen. V.I. Lenin glanced up but he was too busy, perhaps even too indifferent, to remark my leaving.

I stood in the corridor between our offices in the Old Nunnery, listening to Pinsk questioning Lenny.

'I'm going to have you checked out, Lenny.'

'Checked out?'

'You know what I'm talking about. According to Inspector Vadim, you could have passed easily back and forth into the Clinic's boiler-room. Do you deny that?'

'No. Why should I deny it? Last year when the furnaces were working I was disposing of all my garbage that way. I told the inspector that.'

'And the connecting doors are still open. In other words you could have dragged them through this way.'

'Them?'

'Dr Vadim and Joan Fowler.'

'But I didn't, fuck your mother!'

'You knew Dr Vadim?'

'Everybody in the Lermontov knew her. If you saw her, you asked who she was. Any man who claims he didn't is a liar.'

'Did you know Joan Fowler?'

'Intimately,' Lenny said. 'I had her on the table.'

'You bastard,' Pinsk hissed at him. 'Did you ever meet when she was alive?'

'Never. Rich American women are outside my range.'

'What were you doing on the weekend of the 5th/6th? The Saturday night?'

'When Natalya Vadim disappeared?' There was a long pause. 'It's my own business.'

'No longer,' Pinsk said.

I could imagine Lenny's eyes crossing in fury. He dominated his small dead world down in the mortuary. He was not used to being called to account. 'I took off for a weekend in Norway,' Lenny snarled. 'I can give you the proof you want. But listen, I have a wife. I told her I was working that weekend.'

I turned away and walked on into Abby's office. She looked up from the desk. 'Nothing from Lenny?'

'I don't think there will be.'

'What about his assistants? There'll be some sort of record surely?'

'Of everybody who worked in the mortuary over the last few years? You expect records?'

'Yes. Employment records. Not too much to ask is it?' I could hear the edge in her voice.

'Look, Abby,' I said. 'When are you going to stop thinking about Murmansk as if it's Manhattan? We've just come out of a civil war, for Christ's sake. Half the people who fought in it were on the losing side. They were Anarchists. Outlaws. They've changed names. They've gone underground. They've got new papers.' I kept my tone low and reasonable but I had an important point for her here. 'You know what happened to your own embassy in Moscow, yet you talk as if we can sit here and tick suspects off a list like Father fucking Christmas, ho, ho, ho!'

She stood up and walked around the desk to stop a metre in front of me. 'All right Constantin,' she said. 'But understand how hard it is for foreigners too, trying their best to make sense of the whole crazy scene here. We're in an apparently wealthy Western-style society. Mercedes and BMWs, Jaguars and Rolls-Royces are common as at Cape Cod in summer. But half the society is dysfunctional. You have a good working hospital like the Lermontov – and a psychiatric clinic attached that looks like something out of the Marquis de Sade. Some of the best computer minds in the world come from Russia – but the life expectancy of men is medieval and ninety per cent of high-school girls polled say their ambition is to become a prostitute. What the hell is someone like me to make of a country like this?'

'So what are you doing here? Why are you on your second Moscow tour?'

'Because I love the place,' she almost shouted. 'I shouldn't. I should hate it. I should hate its fumbling drunks and racism and unmade roads and its callous authorities and ruthless *racketiry*. And I do. But I still love the place.'

She let her hands fall to her sides and turned towards me. 'That's about the size of it. When I ask for records of everybody who worked in the Lermontov's morgue over the last few years, I ask in hope. Like a Russian. Not in expectation. Like an American. Get it?'

I opened my mouth to speak but she had already grabbed her coat from the chair and stormed out of the room. I can't claim to understand it, brothers, but I had a very disturbing feeling this was somehow all about last night.

39

I DRIVE BACK TO my apartment. I still have the dinner-jacket Vassikin the black-marketeer lent me. I look at the clock and find I'm in good time. Getting dressed, I notice items that belong to Abby, a file on the table, a coat thrown over the back of a chair, nothing much, but just at this moment I don't want them there. I go round picking them up and put them in her bedroom.

Then I stand at the window in white shirt and satin-striped black pants and look down ten storeys to the port. A cruise motor vessel, brilliant with small bright cubes of light, lies at anchor among the dark shapes of cargo boats. *That* night, I remember, it was a tanker. But tying the black tie in front of the mirror even, even with a thumb of coriander vodka by my side and *A Bark for Barksdale* playing in the background, does nothing to recreate that Saturday evening so impossibly long ago. I confess it, brothers, I have this terrible need to wallow. Or, at least, to relive those last minutes I spent alone in the apartment with her.

I work at it. Hard. A conscious evocation of that last evening together. Natalya rising from the bath . . .

But it doesn't work, dammit. I throw the vodka down my throat, pull on the jacket and, without another glance in the mirror, set off for City Hall.

Murmansk needs snow to humanize it. Even with enormous crowds milling around in Union Square, without snow the city has a nakedness about it. It is light well into the evening now as the short Arctic summer rushes upon us, but it's soft light, muted by the thin mist rising from the gulf, a light more charged with memories than any harsh southern light could ever be. Why, I wonder, did all the great painters scurry for the south?

I've taken a cab but we seem now to be part of an impressive convoy of vehicles approaching the City Hall building. Militiamen with all their traffic-control equipment, coloured flashlights, white gloves, armlets, and screeching whistles direct us through the crowd. But it's not only crowds here tonight, of course. There are hamburger stands and rock groups performing, and Union Square is hung and draped and decorated with more banners than we have seen since the heyday of Communism.

Every two or three minutes or so part of the crowd sets up a chant for Madame Badanova and it's answered immediately in a challenging roar from another part of the crowd. And suddenly all the confusion becomes clearer and you see that the militia are holding two vast hostile groups apart to allow our cars and taxis to approach the building. On my left are Madame Badanova's supporters, a friendlier, less menacing lot, I would say, than those on the other side. The bare tattooed arms are prominent here on the right, the short sheepskin or black leather jackets, the painted faces mutilated with rings through nose and eyebrow. And some normal everyday folk of Murmansk City too, I'm bound to admit. Black and red are the colours of this group and large white discs are waved above the heads of the crowd with the thick plain X of the soon-to-be-revealed candidate.

I mount the polished sandstone steps and show my invitation to the militia sergeant. He lets me through the smoked-glass doors but inside there is an almost equal throng of people, better-dressed than those outside, I have to admit. Almost every man here is wearing a black tie; the women are all in sequinned or red-sashed evening dresses and expensive pumps bought in Moscow or Petersburg.

Over the tops of heads, bald or carefully coiffed, I see Jay Dellerman. In her long black sleeveless dress she is slithering very efficiently through the press of people.

'God, Constantin,' she rolled her eyes. 'What a crush! Here's your boarding-pass to the actual ceremony in the main salon. All the rest of the well-dressed *hoi polloi* get to see it on the wide screens in any room they can force their way into.'

She gave me a ticket with a row and seat number. 'Looks good,' I said, glancing at it.

'Front row, centre seat next to the aisle. Madame Badanova insisted. As electoral commissioner, you can't act on stage, but you do get the best seat in the house.' She waved a second ticket just under her chin and looked around ostentatiously. 'You didn't bring a guest?'

'No,' I said, puzzled.

Still pretending to look over my shoulder . . . 'Not a beautiful black FBI agent in sight,' she murmured.

'You're well-informed about the electoral commissioner's colleagues.'

She turned down her lips in a grimace-smile. 'It's my job.' She took my hand and led me through the crowd towards the bank of elevators and waved over one of the sergeants. 'The main salon for Inspector Vadim.'

'Yes, Miss Dellerman.' The sergeant reached out and pressed a button. Outside I could hear the chants increasing in volume. It was impossible to make out which candidate the chants favoured. Jay cocked her head, listening.

'How many candidates are expected to declare?' I asked her. 'I've seen posters up for about twenty-five separate parties.'

She smiled. 'You must know the way in your own country, Constantin. Anybody who can get the backing of a few city council members and can afford to get a thousand posters printed stands as candidate. Among them, lots of guys doing time.'

'But most of them don't stand a chance. So why are they doing it?'

'Not all the tinpot, thousand-poster candidates just fall by the wayside. The smaller ones, maybe. But for anybody likely to pick up a few thousand votes, the election funds of the main contenders, Madame Badanova and Candidate X's Party for New Russia in this case, are dipped into. The minnows take the money and pull out, endorsing whichever candidate pays them.'

'And Madame Badanova goes along with this, too?'

'She's refused.' Jay shrugged. 'She says it's buying votes. Nothing more or less.'

'What do you think?'

'It's also my job to point out the political risk. It means all the spare votes are snapped up automatically by Candidate X.'

'So back-alley pay-offs are a built-in part of the game.'

'As I told Madame B – if she wants to play, yes.'

This wasn't the place to debate much-needed reform of the Russian State. 'Is she here yet?' Lights were flickering on the elevator control panel in front of us.

'Of course. She's been here all day working on her speech upstairs. For the moment, she still occupies her late husband's gubernatorial penthouse apartment.'

'And Valentin Fortunin, will they be bringing him straight from gaol for the ceremony?'

'Assuming Fortunin is Mr X, I guess so.' The lift had arrived; the sergeant was holding the door open. She held my look. 'See you after the show.'

I inclined my head and she was gone, slipping bare-shouldered through the crowd like a dolphin through water.

As I came into the main salon I was surprised at the number of American voices around me: young businessmen, probably members of the new organizations set up by the US Aid and Trade Bill. With their American wives or Russian girlfriends, they collected in small groups before they made their way to their seats.

These were comfortable wooden armchairs arranged in two blocks on either side of a central aisle in the huge square room. Less than half the guests were already seated, mostly slewing in their seats to see who was coming down the aisle. The rest made their way with a deliberate slowness, checking tickets against row after row, giving ample time to see and be seen.

Gradually, with many pauses to greet acquaintances, greetings which varied from discreet handshakes to hugs and backslapping and shouts across the width of the main salon, the audience took its place. Cigars were lit. Champagne corks popped. A lot of people here were planning to celebrate *something* in style.

In one knot of young men and attractive women, I saw Sasha Roop. He was waving a cigar in one hand, a bottle of champagne in the other. Catching sight of me, he left his friends and sashayed between the rows of still empty seats. He clamped the cigar expertly in his teeth and pulled out another, offering it to me. 'Think of it as the pipe of peace,' he said. 'It's the best I can do.'

Guardedly, I shook hands with him.

He turned towards the stage. 'Now that you've become an admirer of Lukas, you'll enjoy the heads he made for the pageant.'

'Which side are you rooting for, Sasha?' I asked him.

'Must get back,' Sasha said, ignoring the question. 'May the best man win.' He grinned. 'Old Russian saying, I believe.'

I took my centre-aisle seat. Curtains hid the stage from view but I could hear, behind them, the last-minute touches being added.

The music, when it began, was Alexei Stolpin's new and highly popular *Medley: Russian Land and Russian People*. It visibly settled the hall and behind me I could hear the shuffling and loud voices diminish. When the house lights dimmed almost all the guests had taken their seats.

The Stolpin came up now to fill the salon with its powerfully Russian resonances of folk-song and soldiers' choirs. It was irresistible stuff. Feet started stamping in time to the music. You would have thought that we were, all of us seated in this great hall, a citizenry united.

Silence fell as the music faded. The curtains slid apart on a darkened stage. A dinner-jacketed man in his seventies, with sleek Caesar-cut white hair and alert blue eyes, came out from the wings and walked to the microphone. Thumb and finger on his bow-tie, he surveyed the crowd and gave us a smooth, self-deprecating grin. For a moment there, I thought he was about to offer us a rendition of the opening lines of *My Way*.

Instead he introduced himself as Vladimir Zinoviev, senior official of the Justice Department in Moscow, chairman of the troika supervising this election. 'To make up the troika,' he said, 'allow me to introduce Inspector Constantin Vadim whom you will all know, if only through the recent tragedy which has befallen him.'

There was a subdued respectful outbreak of hand-clapping. I stood and turned towards the guests and clapped back in the Russian fashion that foreigners find so amusing.

'The third member of our trio is the distinguished militia officer, Captain, now Major, Boris Pasko, who, for the past years, has ably run the Missing Persons Bureau here in Murmansk. And who, we can be sure, will pursue any missing votes with the same relentless enthusiasm for success with which he seeks out missing persons.'

Pasko rose. He was a few rows back and I had not noticed him. He wore his best militia dress uniform, but he still managed to look as though a bear had slept in it last night. He finished acknowledging the applause and turned to acknowledge me.

In my pocket my pager began to vibrate. The message read: *Call me, Chief. Urgent – Dronsky.*

I got up and moved quickly to the back of the salon. The Moscow man, Zinoviev, was presenting Madame Badanova. I glanced quickly over my shoulder. A spotlight picked her out seated on a dais on the centre of the stage. She was wearing a dress of yellow and green satin. From her supporters, the applause mounted reassuringly. Overwhelmed by noise, I slipped past the sergeant, out into the corridor, found myself a quiet corner and dialled my cellphone.

It rang once. 'Dronsky,' the familiar voice said.

'It's me. Constantin.'

'Where the hell are you Chief? What's going on?'

'What do you mean, what's going on? I'm at City Hall. It's declaration night.'

'I'm talking about Abby. Have you two had a fight?'

'Not really. This morning, she got a bit hot about something. I don't know what.'

He was silent.

'Is that what you paged me about?'

'Chief . . .' The voice was patient, but with effort. 'She came here to visit this afternoon. I told her it wasn't a good idea for the two of you to be sharing the apartment together.' I could almost see him shaking his head resignedly. 'You never do understand, Chief. A woman needs a little space.'

'You mean I'm crowding her.'

'In a manner of speaking.'

I thought about that. 'Last night, we had a few drinks,' I said defensively.

'I know.'

'But this morning I thought we were on the best of terms.'

'All the same, you should think about making a change.'

'You want *me* to move out of my apartment? You want me to move in with V.I. Lenin?'

'Just pack your things as soon as you get back tonight, Chief, and move into the office. Don't worry about the cat.'

'You mean a couple of days,' I said, grimacing at the horror of it, 'and we'll be watching TV together while I scratch him companionably behind the ears?'

'Who knows? How about tonight for the move?' he said. 'OK, Chief?'

'Where's Abby now?'

'At the Nunnery.'

'OK . . .' I was about to ring off. 'Hold it, Ilya. Is this what she asked you to tell me?'

'I suggested it was a good move. She agreed. You'll do it?'

I was baffled. 'If you think it's best.'

'I do.'

When Dronsky speaks like this he has a sort of natural authority. The natural authority of solid common sense. I knew I wasn't going to cross him. Not on solid common sense – even if it meant waking tomorrow with the reek of fishburgers in the nostrils. 'I'll move out tonight,' I said.

I returned to the main salon. The applause was thunderous. Men and women were on their feet, shouting, waving bottles of champagne. Standing just inside the door, I couldn't see much of what was happening on the stage. Some sort of children's pageant was marching across it. Young children dressed as serfs carried black poles on which were spot-lit latex heads of famous writers, fashioned, I'd no doubt, by Lukas Roop. I saw Gorky go by, quickly followed by Sholokhov. I saw the plastic head of Murmansk's adopted writer, Mikhail Lermontov, float past on a black pole carried unsteadily by a girl of about seven. The theme, outlined by banners, was the Triumphant March of the People's Artists.

Will we never outlive these mind-numbing myths? Quite as often as our great writers have illuminated our world, other Russian writers have conspired to conceal its grim truths. 'Left, left, left!' sang Mayakovsky but failed to mention that that road led straight to Stalin's death-pits. Lermontov, I take to more naturally, perhaps because I understand him less. *A Hero of Our Times,* he calls his novel. But the hero is a hero-villain, as Russian a Russian as you could ask for. Maybe here, we begin to touch upon the truth, brothers.

Then suddenly, from the ceiling, powerful spotlights cut through the smoke filled air in Madame Badanova's green and yellow colours. To the right, red and white lights beamed down on Candidate X's side of the stage. On tip-toe, and stretching my neck, I could just see Madame B standing at one end of a long table, waving vigorously to the people in the auditorium. I couldn't help noticing that the green and yellow spotlight confused the greens and yellows of her satin dress.

I changed position to get a look at the other end of the table. It took me remarkably long seconds to realize that Candidate X, red-lit and beaming like Beelzebub at his triumphant emergence from darkness, was the old friend of my youth, *Roy Rolkin* himself.

40

'MADAME BADANOVA IS giving a drinks party in her apartment,' Jay Dellerman said, slipping into the seat next to me. 'You're among the honoured *invités*.'

Around us it was a chaos of champagne toasts and stamping feet and snatches of song. Madame Badanova and Roy had left the stage. The children's pageant continued, unnoticed by the guests in the auditorium.

'Are you OK?' Jay said, looking at me.

'It mustn't be allowed to happen.'

I was shell-shocked. Roy Rolkin as Governor of Kola! It was a grotesque idea. For a country that was supposed to be stumbling towards a workable democracy, governors like Roy Rolkin would set us back years.

'It mustn't be allowed to happen,' I repeated. 'What happened to Valentin Fortunin?'

'Nothing,' she said. 'He's still in gaol. It was all a carefully organized smokescreen by the opposition. While Madame B's supporters believed Fortunin would be a walkover nobody thought it necessary to pull out the stops.'

This was Roy. I could see him planning it. I could see that contented cat-that-got-the-cream smile as he watched Madame Badanova's organization mark time, safe in the belief that they had only the criminally well-connected but none too bright gaolbird, Fortunin, as opposition.

'At least now we know where the real opposition is,' Jay said. 'He's standing there in front of us.'

I think I scowled at her. 'You don't know Roy,' I said. 'He's a will-o'-the-wisp.'

'Roy . . .? I don't know *Roy*? Meaning *you* do?'

'All too well. We're blood brothers.'

'What!'

'That's according to Roy. We grew up together.'

She looked at me anxiously. 'Which camp does all this leave you in?'

'You have my word for it, Jay,' I said fervently. 'Even more strongly in Madame Badanova's camp than ever.'

We joined the party. Noise crashed around my head, reminding me painfully of the bad night I'd had last night. Madame Badanova was in the middle of a press of enthusiasts and waved to me cheerfully.

But Jay Dellerman was anxious. The more I told her about my childhood and teenage years with Roy Rolkin, the more anxious she seemed to grow. I could see this in every movement. That extraordinary self-contained element that I had noted when I first met her had dissolved. Why am I so often more wrong about people than right?

We crossed the room to sit at a side-table furthest from the band.

'If Roy Rolkin were elected governor, what would his real programme be?' Jay asked. 'What would be his priorities?'

'You heard his campaign speech tonight. To make Murmansk Dynamo into a team that no longer loses in double digits every Saturday.'

'Be serious, for God's sake.'

'I am. Sport, booze and girls are Roy's priorities. Beyond that he'd continue to line his pockets and his associates' pockets with whatever came along.'

'Clever,' she said. 'The sport angle. Stadium ward is the biggest ward in the city. That whole district's going to be packed with fans. Pumping money into Murmansk Dynamo is like buying votes.'

'One of Roy's gifts is to pare things down to essentials. If Stadium ward is that important to this election, I'm not surprised he's already got it singled out.' I paused. She was leaning across the table staring at me intently. 'Why are you looking at me like that?'

'Among other things, I'm wondering how far you can be trusted. Trusted to tell you the truth.'

'What truth?'

'Madame Badanova's campaign was flagging before Roy Rolkin announced tonight. I've been working on the figures.'

'They look that bad?'

'Short of someone quietly stealing thirty thousand Rolkin votes, we're going to lose in the city. And the city has eighty per cent of qualified voters in the whole Kola region.'

'You're not suggesting *we* steal the votes?'

She flicked back her hair. 'Screw politics,' she said. 'At least for tonight. I want to hear more about you, Constantin. You don't seem to fit any of the Russian moulds.'

'I fit all of them, only too well,' I said. I poured champagne for her. 'What about you . . .?'

'You've seen lots of American girls like me. We're all over Russia. Advisers, consultants. Mostly we're just Russian-speakers who lay claim to vote-winning experience we don't have. You'd be astonished at the number of phoney CVs girls like me carry around. My own CV makes claim to have managed three separate winning Congressional campaigns.'

'Not true?'

'No. I worked on all three but the only time I got into the key policy meetings was when I brought in the coffee. CVs like that hold up the Western world these days. Why should Russia be different?'

'You sound as though you're saying you're here while the bandwagon rolls. But that's all. A moment ago you were wondering how far *I* could be trusted.'

She pursed her lips. 'Look, Constantin, your country is in a mess. Recurrent economic crises . . . the regions threatening to go it alone – Siberia already gone . . . politics the most dirty and dangerous trade going. In Russia, I'm my own woman, Costya. Madame B is jungle smart, she knows that. I don't even try to keep it secret.'

I knocked back my glass of champagne. 'I have to go,' I said.

She made a faint disappointed moue with her lips but was already rising to her feet. 'Drive me home, OK?'

I enjoyed the drive. We talked a bit more about Madame Badanova, about the election. I couldn't go back to my apartment and talk to Abby. She had no interest in the election – found the time I spent on it slightly weird, I expect, while we were investigating matters of life and death. But, for Russians, politics *is* a matter of life and death. Always has been. In the twentieth century, thirty or forty million Russians found the grim truth of that.

I drove through a quarter of Murmansk that had been bombed during the Civil War but was close enough to the city centre to merit rebuilding. Along the length of Turgenev Street new apartment blocks were rising on either side . . . 'Here we are,' she said. 'Thanks for driving me home. Come and see my new apartment.'

The apartment block Jay indicated I stop outside was still being worked on. The whole of the front hall was grey concrete lit by strings of builders' lights. Scaffolding caged one side of a staircase wall where plastering had started. The untiled floor was thick with dust from crumpled cement bags. Late as it was I could hear an electric drill at work, and a few odd snatches of song from the floors above.

'Jesus,' I said. 'You live here?'

'It's going to be brilliant,' she smiled. 'But not yet. The company was on a penalty clause. The date passed and the builder committed suicide or went off to the Crimea for the winter. About twenty apartments are finished. I'm one of the lucky ones. They're working way past midnight to get the public parts finished.'

We climbed the stairs to the third floor. Large rectangular holes in the outside walls offered a view of the street below. Someday they would be windows. Up here on Jay's floor, the corridor had at least been swept of cement dust. Multicoloured cable trailed everywhere and the walls gave off the peppery smell of drying plaster.

'Not bad,' I said.

She gave me a bleak look. 'Just wait.'

We entered a superb apartment. My flat in Gorshkov Tower would have fitted into the main room alone. I looked around while Jay disappeared to make coffee. The furniture was fresh-looking, painted Swedish. One whole wall was covered with books. Impressed, I stepped up closer. I frowned. The books were English, Russian and French but I found none of the titles familiar.

I reached for one at random. It was in English and entitled *Walter*. Inscribed below the title was Anonymous. 'Of its genre,' she said, coming back into the room, 'extremely well-known.'

'Is it a novel?' I said. I have this pride about my English studies. I was, to be truthful, slightly piqued that I didn't recognize the book.

'Autobiography,' she said.

'Who was Walter? Walter Pater? Raleigh? Walter de la Mare?'

'No-one knows. It's Edwardian pornography at its most fascinating. A true insight into the English at work and play.' She waved her hand to the bookshelves. 'I'm a collector,' she said. 'Of serious pornography. Strange what gems can still be found in Russia even after the puritanism of the twentieth century. But then, in such times, pornography often flourishes best. Look what I found in the Tishkin flea market in Moscow last time I was there.'

She took down a large-format book with a dull grey thin cover without any sort of title. 'Published under plain wrapper,' she said, 'in 1932.' She flicked the pages. I saw Aubrey Beardsleyesque drawings of men and women, men and men or women and women in every sexual entanglement imaginable. Then the men's faces. Stalin, of course was unmissable. The sycophantic Voroshilov, the sinister Yeshov the poison dwarf, the sad-faced Kalinin whose wife was heading for the Gulag.

I grunted.

'You don't find it amusing?'

'I don't find anything that gang of mass-murderers did amusing.'

'I'm sorry. I struck a wrong note.' Casually, starting with the skirt, she began to undo the buttons of her dress. 'Nevertheless a piece of quality Russian twentieth-century porn like that is a collector's item.' She moved, making the material flare away from her legs. She walked into the bedroom. 'I have to take a shower,' she said.

I stood looking at the door slowly swinging open. In a mirror I saw a flash of naked flesh. 'Perhaps,' I said, loud enough for her to hear beyond the half open door, 'we should talk about the election.'

'OK,' she called. 'Come through.'

I heard shower water fizzing against glass. 'Come and talk to me.' Her voice rose over the hissing and gurgling of water.

I walked through the bedroom from where I could see into the small tiled bathroom. I could see her outline, behind the glass, the image of a thousand advertisements for soap and shampoo and age-defying gels. She turned, came close to the glass and mouthed the words: *Join me?*

I fell back a step. 'No,' I said. 'No offers, Jay,' I shouted above the hiss of water. 'No offers I can't refuse. I'm already suffering enough guilt for a dozen sorely tempted saints.'

I turned and walked back into the other room and sat down, pulling the copy of *The Autobiography of Walter* from the bookshelf. He, Walter I supposed, was in a graveyard on the English coast. Two finely built fisherwomen were laying flowers on two very recent graves. He was admiring their bodies as they arranged the flowers. He liked strong arms, our friend Walter, and deep bosoms. A few seconds' conversation revealed they were sisters who had just buried their husbands who had been taken by a fierce summer storm at sea. Walter didn't hesitate. He offered them two shillings each. They were poor women in need of anything they could get now that their menfolk were gone. The women consulted between themselves and came back, one blushing furiously, the other white-faced with anger – and agreed his price.

I could hear Jay moving about in the bedroom. I felt a shame I couldn't define. I stood up and called out to her. 'Listen, Jay,' I said. 'I'm washed out. I'll call you tomorrow.'

She emerged almost immediately, swirling a blue robe round her bare shoulders, and stood tying the belt. 'It's not late,' she said.

'No,' I felt as if I was hopping from foot to foot. 'But it's getting later.'

'Undeniably,' she said. 'You know, the crazier you get, Constantin, the more I find I like you.'

'You ain't seen nothing yet.'

'Don't worry about it, Constantin,' she said. 'I'm a good loser, OK?'

I nodded and turned towards the door.

'You want to take *Walter* with you?'

'No,' I said. 'No thanks.'

'Take these, instead.'

She had something in her hand. She held it up. A set of house keys. 'Keys to the apartment,' she said. 'Anytime you want to use them.'

I'm not sure how I reacted but she smiled. 'Not for now, of course. I can see that you won't want to make use of them just yet.' She paused, again with a faint smile. 'But the time could come . . .' She swung them gently to and fro at the level of my bow-tie. Then dipped her hand and deftly let them drop into my side pocket. I moved to take them out but her hand was already covering the pocket.

A Russian gentleman, I thought, should not refuse. Worse than that, a Russian gentleman could make a hell of a fool of himself wrestling with a half-dressed woman to give her her keys *back*.

I kept the keys.

Driving home, I called the Nunnery. Anna Danilova answered. Didn't she ever go home?

'Do you know the whereabouts of Agent Cunningham?' I asked cautiously.

'She called in to say she'd be having dinner with the consul, Mr Bridger.'

This would give me time to get back to my apartment, pack my things and get back over to the Nunnery. Kola's only sophisticate had suffered enough embarrassment at the hands of American women for one evening. The enigmatic Abby Cunningham would be more than I could take.

'Before she left she put an envelope addressed to you on your desk,' Danilova was saying.

I asked her to get the message and read it to me. A minute later she was back on the other end of the line.

'What does Agent Cunningham say, Anna?'

'The message, very well.' I could hear the crackle of paper and the crackle of Anna's disapproval. 'Message reads, Inspector . . .' She cleared her throat. 'Message reads: *The black chick says she's really sorry.*' There was a pause. 'End of message.'

I got to my apartment. Once in, I poured myself a drink and pulled out a duffel bag. Using one hand (the glass occupied the other) I pulled open drawers and threw socks and shirts into the unzipped mouth of the duffel. On the bed next to it I placed a couple of suits. Picking up the bag, I went back to the kitchen to refill my glass.

Passing through the living-room I looked up at a sound to my right shoulder. Abby was standing in the doorway of her bedroom. She wore jeans and a sweater. No shoes, no make-up. 'Hi,' she said.

'Hello.'

She leaned against the door-frame. 'Did you get my note?'

I nodded. 'Sorry for what?'

'You know.'

Was she sorry for forcing me out?

'You don't have to go,' she said, adding to my confusion.

'Dronsky thought it best.'

'You're a big boy now, Constantin. You can decide.'

'Not without a drink. Will you have one?'

'Coffee.' A beat as she glanced at me. 'For you too, uh?' She came into the room and took the duffel from me and dropped it on a chair. 'It's late. Think about moving in the morning.'

'Maybe . . .'

I made coffee and we sat and talked about the coming election and what it might mean if Roy Rolkin won control of Kola. I told her, what I knew to be true, that any lead that Madame Badanova was relying on as the wife of a successful mayor was probably already close to being wiped out. Roy Rolkin had no scruples. He also had a huge network of new business contacts in this city. And the secret police, beginning to re-form as the new Missing Persons Bureau, was still staffed by his old friends.

'There's an American on Madame Badanova's staff . . .' She brought it up.

'Jay Dellerman? You know her?'

'We keep a track on all Americans involved in Russian political organizations. She's moved around quite a bit in Kola politics.'

'Are you saying watch her?'

'No. Although I gather she's easily watchable.'

'Some would say.'

When we parted for the night she extended her hand and shook mine. 'Sorry again,' she said, standing in the doorway to her bedroom.

'Abby . . . Sorry for what, for Christ's sake?'

But she had already closed the door.

41

ROY ROLKIN'S CHAUFFEUR picked me up at eight o'clock the next morning. Standing in the doorway of my apartment he was all nickel-toothed Monday morning smile.

'Listen,' I said. 'Tell Roy I don't have the time.'

'Twenty minutes,' the chauffeur pleaded. 'He knows you're a busy man.'

'Where is he?'

'The Arctika. He's taken a full floor there. Penthouse.'

I looked over my shoulder. Abby was in the kitchen. 'I'll meet you at the consulate,' I said. 'I'll be there in half an hour.'

She appeared briefly in the doorway before I left with the chauffeur.

'Is that yours?' the chauffeur said as we waited for the lift. 'Fuck your mother! No wonder you don't have time for an old friend.'

As we drove I saw that Roy's people had been busy. Posters of Roy were up everywhere. *This is Candidate X*, they screamed in their red, white and black. *Uncle Roy is your candidate*. People with huge lapel buttons of Roy's face walked the streets. The radio announced that the first polls with Roy's name substituted for Candidate X had cut deep into Madame Badanova's lead. She was still well ahead with forty-nine per cent to Roy's thirty-nine. But Roy's star was rising.

His office was much as expected, large, a picture-window view over the hills, furnished in leather and hung with posters of himself. Somehow, sitting behind the broad desk, barrel-chested in the blue and white shirt of Murmansk Dynamo and a blue baseball cap, he didn't look as ridiculous as he should have. This, I think, is because anybody with eyes as oddly shaped and startlingly alert as Roy Rolkin's doesn't encourage you to think he looks ridiculous at any time. He got up and clasped me in a bear-hug and led me to a red leather chair in front of the desk. 'Now tell me what the fuck you're doing,' he said amiably, 'working for the opposition.'

'It's the choice I've made, Roy. That's all there is to it.'

'But why, for Christ's sake? What's in it for you?'

'I suppose it's her policies,' I said. 'Good enough?'

'Not good enough, fuck your mother,' he said. 'Not good enough at all. We're brothers, right? As good as.'

I stared into those intimidating eyes. 'It's simple. I don't want you running this city, Roy. Just look at your posters. They're a disgrace. A Red-Nazi pastiche.'

'It pulls the votes,' he grunted. 'It doesn't mean anything. Coffee, cognac or both?' he asked, getting to his feet.

'Neither,' I said. I stood up. 'We're finished, Roy. We're on different sides of the fence.'

'What fence? If there's a fence we're on the same side, always have been.'

I knew what being on the same side of the fence as Roy meant. Flattery, drinks, gifts . . . then requests for the sort of co-operation you wouldn't want to give . . . then the deeper nastiness you suddenly found you couldn't really avoid . . . and the cool and totally effective menaces if you thought you could try. No, a man doesn't rise high as a secret policeman without learning to get his way. 'I just want to put my cards on the table, Roy,' I said.

'Anyway,' he said petulantly, 'I'm a reformed character. Ask anybody that's worked with me in Budapest.' He looked up, sniffed and grinned.

'What sort of reformed character chooses a man like Pasko as his electoral commissioner?'

'Listen, I had some old favours I owed him, fuck your mother. He was my deputy in the Nunnery at one time.'

'I remember.'

'So I remember when I owe somebody something. Where's the crime in that?'

'Depends what you owe them for.'

'Very funny.'

'Roy, I just don't want there to be any doubt at all . . .'

'Between friends, always the best way,' he said piously.

He was unreformable. 'We don't look at things the same way any more,' I insisted. 'Haven't since we were kids, for Christ's sake. I'm looking for a different kind of life for the people here, Roy. Different from the one you'd want to aim at. OK, I'm a small cog in the wheel, but any contribution I can make to that new life I'll make. I'm a hundred per cent behind Madame Badanova . . .'

'You really mean that?'

'I mean it.' I walked to the door. 'And one hundred per cent for Madame B, Roy, makes me one hundred per cent *against you*.'

'Costya,' he said as I pulled open the door. 'I need you on my side.' He came forward. 'Ask yourself, who am I going to get to guide Murmansk's climb to the top of the league?'

'Murmansk Dynamo – top of the league? You can't be serious. Last game they lost eight nil to Norilsk.'

'I'm serious, OK? I'm buying the club, Costya. I'm going to pump money into it for first-class players. For an international manager from Italy or England. We're never going to be beaten by Norilsk again.' He paused, his finger in my chest. 'And I want you to be Director.'

He was smiling broadly at his *coup de théâtre*.

'No, Roy.' I swear his eyes really did seem hurt. 'No. Go shove your bribes in someone else's pocket. I'm electoral commissioner for Madame Badanova. Any lost votes, burnt votes, over-votes and I immediately inform the Moscow commissioner.'

'Who?' Roy said. 'Frank Sinatra? Old blue eyes?'

I started to laugh. You can't know a man as well as I know Roy Rolkin without being on the same wavelength about a hundred trivial things. We both loved the team of losers called Murmansk Dynamo. And clearly we both saw the Moscow electoral commissioner as a smooth Sinatra lookalike. I raised a hand in a V.I. Lenin salute as I turned to the door.

'Listen to me, Costya,' he said. 'I'm going to make myself governor of Kola, fuck your mother.'

'Goodbye, Roy.' I opened the door.

'But more than that, Costya,' he said. 'If it has to be without the help of my oldest friend . . .' Something in the timbre of his voice made me glance back. 'I'll still do it . . .' He was running at me. What the hell was he doing? Dropping to one knee, he slid across the carpet, arms wide, singing me out of the door, *'My Way'*!

Abby was just leaving her car as I was dropped back at the Nunnery. 'What did your old pal want?' she said. 'To cut you in?'

'He says he's going to win. Trouble is, I have an uneasy feeling he may be right.'

The American consular staff, almost all women, middle-aged,

dressed for work in skirts and mostly flat heels and shirts of plain colours, nodded good morning as we crossed the tiled entrance hall. Scent wafted by me as one of the consular assistants passed. A coffee trolley serving doughnuts and croissants was trundled across the flagstone floor by a man in a neat blue overall uniform with a United States flag on his right arm like an astronaut or the pilot of an F36. The Americans, I thought, know how to make their employees *feel* good.

We had stopped by the coffee trolley and were getting into line with four or five others when I heard Miles Bridger's voice from halfway up the stairs. 'Abby,' he said. 'Could you and the inspector come up for a moment?'

We left the line for coffee and followed Bridger up the wide stone staircase.

I'd never been to Bridger's office before. But I had, of course, been in this room. It was, not surprisingly, the best room in the house, the old Mother Superior's office. He had kept the atmosphere of book-lined elegance that dated from the period of World War I. The furniture was of the same period – and the carved desk I had no difficulty in recognizing. Roy Rolkin had used this room as his office when he was in charge of the secret police here just eighteen months ago. We sat down opposite the consul. Miles Bridger moved easily round his desk, tall and comfortable in a dark blue chalk-striped suit and a tie made up of red shields with the word *Veritas* – truth, inscribed on them. The bellied drinking-mug which held his pens was decorated with a similar red shield and three open books inscribed *Veritas*. Below an encompassing garland the word Harvard was written on a scroll.

'The university,' he said. 'Harvard University,' he added in case I'd missed the point.

'Murmansk,' I said. 'Class of '96.'

He smiled, taking the mild rebuke easily. Then the smile faded. 'I've just received my last quarter's accounts back from Washington.' He tapped his keyboard and spun the monitor so that it faced us. Abby got to stare closely at the figures. I stayed where I was. I knew the columns would mean very little to me even if I were near enough to see them. What I really needed was one of the croissants Bridger had on his desk, some coffee and maybe a cognac to lace it with.

'The last quarter,' Bridger was saying, 'shows a black hole.' He pointed to the columns. 'It's what I suspected.'

'What sort of black hole?' Abby said, her eyes following his finger as it stopped centre screen.

'Fifty-five thousand dollars.'

'Is this all down to Joan's department?'

'At a guess I'd say a large part. Maybe the whole sum. Take the month before she disappeared . . .'

'Was murdered,' I said.

He acknowledged my correction with an inclination of the head. 'In that month, Joan's department records a payment for security of five thousand dollars. That was unusual.'

'Do we know what sort of security?' I asked.

'Uncertain. Of course, like every other large concern in the city the consulate uses a security company. But this payment was different. To an outfit called Kola City Security Services. Invented simply to clear this cheque, I guess. The bank order was cleared immediately. It was the only transaction Kola City Security ever passed through the account.'

'Do we have information on who opened the account?'

Bridger looked down at me. 'It was opened by a Russian woman. The name has already been established as false.'

'A description?'

'Yes,' he said slowly. 'I think you'd recognize it immediately, Inspector. As your wife.'

I got up and walked to the window. Natalya couldn't possibly have told me what she was doing, however good the cause. I'm a militia officer who doesn't baulk at the odd gift from a black-marketeer like Vassikin or the loan of a dinner-jacket. But embezzling a US consulate account for over fifty thousand dollars over the last few months, that was something different. Entirely different.

'I don't think we can take this further at the moment, Miles,' Abby was saying. 'It's pretty obviously related to the investigation, probably as the source of the money Joan was apparently using to pay for the transfer of the children. The next step is to know more about the purpose of the transfer.'

'Whatever the purpose, it's still embezzlement of consular funds.'

'Of course.' She stared him hard in the eyes.

I didn't blame him for breaking away. He looked down. 'I've reported it to you, Abby. That's all I'm obliged to do while an investigation is in progress.'

Abby nodded in that considered way that made you wait on her

279

next words. 'That reminds me I had something to raise with you, Miles.' She reached into her bag. 'Captain Dronsky has lots of time on his hands at the moment. He's been checking the original search made by Missing Persons Officer Pasko of Joan's flat. Pasko blundered about destroying more evidence than he found. But fortunately our Lieutenant Pinsk was there part of the time. He was able to list the two boxes of personal items that were passed on to you.'

'Photographs,' Bridger said. 'Letters . . .'

'Three tied bundles . . .' Abby was reading from her list. 'Photographs . . . Seven bound. Thirty-two loose.'

Bridger stood with his eyebrows raised questioningly.

'And a notebook. A sketch-book I guess you'd call it. Pinsk notes it has several crayon drawings in it.'

Bridger gestured bafflement. 'I handed everything over to you at the time.'

Abby pulled a notebook from her purse, opened it and studied it a moment. Bridger was looking at her, trying, I thought, to give her a long curious glance. Succeeding only, I thought, in looking worried.

'Yes, here we are . . .' Abby said, although I was pretty sure she could have done this from memory. 'A sketch-book with six crayon sketches, pretty conventional views of the port.'

'So . . .' Bridger began.

'And a seventh.' Her timing was perfect. 'In pen. Part map, part sketch. A map of a graveyard, it's all recorded here by Lieutenant Pinsk.' She brought her head up slowly. 'What happened to the last sketch, Miles?'

He puffed his cheeks. 'I handed you all there was, Abby. I'd barely flicked through the sketch-book. How was I to know there was a sketch missing?'

'Sure,' she said, giving him a big, not very reassuring smile. 'But let's not worry about it just yet. I think we're going to be able to lift a pretty good impression from the underpage.'

'What was all that about?' I said as we came out of his office. 'I didn't know anything about a missing sketch.'

'Something that came up while you were at the lake,' she said vaguely.

'But you're going to be able to raise an imprint?'

'Already done,' she said briskly. 'It's a map of a graveyard with one area, to the east, shaded in.'

'We don't know the significance of the shading?'

'No.'

'And we don't know where the graveyard is located?'

'Not yet. Let's get some coffee.'

'Slow down. Do you really think Miles Bridger tore out that page?'

'Could have been Pasko, I suppose, *after* Pinsk had recorded the sketch in his list.'

I had the strong feeling she had information she wasn't letting me in on. 'But you don't think it was Pasko?'

She stopped and turned to face me. 'I don't know, Constantin. On balance, I think Miles Bridger might very easily have torn out that page. But I know that we're going to need a lot more than we've got to nail a senior member of the US consular service.'

42

I TOOK MY COFFEE and the green folder Pinsk had given me into my office and I locked the door. Searching in the inner room, Dronsky's room as it had been, I found a clear bottle and poured a thumb or two into my coffee. The green folder carried a label. It read *Post-Mortem Report on Dr Natalya Vadim*. I knew it had to be read.

I didn't dwell on the Latinate descriptions. She died of carbon monoxide poisoning, suffocated in a length of rectangular, shiny galvanized ducting. Severe bruising to the neck and oakum particles embedded in the skin indicated restraint with a thick hempen rope, probably attached to one of the iron rings set in the boiler-room wall. She had heavy bruising all over her breasts and inner thighs. But no semen was found in her body.

I downed the coffee and poured vodka into the cup. Then pushed it to one side. Some things I didn't want to blur. Things like the thick hempen rope. I wanted to remember that when I finally came face to face with him.

Or had I done that already? Miles Bridger had almost certainly torn the final sketch from Joan's book. But we couldn't read any significance into that until we knew exactly what was in the sketch. A graveyard, gravestones meant nothing in themselves. Pinsk's sergeant who had originally recorded the number of sketches in the book had only the haziest memory. So why had Bridger torn it out? If he *had* torn it out. Then I had to ask myself, if Miles Bridger was the man, how had he come to know about the Clinic boiler-room? But wait. We had already decided the abductions would have needed an accomplice. So was it possible Bridger worked with someone, someone who knew the basement of the Clinic? Someone who kept the keys in fact, making the whole revelation of the tunnel nothing but an elaborate red herring. And that someone? Potanin, who else?

* * *

I did not tell Abby where I was going. I felt I needed *not* to tell her. I took a Kamka from the Nunnery car park and drove the short distance to the Lermontov Clinic.

Potanin wasn't pleased to see me. Perhaps he was just busy, perhaps he had rounds to do. Perhaps he was just anxious to get upstairs to the down-filled mattress of Maklova, the manageress. But he wasn't pleased to see me.

I had to remind myself that I had no evidence against this man. No more than supposition. 'Tell me, Potanin,' I said. 'Do you know the American consul, Miles Bridger?'

He stood at the window, the light whitening out part of his face. It reminded me that the view from that window was directly down into Natalya's office in the block opposite.

'I know of him,' Potanin was saying. 'I've seen him on a few occasions organized for charity. I've never met him.'

I nodded. 'Never had *contact* with him? With Miles Bridger . . .'

It was as if I had struck a large soundless bell whose violent reverberations were passing through the room. 'Contact?' Potanin said.

'You said you'd never met him.'

'No.'

'I'm asking did you ever have any contact with him . . . any sort of contact. That was the question. Natural enough follow-up, I'd have thought.'

'I don't know what you're talking about.'

Nor did I. But I wasn't prepared to let go just yet. 'You've met his wife, perhaps. Isobel, the Englishwoman.'

'I've never met his wife.'

'No contact with her either?'

'No, Inspector . . . I never even knew he had a wife.'

I raised a hand. 'Listen to me, Potanin, I know you're lying about something. I don't know what it is but I know you're lying. Did you ever meet Joan Fowler?'

His grey face was blank.

'Joan Fowler, did you ever meet her?'

'Once. Once only.' His hands were shaking now. He reached for the vodka glasses on a shelf and his long, uncontrolled fingers made them clatter together.

'About six weeks ago. I could look it up for you. It was at another of the consulate's charity evenings. I'm often invited to these things.'

'Did you speak to her? Alone, I mean?'

'Perhaps a few moments. I can't really remember.'

'Did you find her attractive, Potanin? Glossy perhaps, as American women can be? More glossy than your friend, Maklova.'

He took a deep breath and looked again towards the vodka shelf. 'I found her pleasant . . .' the colour jumped into his cheeks. 'I didn't find myself overwhelmed with murderous lust, if that's what you mean.'

He stopped, letting his voice drop. 'I'm sorry,' he said. 'An outburst. We're all under strain.'

'You would know,' I said. 'When I've one or two other pieces fitted together, I'll be back.'

I saw his throat tighten, but his eyes stayed on me, unmoving.

I turned and reached for the door-handle. The vodka glasses were rattling under his fingers before I got the door open wide enough to leave.

I walked slowly down the stairs almost oblivious of the mumbling figures that jostled forward, the stench of cooked cabbage and urine. The shock waves from that silent bell had been unmistakable. And it was the question about *contact* with Bridger that had done it. So what sort of contact had they had – and about what? This time I knew I had to suppress my instinct to go back up and bring it out of him. If those long thin fingers had attached the rope around Natalya's throat, this time I would prove it. To myself first and last. And then I would decide what steps I would take in the retribution.

Fanya Karpova, Natalya's friend, was in my office when I got back to the Nunnery that evening. 'You never seem to be at home,' she said. 'I thought I'd track you to your lair.'

She stood up and put her arms around my waist. 'You know how I felt about Natalya,' she said. 'When I heard about that furnace-room, I was devastated.' There were tears in her eyes. She released me and sat down opposite the desk.

'You want some coffee?' I said.

She shook her head. 'No. I won't be staying. I just came to say . . . to say something about Natalya. Perhaps even to say that, if I'd thought about myself less, I might have helped her in some way.'

'I don't think you would have changed the final result,' I said carefully. 'And it's the final result that counts for all of us.'

'Sure.' I could see her hesitating. 'There's something I want to tell you, Constantin. Something I should have said before. Natalya was involved in something with Joan Fowler. She tried to recruit me.'

'Did she tell you what she was doing?'

'Something illegal, I know that. It involved trips to the border. There was one arranged for this coming Wednesday. I was to fill in for Joan who had some consular business she was going to have to look after in Petersburg.'

'What did you say?'

'I said no. The only time I ever refused Natalya anything. Perhaps if I'd agreed . . .'

'I don't think so, no.'

'I already had my suspicions about Natalya and Joan and I wasn't prepared to stand in for her. Jealousy can twist you completely out of shape if you let it,' she said. She stood, looking down at the floor. 'I just couldn't accept that she might find Joan Fowler a more exciting prospect than me.' She looked up quickly. 'There I go again. I came here to bring some word of comfort to you – and I immediately do the reverse.'

I shook my head. 'We still don't know for certain,' I said, 'about Natalya and Joan.'

'We do. The voice on the phone . . .'

'Could have been anybody,' I said.

'But it wasn't,' she said bitterly. 'It was my spy.'

'Spy?'

'Mikhail,' she said. 'He followed Natalya like a dog. When he found out about Joan he was out of his mind. In the end he even made the call.'

'The crazy phone call to the Nunnery – that was Mikhail?'

'He told me later, after you found Natalya. He was drunk. And mad at you.'

'Why me for God's sake?'

'He said he'd gone to your apartment. You'd been so patronizing, so sure that Natalya loved you and only you. He wanted to hit you – hard.'

'He did,' I said.

'Go easy on him. He regretted it immediately. But he was at his wits' end like all of us.' She leaned forward and reached up to kiss me on the cheek, as she used to in the old days, the old days less than a month ago.

*   *   *

285

I slept that night in Dronsky's bed at the office, the doors barricaded against a flying visit from V.I. Lenin. Abby, I assumed, was sleeping the sleep of the just in my apartment.

I say I *slept* the night but it was a thin, disturbed sleep. I had turned in early, not much after ten, but by three o'clock I was awake, heavy-lidded but restless.

I lay propped up with my hands behind my neck, drifting in and out of sleep and conjuring images of Potanin and Miles Bridger. One, or perhaps even both of them, were involved in all this. Bridger, I supposed, might conceivably have known about and even supported Joan Fowler's use of consulate funds to ensure those children were taken to safety in Norway. If so there would be no point in implicating himself now. All he had done, on this scenario, when Natalya and Joan were alive was to connive at the idea of good works by stealth. He stood to gain nothing by admitting it now. So did that explain how Miles Bridger fitted in the scheme of suspicion and exoneration which is a major part of any investigation?

And if that was so – what about Potanin? It wasn't hard to see him as something of a buffoon, a man who had faked his American qualification but was none the less performing a valuable service as director of the Clinic. In post civil-war Russia, adopted identities and adopted qualifications were far from unknown.

But there was another way of seeing Potanin too. As the man who had the keys to the furnace-room. As a man who had known both Natalya and Joan Fowler – as a much more organized and smarter figure than he projected with his dusty files and tattered clothing ... Perhaps I'd fallen asleep again. The ringing of the phone in my ear became mixed in my mind with a high-pitched screech from V.I. Lenin.

I had lifted the phone to my ear before I was fully awake. The digital wall clock said four a.m. It was Jay Dellerman's voice. But different. No long lazy vowels. This was tight, urgent. Jay Dellerman was scared. 'I want you to come over,' she said.

'What's happened?' I was pushing the confusion of blankets aside. 'How the hell did you get this number?'

'You left it on the answering-machine at your apartment. Forget that. Just come over.'

I sat up and swung my legs out of bed. 'What's happened?'

'Nothing's *happened*,' she said tensely. 'Nothing big or dramatic. Or at least not yet. But I've suddenly realized the position I'm in and

I'm very, very scared, Constantin.' She paused. 'Please. I must talk to you.'

I had an uneasy feeling about this one. I've read quite a bit of modern American crime fiction, brothers. When the beautiful girl asks someone round in the middle of the night it's either for sex or sorrow. After last night Jay must have known sex wasn't a likely runner.

My reluctance must have shown in my hesitation.

'I've been stupid,' she said. 'Maybe very stupid. You too, if it helps any.'

'Tell me.'

'I need your help, Constantin. I think I'm in danger. In real danger. Will you come over? Now?'

It was cold, bitterly cold with snow flurries in the air. Spring was playing hide-and-seek. There was no sign of the occasional builder's van or plumber carrying lengths of copper tubing I had seen when I was here with Jay at a much earlier hour last night. Much of the quarter seemed bleak and empty. I should have brought someone with me.

At first glance Turgenev Street looked like Stalingrad on the night of victory. But the buildings were not in ruins – they were just half-completed. And the big steel toads squatting by the roadside were not tanks but builders' tips.

I drove down towards the end and stopped in front of Jay's apartment block. The entrance hall was still missing all doors and windows and the snow was dancing in under lines of fairy lights. I got out of the car and picked my way across the rubble-littered sidewalk. Murmansk builders don't live in fear of being sued by the passing public. Broken piles of brick, shallow service trenches, planks with ugly-looking nails were apparent everywhere.

I stood for a moment in the entrance to Jay's block. Three floors up, there was a light shining at a window which I guessed was Jay's. There were other lights but no windows to front them. These, descending vertically, I took to be the stairwell. In the wind that whipped the snow, empty cans of builders' mastic rolled hollowly across the broken pavements; water from a leaking fifth-floor spout skittered across the sidewalk, causing me to spin round and go for my gun holster.

But of course I didn't have a gun holster. I had a fur-lined leather jacket and a size XX T-shirt with Women Against Violence printed across the chest. But a gun holster I had forgotten.

The enemy you know is finite in his power to threaten, frighten or dismay. Not so the enemy you're far from sure about. I stepped into the cement cathedral that was the lobby of Jay's block and listened for the reassuring whine of electric drills, the noise of hammering or sawing. But tonight the whole building was silent.

Before I started up the bare cement steps I chose myself a piece of timber, thick as a baseball bat and with one or two bent ten-centimetre nails adding menace to the striking end. I moved up quickly now, step by step, alternately in bright light or near-darkness according to the placing of the rope of bare bulbs, my mind full of demons and danger.

When the whistling started above me I was electrified by fear. The strange toneless sound of a man whistling came along the corridor from roughly Jay's apartment to the head of the stairs. One thing I knew. This demon couldn't whistle in tune. I pressed myself against the wall but there was no way to avoid him seeing me with a light-bulb shining into my face.

I could hear the scrape of his footsteps now around the next dark bend in the spiral. I lifted the piece of timber in my hand. When he appeared the whistling stopped. He was wearing a dark workman's overall and a rabbit-skin hat with earmuffs. In one hand he carried a metal workbox.

Relief made me lower the piece of timber to my side. I blinked in the bright light and lifted my hand in greeting. I had just time to read Kola TV Installations in yellow on the back of his overall before he turned the next corner and was gone.

I climbed quickly the remaining steps to the third floor, reassured, now that I had actually seen a workman still in the building. I hurried along the corridor, chaotic with cable and unfinished plastering but well enough lit by overhead lights.

The crumpled heap halfway along stopped me. There was a pile of dirty overalls there, all blue, all carrying the name Kola TV Installations on their backs. I looked back again towards the stairhead. The workman's footsteps had long faded. The prickly edginess I felt before I saw the workman reasserted itself.

Jay's apartment showed a light in the transom above the door. I rang and waited for an answer. Did I hear the tuneless whistling again in the courtyard below? Easily confused with the wind that whistled its own soulless tunes, Constantin, I told myself.

After a few seconds I rang again. Still no answer. No sound from inside.

I had Jay's keys in my pocket, casually transferred from my dinner-jacket with the intention of returning them to her. Taking them out, I looked at them and felt a surge of irritation. Was all this – the late-night phone call, the pleading voice – just a romantic device to get me to the apartment? So that I would use the keys and walk through to the bedroom and find her, lazily stretched across the bed. I didn't think so.

Inserting the Yale key, I opened the door.

The smell of blood was sickening to me. Jay's collection of pornography was scattered, bloodily, about the room. The door to the bedroom was open. From where I stood, I saw she lay on the bed, spread-eagled.

43

IT WAS MORNING. We stood, Abby and I, among the bloodied books in the main room while flash bulbs hurled blue light about the bedroom.

'She like this stuff?' Abby said, gesturing to the books. The illustrated volume of Stalin and his abettors romping through the halls of the Kremlin lay open, stained, appropriately with blood.

'She collected it,' I said defensively.

'How many times were you here?'

'Just once before. Don't make anything of it.'

'We have to,' she said. 'She called you, didn't she?' Abby opened her notebook and read: *'I've been stupid. You too.* Still no idea what that means?'

'I've tried,' I said. 'But I get nothing.'

'You hadn't had some sort of romantic tiff? That fits. Jay was looking for a reconciliation. You'd both been stupid . . . But let's kiss and make up?'

I shook my head at her. 'For Christ's sake, you're wasting your time, Abby. Worse than that, you're wasting mine. Jay was scared. Very, very scared. Why or what of, at that time of the night, we don't know.'

I walked over to where a crime-scene man was dusting the front door. 'What strikes me, first of all,' I said, 'is that this was an unfinished building. No gates, no real security. Yet at four, four-thirty in the morning, a woman opens the door to someone. See here, there's no sign of forced entry.'

'You have to ask yourself how many guys she handed out keys to,' Abby said. 'You don't imagine you were the only one.'

From the bedroom a round, stubble-cheeked doctor emerged. 'No dispute about the time of death. It was a few minutes before the inspector arrived. Say four-twenty this morning. Actual cause of death is strangulation rather than bleeding to death as you might think. No sign of semen but it was clearly a sexual attack. There was a knife used, pretty freely.' He paused. 'It wouldn't have been an easy exit for the girl.'

'Can we move her now?' Pinsk asked from the doorway. I turned away while Abby went in to make a last check.

I walked slowly to the front door and looked down the corridor with its exposed pipes and cables. Pinsk had joined me and was lighting a cigarette. He glanced at me and offered me the packet. 'You know, Chief,' he said. 'We're going to get him for this one. I'm sure of it. As soon as the witness sobers up . . .'

'Witness?'

'Sorry, Chief. You were busy in the apartment when we found him. A drunk. He was sleeping on the floor below. He's muttering about seeing a car. We're sobering him up at the Nunnery now.'

We walked to the nearest unglazed window. Two unmarked vans had just pulled up. Builders were tumbling out of the back. 'See if you can find out what the working system is here,' I said. 'Is there one company for each trade? If so who runs them? Or are they all freelance? We're looking for who else was in the building around four a.m. In particular we want to know who was the television engineer working here in the middle of the night.'

'I've been onto a man named Danny Markov who runs Kola TV Installations,' Pinsk said. 'He says his team finished work at just after midnight the night before last. Leaving the overalls was an oversight brought on by enthusiastic bonus celebrations. He claimed they were the only team who had finished their contract on time.'

'You're saying there was no TV engineer here last night?' The chill feathered up my back. 'You're saying the man I passed on the stairs was our vek?'

Pinsk rolled his eyes. 'Looks like it, Chief. Anything in the way of a description?'

How could I say that I was so relieved the tuneless whistler was a workman in overalls and carrying a toolbox that I hadn't tried to look past the flaps of his snow-hat? I shook my head. 'At that stage,' I said casually, 'I just passed a man on the stairs. I had no reason to be checking him over.'

I drew once or twice on my cigarette and flicked it out through the gap where a window would sometime be fitted. Then turned as Abby appeared in the open doorway of Jay's flat. 'I think you'd better come and look at this,' she said coolly.

I had already started down the corridor when it struck me that

291

her reaction had been a little too cool. Forced cool, you might think. 'What is it, Abby?' I said as I reached the front door.

I could see through to the bedroom where she was standing by the bed. Two crime-scene officers stood, like her, staring down. The bedclothes had been turned back.

The first thing I noticed was the way in which the blood, filtered by blankets had stained a large area of sheet a pale pink. Then I saw that in the middle of the bed was a child's doll, the sort you buy anywhere with three or four outfits to dress it up in. This one was wearing a dark jacket and skirt and pumps.

It had been an old KGB trick to threaten a woman by hiding a black leather glove in her bed. The purpose of the doll was, equally, to menace. In the toy shops, the dolls come with three or four outfits and in three or four racial types. This one was Afro-American, with dark bright eyes, a honey-toned face, and a broad pretty upper lip.

44

ABBY DROVE BACK to the Nunnery with Pinsk. Before I left Jay's apartment I wanted to speak to Madame Badanova before she read it or saw it on mid-morning television. I sat down among the mess of bloodstained pornography and called her number. Telling her what had happened was not easy.

I could hear over the line the sharp intake of breath. 'My God, my poor Jay. Was this a break-in – a robbery? The sort of thing we hear about that goes tragically wrong?'

'No. At least there was no sign of a break-in.'

She thought about this. 'You're saying it was someone she invited into the apartment herself? Even perhaps someone she knew?'

'We don't know at this stage. But it wasn't a random lunatic. Or a break-in that went wrong.'

There was a long pause. 'You mean Jay was sought out by someone. Is that what you mean?'

'Yes. I'm sure of it.'

'Constantin . . . What a business politics is in Russia!'

'What are you saying?'

'I have to believe this is something to do with the work she was doing for me,' she said soberly.

'What was she doing that she wasn't doing last week?'

There was a long pause. 'The declaration took us both by surprise,' she said. 'I knew Roy Rolkin was a much more formidable opponent than the gangster Fortunin would ever have been. So I asked Jay to use all her contacts to find out what we could about Rolkin.'

'What would be the point of that? You were going to *blackmail* him?'

'Blackmail? No . . .' Her voice toughened. 'I was prepared, I must admit it, Constantin, to make public any information she might dig up. Anything that might force Rolkin to withdraw. Did she find something that Rolkin thought would do him damage?'

I grunted my doubt that Roy was behind Jay's death. Madame Badanova didn't know Roy as I knew him. Certainly there was plenty in his past that was unsavoury or downright criminal. But Roy's response would have been more to bluff and bluster and confuse the issue. It was a technique that had mostly worked well for him.

'So you think I'm completely off-track?' Madame Badanova said, interpreting my silence. 'You must decide, Constantin. You're the investigator.'

Abby was waiting for me just inside the consulate hallway. I told her about the phone call to Madame Badanova.

'So she thinks it could have been someone from Roy Rolkin's camp?' she said as we crossed the lobby. 'He's *your* friend. What do you think?'

An irrational sense of loyalty rose in me. 'With Roy you can't easily draw a line and be sure he wouldn't cross it,' I said. 'But setting a lunatic on a woman like that, I'd say no. Not Roy.'

'A less than resounding endorsement for an old friend.'

'I'm saying no . . . Roy wouldn't do something like that.'

'You're also saying you're not absolutely sure,' she said, as we walked towards the door to the basement.

One or two of the women of the American consular staff stopped and looked with curiosity as I opened the heavy, unmarked door set under the staircase. Very few of them had any idea of what had once gone on in the basement below.

I let Abby in past me. She flinched at the sharp waft of cold, carbolic-tainted air. There were no new American radiators on the landings here.

Our heels clattered on the stone steps. At the bottom Pinsk was waiting. 'I've got him in number one cell, Inspector,' he said. 'He's not under arrest. Shall we take him up?'

'Is he sober?' Abby asked.

'Enough. It'd take a week to dry him out properly.'

'Let's have the first words with him down here,' I said. 'It'll give him a sense of occasion.'

Pinsk led the way down the stone corridor to the first cell. The door was open and the thick stench of an unwashed man billowed around the entrance. I couldn't help thinking of those showered, starched women clerks up on the floor above.

Feodor Chaplin was a small man in a torn grey parka and a

rabbit-fur hat with flaps. He sprawled on the wooden bench, one hand cupped round his glass of tea. His red-rimmed eyes blinked when he saw Abby. I could see the struggle to take in this tall dark-complexioned woman in the business suit more appropriate to the New York Stock Exchange than this grim basement cell. Carefully he placed his tea on the floor and stood up, but his balance went and he hurriedly shuffled his feet to recover his equilibrium.

Abby looked doubtfully at him, his body slumped like a marionette on loose strings. 'I'm not sure he can hack it,' she said to me in English.

The man had caught the doubt in her voice. 'I am not drunk. No longer drunk . . . I'm drunk no more. That much I promise you. Ask me to walk a straight line.'

'No,' I said.

'Ask me to count then. The ordinals if you prefer. The First Noel, the Second Coming, Third Reich, Fourth Republic, Fifth Amendment, Sixth Party Congress . . .'

'Seventh Heaven,' I said. I turned to Pinsk. 'Let's get down to business.'

'These are two senior inspectors investigating this matter, Feodor,' Pinsk said. 'Now keep yourself sharp for their questions. No falling asleep or it's a kick in the ass that wakes you. You can sit, but sit upright. No sprawling about on the bed.'

Feodor sat and Pinsk brought in a chair for Abby.

'To start us off, Feodor,' I said. 'Just tell us what you do for a living.'

'I drive a bus,' he said.

I heard Abby's grunt of alarm.

'But I'm not always in this condition, madame,' he said earnestly. 'This is very much an exception. Yesterday was my day off. And today I'm not on duty till noon.'

'Are you clear-headed enough to tell us what you saw last night?' Abby asked him.

'Clear as a bell. And I want to apologize, before you two senior investigating officers and to Lieutenant Pinsk here, for the confusing and roundabout way I've told my story so far. Under the Soviet Union I was an assistant teacher of elementary economics and political studies, so I know a thing or two about clarity of presentation when dealing with facts.

'First and foremost I'm not going to try to disguise the fact that I had been heavily engaged with the clear bottle during the evening . . .'

'You'd been drinking?'

'Yes.'

'Where?'

'At the bus-station canteen. In the company of a few friends. It was late, perhaps even after midnight when I set off home. Turgenev Street is on my way. Somewhere in the middle of the same street I was overcome with an unaccountable and irresistible fatigue.'

'What did you do?'

'It was a harsh night. A hard wind off the river. And the return of the snow. I decided to take shelter in one of the half-built apartment blocks there. Chance had it that I had with me a good slice of sausage and a half-litre of Kuban, so I was in no real danger.'

'Of sobering up?' Pinsk said from the door.

Feodor lifted a finger. 'Now that's unkind, Lieutenant,' he said. 'At all events I made myself comfortable, as an old soldier can. I settled down and, despite the cold, fell into a deep sleep.'

'But something woke you,' Abby said.

'It was a car. It drew up just down in the street below me.'

'In Turgenev Street?'

'No. I had selected a position more to the side. My actual viewpoint was down into the alley beside the block, not visible from the street.'

'What sort of car?'

'Black.'

'But what make?'

'American. A Mercedes was my first thought.'

'A Mercedes isn't an American car,' Pinsk said from behind. 'Concentrate now Uncle, or you'll deserve that kicking.'

'The car was black. The man that got out was well-dressed. Hatless. Probably quite tall. He pointed one of those gadgets that lock the doors and disappeared into some opening, I couldn't be sure which, of the apartment block below me.'

'What time was this?'

Feodor frowned and pulled at his lip. 'As to time,' he said, 'I have to admit the situation is not crystal clear in my mind.'

Abby glanced at me in exasperation. 'Jay wasn't the only one living there, was she? This guy may have been on his way in. Nothing more than that.'

'In that case why did he come out again half an hour later?' Feodor said, his eyes suddenly bright.

Abby sat back and fixed him with a glare. 'Now *this* you *are* crystal clear about?'

'Memory, like sunshine, bursts through cloud, as we Russians say.'

'You got another look at him?'

'Not much this time, Inspector. He was running as fast as he could go. He got into the car and slammed the door. The engine started and the tyres squealed. No way to treat a fine American Mercedes, I said to myself.'

Moments later we stood outside the cell.

'What d'you think?' Abby asked me. 'The only thing he seems crystal clear about is that it was an American Mercedes.'

Pinsk put his head round the cell door. He jerked his thumb over his shoulder. 'Another ray of sunshine,' he said. 'A real ray, if Feodor's not making it up.'

We went back into the cell. Feodor sprang to his feet and sat down quickly again.

'Tell the investigating officers what you just told me,' Pinsk said.

'The ratio of a circle's circumference to its diameter. Expressed as pi or 3.14159.'

'I think he's just left the real world,' Abby said.

'The car number,' Pinsk said. 'He saw the car registration.'

'I saw *part* of the car number, your honour,' Feodor said to Abby earnestly. 'The first figures were 3141 which I instantly recognized as the beginning of pi. The other two numbers, I have to tell you, are lost on me.'

We sat in the white hospital room in the Lermontov, Dronsky, Abby and myself. Pinsk had set in train the search for a list of all cars with 3141 in their registration. At the same time he was trying to impose some order on the chaos of builders' responsibilities at Jay's apartment block. There seemed no doubt that the man I had passed on the stairs was not a television-aerial engineer; little or no doubt that he was Jay's killer.

'Last point,' Dronsky said. 'And most important of all.'

I had already stood up to go.

'Which point is that?' Abby said, frowning.

'None of us disputes the meaning of this doll?' Dronsky lifted his Groucho Marx eyebrows to Abby. Her face had hardly moved. 'So he's telling us, as clearly as he can, that if we continue to come after him Abby will be his next victim.'

'Except she won't be,' Abby said.

I thought of the shadowy Scorpio, clever, lustful, devious.

'You're alone now at the Chief's apartment?' Dronsky was asking her.

'On your suggestion I moved out yesterday,' I said.

'So . . .' Dronsky adjusted his injured leg. 'I'll start again. I suggest you move straight back, Chief. I think from now on, you should see yourself as Abby's shadow.'

I looked at Abby. She pursed her lips and lightly lifted her shoulders.

Mayor Osopov's office was a corner room in the City Hall complex, markedly lacking the grandeur of the governor's penthouse above, and thus quietly reflecting the comparative power and influence in the city of regional governor and mayor.

A man with teeth too small for his face, Osopov sat fatly behind a desk stacked with files and papers. A PC stood, switched to a blank screen, on a table to his right. I had heard from Natalya that the fat man liked to give an impression of high-tech efficiency. It was his first appointment of the morning, probably before his first pick-me-up, and I could see the impatience in the drumming of his fingers. Colonel Sonya Fetisova sat on his right. Her small eyes and red puffy face, and her civilian dark jacket and trousers would have made her a clear first choice in a James Bond audition for the head of SMERSH. Head of the Juvenile Penal Colony Administration on Kola, she had responsibility for the welfare of tens of thousands of children and had clashed with Western journalists and children's agencies many times. As I closed the door behind us, I saw Sonya Fetisova round the desk and waddle across the office. 'Constantin,' she greeted me. 'Still as handsome as ever. It's too long since we last bumped into each other. We should share a thumb or two of good vodka together sometime.'

Osopov placed his large hands flat on the file in front of him. 'I've studied your preliminary report,' he said. 'All this adds up to a considerable indictment of your American colleague, Joan Fowler and Dr Vadim, I'm afraid to say.'

'Maybe. Maybe not,' Abby said. 'I think we should be most concerned about why Dr Vadim and Joan Fowler found it necessary to remove children from the territory of the Russian Federation and transport them to the West.'

'What sort of numbers are we talking about?'

'We don't know. There might have been just one or two crossings, or considerably more. We do know they used a group of ex-soldiers . . .'

'Bandits,' Fetisova twisted from her lips.

Abby shrugged almost imperceptibly. 'We don't know their identity. Let's say a group of ex-soldiers from whom they obtained the children.'

'You mean they bought the children?' Fetisova said, affecting incredulity. 'They were engaged in a market in children?'

'It's in my report, Colonel,' Abby said coldly.

'Of course. But I can still find it shocking, Miss Cunningham. I can still find it shocking even if we have not yet established their end purpose. Was it for philanthropy or profit? Perhaps we'll never know, unless you were aware, Constantin, of what your wife was engaged in?'

I suddenly saw clearly why Natalya had told me nothing. It was not only to protect me from involvement. She had, as always, faced the possibilities and consequences of what she was doing. She had known its dangers. But she had already worked out that if I were to be of any use when a crisis arose, I would have to be free and untainted with any connection.

'*Were* you aware, Inspector?'

'If I'd had any idea,' I said, anger raging through me, 'Natalya would not have suffocated in a basement at the Lermontov. Does that answer your question, Colonel? Because if it doesn't . . .'

'Constantin . . . Costya,' she lifted both hands. 'We're old friends. We mustn't fight, you and me. I was asking a question which had to be asked. You, as a policeman, understand that. I accept your answer. You knew nothing.' A sly smile touched her lips.

There was silence in the room. Even Osopov looked down, industriously scratching the palm of his hand. 'The source of your information about your wife's activities then?' he asked in a subdued voice.

'Special Agent Cunningham has already reported to me that a certain Lukas Roop was the source, Mayor Osopov,' Fetisova said. 'I've had a check run on him. A labourer nowadays, although he was once a teacher according to the record. There are prior incidents although nothing serious. My impression is that he's what we used to call soft-headed.'

Osopov glanced at his watch. 'Very well then. Let us review what we have.' He leaned towards Abby. 'You tell us, Miss Cunningham, that you believe that these children, *if they ever existed*, were *perhaps* taken to the Norwegian border. And we only have the word of one unfortunate that these events occurred.' He paused. 'There is apparently a band of men involved. Possibly ex-soldiers. But does anyone know where we might find them? Or even for certain if they exist any more than these children do? Really, what is the city to do? Send men to roam the lakes and marshes in search of wandering children? I don't think so, do you?'

'We're asking for the fullest possible check on numbers in the children's penal colonies,' Abby said firmly. 'The fullest possible independent check. I believe these children come from the penal system – and I believe that someone in the system has been falsely recording them as escapees.'

Fetisova stood up. 'Enough of this,' she said roughly. 'It is nothing but insulting speculation. I've spoken to all my commandants. They have checked with all their officers. I repeat. We have *no* child escapees on record in the Kola penal region. That is a *fact*, Miss Cunningham.'

Osopov pouted his fat lips and spread his palms wide. 'And I think we all have to accept that it's a fact more solid than myths of wandering children.'

45

'THE BASTARDS,' ABBY said as we crossed the paved area in front of City Hall. 'The kids Natalya was smuggling across the border came from the camps, I'm convinced of it. We went through our routine and there wasn't a flicker of fear to be seen on either of their faces.'

'They hold all the cards, that's why. They're playing with us.'

'Well the time for games is over,' she said sharply.

'So from now on we'll get nowhere unless we follow this ourselves,' I said. 'Direct action . . .'

She glanced at me sideways. 'The Russian way?'

'The Russian way,' I said. 'I believe there's a good chance tonight was the night of their next operation.'

'Even if you're right we don't know it's still on.'

'We know Natalya and Joan would have no chance of cancelling,' I said. 'So it's a possibility. Let's find out.'

'To do that we need Lukas,' she said. 'He's the only one who knows how to find the rendezvous with the men who supply the children. He never said where it was?'

'Somewhere in or near the abandoned hulks. That's all.'

She nodded. 'OK,' she said. 'Since we're doing this the Russian way – let's get him to take us there.'

The call came from one of Pinsk's team at three that afternoon. Lukas Roop's van had left the helicopter hangar. It was being followed by a militia surveillance car and had now started north down Pushkin Boulvar.

By three twenty Lukas was transferring his vanload of first-quality models to the couture clothes shop Lost Innocence on Festival Street. Abby and I were by then sitting in an unmarked car three vehicles behind his parked van.

For a few minutes we watched Lukas carrying the models into the shop. He wore a parka over a thick sweater, jeans and a pair of scuffed running shoes. There was a special care, a delicacy about the way he handled the latex models.

Abby gave me a cigarette, and we fell to the mindless ruminating all surveillance officers depend on to pass the time. 'Lost Innocence,' she said. 'What sort of name is that for a women's clothes shop?'

'Thomas Paine,' I said. 'Anglo-American revolutionary writer. "Government, like dress, is the badge of lost innocence." If I remember rightly.'

'Goddam smartass,' she muttered. But she lit my cigarette.

In the shop we could see Lukas haul a pack of papers from the back pocket of his jeans and offer them to the owner for signature.

I stubbed out my cigarette. We got out of the car and met him just as he was leaving the shop. For a moment he hesitated shyly. 'Constantin,' he extended his hand. 'Miss Cunningham.' He shook hands with Abby too. 'Is this a coincidence? Or perhaps not?'

'Let's get a cup of coffee.' Abby pointed to the café next door to Lost Innocence. 'We have a favour to ask you.'

I watched the bewilderment rise in Lukas's snub-nosed, very Slav-looking face as we walked into the café and sat down.

'I have an apology to make, for Sasha,' Lukas said to me. 'He's very protective. He . . .' Lukas glanced at Abby, hesitating.

'Agent Cunningham knows,' I said. 'She knows I took you up on the lake.'

'Sasha lost his temper. As I say he's always been very protective. I'm sure he'd want to apologize.'

'He already has,' I told him.

We ordered coffee and he looked from myself to Abby. 'You mentioned a favour I could do you, Miss Cunningham.'

'It's to do with the story you told Constantin. About the night Dr Vadim and Joan Fowler disappeared.'

'About going to the old hulks up river?'

'Yes . . .'

He looked towards me, puzzled, worried. 'My job was to drive the van, nothing more.'

'There's nothing to worry about, Lukas. We just want you to take us to the place you took Joan to that night.'

'Why would you want to go there? The men Dr Vadim and Joan talked to will be long gone.'

'It's just part of the investigation, Lukas,' she said. 'Inquiries like this are often a matter of filling in holes. Gaps in the narrative of events. We're trying to do that.'

'I can tell you how to get there.' Arms and legs seemed to be moving in all directions. He pulled shop invoices from his pocket and a pencil. 'It's not difficult.'

'No,' Abby said. 'We want you to take us there, Lukas.'

A dozen body movements seemed to stop. 'Sasha won't like me doing that,' he said.

'I spoke to Sasha at the election declaration,' I said. 'He seemed friendly enough.'

'He wouldn't like it, Constantin. You know I'd like to do anything to help. But you mustn't ask me this.'

There was a long silence. Coffee-cups clattered on the metal table tops. Slowly, it seemed, Lukas and I both turned our heads towards Abby. She spread manicured fingers wide on the table in front of her.

'We need you to show us, Lukas,' she said. 'Vague directions to the area aren't enough. We need you to show us the exact ship where Joan Fowler collected the children the night she and Natalya disappeared.'

'I don't know if I'll remember.'

'You will,' she said. 'Or I make sure you're thrown in gaol for non-co-operation.' I marvelled at the hard light in her eyes.

'Just give me time to think about it,' Lukas pleaded. 'Let me call Sasha.'

She shook her head. 'We're going tonight,' she said. 'No time to think about it. We're going right now.'

First we went back to the Nunnery, Abby driving the unmarked militia car, and I accompanying Lukas in his van. Throughout the short drive he was entirely silent. Once or twice he looked across at me, his expression clearly accusatory.

Later, while he drank tea under the eye of Danilova and Pinsk, Abby drew me into her office. 'He knows something,' she said. 'Lukas knows something.'

'All Lukas knows is that he's terrified of Sasha,' I said. 'If you saw the two of them together . . .'

'Maybe. Maybe it's something about Sasha he knows.'

I went back into the other room. I could only look away from the appeal in Lukas's eyes. As it got dark outside, we gave him more tea and even a shot of Georgian cognac. It wasn't difficult to see that he was worried about Sasha, terrified even. When he asked to call for perhaps the fourth or fifth time, I told him it was best this way. 'When you get back,' I said, 'you can tell Sasha you had no choice.'

Abby had come to join us, leaning against the door-jamb. I glanced at her but there was no softening in her expression. I was only telling Lukas the truth.

At six o'clock we led a slightly hunched, worried-looking Lukas out to his white van. There was a cutting cold in the air. Spring, it seemed, had changed its mind. There was every chance of snow again before the night was out.

Abby had been back to the apartment to change into jeans, sweater and a thick parka. She brought boots for me and an oiled-wool sweater that smelt like a cowshed but was very effective against the weather in our part of the world. Over it I wore a civilian parka. Ducking into another room, I checked my gun and spare rounds under the considered gaze of V.I. Lenin. I remembered that black doll with the bright brown eyes.

46

IT WAS DARK when we took the highway south through the Murmansk outskirts, Lukas and myself in the white van, Abby and Pinsk in the unmarked Kamka behind. There was little snow along the sides of the highway but it still lay thick and suddenly bright in the moonlight on the higher reaches of the hills across the river.

For the first ten minutes Lukas was silent, driving with an intense and careful concentration as if he had a load of valuable porcelain in the back. 'In Rostov,' he said suddenly, 'it's warm by this time of year. Hot even. On the south beach people will be swimming.'

It came to me that he'd mentioned the sun and the beaches of Rostov before as a prelude to talking about his childhood. I wanted to encourage him. 'So it was good, was it – life in Rostov?'

He shrugged. For a long while he was silent, whether recollecting those days in the sun or deciding whether he wanted to talk more, I couldn't tell. Then he glanced sideways at me and back to the road ahead, speaking as if I had put a different question to him. 'We lived first in Rostov itself. Then in Novocherkassk a few miles up the Don river when my mother found work in the champagne factory there. For most people it was a good life in the south.'

'For most people?'

He glanced at me in that flinching way he had. 'For most people, yes, why not? Things are always easier in the sun.'

'But in Novocherkassk,' I said, 'you lived in the same house as Andrei Chikatilo.'

'I never asked you how you knew that, Constantin,' he said in a flat tone.

The question reminded me that he had never called me Costya like all the other boys at Primary 36. 'I'm a policeman,' I said vaguely. 'I have access to documents.'

'Was it *that*, me living in the same house as Andrei, that made you think I had something to do with abducting Dr Vadim?'

'Perhaps.' I let the silence ride for a long time. 'Knowing a man like Chikatilo,' I said. 'It's something that must haunt you.'

'Haunt me? No. Why should it? I told you. The Andrei Chikatilo I knew was a kind, considerate man.'

This was hard to take. 'You're telling me there was another Chikatilo?' I said. 'One we don't know about.'

'There was.' His head snapped forward angrily. 'Afterwards we began to understand. We learnt what pressures he lived under. How many times did he resist it, do you think, that urge to kill?'

'Jesus Christ,' I said. 'You're not saying we should be grateful for the one or two occasions he might have resisted the urge to murder and mutilate?'

'No, but I'm sure there are a lot of young women who would be, if they only knew.' We followed a curve in the river. 'Andrei was two separate entities. Many of the old Slav stories teach us that we all are. You too, Constantin. It does no good to pretend otherwise.'

I had no wish to cross him. But I found myself absorbed by the notion of someone who had actually known a serial murderer. 'How long did you live in the same apartment block as Andrei Chikatilo?' I asked him

He shook his head. 'It wasn't a block,' he said. 'It was a house. A house that dated from before the Revolution, with tall windows and doors and a wide marble staircase. As children we played there all the time. People living there had rooms rather than flats. Sometimes a mother and two or three children to one big room. A kitchen and lavatory shared by six or seven other people. We lived on the third floor. Andrei lived above us on the top floor.'

'You call him Andrei.'

'What else is there to call him? I was a child, I addressed him respectfully as one did in those days, Andrei Romanovich. Today I don't think of him as Chikatilo. If I think of him, I think of him as Andrei.'

'You think about him a lot?'

'All the time,' he said. 'I try to understand the riddle: how can there be two Andreis? How can two men inhabit one body? I read all the accounts of the investigation, the findings of the bodies one after another, slashed and mutilated, frozen mostly under the snow. But what I *remember* is the man who came from upstairs, a tall, quite well-dressed man with an imitation leather briefcase, a man who sat down on the marble stairs with me and handed out chocolates.'

'This man murdered your sister.'

'I told you before – there was no proof,' he said tautly. 'There was no *proof*.'

'She was included in the list of victims by the militia.'

'But he never confessed to killing her. Isn't *that* important?'

I glanced at him and saw that his face was white. His hands on the wheel had tightened again. 'Andrei was not the only man who ever abducted a young girl,' he said. 'There must have been others, perhaps several, in Rostov or Novocherkassk. But the police wanted to clear their inquiry sheets, that's what they do, isn't it?'

'It happens,' I said.

'They find a man who has confessed to three or four crimes and they add six or seven unsolved crimes of a similar nature.'

'Listen Lukas,' I said. 'Andrei Chikatilo didn't confess to three or four. He confessed to fifty-two brutal killings. And was finally executed for them.'

We drove for a while in silence. From time to time as the road curved a shaft of moonlight fell upon his face. I could see the surges of emotion crossing his face, but I couldn't understand. What was he doing? Was he trying to defend the man who had murdered his sister? Tears trickled down his cheek.

Ahead the moonlight glistened on the black road. 'My mother, Rita,' he said quite suddenly, 'drank like a man. She wasn't really happy unless she had a half-litre of vodka on the table in front of her. The champagne she earned from her overtime, she exchanged for vodka.'

'Did Chikatilo or his wife ever come down for a drink?'

'His wife sometimes. But he didn't drink. He was an aloof man towards adults. A teacher at one time, then an engineer. People respected him, often drew attention to the neatness of his clothes. In summer his suits were always neatly pressed and darned, by Andrei himself, all the other women in the house said.'

'Tell me about Yelena,' I said. 'She was fourteen when she disappeared.'

I heard the breath soughing from his body. 'She'd take the *Elektrika* to Rostov to hang around the station there. She told me.'

'Are you saying she picked up men?'

'She and Svetlana, a friend of hers, always went together. Svetlana told me they picked up men coming back to Rostov from factories in the suburbs. They took them onto the wasteland near the station. Svetlana said they gave the men oral sex for three roubles.'

'Do you remember the night Yelena disappeared? Your mother was out?'

'She'd be at the miners' club drinking with the men.'

'And you?'

He made a casual shrug of his shoulders. 'Hanging around on the staircase probably. Playing knucklebones or reading. I liked to read, even then. Sometimes one of the women in the house would give me a piece of sausage and a glass of tea if it got really late.'

'Was Chikatilo at home?'

'He was upstairs. I could hear his wife Feodosia shouting at him. She always shouted at him. For stupid little things. For nothing.'

'But he went out that evening, didn't he?'

What was I doing? Why was I pressing so hard? I knew Yelena had been killed by Chikatilo. Lukas knew. It was something, for whatever reason, he wanted to keep to himself. But I wouldn't let him. Why was I so reluctant to let go?

'Yes,' Lukas said. 'He went out that evening. Some work he had to take care of. He was carrying his briefcase when he came down the stairs. For a few minutes we sat on the top step and played knucklebones. He told me he had to get out of the flat for a while. He told me his wife always became angry each month when she was losing blood.'

The thought chilled me. 'He told that to a ten-year-old boy?'

'We talked about all sorts of things.'

'And you played knucklebones with Andrei Chikatilo the night your sister disappeared.'

The van engine seemed to throb violently and we swerved towards the edge of the road. For a moment I thought we were going into a skid but he controlled the van and brought it to a stop in a lay-by. I stuck my head out of the window. Abby and Pinsk in the Kamka pulled over a hundred metres behind us.

Lukas's face was running with tears.

'I'm sorry,' I said. There seemed nothing else to say to this strange, fragile man.

He wiped his eyes with a handkerchief. 'While we played

knucklebones, we talked. He told me he had heard stories about my sister. About Yelena. About her going with men. He was deeply worried, he said, that the stories might be true.'

'Worried?'

'It's possible he was speaking the truth. Why not? Girls with disorderly sex lives were committing a criminal offence in the Soviet Union, remember. Andrei told me she could be arrested. I imagined the authorities putting Yelena in the big stone prison in Novocherkassk. Leaving me alone with my mother.' The horror of that thought was evident on his face.

'You were afraid of your mother.'

'When she was drunk, she was violent,' he said. 'Many people are when they're drunk – even you, Constantin.'

I suppose I could see it clearly enough now. 'Chikatilo offered to go out and find Yelena,' I said. 'He told you that you must never mention this conversation to anyone. It must never be known that Yelena was a station girl.'

He didn't answer. He started up the engine and pulled out onto the road.

Our journey took us barely ten kilometres from central Murmansk along a narrow but decent enough road that follows the river. There is no real break between the city and the wilderness, and in the dark you only just see the huge polluted cloud we call Anastasia. But the area has its marvels, the first of which is the long beach that runs below the cliffs. Up here in the Russian north this whole area, dependent on maritime transport, has no ship-breaking industry. The result is apparent along the beach. Dozen upon dozen of World War II merchant ships, sunk by the Luftwaffe in Murmansk Harbour and towed up river, rust and rot along a five-kilometre strip of riverside. Nowhere in the world is such a collection of scrap iron to be found, Liberty ships built in San Francisco, tankers which began life in Liverpool, bright red rusting hulks in the sparse sunlight of our northern climate, black crouching iron rodents in the darkness of a moonlit night.

We came off the highway and took the slip-road down towards the beach.

It is a Dickensian waterfront. Some ships have rolled on their sides, their dented funnels eating into the sand. Some flat-bottom cargoes sit upright almost as if they could float away with the morning tide. All are connected by an intricate pattern of narrow walkways of rope and plank.

The beach is known to the militia as a rookery, the hangout of deserters and ex-Anarchist soldiers. You come here for a good and proper reason – or you're unlikely to return.

My heart jumps to my throat as I think of Natalya here some nights by herself. We have left the Kamka two hundred metres back along the road. Abby and Pinsk have transferred to the back of the van and are lying on a pile of blankets smoking cigarettes. The white van is parked in the full moonlight where the beach road runs out. This, Lukas tells us, is the signal for someone to come out to meet us. But tonight I can see that he is desperately afraid. Sitting in the van, the engine turned off, he shivers uncontrollably every few minutes. It's like a spasm.

'It'll be OK, Lukas,' I tell him, thinking what in God's name do I know. 'It'll be OK. They're expecting us.'

He turned to me, his face more fearful than ever.

'When we're approached,' I told him, 'you stay in the van with Lieutenant Pinsk. I'll go with whoever comes for us with Agent Cunningham.'

'These are hard men,' Lukas said in a low voice. 'Hard men likely to kill us all if they suspect a trap.'

'There is no trap, Lukas. We have the dollars. If they have the children, we're going ahead with the deal.'

He looked at me in astonishment, then away quickly as he saw some movement among the dense, irregular shadows of the hulks.

I brought up the nightscope I was wearing round my neck. It gave a strange, rust-red glare, a rectangle of half-light in the darkness around us. Very slowly I panned the ships immediately in front of us. I picked up at least five men, blurred, reddish figures all moving towards us through the cubist shapes of the moonshadow.

'Is there anything we should do. Any move we should make?'

'There's a signal,' Lukas said reluctantly. 'I flash my headlights three times.'

'OK.'

The beams reached out three times across the grey pebble beach.

I got out and waited for Abby to join me from Pinsk's Kamka. Lukas, his head making nervous, birdlike movements, remained at the wheel of his van.

'I don't think,' Abby said as we trudged across the beach, 'that I've ever seen a weirder set-up in the world.'

'During the Hitler war,' I said, 'Murmansk was the route for all Anglo-American seaborne supplies. Food, jeeps, Spitfire fighters, heavy trucks, they all came by Arctic convoy to Murmansk. The ships the Germans sank couldn't be left to choke up the port. There they are.'

We approached the jetty. God knows how many pairs of eyes watched us, how many weapons were levelled on us, but I could only see one man now.

'Unarmed, this would take some courage,' Abby said. She was thinking of Joan and Natalya.

The man stepped out of the shadow and stopped. He stood on the deck of the nearest cargo ship in a shaft of moonlight which also showed the rusted metal letters of its name riveted to the bridge. *USS Rodney K. Ball, San Diego.*

Scrambling over the sloping deck the man gained a rope and plank walkway, crossed it, ignoring the dangerous swing he set up, and arrived at the jetty. He wore the hood of his parka up. His face was in shadow, the moon behind him. 'I didn't expect a man,' he said. Then looked across at Abby. 'Who are you?'

'Another American,' she said.

This seemed to reassure him.

'We'll do the same trade as agreed,' I said. 'Same price.'

'Where are the two women?'

'You don't keep up with the news, friend.'

'We're not always in town.' He spat onto the jetty in front of his feet.

'My name's Costya,' I said.

'You have the money?'

I hesitated. 'As agreed. In dollars.'

He grunted and turned for the walkway. 'Hang on tight. Go over the side and you'd have a cold swim tonight.'

We moved across the best part of half a dozen ships, each giving an eerie indication of being partly occupied, a candle in a wheel-house here, or a low kerosene lamp illuminating a descending companionway there. But never did we see a living soul except the back of the man leading us across the decks. Most of the ships were badly torn with great holes in the deck plates which offered further dangers, but the rope bridges were by far the most terrifying. Two hands were necessary and it was safer, or felt safer, to slide them along the ropes, never letting go as the planking beneath our feet began to buck and twist ecstatically.

Abby, I saw, just in front of me, took each crossing from ship to ship a good deal more coolly than I was able to. But then maybe she could swim.

I looked down as my stomach lurched at the slow swell of black, moonlit water beneath me. Abby had stepped onto the ship ahead. Our guide had stopped and half turned towards us. I felt we were at the end of our journey.

The man's face collected the moonlight. Sharp shadows outlined his nose and chin. His lips were twisted in a smile of contempt as he watched me trying to make the last metre or two. I could almost hear his thoughts: if I were a bodyguard, I was not a bodyguard to be reckoned with.

We assembled on the stern of a long narrow ship. I could see, looking towards the bow, an open hold forty or fifty metres long by perhaps ten metres wide. Now that I was able to direct my thoughts more I could see there was a pale fiery nebula across the top of the hold, and even from time to time a thin column of sparks and smoke rising through it.

We went down a narrow staircase with the cowled man in the lead. I could hear raised voices. As we got closer to the bottom I could feel the air temperature rising and in front of us the ribbed iron hold of the old ship opened up, full of shadow and dancing light and the figures of men moving about their business.

A huge fire burned in the centre of the hold. A tattered but once beautiful silk curtain hung over what I took to be a wide hole blown in the hold and offering perhaps an alternative means of escape. Twenty or so men in groups of two or three sat cross-legged eating from tin bowls and washing the food down with gulps of vodka. There was a lot of laughter and shouting. But the men fell silent when they saw us enter.

The neighing of a horse caught my attention. Past the fire a stabling area had been created, with bales of hay stacked to confine perhaps twenty horses. Two or three men were moving between them with buckets of oats and water. There were children too, forking hay and pouring water into troughs.

I had been so absorbed, puzzled by the horses, that I found

myself surprised to be confronted by a thin, wizened fellow, bearded and almost bald but somehow with a lively authority about him that announced immediately that he was a leader.

'I'm called Venya,' the man said. Our guide had slipped round to the other side of the fire. He gestured. 'These are my men.'

Four or five figures had detached themselves from the fire to form a loose ring around us. They were, I saw, all armed with revolvers in their belts or machine pistols hanging from their shoulders.

'Where are the women?' Venya asked. 'The doctor and the American woman?'

'I think you know,' I said. 'I'm Constantin Vadim, the doctor's husband.'

He nodded gravely. 'I've seen your picture. I carried out your wife's last order because I had no way of knowing if others would come to collect the children.'

'You did the right thing,' I said. 'This is an American who's running tonight's deal.'

Venya looked Abby over. 'As long as she has the five thousand dollars.'

'She has,' Abby said. 'What have you got in exchange?'

'Five girls, four boys,' the little man said. 'We followed your instructions to the letter.'

'Just tell us, friend, exactly how you followed instructions,' Abby said. 'We're not doubting you. But then, on the other hand, we won't be handing over any money until we're sure this is a straight deal.'

Venya looked at me for a moment. Three or four of his men had risen from their places beside the fire. Venya gestured behind him and they fell back. 'You're new to all this.'

'We are.'

He laughed, showing small teeth sharp and pointed. 'This morning,' he said, 'at six-thirty as we'd been told, a truck left Kola 27. The Juvenile Penal Colony at Nivka.'

I stood back and watched the men around the fire. They strolled about with their skewered kebabs or bottles of beer.

'And where's that?' Abby said. 'Where's Nivka?'

'Come and sit,' Venya said. He turned and a group of men moved away from the fire, vacating seats and benches.

We sat and accepted the offer of vodka to toast the success of the night's trade. 'Nivka,' the man's tongue flicked along his sharpened teeth. 'Nivka is the end of the line. Due west of Olengorsk. The road runs out at Nivka.'

'And the camp?' I said.

'That's tucked away in the marshes beyond the river Lovozero.'

'What were your instructions?'

'To pick up the truck as it left Nivka. To move in at the fit and right time and to take the children with a minimum of bloodshed to driver or guard.'

'*Those* children?' I pointed to the shadowy figures in the make-shift stable.

Venya laughed. 'They love horses. Kids love horses, Costya. Calms them wonderfully to give them a horse to look after.'

'So you picked up the trail sometime after Nivka early this morning,' Abby prompted him.

'It's not a complicated operation,' he said. 'A quick radio call ahead and the ambush was set up.'

'But you use horses. How can they keep pace with a truck?'

'They can't. We use the radio for that. And once a truck's ambushed we move off the road. Then there's nothing like horses for a getaway over these marshes. You'd need a hovercraft to keep up with them.'

I looked from Venya to his men and back again. 'You're happy to go against the system, Venya?'

'I'm an Anarchist,' he said. 'I fought on the Anarchist side in the Civil War. Whatever belongs to the government belongs to us all.'

'And the children?'

'The two ladies,' he said, 'they promised me the children would come to no harm.' He stopped, daring me to contradict him. 'I believed them. Was I right?'

'You were right,' Abby said. 'So shall we do the deal?'

Venya turned and put two fingers in his mouth. Perhaps because of the filed and capped prison teeth, his whistle was incredibly sharp. 'Bring over the children,' he called out to the men looking after the horses.

The children assembled for our inspection. They, in turn, nervously examined us. As they were lined up by the two stablemen, I saw that their clothes were neat but drab, their faces clean, the girls with short hair newly washed, the boys' cropped close. There were, as Venya had said, nine altogether, five girls each of about ten years, and four boys perhaps slightly younger.

They were well-fed and apparently well-cared for. There was colour in their cheeks and a brightness in their blue Russian eyes. But they looked at us, and particularly at Abby, with a prison caution. I have never been to one of the children's labour camps for which the Kola Peninsula is notorious. Even militia officers like myself in Street Offences, who deal with abandoned or escaped children regularly, are not allowed near the camps. Occasional, highly prepared visits are arranged for the press. Selected children are paraded for the photographers, their faces glowing with health. Each child interviewed makes improbable statements about the re-educative process, statements he or she has learned by heart. When the visit ends we can only guess what the real conditions are like in one of these remote and frightening camps.

I looked at the children in front of us. Brushed and washed like that, they might well have been a group prepared for the press. 'You're from Camp 27,' I said. 'Nivka.'

There was a ripple of nods along the line.

'And where were you being taken to in the truck?'

Nobody knew. Then one of the girls, slightly older than the others perhaps, shrugged a second time. 'Somebody said we were being transferred to a hospital in Murmansk.'

'A hospital?'

'To cure us.'

Several of the Anarchists gathered round now. 'To cure you of what?' Venya said.

The girl had said all she intended to say. 'Of whatever they put us in the camp sickbay for in the first place.'

'You've been in the camp sickbay?'

'Plenty to eat,' one of the boys said. 'All we wanted.'

Abby put her arm round the girl. 'What's your name?' she asked her.

I could see the child's mouth tremble. 'Irina,' she said. 'I'm called Irina.'

'Do you have bags or anything? Any belongings?'

'No.'

'Any papers?'

The girl reluctantly took out a single sheet and handed it to me. Russians, even prison children, were afraid of parting with their papers. I looked quickly at the sheet. It covered all nine of the children, detailing them as Boy 1, blond hair, one metre twenty-seven tall, age 7. Girl 3, dark eyebrows, blue eyes, one metre forty, age 9. Each child had a brief comment next to the initial description. *Quiet, good behaviour, born . . . Novgorod, Moscow, Smolensk . . .* There were no names, no camp numbers. 'Do you know what it says?' I asked the girl.

'It says we're going to a new hospital they've built. It says we've been specially chosen.'

I handed the girl back the paper. Abby was taking their names. Some of the youngest had difficulty remembering their exact ages and birth dates. It was a long time since any of them had known birthday celebrations. If ever. 'Can any of you read?' I asked.

'No.'

Abby drew Venya aside. 'We'll take them,' she said. From inside her parka she took a billfold. 'Five thousand dollars,' she said.

'Fifty-five hundred.'

'Not a dollar more than the price you agreed with Dr Vadim. Five thousand. In hundred-dollar bills.'

Venya took the money and began counting it. The children watched him uncertainly.

A slave market, I thought. Or perhaps because we were in Russia, a serf market. I remembered, as a child, going to a town which might have been Vladimir with my father. He had shown me a wide market-place. The site, he said, of Tsarist Russia's biggest serf market, even bigger than Moscow's. I looked at Abby. Was she aware in the same way I was that she had just purchased these human beings? Was she thinking of Augustus Cunningham and the $325 ticket round her great-grandmother's neck? I caught her eye and a quick grimace. She was.

The children looked from Abby to me, too cowed to ask what was happening. Venya finished counting, lifted the money in the air for his men to see and cheer.

'They're all yours,' he said, his teeth glittering. 'Take them away.'

'One more question,' I said.

'If I can answer it.'

'You met Dr Vadim and the American woman several times. Did you talk?'

'We talked, yes.'

'How did they know when a convoy of children was due to leave a camp?'

'That, I can't tell you,' Venya said, and I believed him. 'They gave me times, dates, names of camps the children were leaving – and left the rest to me.'

'When you . . .' I paused, skirting the word *kidnap*, 'When you pick up the children, where are they headed?

'To Murmansk.'

'Do you know where?'

'No. Our military operation usually takes place a long time before they reach the city. Most camps are well off the main highways of course. We intercept the convoy carrying the children on one of the feeder roads.'

'People get hurt?'

'Sometimes. Camp guards. We don't shed too many tears for them. Who would spend his life penning up innocents?'

'They may not all be innocents, brother,' I said.

'Perhaps not. But if they're not innocent, it's because others are guilty.' He laughed. 'But you didn't come here to debate the state of Russian society.'

'You must have thoughts about it,' I pressed him. 'What do you think the two women were doing?'

'No harm to the children. That I can say from my own observation. Besides, ask anybody here, Venya likes children. As I said, I wouldn't be doing this if I thought any harm would come to them.'

'Have you and the two women any more meetings planned?'

'Not unless you've got instructions for me.'

I shook my head.

'You can always contact me . . .' To my surprise he produced a business card. It read *Venya* and gave a mobile-phone number. 'If you wish to come yourself, come by daylight or you'll get your throat cut. Ask for Venya. Say you come to talk about children.'

We shook hands. The children walked together in a huddle, following Abby and our original guide in the cowl.

I looked back from the entrance to the hold. The Anarchists had gathered round Venya, slapping him on the back. At least three of them were pouring vodka into an overflowing half-litre glass.

It was a nightmare journey back across the walkways between the boats. Again there was evidence of habitation, lights and cooking smells, but we saw no-one. I suspected that for Venya this was more than a temporary headquarters. There were probably tens, perhaps hundreds of villains of one sort or another here. But nobody came out to challenge us. An extraordinary discretion seemed to have descended on the denizens of the old merchant ships. On the beach there was no doubt in my mind that it was Venya's writ that ran.

The drive to the Norwegian border took nearly three hours. Abby stayed in the back of the van with the children, distributing chocolate and sodas. I sat next to Lukas in the front. Pinsk, in the Kamka, kept a distance of six or seven hundred metres behind us. From time to time I looked through the small grille behind my seat. The children were calm but silent and unforthcoming. Abby scrambled over and sat close to the grille. 'I can get nothing out of them,' she said in English. 'Each one carries the green KOLA tattoo on their shoulder. They describe the camp as a hellhole, the worst camp they've ever been in, run entirely by the older boys and their girlfriends.'

'If it was that bad,' I said, 'how do they look so well-fed?'

'The girl that speaks for them says they spent almost a month in the camp sickbay before they left. They were well-treated there – and well-fed.'

'What were they there for?'

'She didn't know.'

'Could it be that they were being used as some sort of medical guinea pigs?'

I saw her dark eyebrows rise and fall. 'God knows,' she said and dropped back into the shadow.

We took the highway west, crossing the Pechenga river at the town itself, then taking the secondary road towards the border.

About three kilometres out of town Lukas extinguished his lights and slowed down, his head craning to the left every few minutes as if he were hoping to catch a glimpse of some landmark in the moonlight.

The frontier was boldly marked. In Soviet days we would have been stopped long before this, but we passed through the final notices saying *Norwegian border ONLY* without any sign of the border police.

Lukas, who had preserved a guarded silence throughout most of the journey, spoke as we approached a massive final warning sign. 'There's a roadway through the woods here. It leads to a worked-out nickel mine.'

He gestured left with a nod of his head and almost immediately I saw an opening in the trees. Swinging the wheel hard, causing squeals of alarm from the back of the van, Lukas drove, too fast, I thought, up the narrow road which frost and snow had reduced to little more than a dirt track. He was, I felt, a very frightened man.

We reached the nickel mine and Lukas pulled in among some collapsing buildings next to the shaft. Almost immediately four or five flashlights were pointed towards the van.

In the back, the children were silent. I signalled to Abby with a rap of my knuckles on the panel behind my head and got out of the van and walked towards the lights.

The shape of a man was outlined as he came forward. 'A trouble-free journey, I hope,' he said in English. He looked towards Pinsk's Kamka which had pulled up behind us.

'I'm the doctor's husband,' I said. 'Natalya and the American woman were unable to come.'

His eyes never left my face as he nodded twice. He was a big, fair-haired man with a friendly bearded face. 'I've read the newspapers,' he said.

'It's good you came all the same.'

'We had to take the risk,' he said. 'Perhaps you still had the children from last time. We had no way of knowing whether someone else would come tonight.'

'I need to ask you some questions,' I said.

'Have you anything to prove that you're who you say you are?'

I offered him a photograph of Natalya and myself together.

'What questions?' he asked as he passed it back to me.

'Very basic questions. They might seem strange coming from Natalya's husband.'

'You mean you weren't aware of what she was doing.'

I hated admitting it. 'No. She thought it best.'

He scratched at his blond beard, nodding agreement.

'How do you pass across this border?' I asked him. 'I'd heard it was airtight.'

He gave a half smile. 'Some Norwegian children's societies have been doing it for ten years now. It used to be impossible. Today, even Russia doesn't defend its borders as once it did.'

'And these Russian children, where do you take them?'

'To a hospital first. They're examined as soon as we cross the border.'

'Why examined?'

'The children themselves all report that they've been brought here from children's camp hospitals. They were, we were told, desperate cases.'

'What did that mean? Desperate cases of *what*?'

'Neither Natalya nor the American woman ever said more. And we never asked. We accepted that the children were in great danger. Obviously not to their health. The children we've smuggled across have always been proved to be in excellent health.'

'And after the Norwegian hospital?'

'They go to families in various countries in the West. Many to Norway. Some as far as Canada or America.'

I felt a deep sense of shame that we were trading our children across the border like this. And a deep sense of confusion about what might happen to them from here on. But I looked at the open face of the Norwegian leader and couldn't believe he was a link in a trade of children that ended in New York or Chicago or Paris.

In the moonlight and by the cautious light of the torches carried by the Norwegians, we brought the children out into the clearing. Some had been asleep and stumbled about shivering and with trembling lips. The older ones adopted a stolid, defensive look. Abby had told them all there was to tell them in the van. There was no more to say.

'So what have we done?' Abby looked quizzically at me.

'What do you mean?'

'A Russian militia officer and an FBI special agent have aided and abetted the kidnap and smuggling of a group of children across the Russian border. You tell me, Constantin, has this been a good night's work?'

Some of the Norwegians, I saw for the first time, were young women. For a moment I didn't answer Abby as I watched them bending over the children, whispering reassurance in Russian.

I turned back to Abby. 'A good night's work? I believe so. It might lose us both our jobs,' I said, 'but yes, I think it's been a good night's work. What about you?'

She knew how heavily charged the question was. 'I've seen enough to know which side Natalya was on.' She hunched her shoulders. Taking a camera from the pocket of her parka she took photographs of each of the children.

We stayed to watch the Norwegians form them up in pairs. Abby bent over and gave Irina a kiss on the forehead. I saw Abby swallow hard; the girl was crying. 'It's going to be all right,' Abby said. 'You're going to a different life. A happy life.' Most of the other children were crying silently. The bearded leader waved goodbye. The moon slid behind a cloud and within seconds all we could see were pinpoints of flashlights growing dimmer through the trees.

47

OUR RUSSIAN SYSTEM is unchanged since Yeltsin's day. Unchanged since Brezhnev's day. Children without families take two courses through life. One is the freedom of the streets – a few to be gathered up by street patrols like mine and put into decent orphanages. The sort of orphanages which now exist solely through the good offices and compassion of American and West European charities.

Most abandoned children face a very different life. They are designated idiots and imbeciles and sent to *Internaty*, nightmare centres of state care. Or arrested for petty crime and sent to children's camps, many in the deserted marshlands of the Kola Peninsula. Here they live lives of pure abuse, from older children and from those who are paid to supervise them. Decent food and vitamins are often denied them. HIV, and more commonly TB, haunt them as the nemesis of neglect.

Everybody says their plight is a disgrace to Russia. Everybody has been saying it since Yeltsin's time.

I approached Camp K27 outside Nivka with foreboding. Permits were rarely granted. I had never visited a camp before. I knew of the frightening reputations of such places. The snow was melting here, sliding down the tarpaper rooftops of the huts in dirty ridges, the icicles cracking and falling as we left our Kamka in the lot and walked towards the administration building.

Within minutes we were shown into the timber main office. 'The captain is doing camp rounds,' the clerk-sergeant told us. 'The colonel's waiting for you.'

As he opened the door for us I saw Sonya Fetisova come round the desk and waddle across the office to greet us. 'Agent Cunningham – good to see you again. And Constantin, we really must get together for that thumb sometime,' she said.

I shivered. This had to be put on a different footing. 'Special Agent Cunningham and myself are here, Colonel, because we have information to offer you about the escape of nine of the prisoners in your jurisdiction.'

She nodded and waved us to seats before she headed back for the chair behind the crudely blue-painted desk.

Every time I see Fetisova I am astonished that a woman, any woman, can be so ugly. Fetisova exceeded any reasonable weight by almost as much again. Her green uniform skirt, I noticed, had the unlovely habit of rising to a fixed place on her hips as she crossed the room, revealing the backs of her dumpling legs in grey nylon hose.

Turned towards us, her face was almost perfectly round, red, weather-beaten beyond her forty or so years, her dark hair liberally decorated with red highlights. From the distant past I remembered that if someone wanted to butter up the powerful President of the Students' Union they should mention her hair.

'Information about escaped prisoners? I thought we dealt with that during our meeting with the mayor,' she said to Abby.

'More than information,' Abby said. '*Evidence* of an escape.'

The colonel's eyes almost disappeared into her puffed, reddened cheeks so that, when they caught the light, they gave off a sly glint which reminded me of V.I. Lenin, man and cat. 'First tell me how you came into a position to offer me such information,' she said. She unbuttoned her uniform breast pocket and took out her cigarettes. 'Presumably you have some sort of informant? Some person no doubt accepting money, dollars, from you. I should advise you that, in Russia, people of this sort are not always reliable.' She chuckled. 'We have a long history, I'm afraid, of police spies in our country. Almost by definition, unreliable. I'm surprised your Russian colleague, Constantin . . .' her eyes flicked contemptuously in my direction . . . 'didn't make this clear to you. So, how exactly did this information come into your possession, Agent Cunningham?'

'I'm sorry, Colonel,' Abby said briskly. 'I'm not able to disclose that. Nor am I obliged to. I, and my deputy, Inspector Vadim, work directly on the orders of the Moscow All-Russia Procurator's Office. I'm sure you understand.'

The colonel took out a cigarette and lit it. The movements were irritatingly slow. It was part of a technique to slow everything to walking pace, to her pace. I had the strong impression she was a worried woman. She smiled.

To concede a smile would have been a mistake at this stage. Abby sat, her extraordinary face set. I stared past the colonel's head to the wall behind her. A wooden-framed notice-board carried the lengthy inscription:

The year 1998 was declared by then President Yeltsin as the year of the abandoned Russian child. In that year over 200,000 children were arrested for criminal offences.

The situation has not improved. It is our duty, citizen colleagues, to stand guard against the rising tide of juvenile criminality.

On the board, pages fluttered in a draught from the poorly constructed hut, duty roster for weekend beginning Sunday. Guard Unit 22 will take responsibility for all four guard towers from 0600 hours. Regulations for hut-cleaning and rodent control. Duty medical officer for the month: Dr G.V. Potanin. *Potanin.*

I felt my eyes bulge.

'I've had no word from Moscow,' Colonel Fetisova was saying.

'And you should expect none,' Abby said. There was a finality in her voice that touched even the colonel. 'My investigation has already been given plenipotentiary status,' she concluded. 'You can confirm that with the Moscow Procurator's Office right away, if you choose.'

The uniformed woman across the desk pressed her lips together, uncertain how to proceed. I shifted my gaze from her and looked out of the window. There was little I could see of the camp itself. Across the empty asphalt space of the appel square, I could see a column of small drab figures marching through the camp gates. They carried shovels on their shoulders, absurdly long-handled for such small children. As the tail of the column passed through, the gates began to close. What part did Potanin have in this whole matter?

'You present me with a problem,' Fetisova said after a few moments. She stood up and pulled the hem of her jacket. 'I am of course responsible for all junior labour camps in the Kola area . . .'

'How many is that, Colonel?' Abby asked.

'That is restricted social information,' Fetisova said sharply. She got up and began to pace the room, even stopped at the window to lean forward to pretend to examine something that had caught her attention outside, presenting again the opportunity to examine the backs of those dropsical knees.

'I have some difficulty with your offer of information,' Colonel Fetisova said, turning to face us. 'Because I have this morning contacted every one of my camp commandants individually. I required a roll-call to be made *immediately*. I have here the result.' She lifted a single sheet of paper from the desk. 'This year there have been *no escapes* from any of the camps in the Kola Camp Administration Area. The last involved two boy prisoners who were recaptured within hours of escape. That was before the New Year.'

'Let's cut the nonsense,' Abby said sharply. 'Not just any camp. Our names are from *this* camp.'

Even the ruddy face of Fetisova paled. 'Perhaps you have names,' she said. 'But what proof do you have that these children have escaped?'

'We have Camp Administration Identity Numbers. We even have photographs,' I added for effect. 'If the children are still here – just show us.'

Fetisova recovered and shook her head in a parody of sadness. 'I'm afraid someone has been selling you what you want to hear. The commandant here at K27 has examined the names you faxed to him this morning,' the colonel said. 'He found your accusation that nine children had escaped from the camp most interesting.'

'Interesting.'

'That was his word.'

'He doesn't deny that the list contains names of children who are prisoners of this camp?'

'No, of course not. Indeed, he informs me all nine children were, until recently, receiving treatment in the camp hospital.'

'Treatment for what?'

'Let's tackle this problem logically, Agent Cunningham. If you'll forgive me . . .' She crossed to her desk and picked up a phone. 'We're ready now,' she said.

The door opened almost immediately. A young captain in green Camp Administration uniform held open the door.

'This is Captain Loshkin, commandant of this camp. If you'll come this way,' the colonel said, waddling through the doorway in front of us, 'I'll show you your nine escaped prisoners.' She looked at the young captain. 'I'm afraid someone has been having a little game at our city comrades' expense.'

The captain, I noticed, managed only the shadow of a smile.

We were given white cotton masks. We walked through the camp lines past the low wooden huts. From open doors the stench was unendurable. A glance through one or two of the windows showed children crowded onto bunks, matchstick legs swinging, young mouths surrounded with the sores of malnutrition.

The captain gestured to the hut we were passing. 'Tuberculosis is our major problem,' he began but fell silent under Fetisova's glare.

'This is not a medical inspection, Captain,' she said. 'Even less a sightseeing trip.' She turned to us. 'What we do here is a good job under exceptionally difficult circumstances.'

Abby stopped dead at the entrance to a hut. 'Good God, Colonel,' she said, her voice only just controlled. 'What sort of warped outlook do you need to be proud of a job like this?'

But Fetisova, as I could have told Abby, was not easily put down. 'Are you offering a public insult to the Russian Camp Administration?' she said slyly.

'No,' Abby said. 'A purely personal one.'

The huge cemetery was on a remote part of the camp on the side of a hill. I felt Abby tug my arm. 'It's the one,' she said. 'The one in Joan's sketch. Or at least the map that was missing from her sketch-book.'

In the section we were led to there were perhaps a hundred mounds of earth surmounted by crude wooden crosses. We removed our masks in the open air and walked, Fetisova and Abby in front, myself and the captain behind, towards a corner of the graveyard where the mounds of earth were not yet overgrown by moss. Up ahead they made a bizarre couple, the colonel and Abby, almost a denial they shared the same sex. The one in a heavy green winter uniform, uncomfortably hot in the sudden spring sunshine. The other, slender in a pale linen suit, tote bag on her shoulder, jacket held back by her hands thrust casually into the skirt pockets as she paced up the slope ahead of us.

'I thought Dr Potanin was a psychiatric specialist,' I said to the captain. 'Not a medical officer.'

'The doctor began here in that capacity,' he said. 'But our requirement was for medical generalists. I understand Colonel Fetisova managed to persuade him to do an occasional shift here as a general doctor.'

'And he's been on duty this month?'

'He comes out midweek for Wednesday sick call.'

We closed on Abby and the colonel just ahead of us. Over to

the left, a small group of children of about twelve or thirteen were digging shallow graves under the supervision of a single guard. I saw the colonel turn towards the captain and narrow her eyes meaningfully. The captain understood. He crossed quickly to where the children were working and spoke rapidly to the guard. The detail was dissolved in minutes, the shovels abandoned, the children formed up and marched quickly downhill.

Colonel Sonya Fetisova relaxed. She stood, her hands on her hips, her skirt riding up on her swollen rump, her red-braided cap pushed slightly back on her two-tone hair. 'You see, Inspector,' she said, addressing me directly for the first time, '*somebody* has made a considerable error.'

She glared at Abby and left us in no doubt who she thought the somebody was, or at least who that somebody was going to turn out to be. 'Let's have a look at your list,' she said. She looked down at the line of the newest graves. 'Irina Laktova . . .' She pointed to the nearest wooden cross. *Irina Laktova 2005-2017. With God.* 'There,' she thrust the list into my hands. 'Check them out yourself.'

She turned away, affecting to lose interest.

I glanced at the list to refresh my memory, then quickly along the lines of graves. All the children we had driven to the Norwegian border last night seemed to be there, in the ground.

'What was the cause of death?' I said.

She frowned, a *do you have to prolong this nonsense* frown. 'You have the death certificates, Captain?'

The young captain handed me a sheaf of printed papers, cheap paper stock with brown wood stains dotted across each page.

'An attack of E-Coli,' I said, reading the cause of death.

'Now eradicated,' the captain said automatically.

Fetisova's smile was triumphant. 'You can see how surprised I was when you talked of information regarding an escape. And offered *these* names.'

'Not information,' Abby said. 'Evidence.'

'The evidence lies there, in the earth,' the colonel said. She waved a fat hand across the burial mounds.

Abby had been standing slightly apart and above the rest of us, on a sloping path that led up to the stone boundary wall. 'Are *you* empowered to sign the certificate of exhumation, Colonel?' she said casually.

Sonya Fetisova's mouth opened. 'Exhumation,' she said. 'You're asking for exhumation?'

'I'm asking if you have the power to authorize it,' Abby said with that cold, hard snap in the movement of her lips that I'd seen once or twice before.

'Out of the question.'

'Perhaps the current medical officer, Dr Potanin, will,' I said.

Abby looked at me with interest.

'He has no authority,' the colonel said dismissively. 'He is under my command when he attends here.'

'The medical officer has no authority and you yourself refuse to give it?' Abby said neutrally.

'Exactly.'

'Then, instead, perhaps you'll allow us to talk to some of the men and women under your command?' I said. 'No difficulty there, is there?'

'You want to talk to staff at random?'

'More specifically in the sickbay.'

Her mouth tightened. 'I can only think that that would disturb the smooth running of the camp schedule. Apart from that you, as visitors, would be subject to an unwarranted risk. I can't authorize that.'

'So you're refusing to co-operate?' Abby took over. 'On questioning the staff and on the matter of exhuming the graves? Is that the situation?'

I watched Colonel Fetisova. She bristled, then relaxed slowly. 'The situation is that Camp Administration regulations state clearly that I decide what happens in my camps, unless otherwise directed by the mayor of Murmansk or the governor of the province. You are possibly aware that the Kola region has no governor at present, Agent Cunningham.'

'The election results on Sunday will change that one way or the other,' I said.

'Then we must see if the new governor is prepared to endorse this distasteful business,' the colonel said comfortably. 'Until then Mayor Osopov's word is law.'

48

A MILITIA DETAIL HAS picked up Potanin and brought him to the Nunnery. Abby and I take him into her big office. She is behind the desk. I lean against the wall to his side, but almost out of his sightline from the chair he sits in. Potanin's face is unshaven as usual, but white and drawn. He carries a brown cardboard file under his arm. He wants, he says, to make his part in this whole business clear. He is very obviously afraid.

'This whole business?' I say from my place against the wall.

'The market in children.' He puts the file on the desk in front of Abby. 'Please read that, Miss Cunningham. It will tell you how it all began.'

'You tell me.' She pushed the file to one side.

'Do you have a drink here?'

Abby looked from him to me with exasperation.

'It sounds like a good idea,' I said. 'Abby?'

She nodded, resigned, and I went into the other office to collect a bottle and glasses. When I came back and set them on the table Potanin was speaking.

'A year or more ago . . .' Potanin took the glass I pushed towards him. 'A year or more ago, I was called to see Colonel Fetisova at the Children's Prison Service. I attended her office in the city and was well received with cakes and a very fine Kuban vodka. Nevertheless I was afraid. It's not every day one is called to the office of a senior prison service officer.'

'What did she want?' I asked.

'Two things. She first, she said, wanted to confirm my qualification.'

'That must have been embarrassing for you.'

He gave a spectral smile. 'You might have thought so.'

I turned to Abby who was frowning at this exchange. 'Dr Potanin's qualifications are all considerably less than they seem.' I heard a quiet groan from Potanin. 'Indeed you have no real right to the title doctor. Isn't that so, Doctor.'

'What did Colonel Fetisova conclude?' Abby asked.

'On my second visit, a week later, she said my qualifications had been checked and found impeccable.'

'Now this was a surprise to you.'

'Of course it was. But I'm a Russian. I knew what we had here was a barely veiled threat. My qualifications would not be exposed in certain conditions.'

'Which were . . .?'

'I was offered – and expected to accept – a post at K27, the children's camp at Nivka. Visiting physician. One day a week. A handsome salary.'

'And your silence about anything you might see.'

'That was implicit in the arrangement.'

I sat on the edge of the desk. 'What did you see?'

'Misery and ill-treatment beyond my imaginings. Undernourished children in constant danger from diphtheria and tuberculosis. A regime of intense cruelty and deprivation based on the authority of half a dozen licensed teenage thugs. The prison guards seldom stirred from the guardroom in winter. What I saw, Inspector, was close to a death camp.'

I refilled Potanin's glass.

'Last winter we lost nearly twenty-five per cent of the children. Twenty-five per cent! Disease mainly of course. But beatings, murder too.'

'This is not what you came to tell us.'

'No. I'm not made of clay, Inspector. And yet I was very conscious of the risks if I spoke up. A coward's dilemma.' He tossed back his vodka and breathed out through his teeth. 'But something else was happening in the camp too. The sickbay was built apart from the main detention huts. Working there I was required to go through the camp and pick out the fittest children. Not the sick. Not the most needy, but the fittest.'

'And they were taken into the sickbay?'

'Exactly.'

'What for?'

'Feeding up. Delousing. Reclothing. Colonel Fetisova would come to winnow out any child with scars or missing teeth. Only the best-looking stayed on.'

'And then what?'

'After perhaps a month, when they were as healthy as a normal child should be . . .'

'You were required to sign their death certificates.'

'Without being allowed to examine the bodies. Yes.' Potanin looked down. 'After a while I couldn't pretend I didn't know what they were destined for.'

'And you kept quiet because your comfortable life at the Clinic would never survive Fetisova revealing that all your qualifications were worth nothing,' Abby said, the contemptuous note clear in her voice.

'No, Miss Cunningham,' he said softly. 'I kept quiet because I have a young sister who was sentenced to three years in a juvenile labour colony in southern Russia somewhere. Ninety per cent of prisoners contract TB. My sister would certainly have been released a cripple, soon to die. Instead Fetisova offered me her transfer to community service for the remainder of her sentence. My silence keeps my sister out of a TB colony, Inspector.'

Abby slowly took out her cigarettes. Unsure of her, Potanin turned to me. 'I tried to do something, Constantin, shortly before your wife was abducted. I wrote a series of anonymous letters to the American consul here in Murmansk.'

'To Miles Bridger?' Abby said, her head coming up.

'I made clear in my letter that I had no idea how high the management of this market in children went.'

'Did you ever see any action on the information you'd given? Were any changes made in the camps?'

'No. But immediately after the first letter, all key members of staff were interrogated by Fetisova herself and reminded of the consequences of what she called betrayal.'

'You're saying Miles Bridger passed your information straight to Fetisova?'

'He did. Whether innocently or in connivance with her, I don't know.'

'And that was the end of it?'

He hesitated a long time. 'No. One night in January I met a member of the embassy staff at a Lermontov gathering. I was drunk; she seemed sympathetic. I took a risk, a fool's risk. I told her what I thought was happening.'

'Joan Fowler?'

'Yes. Within a month Fetisova announced there would be a complete blackout on news from the camps. Her excuse was that bands of Civil War deserters were roaming the area and attacking our food convoys. It was true about the attacks by roaming bands of deserters, of course. But they weren't looking for food.'

I found myself taking deep breaths.

'I am asking for temporary protection. Too many who tried to do something about this obscene trade are already dead. I'd sooner put myself in your care than offer myself as a target in the city.'

Abby nodded towards Potanin. 'I'll assign you two men. We'll take a statement from you and check it out.'

'You'll ask why the consul Mr Miles Bridger took no action?'

'I certainly will.'

Miles Bridger was calm on the outside. How deep it went I couldn't tell. 'I have to be clear, Abby,' he said, 'what it is you want of me.'

'An explanation,' I said, before she could answer. Looking at him I could see a hollowness about him I hadn't seen before. A shifty, greedy look which fitted the idea I now had of him. 'An explanation of the fact that you passed on to Moscow none of the information supplied to you about burials in Nivka Camp.'

'I don't pass on baseless rumour, Inspector. I don't pass on tittle-tattle. Abby will tell you how much rubbish passes through our consulates. Your country has emerged from a bitter civil war. There are denunciations daily. Still, a year or more later. Frankly I don't even remember the material you're talking about. I certainly don't owe you an explanation for not acting on it.'

'We have another problem, too,' Abby said in that steely voice she could conjure up.

He looked at her coldly.

'The personal possessions of Joan Fowler . . .'

'The ones I handed back to you?'

'The page torn from her sketch-book . . . It contained the map of a graveyard at Nivka.'

He lifted his shoulders. 'People do that with their notebooks, Abby,' he said. 'They tear pages out when they're dissatisfied with what they've sketched. Good God, it's a common enough thing surely!'

'But Lieutenant Pinsk's meticulous notes didn't mention missing pages,' I said.

Bridger turned back to Abby. 'Really, what is going on here? I have to tell you I don't at all like the tone of these questions.'

332

'OK, Miles,' Abby said in a quick change to a friendlier tone. 'Good enough.'

I stared at her. Was she letting him off the hook? He was nodding to himself and her in a way that excluded the blunt Russian oaf leaning against his wall.

'But one thing,' Abby added, as she turned for the door. 'Have you come across the Children's Penal Service boss, Colonel Fetisova?'

'More times than I like to remember.'

'You didn't pass her the anonymous letter on the empty coffins.'

'Why should I?'

'It's her bailiwick.'

'I believed,' he said patiently, 'that the letter was the work of a crazy. Empty coffins . . . Honestly, what would you think?'

'Memory, like sunshine, bursts through cloud,' I said.

'What are you talking about?'

'A moment ago, you couldn't even remember receiving the letter.'

'Half an hour in the basement downstairs . . .' I said in the passage outside Bridger's office. 'Just give me half an hour with him.'

'I know how you feel,' she said with a complicit smile. 'I'd take him myself if I could. He's in, I'm sure of it.'

'But is he the killer?'

'No, I don't think so. He's a link in some sort of chain. I think our vek is way down the line from Miles Bridger.'

'So what do we do? Short of breaking into his apartment?'

A familiar look of alarm crossed her face and she increased her speed down the corridor. 'For Christ's sake,' she muttered.

I caught her up and grabbed her arm. 'What is it?' I said. 'Ten seconds ago you were talking about beating the shit out of him in the basement.' She was swung round to face me. 'You hear what you want to hear. I said *short* of breaking into his apartment.'

For a moment she breathed heavily, then looked down at my hand on her arm. I released her. 'What we do,' she said, 'is put a twenty-four-hour tail on him. We get Dronsky to push through a tap on his line. We make it all very obvious in a bumbling sort of way. Line clicks, surveillance car following too closely. We hope to bounce him into making a run for it. Then we pick him up and I hand him over to you and Dronsky for questioning.'

'I don't need Dronsky,' I said.

She grimaced. 'Oh yes, you do.'

Twenty minutes later we were clambering over the builders' rubble in the half-built block in Turgenev Street. The sergeant in charge of the crime-scene specialists was waiting for us, a thick folder in his hand, at the door of Jay's apartment.

That sick smell of blood was gone, cleared by open windows. The books had been stacked in one corner and I saw through the open bedroom door that the bed had been stripped to leave just a lightly stained mattress. 'What do you have for us?' Abby asked as she shook hands with the sergeant.

'In the matter of fingerprints,' he said formally, opening his file and handing her photographs of dusted prints, 'the door as usual yielded most. People don't just use handles. They push at doors. They close them by taking hold of the edge and pulling it towards them. They slide their hands up them as they stand talking between the two rooms.'

'Anything recent, other than the victim?'

The sergeant coughed. 'Plenty from the inspector here,' he said, with a half smirk at me. 'All over the door . . .'

No cause for surprise there.

'. . . and one good palm print on the shower glass.'

Abby raised her eyebrows in interest.

'I'd forgotten I actually walked into the room,' I said. 'She was in the shower. I couldn't catch what she was saying.'

'Anything else that looks recent?' Abby turned towards the sergeant.

'Some bloody smudges from the taps in the bathroom. Lot of work to be done on them before they'll produce anything. We drained the U-bend and found a dilution of blood there, too. Looks as though the vek washed his hands before leaving.'

'But nothing we can get our teeth into.'

The sergeant was the sort of man who leaves the tastiest morsels to the end. He took two copies of a picture from his folder and handed us one each. At first it was difficult to see what they were.

'Footprints,' he said as I turned the picture right way up. 'All around the bed. I'd say they were a leather shoe, a man who comes down hard on the right heel. Size 44. That suggests a pretty tall man.'

Abby was studying the pictures. 'Are these copies?' she asked.

'All copies,' the sergeant said. 'You can keep the whole folder.'

We followed the sergeant into the bedroom. The walls, I now saw, were spattered with blood. There was a large stain beside the bed. Yellow tape had been stuck to the pale grey carpet to mark out two or three areas. The bloody footprints were clear enough. I found them somehow especially chilling to look at and I jumped involuntarily as Abby's mobile sounded.

She took it from her purse and walked into the other room.

'How far did the footprints go?' I asked the sergeant.

'The prints themselves ran out pretty soon,' he said. 'But distinct traces of blood were found on the carpet outside. And on one of the overalls in the pile in the corridor. I think he cleaned off his shoes there.'

I looked up. Abby was standing in the doorway. 'That was Pinsk. Miles Bridger's Lincoln has a registration containing the figures 3141,' she said.

49

THE AMERICAN CONSUL leaned forward, hands flat on his desk, his shoulders hunched. He was a big man without being excessively tall. I would have said 44 was about his shoe size.

'You understand, I'm sure, Abby, that I'm not prepared to go on answering your questions throughout the whole working day. Whatever it is can wait until tomorrow. I have a particularly heavy workload to catch up on this afternoon.'

'Your workload will have to be put aside,' Abby said. 'Just to get this clear, this is an FBI investigation into the death of Jay Dellerman.'

'For God's sake, Abby. I knew Jay. She used to work here. I was as shocked as anybody who knew her. But you can't simply walk in here and expect me to drop everything I'm doing . . . Go ahead and I'll instruct my staff to give you full co-operation. But, beyond that, I can't see what this has to do with me.'

'Let me tell you then,' Abby said crisply. 'Your car was seen outside her apartment block at approximately the time she was murdered. Does that explain what we think it's got to do with you, Mr Bridger?'

I'd never seen such a sudden collapse of vertebrae. His back seemed to curve. His neck fell forward until he was looking down at the surface of the desk. 'May I ask,' he said, his eyes still cast down, 'how you know it was my car?'

'It had your registration plate on the tail. Good enough?'

He pushed from the flat of his hands and stood upright. 'I can explain it,' he said.

There was a heavy silence in the room. I felt this man was infinitely wily. Was he the Scorpio – clever, devious, lustful? How in God's name was he going to explain the fact that his car was there at four or four-thirty the night Jay was murdered?

'I went to see her,' he said. 'I went to see Jay.'

'At four in the morning?'

'My wife has difficulty sleeping. The first few hours are uncertain. After about three o'clock she often takes a very strong draught.'

'Propteknol?' I said.

'Yes. Propteknol. It's the latest and the most efficient.'

And the drug that left traces in the bodies of Natalya and Joan, I reminded myself.

Abby had taken her black notebook and was scribbling notes.

'I was having an affair with Jay,' Bridger said heavily. 'Had been since she worked here at the consulate. But I hadn't seen her for weeks. Problem was, Jay wanted me to leave my wife and I refused. It's a very old, old story, Abby. I'm sure you've heard it before.'

That wasn't quite how Jay had told it to me, but she might well have decided that half a story – her half – sounded better than the full front page.

'Did Jay know you were coming to see her?' I asked him.

He hesitated. 'Yes. I called her. She was not very enthusiastic.'

'You went all the same?'

He shrugged. 'I was missing her. I'd been drinking. You know, all the base excuses.'

'You wanted sex,' Abby said.

'I don't deny it. I wanted to talk, too.'

'And what happened when you arrived at the apartment?' Abby asked.

'I didn't stay long,' he said. 'She wasn't prepared even to let me in.'

'You didn't have keys?' I said.

'As a matter of fact she did once give me a set of keys. But that was to her old apartment down by the port. I was never favoured with the offer of keys to this one.' He looked up at me. 'You evidently were.'

In the consul's changing-room the Russian valet was uncomfortable about allowing us in to look around.

'I should first ask the consul's permission,' the small fat man in the green and black striped apron said.

'It's late. The consul's gone home,' Abby said. 'And this is urgent.'

'This is his private changing-room. It would be better if you could wait until tomorrow.'

'Just open up the shoe cupboard,' I said. 'We'll be out in five minutes.'

Muttering to himself, the valet took a small brass key and opened a cupboard behind him. In the top part there were two or three dark suits and a dinner-jacket. On two shelves below were five or six pairs of shoes. I reached in and triumphantly lifted out a pair. But I knew before I looked at the size stamped in the instep that they were not big enough to fit the blood prints on the grey bedroom carpet in Jay's flat.

We made our way slowly back to Abby's office. 'I thought,' she said, 'that we had him.' She shook her head. 'It's too much of a coincidence. He was there in the middle of the night more or less *exactly* the time she was killed. There's something we're not seeing, Constantin.'

We reached her office door. 'Let's take a cup of coffee with maybe something in it before we go back to your apartment.'

It was the first friendly approach she'd made since the night we got drunk together and I was sorry to turn it down. 'Madame Badanova asked me if I'd call in at her campaign headquarters . . .'

'At this time of night?'

'She says it's important. I arranged with Pinsk to drive you back to the apartment. Make sure you lock up. And don't answer the door to anybody, however highly placed they are in the US consulate in Murmansk. I should be back in an hour or two.'

'I won't wait up,' she said.

As I drove through town on the way to the Palace I saw members of the special Electoral Police squads reeling in and out of late-night bars and restaurants along Pushkin Boulvar, enjoying the hospitality they were expressly forbidden to accept.

'Our duties give us considerable powers,' Zinoviev, the Moscow electoral commissioner, had told me. 'But it is rare to use them. The Electoral Police are highly experienced and we may safely leave the supervision to them. What is important is to be seen to be the eyes and ears of Russian democracy.'

Less than half an hour later I parked in the empty-looking parking-lot of the Admirals' Palace. Madame Badanova met me in the timber-lined hall. She wore about half her usual complement of make-up. Her hair was brushed back severely. She looked, not unwell, but certainly very different. 'I feel very guilty,' she said, 'drawing you away from your investigation.'

'It's going forward,' I said. 'What was it you wanted to see me about?'

'Yes, Constantin.' She took my arm as we passed into the empty map room of the Palace with its huge wall map. In silence we walked the length of the Norwegian coast, crossed effortlessly to Scotland and headed out into the Atlantic towards the eastern seaboard of the United States. 'I've come to an important decision, Constantin. For me, a very sad one. But I wanted you to know first. I've decided to withdraw.'

'From the election? You're going to pull your candidature?'

I could see her eyes were puffy with tears. 'Whether or not he had anything to do with Jay's awful death, I've come to the conclusion I can't fight Roy Rolkin. I would fight him to the end if I thought there was any chance of winning. But there isn't.'

'This is what the polls are saying?'

'It's the way they're going. Inexorably.' She paused and I could see how miserable she was about her decision. 'There's no way out of this. He's got the Stadium ward vote. He's promised to use ten million dollars of public funds to build Murmansk Dynamo into world-beaters. And the public are falling for it. Stadium ward alone, Constantin, will lose me this election.'

'But the election's nearly on us. Won't you see it through to the end? You can't know the result until the last vote's cast.'

'I think I can, Constantin. A registered voter is free to vote in any ward he chooses. On election night Dynamo are playing at home. Registrations in Stadium ward have been pouring in all day. Roy Rolkin could clear between thirty and fifty thousand votes by that one promise.'

'You can't announce you'll do the same?'

'The press would slaughter me. And rightly so. I was overconfident, Constantin. I see that now. I should have found a seasoned politician to take over from my husband. I should have spoken for him, marched for him, raised funds for him.' There were tears in her eyes. 'Instead I pushed myself forward. I thought Anton's name would carry me through. Now, like a damn fool woman I've handed Roy Rolkin what Jay used to call a home run.'

'You've not lost yet,' I said desperately.

'I've been outmanoeuvred, Constantin. Outplayed. And the death of Jay on top of it all ... My God,' she said, under her breath, 'I hate politics!' We were standing by the window. She turned me slightly until we were looking out across the gulf. 'I hate the betrayal involved!' With her free hand she pointed to the unlit tower blocks above the distant city, silhouetted by the weak flicker of the northern lights. 'My betrayal of all the people who live up there fighting to rebuild their lives in cold and semi-darkness. All those people who had put their trust in me.'

'You mustn't withdraw,' I said. Not for the first time I felt very close to this woman. 'Trust me,' I said. 'I'll think of something.'

But the truth of the matter was, I already had.

When Madame Badanova left me in the map room to attend to some business with her election committee in the rooms above, I slowly walked the breadth of America. I crossed the broad Pacific until I reached Vladivostok. At that moment, brothers, I was totally preoccupied by the problem of dividing myself, splitting myself in two. I have the answer to her dilemma, I'm sure of it.

But I am also a man with a mission to find the vek responsible for the death of my wife. To find the man who forced her to climb into that gleaming gas flue and almost certain death. When I find him he will burn in hell. I've already decided there will be no trial. No obscene arguments traded back and forth between defence and prosecution in front of a robed, nodding judge. There will be no slavering descriptions in the press of her occasional sexual experiment with other women. No, brothers, he will be dispatched, *painfully*. As I see it in those moments before sleep, he will be dispatched by fire. I dream of lighting one of those great iron furnaces under the Lermontov and trolleying him into it like living entrails. And I'm crazy enough to think that the Shakley Brothers, of Sheffield, England, those stern Victorian boiler-makers, would, if not nod their approval, at least purse their lips neutrally and look the other way.

This then, is the revenger's tragedy. He has become a figure of political importance. He has the power to intervene decisively in this election. Before she died, hadn't Jay already whispered the words in my ear. In jest at that time. But they came back to me now: *there was only one way for Madame Badanova to win this election from Roy – and that was for someone to steal thirty thousand votes cast on Sunday in Stadium ward.*

When she came back an hour later, Madame Badanova refused to countenance it. 'I'm fighting a man who fixes elections,' she said.

'A man who uses public money to buy votes. Am I to go one step lower and *steal* votes?'

'I don't see an alternative,' I said. 'I know what the rule of law is. I've talked to Natalya a thousand times about Russia's need. But the law has to be even-handed, or as even-handed as men can make it. And both sides have to play by its rules.'

'And you still propose to steal thirty, forty thousand votes from Stadium ward?'

'I'm going to think about it,' I said. 'I'm going to think hard about it. And I'm going to ask you, in the meantime, not to concede the election.'

50

ABBY LOOKED AT me as if I were crazy. She was dressed for work, hair brushed back, make-up applied. I stood there, ridiculous in my crumpled suit in the dawn light, unshaven, my tie pulled, desperate for a glass of tea.

'You're going to steal thirty thousand votes?'

'I didn't say that. I was explaining the dilemma we were in. We need Madame Badanova as governor. The investigation needs it. With her permission we'll be able to do the exhumations at the camp. With her permission Fetisova will be forced to allow us to question whoever we want to question.'

'And for that you're prepared to *steal votes*?'

'To find the man responsible for Natalya's death, I'm prepared to do *anything*.'

Did it matter what Abby thought about the way things sometimes have to be done in Russia? Abby was an outsider. She didn't understand. This was my city. But all the same I knew I should never have told her, never have mentioned it. 'I was explaining the nature of the dilemma, for Christ's sake,' I said. 'I didn't say what I'd decided to do about it.'

She walked two paces towards the kitchen, swung on the toe of her black high heel and walked two paces back to stand in front of me. 'Do I have to remind you, Constantin,' she said icily, 'that we are the *upholders* of the law?'

This was too much. 'Do I have to remind *you*,' I responded, 'that in Russia things never work out so chessboard neatly.' I blinked and stopped a yawn. That hadn't come out as forcefully as I would have liked. I was exhausted. A man could only take so much. 'We live with a lot of grey here,' I added. But that sounded apologetic too.

She took her briefcase and headed for the door. In the hallway she stopped and turned. 'Just tell me this, Constantin. What do you think Natalya would have said about the idea of stealing thirty thousand votes in the middle of an election?'

I flinched. She stared at me, waiting for an answer. She thought she'd clinched the argument. But again, it wasn't strictly black and white. 'Natalya was an activist. In the last resort, Natalya would have done whatever was necessary.'

'She also believed in the rule of law.'

Anger flared in me. I tried to push it back but it erupted like battlefield smoke and flame. 'How in God's name do you know what she believed in!'

'OK . . . During this case, I've talked to everybody who knew her.' She took a deep, angry breath. 'Maybe I know her better in some ways than you do. Natalya would not have endorsed the destruction of legally cast votes.'

I couldn't help it. I blew up. 'What you know about Natalya is second-hand. What you know about what she would or would not have done is pure hearsay. Roy Rolkin has to be stopped. I'm telling you – Natalya would have seen the necessity.'

I saw her make an effort to bring things back into balance. 'What I'm saying to you is that this is a crazy idea,' she said evenly. 'I want you to tell me here and now that you're giving it up.'

'I can't tell you that,' I said stubbornly. 'One way or other, I haven't decided yet.'

She nodded slowly. Her expression, I saw, was no longer angry. 'Listen, Constantin,' she said. 'As of this morning, I want you to stay away from the investigation . . .'

'What!'

'Just let me tell you the stage we've reached. The stage we've reached all working together.' She paused, eyes glittering. 'An FBI report from the Loadman Bank, Boston, informs us that Isobel Bridger has had over six million dollars paid into her account there in the last four years. All money passed through a numbered account in Zurich.'

I felt that burble of triumph that the first major crack in an investigation brings. 'So we've got them.'

'We would have, if they hadn't made a run for it during the night. I've been half the night at their apartment with Pinsk . . .'

I felt a lurch of guilt. I should have been there. 'Did you find anything?'

A single quick shake of the head. 'Bridger saw the dam bursting. The apartment was stripped of anything incriminating.' She paused. 'An expert job. Papers and photographs shredded and burnt.'

'You've put out an alert?'

'For both of them, together or separately. I have airports covered, trains, roads . . .'

'The bus station?'

'Even the bus station. But don't get too excited, Constantin. I mean what I said.' She stood in the centre of the room, legs braced. 'Unless you can give me your word.'

I couldn't believe it.

'I want you to stay away from the investigation at least until you've made up your mind what you're going to do.'

I stared at her. 'What I'm going to do?'

'One way or another, about those thirty thousand votes.' She gave a single forceful nod that said something like: that's the way it is.

I listened to her heels click along the hall, the front door open and slam. I didn't feel like that glass of tea any more. I poured vodka into a beer glass, then, as a considered second thought, carried the glass and bottle with me across the room. I collapsed back onto the sofa holding bottle and glass in the air. Either I let Madame Badanova lose the election, let down all those people in the crumbling high-rise blocks . . . Or I was off the case. In the hunt for Natalya's murderer, and in what I knew would be his eventual capture, I was not to play a part.

Dronsky was walking, practising steps with the help of two aluminium sticks. I stood at the door of his room as he hobbled to one wall, turned, and hobbled back. 'What d'you think, Chief?'

'The grace of a ballerina,' I said.

He stopped and looked at me. 'Shouldn't you get some sleep?' Then he started out again for the window.

'I've had a few hours on the sofa. It's no help for my problem. Listen, Abby's fired me. Thrown me off the case.'

He had reached the window. He stood there, his back to me before he made an awkward turn. 'She just called me.'

'For your consent?'

'For my consent. Here, sit down, Chief.' He hobbled to a chair.

I came into the room and sat on the pale green hospital counterpane. 'You gave it – just like that?'

'No, not just like that, but I gave it.'

'You're technically in charge of this investigation.'

'True.'

'So you can change your mind.'

'I can't do that, Chief.' His big brown eyes never left mine. 'I hate to say it but I think she's right.'

'Jesus Christ, Dronsky! A victory for Madame Badanova could unlock this case. From her we'd get permission to turn that camp over. Permission to find out why they're running a reverse *Dead Souls* operation pretending to bury children and shipping them out of the camp. It's central to this case. It's what Natalya was engaged in when she was abducted!'

I watched while Dronsky took out a cigarette. His hair had been cut or rather cropped afresh since I last saw him, and as he bent forward to light his cigarette I saw the fainter light patch of his skull showing through. He lifted his head and exhaled smoke. 'We're getting there, Chief,' he said. 'It's not the way you want to do things but we're getting there.'

'It's not the way I want to do things. It's not the speed I want to do things.'

He shrugged his shoulders. The gesture twisted my gut. Ilya Dronsky was saying I can't discuss this with you.

There was the noise of a trolley in the corridor. He looked towards the open door, hoping some piece of hospital routine was about to break this up. But the nurse pushing the trolley went straight on past.

'Speak to Abby,' I said. 'I can't be cut out now, Dronsky.'

He turned back to me, his eyebrows pushing at his ridged forehead. 'It's not everybody who finds you easy to work with, Chief.'

'Something of a maverick?'

'I'm saying you can't blame Abby.'

'I don't. I blame myself,' I said. 'Why in God's name did I tell her I was thinking of stealing ten cans of votes? She doesn't understand the way things work in Russia. She doesn't know what a disaster Roy Rolkin would be as governor of Kola. Did you hear this morning's polls? He's overtaken Badanova. In one poll he's five clear points ahead. And he still has Stadium ward.'

'So you've decided, Chief? About the votes?'

I stood up. I was too agitated to sit still. I took one of Dronsky's cigarettes. 'I don't know.' I began to pace Dronsky's course to the window and back. 'I don't need telling democracy should be allowed to run its course – the choice of the people is the choice of the people . . . But that's how half the crooked city mayors and regional governors in Russia have got into power. Abby doesn't understand that. She sees me as some sort of danger.'

Dronsky stubbed out his cigarette and stood up again. 'I've got to keep up the exercise,' he said, 'or I'll end up one leg shorter than the other.' He lifted both sticks. 'See? A balancing act. That's what walking a straight line is all about.'

'I may be a danger to myself, for God's sake. But I'm not a danger to anybody else.'

He looked at me, brown eyes and Groucho eyebrows and all. 'Chief, you could blow this investigation away. By accident. That's what Abby's bosses in Washington are warning her.'

'They're talking about *me*? In Washington?'

'You ought to be told, Chief . . .' He turned from the window, his face troubled. 'Abby's fought tooth and nail with Washington to keep you on the case.' Clumsily, still holding onto his sticks, he checked his watch. 'I've got to go, Chief. It's time for my physio.'

I left Dronsky and walked slowly through the Lermontov towards the entrance. People flowed past me, the usual bustle of the big, busy hospital. I used to feel warm, at home, here, but no longer. Since Natalya's death I feel a stranger.

The canteen sells a good coriander vodka as a cure for a man with a bad taste in his mouth, so I turned in there. Glass in hand I fed the phone and called Abby at the Nunnery. I got Danilova. Abby, she said, was out of the office. She had no knowledge of when she might return. The tone was stiff and empty of recognition. Danilova had heard.

I finished my coriander vodka and decided another was needed. I am not one of those who believes his best decisions are made when drunk. Not at all. Beyond any doubt I've made some quite spectacular blunders when influenced by the clear bottle. But, equally, when toying with a fragrant glass of tea. The disturbing truth is *no real difference is discernible*.

Over the years I've brought this matter of decision-making to a fine art. My advice, to myself, is plain. Take a thumb or two of something comforting if the gravity of the decision seems to warrant it. Take a thumb or two more if you find the struggle to decide is particularly uphill. Buy a half-litre to slip into your pocket if the issue seems incapable of resolution – and go in search of the nearest public *banya*.

The Lermontov runs its own bathhouse, a low-ceilinged vaulted temple with wall mosaics of Greek youths prowling the forest with bow and spear and uncalled-for erections.

I booked in my clothes and watch and paid for a towel to wrap round me and conceal the half of vodka I was bringing in. The bathhouse itself was ill-lit by green lights beyond floating levels of steam. Stunned by the heat I felt my way to the furthest corner from the furnace and clambered onto the lowest of a rack of wooden shelves.

I was off the case. I was cut off from the information flow. But I was also a free man. I felt a surge of exhilaration. As a free man I could make my own choices, my own decisions.

It was almost dark down here in the bathhouse and the effect of the heat pleasant rather than dunning. All around I could hear American voices, immediately recognizable, even if you couldn't hear the words, from being lighter than the Russian middle-age tobacco rumble.

First things first. I pushed all thought of the investigation from my mind and got down to work. I drank two or three good mouthfuls of the coriander and thought about stealing thirty thousand votes from Roy's total.

To me it sounded at first good, then better and better still. If the votes were removed, the election would be Madame B's. As governor she would grant permission to exhume the empty graves at the camp at Nivka and grill the colonel on the purpose of her sinister subterfuge. I was more than ever convinced that if we knew the full story of the traffic in children, we would have the name of the killer within hours.

From the steam, an American voice said something about the coming election. Another disagreed. A third said: 'This goddam election is fixed anyway. Rolkin couldn't have more illegal funds available if he printed the stuff himself.'

I think it was at that point that I decided. Was I drunk? I looked at the half-litre and saw my consumption had been modest. I concealed the bottle during my visit to the freezing pool and the beating slab. There, birch twigs thrash you to a level of health and vigour the West is supposed to marvel at. Russians, as I'm sure you know, never cease to marvel at it themselves. Never, that is, until they reach the national average life expectancy of fifty-eight. After that they begin to think twice about press publicity against the coronary dangers of the searing heat and cold-water plunge.

I dressed and called the bandit Venya from the lobby of the Lermontov. Again that medieval image rushed my imagination: Venya at table in his vast, rusting cast-iron hall, a fire blazing, an ox roasting. When he answered, the more immediate vision of the small, scruffy man in a sheepskin jacket holding a mobile phone to his ear blurred the image. 'I want you to steal something for me,' I said.

'But of course,' he said with enthusiasm. 'Come at midnight – bring bags of money.'

I spent the night at Venya's hulk. I was wrong about roasting oxen – it was hamburgers held to the fire on iron prongs, and singing, and dozens of bottles which rolled and gurgled across the uneven floor. In the firelight, there was dancing.

51

POLLING DAY DAWNED. A good clear spring day. This was
a town aware that today was a day of destiny. Flags red,
white and black or green and yellow flew from buildings, cars
and passing trucks. The faces of Roy Rolkin and Madame B
were everywhere – beaming or sombre, depending on the poster
copy-line. Loudspeaker units toured the streets dispensing message
and music. *My Way* seemed to get more air-time than all the
patriotic pieces put together. It seemed to me that, like the devil,
Roy Rolkin had all the best tunes.

As electoral commissioners, Pasko, Frank Sinatra and I drove
round town, the three of us in the back of a large city Mercedes,
the Moscow commissioner maintaining a disdainful pursing of the
lips as if it might offer defence against the waves of body odour
emitted by Pasko. At all the main polling stations we descended
and made our presence known.

Stadium was the fourth or fifth in line. We turned in through the
big gates and came to a stop at the long hut decked with the colours
of the two sides. A large poster, only slightly to the left, showed Roy
Rolkin in Murmansk Dynamo blue shirt proclaiming his intention
of bringing the club into the European Premier League within two
years. The kick-off for tonight was set for six o'clock. When the
fans entered the ballot station before the match, Roy would be
picking up votes at a rate of ten to one over Madame B.

We got out of the Mercedes and were conducted inside the hut by
a sergeant of the Special Electoral Police. The room was large and
simply furnished for its purpose. There were ten separate booths
although only one of them was in use. A single line of people was
passing through the system, marking their papers, disappearing
into the black-curtained booth and emerging with that slightly
guilty look on their faces.

'This is just a trickle,' Pasko said. 'An hour before kick-off and
Rolkin voters will have to be shunted through.'

I didn't doubt him. A group of photographers appeared and Frank Sinatra posed and smiled effectively. In answer to all questions I stated that so far the commissioners had been very impressed by the serious tone of the campaign and the arrangements made for the poll. The other two nodded support.

As we walked back to the car I felt a hand squeeze my arm. Pasko's barely shaven cheek was close to mine. 'All that unpleasantness a while back,' he said. 'All behind us? Forgotten?'

'I've a near-uncontrollable urge, Pasko,' I said, 'to give you the sort of good kicking you no doubt administered many times in the Nunnery basement. After that to throw your already fetid body into the Kola river. Apart from that, I'd say it was all behind us, yes.'

He released my arm and we climbed into the Mercedes, the Moscow commissioner in the front seat now. Pasko's underarm microbes were celebrating the arrival of spring. 'You won't object,' the Moscow man said, 'it's such a fine day, if I roll down the window.'

We broke off duties in time for me to get back to the apartment before Abby returned. The phone was ringing as I let myself in. I slammed the door behind me and crossed the hall to pick up. There were no preliminaries. 'Who are you?' a woman's coarse voice said.

'I'm Constantin Vadim. Who do you want to speak to?'

'The inspector.'

'That's me.'

'Listen.' The voice was harsh but not that old. 'I've read the *Kola Pravda*. The story about these murders. The women found in the boiler-house.'

'That was weeks ago.'

'And the latest one. Slashed to death in her own home.'

'Where do you live?'

She ignored the question. 'Trust me. I know who's guilty of this dreadful thing,' she said.

The voice sounded too cracked or crazed to take seriously. 'Who is it?' I asked her, not really expecting more than a vicious denunciation of a neighbour or employer.

'I need to speak to you in person, Inspector. I need to explain.'

I hesitated. 'Look, come to the Old Nunnery. There's an incident room there for these crimes. You can make a statement.'

'No. I can't come into town. You must come to me. I'll be here at Sin City after midnight.'

'Tell me why I should.'

She cackled. 'You're an honest man, Inspector. I've been told that. You have an honest face. You'll bring my reward.'

'Why else should I come?'

'You'll be surprised to learn who I am. I have an old story to tell.' She paused. 'It happened long ago. An old story to tell about a doll.'

'I'll come,' I said. 'Where?'

The clock in the hall said ten to six. Quickly, I showered and changed into my dinner-jacket. Before six-thirty I was out on the street again, an hour or two to kill before I was due at the central counting station which had been established at the airport.

The woman on the phone had excited me. An old story about a doll!

However much I had pressed her she wouldn't say where we could meet. No more than a vague mutter: 'It'll happen. We'll meet when we're due to meet.'

Did that mean she'd call again, or stop me in the street? Did she really have information to give me? And why me? Because I was an honest man, she'd said.

So honest I had just drawn out my last rouble from the Barents Bank to pay for the theft of thirty thousand votes!

52

The NEW Kola International Airport is about as ordinary an example of Russian box-building as you can envisage. There was an attempt by the authorities, a few years back, to make the place swing with the acronym KIA, placed in eight-metre neon letters over the entrance to the main concourse. It was not until the day before unveiling that somebody pointed out that, to Americans, this meant Killed In Action. A heavy crash landing and several spectacular air misses at about the same time forced a rethink and the huge letters were replaced with a more modest flickering blue *Kola International* as today's reigning title.

For the election the airport had been suitably decked out, not so much with the flags and posters of the opposing candidates as with the Murmansk city colours. Blue and white quartered shields and swagging decorated the goose-necked street lamps and an arrangement of blue and white light patterns played across all the main airport buildings. Patriotic music roared from the loudspeakers and Special Electoral Police were evident everywhere, directing traffic and inspecting ID.

In the main concourse the noise was deafening. Television crews were set up all around the counting tables which were arranged in a circle in the middle of the room. To the strains and sometimes thunder of the patriotic music I'd heard on the loudspeakers outside, fifty men and women tipped the votes from small black metal boxes and arranged them for counting. A uniformed electoral inspector sat opposite each counter, inside the circle of tables, to make certain that no votes were missed. When each electoral district was counted the place and number of votes was recorded on a huge green screen at the back of the platform which occupied one end of the hall.

Each party had been provided with offices and rest rooms above the hall. From where I stood in the doorway, I could see Pasko roaming the circle of tables looking knowledgeable and important.

Roy Rolkin, surrounded by minders, was just coming down into the concourse from his party's offices above. He was wearing a well-cut business suit and carrying a blue Murmansk Dynamo baseball cap. Even at this late stage he was not going to let anybody forget that a vote for him was a vote for saving the city's pride and joy.

Following the signs I climbed a staircase next to the entrance and found myself on a corridor of offices, the doors draped with yellow and green. The security man recognized me. 'If it's Madame B you're looking for . . .' He opened an office door.

'It is,' I said.

I walked into a cloud of perfume and an all-embracing hug from Mariya Badanova who pulled me into her office. Aides operated PCs along the window wall, or argued in self-important huddles in the middle of the room.

'Constantin,' she hugged me tighter, pressing my head into the deep-scented bosom. 'I'll never forget,' she whispered urgently, 'what you've done for me, for my husband's memory and for the ordinary, honest people of Murmansk.'

I struggled free.

'There, I've smothered you,' she said, laughing. 'If I'd been thirty years younger . . .' she wagged her finger skittishly at me, 'you wouldn't have been so anxious to come up for air . . . Now let's have a glass of this very fine French champagne, none of your inferior Georgian growths, this is what . . . let's see, Bollinger 2002. The very best.'

She was already pouring a glass for me before I was able to say my first words.

'Wait,' I said. I put a hand on her forearm and the champagne stopped its scintillating hiss into the glass. 'It's too early for celebrating.'

'Not at all, my dear boy. Look at the results so far.' She turned to the screen and punched a button. It flashed bright green and settled to a yellow on green list of city wards, with totals of votes for Madame B and Roy beside each district. At Gagarin, Marshal Zhukov, Theatre and St Nicholai wards, Madame B was slightly ahead, giving her a total lead of a slender six thousand votes. There were nine or ten of the more far-flung wards to come in during the night but both of us knew from the polls that they were likely to balance out more or less evenly.

The election result would not be announced until dawn but the winner would be known long before that. The two key wards left were Lermontov and Stadium.

'Exit polls from Lermontov ward,' Madame B said, 'show us pulling ahead of Rolkin.' She turned to me. 'He'll need to be fifteen or twenty thousand votes ahead in Stadium ward to win.' She finished pouring the champagne and held out the glass to me. 'But I understand . . .' she dropped her voice although there was no-one close enough to hear, 'that he's not going to get them.' There was a quiet glee in her voice that made me look at her. She was a committed democrat like me. To steal thirty thousand votes was a matter of *necessity*, of *regret*. It wasn't cause for glee. She lifted the champagne towards me. 'I think we should drink, you and I, to our poor Jay . . .'

It hit me like a bullet. It didn't tell me any more about Jay's death but it told me far more than I'd understood about the evening of the declaration when I'd driven Jay home. 'You already knew,' I said, still uncertain.

Madame Badanova smiled and again held her champagne glass to me.

Had she really planned this vote-adjustment exercise from the beginning? Had she seen me straight away more as the simple patsy than the loyal friend? Or maybe just the perfect sculptor's clay to be moulded to a design she had long decreed.

Constantin, I tell myself, this can't be allowed. Even when sober you're acting the drunk. Remember, you're on your own now. What you're going to have to do, Constantin, here and now, is to take charge of your life.

And there's no doubt this has to begin with a big decision about Madame Mariya Badanova. 'You had already arranged with Jay to plant the idea,' I said as coolly as I could. 'You'd arranged for Jay to take me to her apartment and fix the idea solidly in my numbskull that the theft of thirty thousand votes could save the city from disaster.'

She held her smile but said nothing. I ignored the proffered champagne. I didn't take it. Very slowly I saw the lines of her face harden around that smile.

'Then you sat back and let *me* persuade *you* to agree to me stealing the votes.'

She stepped back and put down the champagne. 'I think you're being over-dramatic, Constantin. As I remember it, Jay and I did the figures. And they didn't look good. Not unless . . .'

'A whole batch were lifted from Stadium ward and dropped into the river.'

She leaned back against the desk. The pretence of innocence, even of goodwill, was over. 'I take it that's already been done.'

'Only more or less.'

'Don't play games with me, Constantin. The future of a whole city depends on this.'

'The future of Mariya Badanova depends on this, too.'

'You're surprising me, Constantin. Not pleasantly. Just tell me this. Have you dealt with the Stadium votes?'

'Let's say the operation is half completed.'

For a long moment she was silent. Then she looked up. 'Are you bargaining? Are you asking for money?'

I stared at her.

'No . . . It wouldn't be money. Of course not . . . What, then?'

I thought for a moment. 'Would you agree, if you became governor, to an immediate exhumation of the most recent graves in all the camps under Colonel Fetisova's control?'

Everything seemed slow about the next seconds. In particular, her voice. 'Why should I agree to that?'

'Because I was asking you.'

The full, fleshy smile returned. 'Such a strange request! But then I think of your involvement with children. It does you credit to be thinking of them tonight, on the very edge of victory. Listen, we're friends, Constantin, old campaigners. We both have the good of this city at heart. We're both Russian to our toenails and willing to fight to keep the city in Russian hands. You know with your one-time friend Rolkin as governor, Kola will be flooded with American films, American customs, practices, laws even . . . Koka-Kola will be much more than a TV catchphrase.'

'Would you grant a request for exhumation?'

Her chubby hand reached out and covered mine. 'Tomorrow, Constantin, you can have anything you want.'

'Is that a promise?'

'To a comrade in arms.'

I released my hand and turned to go.

'You're not going. Not before you tell me if the votes are safe.'

'They're safe,' I said. 'Whether they're safe for you or safe for Roy . . . I really don't know.'

I walked down the stairs into a wall of noise. Roy saw me as I reached the last few steps and his bodyguards shouldered a way through for him. He was wearing his baseball cap. 'Costya, rejoice for me. You've seen the way things are going?' He gestured towards the big green screen. 'The fat old bag is maybe five or six thousand ahead. Lermontov ward is just being counted and it looks like a dead heat. Stadium's expected within an hour or two. When it does, thirty, forty, fifty thousand votes drop straight into my lap.' He flexed his knees, grunted and grabbed two-handedly at his groin.

My mobile rang and I took it from my inside pocket. 'Chief,' Venya's voice whispered in my ear. 'All according to plan. Stadium Electoral Police agreed to look the other way for half an hour. At a price . . .'

'Venya . . .' I said.

'There were something like forty thousand votes cast. The votes, minus thirty thousand for you, are on their way to the airport. Documentation has been dealt with. It's simply going to look like a disastrously low turn-out at Stadium.'

Panic struck me. 'Hold everything, Venya,' I said. 'For Christ's sake. I need time. Another few hours to work this out.'

'This is merchandise that should be disposed of one way or another – and quick. It's volatile stuff to carry around, if you get my meaning. Let me know, soon as you can, OK, Chief?' Venya said and rang off.

Roy was looking at the results screen. Lermontov ward was just declaring. For Madame Badanova sixteen thousand five hundred. For Roy, barely three or four hundred less. Pulling his baseball cap to one side, Roy stuck out his tongue and crossed his eyes. 'Who could have thought that the dunce of Primary 36 would make it to be elected governor of Kola?' he asked.

'*You* did,' I said. I pulled him aside. 'Listen, I have things to ask you.'

'OK.' He signalled to two of his minders to muscle us room to speak.

'You know more about Murmansk politics than I do, even after two years' exile in Hungary. I need some answers, Roy. Straight answers.'

'Did I ever give you anything else?'

'For Christ's sake, Roy . . .'

He gave me his narrow-eyed smile. 'Having doubts about your bedfellows, are you, Costya? I told you, by all that's holy, there's only one candidate here stands for decency and the rule of law.'

'I need some background on Badanova and her late husband.'

'You've come to the right man.' He grinned.

'What's the story on Governor Badanov's death? Was his death an accident?'

'Every cloud has a silver lining. I wouldn't be sitting here now if someone hadn't arranged to slip a few litres of water into little Anton's helicopter tank. As I say, every cloud . . .' One of Roy's minders handed him a glass of clear spirit and, as a reluctant afterthought, one to me.

'The day you came to Murmansk you warned me off. I thought you were warning me off working for Badanov. But it was really about going anywhere with him by helicopter. You knew.'

'I'd heard rumours. I didn't want to see my boyhood friend go down in the lake.'

'You didn't arrange it yourself, by chance, the helicopter crash?'

Roy tipped his glass reflectively to his lips. 'Not denying I might have done it if I'd thought about it. But I didn't think of it, fuck your mother. That's life for you.'

'Who did then?'

'Any one of a hundred local *racketiry*, Costya, my old friend. Well, any one of twenty or thirty ambitious enough to own their own private helicopter.'

'What are you talking about? What are you saying happened to Anton Badanov?'

'Air General Badanov as he once was.'

I leaned forward. 'I remember. He commanded an air regiment during the Civil War.'

'The 351st Assault Helicopter Regiment. He made a reputation with his aggressive use of his light reconnaissance helicopters.'

I began to get it. The light began to dawn.

'You thought he made his money from that bankrupt Texas-Badanov jeans company?' Roy sneered amiably.

'I did until a moment ago.'

'He had a dozen good lines going by the time of his death. Building franchises, business permits, but helicopters is where he started straight after the Civil War.'

'He was selling off the army's helicopters?'

'Only the small ones. He had the business acumen to see that his own regimental light reconnaissance helicopters, repainted of course, were ideal for the new Russian businessman.'

'That's acumen all right.'

'The only trouble was, Badanov couldn't guarantee the maintenance was up to scratch. I'd say he had nearly ten crashes in the last three years. On sales of maybe thirty, that didn't look too clever to the *racketiry*. One of the survivors decided it was time to get even – that's my guess, anyway.'

The thought floated into my mind. '351st Assault Regiment,' I said. The faded regimental number on Sasha Roop's hangar. 'You know Sasha Roop?'

'He was Air General Badanov's batman in the service. Brother of that loony we were at school with, Lukas.'

'You think Sasha got a cut from the helicopter business?'

'It's what set him up. When the army investigators finally caught onto the operation, they decided a cover-up was necessary. There were just too many generals involved in similar sales, tanks, heavy guns, personnel carriers, light aircraft . . . Badanov got off scot-free because he could name too many names. The brass looks after the brass. Sasha was given three months' community service.'

'Just three months' community service?'

'For failure to provide an adequate guard for government property. A pushover. Three months' community service and he walked free.'

'So Sasha and the Badanovs have a real history together.'

'The Badanov connection is a very useful one to have in this city. We've got to change all that.'

I thought about it. 'And how will you do that?'

His eyes sparkled. 'By substituting the Roy Rolkin connection, of course.'

53

I HAD PROMISED MYSELF reform. Or threatened myself with it. So the time has come. I'm taking charge of my life, brothers. Facing the fact that it's decision-making time. Whether I want it this way or not, the gift of the governorship of Kola Province is in my hands. The kingmaker's burden. I cannot escape this decision, much as I recognize that decision-making is something I spend a lot of time avoiding. But the way it is, if I destroy the votes, Madame B wins. If I reroute them back to the counting table, Roy wins. Either side is, I'm now convinced, a disaster for the city.

With such a dilemma, unresolvable by logic, there is only one place to go. Only one place that offers the *possibility* of a solution.

I take the Kamka and drive through the southern urban district until I reach Sin City. The miserable remains of Sin City, that is. There's nothing quite so weird as an ice fair after the thaw. At a distance of a few hundred metres the moonlight catches the turrets of medieval castles and onion domed churches, darkness and distance masking the small scale of each building. Closer, the eyes adjust and a slight movement becomes visible, the bobbing of those swallow-tailed turrets and golden domes on their blackwater foundations.

I follow the road to the top of the hill where the gypsy camp has been pitched. Even at this hour fires burn and among the sporadic bark of dogs a burst of card-players' laughter rises through the night. Over everything, the bitter stench of plastic sleeving from burning copper wire hangs on the air.

I turn off the lights of the Kamka, cruise for the last hundred metres and spin the wheels into the bush and scrub beside the road.

It's long after midnight, but fairground camps don't sleep. As I wander between the tents and wooden shanties that have been erected since the thaw, I see everywhere people at work, building fires, repairing ancient panel trucks, sewing canvas and even cooking. A line of undernourished children wait for food at the Salvation Army soup-kitchen. Many have limps or facial disfigurements. Missing teeth are commonplace. Some have the white fleshless look of the Aids victim. They are drawn here from the city because they know the whores and gypsies will always give them scraps. The Salvation Army know this too, and lie in wait with soup and bread and fruit. In Yeltsin's Russia we had half a million abandoned children and unfulfilled promises that the problem would be tackled from the highest in the land. Today we have a million of these *bezprisorniki*. I tear myself free of the grip of such misery.

The site the encampment occupies is small compared with its winter sprawl across the ice. It means the old woman's tent is not difficult to find, tipped at an angle, the bargeboard slipped, the once yellow panes of canvas streaked with mud. But a light burns inside.

I called . . . paused and went in. Under the hissing lamp the old woman sat at her table, slowly drawing on a long cigarette.

I could tell from her eyes that she was stoned, from her eyes and the slump of her old body in her chair. And from the bite of cannabis in the air.

She seemed quite unsurprised to see me. 'Ah,' she said, 'the handsome inspector of militia.' She dipped her head. 'I'm sorry it turned out badly for your doctor wife.'

I remembered in time she was an avid reader of newspapers. I pulled out the chair opposite her across the green chenille-clothed table. 'I need your help,' I said.

She raised her eyebrows, or part-raised them as if the effort were too much. 'I said you'd be back.'

'You say that to all your customers, don't you?'

She smiled. 'What can I lose?' She drew on her cigarette, swallowed and, throwing back her head, let the smoke flow in confusion from her open mouth. I've seen more elegant smokers.

'So, Inspector . . . my help, you say.'

'There are two people, a man and a woman. By chance, I am in a position to do one of them great good – or immense harm.'

'But only one of them?'

'Correct. Through the one I choose, great good may also be done to many others.'

'Or great harm if you choose wrongly.'

'There you have it.'

'Not quite.' She pouted thick lips. 'I must know more.'

'What?'

'These are two people you know well?'

'The man I've known since I was a child. The woman only a short while.'

'Go on . . . go on.'

'They are both elevated personages,' I said. 'One publicly devoted to the good of the people . . . the man avowedly devoted to his own rise. The question is – to which one do I give my support?'

'What do you have?' Her eyes were sly. 'Votes to sell?'

I stared at her.

'A jest,' she said. 'A poor jest in even worse taste. So between these two elevated personages, it's a simple matter of which way to tip the scales. Will it be north or south – winter or summer?'

'Yes.'

'A straight choice. Then we must use the mice.'

'What?'

'Myomancy, Inspector.'

'I've never heard of it.'

'Myomancy. Divination by the study of the movement of mice.'

I lifted my hands, casting long shadows on the chenille cloth. 'Cards, I can believe. At least I can accept chance works through them.'

'But not mice?' Her dull eyes held mine.

'Are you serious? I hate mice. I can't believe they're more capable of making a decision than I am.' I pulled a half-bottle of Kuban vodka from my pocket, uncorked it and drank.

She sat forward, heavy-lidded. 'It's a very ancient form of divination, Inspector,' she said earnestly. 'Deserving of the greatest respect. Tried and tested.'

I pricked up my ears. 'Tried and tested?'

'Don't turn away from it,' she pressed me. 'The Greeks used it for matters of the greatest importance, matters of state, of peace and war even. Through Byzantium it passed to us Russians, making its way up the southern rivers. Will you try it, at least?'

I grimaced. Are all Russians mad? Divination by mice? And yet . . . for centuries apparently . . . 'If you really think . . .' I muttered uncertainly. I took another mouthful of the Kuban vodka, let it explode in my chest and took another. 'All right,' I said decisively. 'The mice.'

She got up and went to the back of her tent where I saw for the first time a bed was made up with a dirty patchwork pillow and worn bearskin coverlet. From under the bed she took a circular shallow box covered with a tattered gold-fringed cloth of dark damassin.

This she placed carefully upon the table. Under the cloth I could hear the nervous scuttle of claws on woodwork. 'First the lamp,' she said. From somewhere just within her reach she brought a small china oil-lamp, its brass shade polished on the underside so that when she lit it, light was thrown downwards. 'Now we must people our landscape,' she said. She rummaged in a leather bucket and came up with a handful of clay figures, from which she chose two cheap fairground representations of a male and female peasant. 'They're both Russian, your man and woman?'

'Russian to the marrowbone.'

'There then.' She flipped off the cloth.

There were perhaps fifty to a hundred of the creatures under a glass lid. More mice than I have seen in my life. More by far than I ever wish to see again. They were, at this stage, remarkably unafraid, unfazed it seemed by the sudden light. They nibbled and scratched and ran this way and that, as mice do.

The box itself was like a Roman arena, a circular area surrounded by two tiers of low arches through which the more energetic of the mice appeared and disappeared.

Very carefully the old woman set the two terracotta figures one at either end of the glass lid which I now saw was scored with stars and circles. Roy stood to my right, on a star, his legs in bulging *valenki*, head and shoulders in what looked like a half sack fashioned to make a cowl. Madame B was to the left, bulky in a nondescript cloth coat, a headscarf tied beneath the chin. This done, the old woman placed her lamp in the centre of the glass cover of the box so that the light was thrown down in two circles – one on Badanova's side, the other on Roy's side of the box.

Still the mice paid no attention.

Then, from under the table, the woman took her drum, the same yellowing instrument she had once used to set the scene with me. She held it on her lap, and looked towards me. 'You described this choice between the man and the woman as one of desperate importance?' Her fingertips were gently drumming.

'No less,' I said.

'Affecting the lives of hundreds?'

'Thousands even.'

She inclined her head and slapped the drum with the flat of her hand.

The effect was spectacular.

Mice ran madly back and forth, scuttling under the arches, jumping over each other, squeaking with terror.

A pack of cards appeared on the table. With one brown and seamed hand the old woman was turning the cards, with the other she knuckled the drum on her lap to a crescendo.

While the mice squeaked and scuttled, the marijuana smoke layered and wove itself above our heads and the drumbeat rose to a thud that seemed to fill space and time, I found myself dragging out my bottle of Kuban vodka.

'You're prepared for betrayal?' she said.

'Well prepared,' I necked the bottle and drank. 'But who is it? Who's the betrayer?'

'We shall know,' she said. 'We shall know when the mice speak.'

'Speak?'

'Watch them now as I put the question.' She threw back her head and beat wildly on the drum. As a loud hissing came from her rubbery lips, I saw the mice go mad with movement, crowding, jumping each other, racing for the protection of the arches, to avoid the corner where the Badanova effigy stood. But then, I saw, they were, equally (or not, I couldn't guess), tumbling over each other to avoid the corner where Roy Rolkin was placed.

With a final flat-handed slap on the drum the old woman threw the cover over the box and sat back exhausted. 'There can be no doubt,' she said. 'No doubt about your woman at all. Not one mouse would remain within her circle of light. Not one.'

'What are you saying?'

'She is purely evil,' the old woman said. 'The woman is purely evil. The mice leave me in no doubt.'

'And the man?'

'He is cloaked from us, handsome inspector of militia.'

'You mean you don't know?'

'You saw the mice,' she said angrily. 'They ran in terror this way and that. The cards, you saw the cards?'

'No . . .'

'In sequence! When a well-shuffled pack falls in sequence, an even balance is indicated. This man carries both good and bad in his heart.' She took a deep, hissing breath. 'But the woman ...' she said, bringing her head up so that her leathery eyes stared deep into mine. 'Beware the woman.'

The hypnotic effect of those dark eyes bore almost the strength of Kuban vodka. I felt myself being pulled towards madness. Towards mice, marijuana and madness.

'Of the two,' the fortune teller said, 'there can be no doubt. You must go with the one you know. You must choose the *man*.'

I placed rouble notes on the table, ten or twenty. 'You're about to say I'll be back.'

She shook her head, expelling a plume of weed smoke. 'No, young man,' she said. 'You won't be back. You won't be back. Ever.'

I moved to the flap of the tent.

'Before you leave Sin City,' she said, 'there's someone here. Someone who talks about you. Perhaps she has things to tell. Will you see her?'

I stood uncertainly. 'I don't understand you.'

'She works here. Plies her trade,' the old lady said with an unlovely leer. 'You've already spoken to her – she wants to tell you a story. About a doll.'

I looked down at her. 'You couldn't *know* I'd come tonight.'

'Of course I couldn't. Why do you insist on giving me more gifts than I have?'

At the open flap of the tent, the old woman signalled to a bundled figure waiting in the shadows of an old traction engine. I walked forward as she hesitated, then came towards me. 'Have you spoken to the Americans about the reward?' she said.

'I will,' I said.

'Come with me.'

She led me through the tents and propped-up vehicles, the grazing horses and the general indescribable squalor of the place, towards a small corrugated tin shack. She was not a bad-looking woman, but worn now. Quite tall, probably slim under the thick cloth coat, but there was a greyness about her face which even the flicker of a neon sign as we passed did nothing to disguise.

With a spring suddenness a few drops of rain turned into a downpour. We stood for a moment in the plywood ruin of a miniature Disneyland castle.

'I have to know,' she said. 'There really is a reward?'

'The American consulate is offering ten thousand dollars,' I told her.

She shook her head in wonder. 'Listen,' she said. 'I owe nothing to my family. I'm not ashamed of meeting you.'

'Your family?'

'My name is Valya Roop. Rita, the mother of Sasha and Lukas, she was my elder sister.'

The rain strengthened again, rattling like gravel against the tin huts around us. Muddy water rose from the sparse blades of grass in glistening crowns.

'Queen of Heaven,' she said. 'Come and shelter.'

We ran across the grass road. Her hut was open-fronted but cleverly porched in corrugated iron to prevent the worst of the rain being swept inside. A second woman was sitting on the bunk at the back of the dark space, tending a samovar.

'Leave us, Tatiana,' the tall woman said.

'Of course, of course.' Tatiana was on her feet, dusting off the bed, eyeing me, and thumping the bed with the flat of her hand.

'Tatiana,' the woman said. 'He's not a customer. He's a police-man.'

Tatiana absorbed this new information and began to edge out of the door. 'Even policemen,' she was saying, almost to herself, 'have needs to fill.'

Despite the grey hair and lined face, I saw now that Valya was in little more than her early fifties. Motioning to me to sit down on the bed, she took a stool from under a metal table and sat opposite.

I could feel the raindrops trickling through my hair. 'You said you have something to tell me,' I said.

She arranged herself more comfortably on the stool. 'You have to understand. We live a life here free from the daily news. It was only a few days ago that I heard about the death of these women in the Lermontov basement.'

'One of the women was my wife,' I said.

'It's why I called you.'

I found I was struggling hard to maintain some sort of pro-fessional distance. By whatever trick that longing plays, I felt more acutely the loss of Natalya here in this pathetic, rain-lashed brothel-room than I had since she died.

'I saw an old newspaper. It was only when I read the story about the rubber dolls,' she said, 'that I made the connection to Sasha.'

'What connection?'

'I knew immediately Sasha was the man you were looking for.'

I was cautious. 'What makes you think he had anything to do with the death of my wife and the other women?'

'You know nothing, Inspector. The militia never do. Not the important things.'

'You'll tell me.'

She looked at me cautiously. 'You're not trying to steal my reward?'

'I want to find out who was responsible for my wife's death. I'm not here to steal your reward. So what makes you think Sasha is implicated?'

She took a deep, decisive breath. 'The first two, your wife and the American woman, were found in the Lermontov basement. One of those locked-door mysteries, the newspaper said.'

I kept my face still and let her go on.

She leaned forward. 'People have forgotten that there's another door. One that leads to the mortuary.'

'How in God's name do you know that?'

'I worked there for almost a year,' she said. 'Mortuary laundry-maid. The same time Sasha was given his army punishment. Community service in the mortuary.'

'He worked there for three months as Lenny's assistant?'

'Burning human rubbish. At that time Sasha used the passage to the furnaces every day.'

My stomach turned over. In the tin hut, with the rain beating down, I looked on her in a suddenly different light. In a simple stroke she had linked Natalya and Joan's place of imprisonment with the dolls.

'You're listening now, militiaman.'

'What can you tell me about motive?' I said.

'What man like Sasha needs a motive to rape and murder a beautiful woman? You must know of his record. When his mother died, he was placed in an *Internat*. If he wanted a girl there, he did what the rest did, he beat her and took her. No, it's not motive you should be asking about. It's the dolls.'

'We know about the dolls,' I said, far too glibly. 'We know Sasha manufactured them. He came forward himself.'

She laughed at me. 'Of course he would. But I'm asking you why should the killer put out a doll for each woman?'

'We still don't know.'

She lifted her head triumphantly. 'It baffles you. You still can't guess why they were placed, like that, dressed in the victims' clothes. You'd never seen anything like it, had you?' She left time for a calculated pause. 'But I have.'

'In those days, I lived down the street from my sister Rita and her family in Novocherkassk. It was before Sasha was born, of course. But Rita was already drunk most of the time. So fat even a Russian workman wouldn't look at her. She was out every night drinking, left the children, Yelena and Lukas, in the house with a fiend roaming the attic upstairs.'

'Andrei Chikatilo.'

Her eyes opened in surprise. 'You know?'

'I know that Yelena disappeared. She was one of Chikatilo's victims. There's no real doubt about that.'

'He was the most sinister man I ever met,' she said. 'Quiet-spoken in public places. Even before he was arrested I knew he was a madman for sex. I wasn't working in the tractor factory any more. I was already living a "disorderly sex life" as the police charge-sheet used to say. Chikatilo asked me often enough, offered me good money, but I never went with him. In my business you develop an early eye for trouble. And Chikatilo was trouble. Of course this was years before he was caught. I told my sister enough times to keep Yelena out of his way, but she was too drunk to take any notice. The last night Yelena went out . . .'

'Chikatilo knew where she was going, because she always went to the station in Rostov?'

'No . . .' She paused. 'He knew because Lukas told him where she was going.' Her breathing missed a beat. 'That night, Lukas had gone with her.'

'You can't know that.'

'Several of the station girls told me. I believe Lukas led her onto the wasteland where Chikatilo was waiting.'

'Deliberately?'

'Chikatilo had no doubt offered the boy a few roubles. Lukas of course never suspected for a moment that Chikatilo was the man who was terrorizing the whole of Rostov Oblast. He *liked* Chikatilo. He knew his sister sold herself for bom-bom. In those circumstances, you might say: what was more natural than to take him to her?'

I bubbled air and bewilderment through my lips. My God! A child I'd been at school with! But a life I'd never dreamed of.

What could be more natural than selling your sister for a few roubles? Or was this woman as crazed as the rest of her family, so beaten and battered by circumstance that she had no scruples about lying for a reward?

I hadn't realized that I had begun that restless ex-smoker's patting of the pockets until the woman gave me a cigarette and lit it for me. I needed something more but she had no half-litre to offer. Yet even the pause was welcome. I drew deeply on the cigarette and listened to the patter of rain on the corrugated roof.

'Families like ours,' she said, her voice lower, 'could very quickly drop to the bottom of the Soviet pile. Our father had originally come up from Petersburg to work in the submarine yard here, a Communist party member, twice chosen delegate on Moscow May Day parades. Rita and I grew up here in Murmansk. She was ten years older than me, a wild one while I was shy and nervous.' She laughed. 'In those days!'

'How was Rita wild?'

'Drinking, going with sailors. In my father's position he felt it was unwise to keep Rita at home. She was epileptic too, you see. So it gave him the right to send her to an *Internat*.'

'In those days we treated our children like dogs,' I said. 'What's changed?'

'My father had his position to consider,' Valya said tartly. 'It was not possible to have a teenage daughter hanging around the port here, taking money from foreign sailors.' She leaned forward. 'Many of them Indian and black.'

'You mean your father was able to have her put away in an *Internat* as an epileptic rather than a girl with a disorderly life.'

'It was better for his position. In those days families had pride. The party demanded certain standards of behaviour.'

I bit on my tongue. 'Go on,' I said.

'Rita left the *Internat* when she was eighteen. She married another inmate and, after a few years, moved down to Rostov. She used to write to me about how the young men down there all liked northern girls. She'd just had Lukas and was probably looking to me for help. Anyway, I moved down there. I took a job in the Rostelmash tractor works and at first I was happy. Fifteen years old, in the sun and warm wind for the first time, money in my purse . . .'

'What happened?'

She laughed. 'History happened, Inspector. The devil Gorbachev became our leader. He was no Communist. Things began to change. But things had already changed for me too. I married a brute. When he could no longer afford vodka he sent me down to the bus station.'

'And Rita?'

'Rita's life was already collapsing. When her husband was killed by those heathens in Afghanistan she was already drinking a half-litre a day. She'd moved to that house by then, in Novocherkassk. She'd had a hard life in the *Internat*, I know that. She blamed our father for putting her there, she blamed her husband for dying and she blamed Lukas, her son, for being a male child. Even when he was small, five or six, she used to prod him, you know what I mean? Scream at him for being shaped like that.'

'For being a male?'

She let her head dip forward. 'Yes. For being a male.' The memories came back too forcibly. She took a moment to calm herself before going on in a quieter voice. 'Yelena, Rita's daughter, fought back. Even at thirteen, you understand, Yelena was a spitfire. By then, of course, Andrei Chikatilo and his wife had taken the top floor of the house. Who was to know what a fiend Rita and her children were living with? Girls' bodies began to be found on strips of wasteland everywhere. Their eyes dug out with that knife he always carried. For trimming pieces of leather from his shoes, as he claimed in court.' She stopped. 'Who was to know what a fiend the man was?' she repeated slowly.

'Nobody in the house suspected Chikatilo?'

'Not at that time. Not until much later.'

'Not even you?'

She shook her head. 'If I was worried about violence in the house, it was Rita who worried me.'

'Her violence.'

'Drunk or sober, she was violent. That's not what I meant. By now she was doing things to Lukas that a mother shouldn't do with her son. You understand me?'

'Yes,' I said. 'I understand.' I thought of the lanky, awkward child at Primary 36 in Murmansk. I bitterly regretted not showing him more friendliness. 'She took him into her bed. Is that what you're saying?'

She looked at me pityingly. 'There was one room, Inspector. One bed. Yelena and Lukas and his mother had slept together all their lives. The difference was by then that Yelena was out every other night working the train station at Rostov. And Rita was mostly too drunk to know her son from Yuri Gagarin.'

I had a sudden chilling picture of the boy, waiting the evening out on the broken marble staircase until his drunken mother returned with her horrifying demands on him.

'One Sunday afternoon,' Valya said, 'when I called round to see Rita and the children, Yelena was not at home. Rita was badly hungover, still rolling about on the bed. I made a glass of tea for her. Lukas, I could see, was red-eyed, the side of his face bruised. "I've had the militia here," was all Rita said.

'I thought at first the neighbours had reported her for beating Lukas. But it wasn't that. It took time and some vodka in the tea for the story to come out. It seems Svetlana, Yelena's friend, had seen her and Lukas go off into the wasteland by the station. The militia had come to question Lukas. He told them they had taken a short cut through some woods to the station, that he left her in the station square there when he went home.'

'Why were the police suddenly interested in a station girl who hadn't come home?'

'Rostov in those days was a city in fear of its own shadow. With new bodies turning up on strips of wasteland all over, the militia were following leads they would have left to rot before. Anyway, as Rita was telling me this, I saw that tears were running down the boy's face. Seconds later he ran out onto the landing and raced down the stairs. Rita was still rolling around on the bed, reaching out for her litre and cigarettes. Mostly she was cursing this great lump of something that had got underneath her. It had become wrapped in the bedcovers. I asked her what all the fuss was about and she dived a hand into the bed. "You'd think by now I'd made a fucking man of him, wouldn't you?" she said. "But this morning, after the police came, he gives me this to say he's sorry about Yelena." And Rita pulls it out of the bed, this great big painted-faced doll!'

An apology. The doll Lukas had given his mother was an apology for telling Andrei Chikatilo where Yelena was that night. Perhaps even taking her to him. I took a deep breath. It meant the young Lukas Roop almost certainly knew, nearly eighteen months before the Rostov police, that Andrei Chikatilo was the Wasteland Murderer.

An incredible burden to live with. Even worse, he knew that he had abetted murder. The doll was his pathetic apology. As the latex dolls were an apology for Sasha's murders? I remembered Abby's conviction that each doll was an apology. What we hadn't got to was the idea that it was an apology for the murderous actions of *someone else*.

Valya looked at me coldly. 'I'll need to get away from here. To go into hiding from Sasha. Will I get a reward?'

Out loud, I was pushing my thoughts along. 'If Lukas knew, from the beginning, what his brother was planning to do . . .'

'Brother?' she interrupted me harshly. She shook her head, rattling the long grey locks. 'Do you militia never listen?' she said in irritation.

'I'm listening now.'

'Do I have to spell it out? I told you what life was like for Lukas. He knew, when Sasha was born, what that meant.'

I felt my stomach churn. 'Lukas and Sasha are not brothers?'

'Who will ever know?' she said, triumphant in her ability to shock. 'The bond could be even closer. As it is in a lot of cases where boys were forced to share beds with their mothers. You militia know nothing,' she said contemptuously.

I sat on the bed, looking at her, thinking (perhaps to protect myself from the physical images of ravening, drunken mothers) of the system that had spawned all this, the foul *Internaty*, the deprivation and the mendacious hypocrisy of a regime that daily proclaimed the superior values of its own social system to the world.

'Rita moved back to Murmansk to have her child, Sasha. In Rostov everybody knew how much trouble she had getting a man. Here, in Murmansk, she could keep her secret. If there was a secret to keep. Lukas was barely fourteen when Sasha was born.' She pressed her hands to the side of her face. 'Lukas would do anything for Sasha. He knew of course that he was probably the father. Murder itself couldn't break a bond like that.'

I was trying to force myself to accept the idea. 'Did Lukas ever talk to Sasha about Andrei Chikatilo?'

'It was a litany. Sasha grew up on stories about him. As a boy he collected newspapers, any bits and pieces connected with Andrei.'

I sat back in the squalid hut, struck almost breathless by the impact the pallid personality of Chikatilo had had on Lukas and Sasha. But of course it's that balance that appeals to us all in our chosen heroes, kindness and cruelty – sympathy and sadism.

'I don't doubt it was Sasha who abducted the women,' Valya said. 'Chose them for whatever reason. Pleasured himself. But Lukas must have found out. He left the dolls. History repeats itself. It was Chikatilo all over again, except this time it was *Sasha* that poor Lukas was apologizing for.'

I ran through the path between the shanties, out onto the stone road and stumbled about among the bushes until I found my Kamka. Reversing onto the road, I pointed it back to the city and put my foot down hard.

Myomancy. Divination by the movement of mice. And stories of mass murderers and incest. Is it possible that *this* is what I meant, brothers, by taking charge of my life?

I skid round a corner in the narrow rocky road, headlights blazing, and terrify a pair of rabbits in my path. They leap and run – one left, one right. Does *that* have a meaning? Lapinomancy? Divination by the movement of terrified rabbits?

I drive, disgusted with myself, with the sordidness of the fortune teller's tent, of the scuttling mice, of my readiness to believe her denunciation of Badanova.

But I drive, too, with the knowledge that Valya has given me. Sasha had worked in the mortuary as Lenny's assistant. He had known of the way into the Potanin basement. So I have my murderer and his reluctant helpmeet – Lukas, his sad, ever-apologetic father/brother. I'm still too shocked by the story to regain my balance. The tyres screech like furies in my ears as I take the bends on the narrow road.

54

I PULLED THE KAMKA to a halt in the short-stay car park. From where I sat I could see people milling outside the airport building, people who had come for the announcement of the result. Earlier arrivals stood, ever-patient Russians, under the blue neon airport sign.

I turned off the engine. This side of the parking-lot was poorly lit and quiet. So quiet that I even heard the whisper of the Mercedes engine behind.

I glanced in the mirror and saw the silvered grille moving, without headlights, towards me. At the last minute the car swept left and came to an abrupt stop across my front. I flicked my headlights but nothing penetrated the blue-smoked glass.

I restarted the Kamka engine to make a quick reverse, but as I looked up Sasha Roop was already out of the Mercedes and standing next to my open window, a large pistol pushing deep into my cheek.

'Turn off the engine,' he said. 'Come with me. We have some votes to discuss.'

I was facing the man who had killed Natalya, the man whom my pedantic obsession even then corrected to the man who was *responsible* for her death. It might have made the slightest difference to my mind; to my gut it made no difference at all.

I could hurl myself at him and risk the big pistol blowing my head open. But hear the truth, brothers. It wasn't that that held me back. It was the mortal acceptance of the fact that, as a dead man, I would no longer be able to wreak vengeance on Sasha Roop.

I must reserve to myself this knowledge I carry. I must show him no signal that we are not talking just about votes. Nothing of the loathing I feel for him must show on my face. I must live to fight another day.

'We'll sit in the Mercedes,' he said. 'It's more comfortable.'

*   *   *

We sat in the rich leather seats, half turned towards each other, pinpoints of map lights shining down onto our heads. The pistol in his hand pointed straight at my crotch.

'The votes,' he said. 'Where are they?'

I shrugged and the pistol came down on my wrist, fit to crack a bone.

'Now let's start again,' Sasha said. 'Where are the votes?'

It was as he was speaking, as my wrist was burning with pain, that I became aware of the ambience of the interior. Not just the feel of leather or the soft whisper of music from the speakers – but the scent.

Guns pointed at the crotch concentrate the mind wonderfully. Until I turned my head towards the perfumed emanations from behind me, I was unaware of the woman in the back seat.

'I'm not in a hugging and kissing mood any more, Constantin,' Madame Badanova said. 'I want an answer.'

'Who would have believed the mice got it right?' I said.

She ignored what I thought might have at least gained me a few moments' thinking time.

'I want an answer,' she repeated. 'And I'm willing to do a lot for it.'

'That, at least, I don't doubt.'

The gun barrel came down on the same wrist and I yelped like a bat-eared terrier.

'You have one possible way of living beyond this evening,' Madame Badanova said, opening her door and moving her fur coat into a position to get out. 'And that's if you can persuade Sasha that those votes have disappeared without trace.'

She stepped down from the car and slammed the door behind her. I had caught, for just a moment, the blank fury on her face. In that moment, I saw her as a woman capable of any excess. I saw nothing of motive, aim or method. But I saw enough to know she would do anything to achieve her ends. In a country of less than average detectives I'm less than average for a different reason. Reading character is something most Russian policemen don't even try. I try, but fail. Sometimes it hardly matters – other times it leaves me with a Magnum .44 pointing at my crotch.

I shifted my attention back to the man holding the Magnum. Sasha sat, his black hair gleaming, teeth bared, staring at me.

'What happened to the votes, Vadim?' he said, prodding my crotch.

'Madame B is as good as declared Regional Governor,' I said. 'The votes are in the river. How can I prove it to you without dredging the deep-water port?'

'Let's hear it step by step.'

'That's it,' I said. 'That's the whole story.'

'You don't like blood, Vadim, I can tell.' His face was split in a wide, unnatural grin. 'I can see a nervous twitch in a man before he moves a muscle. I want to know where those votes are. *I* think you would have kept control of them.'

Sasha had no need of his antennae to make deductions about my moral fibre. Any fool could have seen I was shaking like a leaf. 'Hands locked behind your head,' he said. He was backing out of the car, the pistol trained on my crotch. 'Now ease yourself over into the driver's seat.'

As I struggled to do what he asked, he slammed the driver's door shut on me and rounded the car with impressive speed. Before I knew it he had the passenger door open and the Magnum aimed where it caused me a repetitive spasm of fear.

I didn't see the knife appear in his hand. Only the glint of the blade under the pinpoint light.

Slipping the big pistol into the map holder beside him, he rested the knife-blade on my thigh. 'Drive,' he said. Castration was only a parking-lot pothole away.

We drove up into the low hills outside the airport. Close as it is to the movement of cars and aircraft, it's still a remote and forbidding place. The trees here have been destroyed by acid rain from the great nickel mines to the north so that the road rises through a landscape of stunted pines against the moon.

On Sasha's word I drew the car to a stop. Through the haze of pollution, I could see, to my right, the airport lights about ten kilometres below us, the terminal building with its blue signs, the control tower and the long avenues of light which were the two main runways fanning out into darkness.

You don't think, at these times, of imminent death, brothers. You think of life. You think of an army convoy stopping to ask directions; a militia car wondering if you've broken down; even of Abby and Dronsky or Pinsk and Danilova ... anybody ... arriving unheralded and unexpected. Your daydreams don't need plausibility.

'Get out,' Sasha said, opening his own door.

Every Navy self-defence course I had ever been forced to take had stressed the need to seize *theatrical* advantage before you tried to disarm a man. In the car my range was as limited as my movement. That left one textbook option only and I took it.

I screamed like a madman.

Shock gave me two seconds' grace. My elbow hit him in the ribs. My right hand ripped the knife from his loosened grasp – and as he went for the Magnum, I thrust the blade deep into his shoulder.

He was quicker than I thought possible. Had tumbled from the car, before I could stop him. Scrambled to his feet and stared for a moment, eyes blazing with shocked anger, reaching for the knife now embedded in his shoulder.

But by now I had the gun.

As I threw open my door I saw he was backing for the woods behind him. I lifted the Magnum. His hands came up for a moment, then he turned and ran.

It's a big gun to aim. I brought the barrel up. 'You killed my wife,' I was yelling into the darkness. No cool pedantry now. 'You killed my wonderful wife.'

I saw him, caught in a shaft of moonlight. I fired, three, four shots. I saw him again, for a second only, arms like windmills spinning through the dead trees.

55

H EAT, CIGARETTE SMOKE, television lights, shouting voices . . . the atmosphere in the counting hall derived less from Dante than the 1940s Hollywood musical *Hellzapoppin*. Hundreds of people were pressed together round the circle of counting tables. Journalists with cameras climbed wherever it was possible to climb to get a shot of what everybody knew, when it came, would be the deciding Stadium ward count.

I fought my way across the concourse. One of Madame Badanova's team stopped me at the foot of the staircase to the offices above, a young fat man with the gleam of sweat on his forehead. I recognized him as Voronov, the public relations man. 'She's not up there,' he said, the desperation audible in his voice. 'She's not in her office.'

'Where is she?'

'Nobody's seen her for almost two hours. She could be the winning candidate, for Christ's sake, and she's disappeared.'

'You tried her apartment at City Hall?'

'Not there.'

'Her campaign headquarters?'

'Why would she be there, for Christ's sake? This is where the action is. My God, do you realize we have the whole of the city's press here. We could be declaring her the new governor on an empty platform. I tell you, they'll want blood.'

'Look on it another way,' I said. 'Maybe she's decided she's lost.'

He looked at me as if I'd just poisoned his cat. 'Whose side are you on?' he snarled.

'It's a possibility,' I said mildly. 'Maybe it's just not worth her while to stay.'

He gave me a nervous, snaggle-toothed grin, a silent plea for me to be joking. 'There's Stadium still to come,' he said.

'Stadium's going to swing it,' I agreed. 'One way or another.'

I mounted the stairs. The two armed minders on Roy's door let me through. He was lying on the sofa fondling and being fondled by a young brunette who wore a short white majorette skirt and a sleeveless T-shirt in the colour and design of the Stars and Stripes. Red high heels terminated her long legs. Perched next to her on the arm of the sofa was an Uncle Sam top hat. The television screen was showing a post-match video of a bewildered Murmansk Dynamo playing against an incredibly skilful Italian team. I didn't want to ask the score.

The brunette had rolled away from Roy and was looking at me as if I had spoiled her big moment in life's audition. Which I probably had. 'Listen, Roy,' I said. 'I have something to tell you.'

'It can wait, surely.' Roy's smile was amiable. 'Stadium's vote is about to arrive.' He reached out for the brunette. 'In twenty minutes I'll be governor of Kola in all but name . . .'

'It's a possibility,' I said. It was becoming my mantra for the evening.

'It's a certainty,' he corrected me. 'This is Belinda. Belinda here is on my public relations staff. She was an important figure in the Las Vegas mayoral election. I plan to get her to present me with the governor's scroll of office when the announcement is made.'

'Dressed like *that*?'

'It's symbolic,' Roy said. 'Together we symbolize American-Russian co-operation and friendship. And the need for more aid. *Koka-Kola.*'

'Roy, there's something I have to tell you . . . it's something that just can't wait.'

'Don't get so melodramatic.'

'I think you're going to lose.'

He pulled Belinda closer and thrust his hand down the front of her T-shirt. The Stars and Stripes rippled. 'I'm a Yankee doodle dandy,' Roy sang under his breath. 'Yankee doodle, do or die . . .' But he was looking at me with those hard eyes. And he was squeezing the girl's breast enough to make her wince. 'Lose?' he grunted at me. 'What do you know that I don't?'

'I think you're going to lose,' I said carefully, 'because someone just stole thirty thousand of your Stadium votes.'

There was sudden deadness to his face. 'Is that true?' He sat up, dragging his hand out of Belinda's *décolletage.*

'It's true.'

'You know that for a fact.'

I swallowed. 'A fact,' I said.

He turned his head to Belinda. 'Get outside,' he said. 'This is no place for a fucking woman.' She hurried out on five-inch-high heels. I had the impression that politics, for her, had been a series of rapid exits.

Roy was on his feet. The set of his face was truly menacing. Those eyes. I'd never thought of it before but, apart from the strange green colour, I suppose you'd call them Asiatic eyes. A genetic line left by Genghis Khan and the Golden Horde. 'Are you telling me, Costya,' he said, in a frighteningly restrained voice, 'that *you* have stolen thirty thousand of my Stadium votes?'

'I arranged to steal them,' I acknowledged. 'For Madame Badanova.'

'Friends since we were kids,' he bawled. 'What sort of friend are you, fuck your mother?' He came at me like a squat powerful bullock. Charging across the carpet he hit me with his shoulder somewhere about the solar plexus. I *heard* the air rush from me and crashed back against the wall. Perhaps I blacked out for a microsecond.

When I blinked I saw he had stepped back and was swinging a bunched right fist straight at my head. I did what came naturally. I lifted my left and blocked his swing but an excruciating pain travelled all the way from my wrist, damaged by Sasha Roop, to my shoulder. I yelped.

When I dropped my defence he hit me with the other hand. Another blow that would have brought me to the ground was arrested in mid-air as the door flew open. A broad-shouldered minder stood there, fists bunched, visibly trying to work out what was happening.

'Get out,' Roy snarled at him. 'This is a private matter – between old friends.'

The door slammed closed. 'You stole my votes, you bastard!' It could have been an apple or chocolate bar except for the kick that accompanied it. Viciously aimed between my legs, it was just part-deflected by my raised knee.

In the second the yawning pain made me double forward, I saw him turn for the drawer of a desk beside him.

When my head came up he was holding a small, leather-covered truncheon. Tools of the trade was the term that flashed through my mind.

I struck back. My one advantage over Roy is that I am much

taller. The length of one arm kept him from me. Measuring up, I hit him with my good forearm.

The roar coincided with the dull roar of another goal scored by the Italians. Remarkably we both flicked our eyes towards the set for the replay. But Roy was back in the real world first. Charging with the truncheon raised, he reached me as I ducked the blow and rolled across the carpet. A second later his eighty kilos had thudded down on me.

The truncheon came up and I held his wrist for the vital seconds. 'I'm trying to tell you, you reindeer brain, that I'm planning to get the votes back for you.'

He lowered the truncheon. His face was bright red, sweat trickling across his forehead. His mouth opened. 'Of course you are, fuck your mother. I know that. You wouldn't have told me otherwise.'

We were breathing like hippos, splayed out across each other, when Pasko threw open the door. 'They've just emptied the voting boxes from Stadium,' he shouted in hoarse panic. 'It's the lowest turnout in town. We're thirty, forty thousand short. You can't win!'

Roy looked up. Belinda, statuesque in her red high heels, stood behind Pasko. 'Jesus,' she said, looking down at us. 'Jesus Christ.'

Roy pushed me off him and kicked closed the door. 'You were planning to get them back to me, Costya. When?' The breath was whistling from him.

'I want your word first, Roy, that you had nothing to do with Natalya's abduction. *Nothing*.'

He looked at me, his lower lip turned down. 'You wouldn't accuse me of that, Costya?'

'I've seen things in the past, Roy.'

'Reasons of State is something else. But not a friend's wife. Not *your* wife, Costya. You can't believe that.'

I thought he was going to burst into tears. He shook his head. 'I can't believe this is happening to me.' I stared at him. He had forgotten the Stadium vote. 'Costya . . .' he said. 'Do *that* to you?' He shook his head decisively. 'Anyway, what's this got to do with my votes?'

I lifted myself onto one elbow. 'Just give me a few moments on the phone,' I said. 'I can still get you the votes.' I paused. 'As long as you remember one good turn deserves another.'

He wiped tears from his eyes and grinned. 'You stole them in the first place, fuck your mother. Get on that phone and get me my votes back. Then we'll talk about favours.'

We sat in Badanova's office. I was mopping my nose which wouldn't stop bleeding. The lights were on although the dawn sky was pale against the windows. Abby was at Badanova's desk; Dronsky, his stick against the wall, sat on a black leather and chrome chair to my right. I won't deny some sense of triumph, brothers. I had been thrown off the case but it was me who had linked Sasha to the Clinic basement. It was me who had established that the old military connection between Sasha and Air General Badanov had continued between Sasha and Badanova. Not pro-actively perhaps. But none of us knew it existed before I was dragged into the Mercedes with a .44 Magnum rammed against my cheekbone.

'The report came in about half an hour ago,' Dronsky said. 'The warden in an isolated weather station up in the hills reported a stationary car on the forest road and several shots. He thinks maybe five. Moments before he's seen a white Mercedes up there. The militia sent a patrol up and found blood all over.'

'But no body?'

'No. But they got a doctor up there who said anyone who'd lost that amount of blood would be dead if they didn't get to a hospital tonight.'

I saw Abby, bending to the bottom drawer, glance over the top of the desk. 'What do you think?' she said.

What did I think? I thought of Sasha's black eyes pinpointing in fear as he realized I was going to kill him. I thought of those small ineffectual palms turned up towards me as if they might block the bullets. But had he survived? In the darkness of the wood they had found blood but no body. 'I think he won't get far,' I said.

'We've circulated details to all militia units and asked for a special check on hospitals.'

'And Lukas,' I said. 'You're bringing him in for questioning?'

'Of course.' Abby nodded energetically. 'Pinsk has already taken a squad up to the hangar.'

'You'll tell Pinsk to take it easy with him.'

'He may be feeble-minded,' she said. 'But he's an accessory to murder at the very least.'

'I don't see him that way,' I said.

She shrugged off our differences impatiently. 'Either way he has a lot of questions to answer.'

'Listen,' I said. 'All I'm saying is that he's been stamped on all his life. Sasha was just the last in line.' I stood there thinking about the schoolyard at Primary 36. About the swaggering menace of Roy as he approached the tall, stuttering boy, his hand out for Lukas's lunch money. A rouble or two. The bully's tribute. 'I'm asking you, that's all. Tell Pinsk. Take it easy with him.'

Downstairs the main airport concourse had erupted in a great roar. 'Is that the result?' Abby asked, standing behind the desk.

'No,' I said carefully. 'That's the final delivery of voting boxes.' I paused. 'It appears the Stadium ward vote arrived in two separate consignments. For some reason,' I added unnecessarily.

I picked up the quick tap of high heels and looked up to see Roy in the doorway with the tall American girl behind him.

'The rest of the votes have arrived from Stadium,' he said, looking at me. 'I guess I'm just about to be declared Governor of Kola.'

'And what happened to your opponent?' Abby said, standing behind the desk.

'Special Agent Cunningham, I presume.' Roy bowed, quite elegantly even. 'In Russia, Special Agent Cunningham,' he said, 'there's no long tradition of losers staying around to shake hands with the winner. Badanova has already crossed the border to Finland or Norway is my guess. Come down and watch.' He spread his arms generously. 'History is about to be made.'

'One question, Roy,' I said. 'Before you go and make history. You remember the President of the Students' Union, Fetisova?'

He nodded.

'You knew her?' Abby asked him.

'Carnally,' he said. 'I once had to sleep with her to get a student tourist pass to Helsinki. It was a grisly business.'

'Will you give us permission to exhume the graveyards in the children's camps she controls?'

'Why not?' Roy said. 'Why should you want to do that?'

'The short answer is because Badanova didn't want us to.'

'Then you can be sure you're on the right track. The colonel and Badanova are first cousins, did you know that? I'll send that permission over, Costya, as my first executive act.' He turned and looked at Belinda. 'My second executive act, maybe.'

*   *   *

382

Word came through from Pinsk before we left to go down to the ceremony. At the hangar there was no sign of Sasha – and equally no sign of Lukas. They had searched the woods around but found nothing. The white van had gone.

The declaration carried a riotous admixture of farce. The loud-speakers played Roy on stage with *My Way*. Belinda was promi-nent beside him, looking nearly three metres tall in her red high heels and Uncle Sam top hat. The crowd roared approval and sang and danced on the trestle-tables until they began to collapse under the weight.

The result was to be announced outside where a scaffolding stage had been erected. Hundreds, thousands even, of ordi-nary Kola citizens had come out to the airport to hear the announcement, braving the thin sleeting snow and the dropping temperature.

As an elected commissioner I was expected to join my colleagues on the outside stage. Among a sea of umbrellas I caught a glimpse of Abby on the fringe of the crowd and she waved. Dronsky, I guess, had decided not to risk his newly knitting bones in the press of Roy's supporters.

On the plank stage, the senior commissioner from Moscow produced a roll of paper and the crowd fell quiet. The outside lights dimmed dramatically to reinforce the spots directed towards the stage.

'Fellow Russians . . .' the Moscow man said. *Kola International* in blue neon flickered uncertainly over his head. 'Citizens of Murmansk and the Kola Region. You have spoken – and your voice has been heard. I now read the official result agreed by the Electoral Commission for the governorship election. Mariya Badanova . . .' The roar of voices drowned the numbers. The commissioner's mouth opened and closed again and he lifted Roy's arm. Lights came up all around. Loudspeakers blasted *My Way* deep into every ear. Sheepishly I looked across at Abby, shrugging my detachment from these circus proceedings. Surrounded by gleaming black umbrellas, did she shrug back?

Alarm touched me.

It took me a second or two to register that *this* Abby was wearing a different coat. Another full second to realize that she was totally immobile. Lifelessly immobile.

56

A LONG-SHADOWED DAWN broke across the airport buildings, the beginning of a day of madness, of the sort of panic I'd only felt before when Natalya was missing. Images of Abby flooded me. Images of Abby walking, talking, smoking a cigarette.

Within two hours Dronsky and I were on our way back to the Nunnery. A search of every engineering and administrative building in the airport and the still, dark spaces between the runways had produced no result. When we questioned people who were standing on the far edge of the crowd, several of them had reported a white van which had pulled up a few yards behind them. It could not have stayed more than minutes. When the cheering and clapping that greeted Roy's victory had died down, the van had gone.

Away from the airport we had put a major search in motion. Pinsk had placed a concealed roadblock both north and south of the 351st Helicopter hangar. A large squad was searching the ruined buildings of the North Bay. Most vitally, all militia units in the city and outlying areas were put on alert for the white van. That morning's Kola news would have full details. Roy, as the new governor, had agreed to make an appeal for citizens' help.

Together, Dronsky and I worked it out this way. Sasha, in the woods above the airport, injured, but much less seriously than I had believed, had called Lukas to pick him up in his van. There had been a consignment of undelivered dolls in the back. Alone, or maybe even with Lukas driving, Sasha had seized Abby when everybody was concentrating attention on the announcement of Roy as governor. What we couldn't guess was whether Abby's abduction was to be used to protect the flight of Sasha and Badanova from Murmansk. Or could her kidnap be the prelude to the insane sexual attack we had seen on Jay?

'What do you think, Chief?' Dronsky asked as we drove back to the city.

'I suppose a man with an untreated knife wound in his shoulder could go any way,' I said. 'But I still think Sasha's first stop would be a hospital.'

'Then who was giving Lukas his orders?'

'Or looking at it another way,' I said, 'we don't know if Lukas was in the van at all.'

We were swinging in beneath the Nunnery arch when the message came from Pinsk, who had staked out the hangar. He had taken a squad forward to search it. There was no sign of Sasha, Lukas or the white van. But they had found, hidden in an outbuilding, Miles Bridger's black Lincoln.

I knew I had nothing to contribute to the militia search. Leaving Dronsky to direct the operation from the Nunnery, I drove on south, as dawn broke, out past Sin City to the Admirals' Palace. I was playing a wild card. I didn't really expect Sasha to be holed up there. I had certainly no expectation that Badanova would still be there. But I sensed that somehow there was more to learn from the place.

But the monument to Russia's once powerful northern fleet was even more empty than I'd expected. Perhaps there are few more totally and swiftly abandoned places than the political headquarters of a failed candidate. Computers had been removed but half drunk cups of coffee still stood on desks. The wind swept handbills and posters through the empty rooms. Doors banged and squeaked back to bang again. The lights still burned. In a rush of hope I ran like a madman through the great map room and up to the floor above, shouting Abby's name.

But there was no sign.

I thought of basements. This building had once been a naval headquarters. It would have a secure basement, maybe even a bomb shelter.

I ran down to ground-floor level and towards the back of the house. A door marked Document Room stood open. I could see dark stairs leading down. There were light switches everywhere and I threw them on wherever I saw them. The dark stairs were suddenly brilliantly illuminated. Going down I saw that the basement was on two levels. Before me, the double doors to the document rooms opened onto long empty shelves and grey metal files for protected computer storage. Broad steel steps led past the document room and down to the lowest floor, its concrete casing immediately announcing its purpose.

The steel doors were ajar. I slid between them. I was in an eerie green-lit concrete room of comfortable sofas and drinks tables. Pictures of the massive Soviet northern fleet decorated the walls. The admirals' shelter-lounge. Leading off the lounge there were six or seven individual bedrooms for the most senior officers, then kitchens and washrooms ... The last room was huge. A thirty-by-thirty-metre low-ceiling sleeping quarters for less senior officers. Aisles ran between bunks racked three high. There were perhaps a hundred sleeping berths, but what struck me as immediately strange was the fact that over half of them had obviously been used recently, the pillows crumpled, the blankets tumbled.

For the first time since I had got here, I stopped. I was breathing heavily. I walked down a long aisle between the tiered bunks. The green overhead lights burned down. I could feel the heat. I had turned back to the door when I saw the first scrawl. A childish hand on the wall behind one of the bunks: *Volodya was here. March, 2017.*

I was moving from bunk to bunk now: *Where are they taking us? Lydia Perskova. Help us! A.N.K.*

Then, *Joseph* and *Anya* and *Nicolai* all with their pathetic messages, tossed into the void like message-bottles in a limitless sea. And: *Alexei – my birthday tomorrow. May 15th, 2017.*

Of course this was the place. This was where the children had been kept. Until when? Until a plane was ready? Until enough of them were assembled? In all probability, I'd never know. But it was to this place that the children were brought from the Nivka's sickbays, perhaps from the sickbays of many camps under Fetisova's command. It was from this place that they were shipped into the arms of the waiting West.

I got back into the Kamka and drove. The remnants of Sin City were jumbled below me where they had been hauled from the lake. For a moment I hesitated as I approached the slip-road down to the haze of cooking smoke, but at the last moment I pulled on the wheel. The fortune teller had said I would not come back.

The day wore on. I've never felt a cliché more apt. I began to feel I could take no more of the ringing phones with the hopeless, pointless messages from Pinsk or the other search parties spread across the city. Or endure the crossing and recrossing of the room by V.I. Lenin, parodying the pacing of a man desperately waiting for news . . .

As the sun set between the gaps in the poured-concrete buildings in the hills across the river, I was sitting at Abby's desk, my eyelids dropping and being forced open. Dronsky was retailing to me the false sightings of the white van which every publicized search throws up. V. I. Lenin was now roaming the desktop between us and I was too weak to push him off.

'We're doing all we can, Chief. You could be needed later. Get some sleep.'

I shook my head. 'I can't sleep now, Dronsky. I'll get a beer and some fresh air.' I got up. 'I'll be back in fifteen minutes.'

I went down, out into the cold air. Leaning against the wall beneath the arch, I smoked a cigarette and necked from the bottle of beer. I don't usually drink beer. Beer is for desperate times when I want nothing else but to be drunk and know I must stay sober . . .

Beyond the arch, along the main street, cars and buses travelled home. I struggled with the thought of Abby, with the thought of that moment when I had seen her standing on the edge of the airport crowd, a pace or two behind the mass of rain-slick black umbrellas. Why didn't I think then of the danger? Why didn't I think, just a split second earlier, that our vek was standing under one of those umbrellas, a metre or less from her?

As I tipped the bottle to drink, I found I was staring up at the old rusting lamp above my head, its bulb weak and yellow as gaslight. The iron fitting was decorated in the style of a hundred years ago, the dark green paint chipped . . . but there was something else. A welcome minor mystery on which to focus my skidding mind. Sometime in the last few years, a neat hole not more than a centimetre or two across had been drilled through the old lamp support. As I stared up at it, I saw that whenever car lights passed on the road beyond the arch, a pale yellow glass eye winked slowly back at me. It was, of course, one of the long-defunct surveillance cameras Roy had installed when he was commander of the secret police unit here.

So why hadn't I thought of it before? Why hadn't anybody? Because Jay's apartment block was only half finished. Because half the windows weren't in place, let alone surveillance cameras. But we knew, didn't we, that Kola TV Installations were ahead of the other contractors. They had finished the job. Our mistake was to assume that the job had been cabling up dishes and masts on the roof. But there were a dozen overalls in the corridor. You wouldn't need a dozen men to fit television aerials. So what were they doing? What if Kola TV Installations were a closed-circuit outfit, what if they were a CCTV company fitting security cameras?

Danny Markov was big, bearded and capable. I could see why his men had completed their contract on time. He set up the portable monitor on Dronsky's desk. 'Very latest American equipment you have here,' Markov said. 'High-definition picture and an automatic zoom-and-pull-back camera. You'll see, it's as good as having an operator present.' He fitted the seventy-two-hour tape, pressed the start button and dropped back into a corner.

The footage unreeled with a well-lit corridor in which four men were fitting a door and frame to one of the apartments. The number 64 was scrawled on the door in chalk. Jay's apartment was number 65. The left-hand corner of the screen gave the time as 2400 hours, midnight.

'Fast forward,' I said.

Dronsky pressed buttons and we watched the screen flicker. The four men fitted the door faster than they'd ever fitted a door in real time. When the job was done, one of them drew a clear bottle from his tool-bag and passed it around for them all to take quickened, jerky sips. Seconds later, they were gone.

As Dronsky pressed hard down on the button, the timer flickered through the hours ... 0100, 0200, 0300, 0400 ... 'Slow it there,' I said.

Dronsky took his thumb off the button. The screen now showed an empty, well-lit corridor. The pile of overalls lay between the new number 64 and apartment 65, Jay's flat. For five minutes we stood staring at the screen. Behind us Danny Markov sucked on his pipe.

'There,' Danny said from the corner. 'Someone's in the corridor.'

I glanced back at him, nonplussed.

'Moving forward very slowly,' Danny Markov said. 'Not in shot yet. But watch that wall shadow.'

I saw what he meant. A formless shadow lay angled across the wall, moving forward slowly across the screen, but coming into sharper focus as each step brought the bare light more directly behind him.

Then, just before the newly fitted door, the shadow stopped moving forward. The man must have been within a pace of coming into shot. So close that I could even see cigarette smoke curling forward across the screen.

In the silence I heard my own hissing intake of breath as the figure took another pace. In his black overcoat Miles Bridger was hunched forward, listening, one gloved hand on the wall for support, the other lifting a cigarette to his lips. Drawing heavily on the cigarette, he edged level with the windowless opening just before Jay's door, throwing the butt from him without looking down.

We'd still had no clear shot of his features but as he stood before the door of number 65, he turned slightly, fumbling in his pocket. His face was as haggard as ever I'd seen a face. He bent forward. I could see his lips moving now, talking through the door, perhaps trying to reassure Jay about his call in the middle of the night. As he spoke he was drawing keys from his pocket.

Everything seemed to move at so leisurely a pace. Still talking, he unlocked the door. Perhaps she had the weight of her shoulder against it because I could see it only giving slowly against the heavy pressure of the flat of his hand.

Then, after the slow, inexorable pace of the last few minutes, the next seconds were a whirlwind. From the right of the screen a man hurled himself at the door. There was a second only to see, through the opening, Jay thrown back against the wall behind her, a second to feel my stomach clench at the terror on her face as the man flung himself at her, whirling a cord round her throat, dragging her into the apartment by the neck.

Then Bridger's gloved hand reached forward and pulled the door closed, but not before I had caught one unforgettable glimpse of Jay rolling onto her back and of Lukas Roop crouched above her, his teeth bared, his hands tightening the cord round her throat, shaking her head like a rag doll.

Then, as the camera pulled back into long shot we saw Miles Bridger slink back along the passage until he passed under the camera lens. As he disappeared the camera began a slow zoom back along the empty corridor to the door of Jay's apartment. It didn't take imagination to know what was happening inside.

57

THROUGH THE REST of the evening I sat in Danilova's operations room, listening to the reports from militia squads in
North Bay where the search for Abby was being concentrated. My
own gut feeling was that Lukas would return to the hangar. Where
else did he have to go? However violent, however it had coincided
with his own twisted needs, the role he had been assigned was
minor. He was expendable in the machinery Governor Badanov
and his wife had set up to sell what had been, over centuries, a
uniquely valuable commodity – living, breathing human beings. I
could be fairly sure no hiding-place had been organized for Lukas
Roop, no place prepared for his escape.

But the hangar had been searched for the third time about an
hour ago. In a wide circle round the plant Pinsk had a large
militia squad concealed, with roadblocks north and south of
351st Helicopter. Every vehicle was being searched as it passed
through.

There were, of course, paths through the wooded hills behind
the hangar, but it was difficult to imagine anybody carrying a
woman's body through such uneven broken country, carrying a
woman's body slung round the neck like a wolf, bound, living or
dead. Even so, I had ordered a dog team up there, searching back
and forth through the woods above the hangar all night.

'You'll pass out just as we need you, Chief,' Dronsky warned
me. 'If you won't sleep at least try that thirty-second eye-rest thing
you learnt in the Navy.'

Dronsky is cleverer by half than he looks. I closed my eyes to
demonstrate the impossibility of simply closing my eyes. An hour
later the ringing next to my head brought me guiltily awake.
V.I. Lenin was leaping for safety as I grabbed at the phone and
mumbled my name.

I was speaking to a Militia Captain Rakovsky from District 8,
the port district. 'That all-stations call for a white VW van,' he

said. 'You want to come and look at what's just been driven into the river?'

'Anybody in it?'

'Come and decide for yourself.'

'For Christ's sake!'

'It's not easy to tell. There may be someone,' he conceded. 'We're trying to get some equipment to haul it out.'

A terrible fear gripped me as I waited impatiently for Dronsky to clump down the stairs beside me. 'Jesus, I'm sorry, Chief,' he said. 'Go on ahead.'

This is the moment when policemen become different from other people. Maybe combat soldiers, too. They develop a sort of strained objectivity before death. I took Dronsky's arm and we struggled down the stairs together.

The port area always looks bleaker and colder than the rest of the city. We drove fast with lights on among the warehouses and pulled to a stop alongside half a dozen other blue police Kamkas a few metres from the water's edge.

Captain Rakovsky came over, the collar of his greatcoat turned up round his ears. He shivered theatrically. 'Even in Norilsk they have better spring weather than this. Come and take a look.'

We followed him between the Kamkas until we reached the edge of the dock. 'Tide's out or we wouldn't even see this much.' Rakovsky pointed. Under the lights they had rigged up on the quayside, a few centimetres of the top of a white van were visible, a pale rectangle washed back and forth by a thin glaze of frothing water. 'You think that's the one you're looking for?'

'I'm sure of it,' I said.

Dronsky twitched his cropped head towards the van. 'What makes you think there could be someone in it?'

'Take a look from here,' Rakovsky said. 'Driver's side.'

The militia captain took a powerful flashlight from one of his men and pointed the beam into the dark water. At first it seemed to reflect off the slow swell. Then gradually the eyes adjusted. Through the submerged driver's window a shadowed face, warbling with the water's movement, was briefly visible in the flashlight beam. 'Man or woman, I wouldn't like to say,' Rakovsky said. 'But it's a face. Right?'

'A model?' I said. 'Could it be a doll?' I got down on one knee on the dock to improve the angle. I took the flashlight from Rakovsky and shone the beam into the dark water. I heard Dronsky's voice, tight with hope against hope, asking: 'Is it Lukas?'

The light beam picked up a face. I could see the hair lifting in the lazy currents. I stood up. 'It's a woman,' I said to Dronsky. 'The hair.'

He was aghast.

'I don't know,' I said, in answer to the question he hadn't asked. 'It could be her.' I found myself swallowing hard. 'Who else?'

A clattering behind me made me look round. A yellow tractor was rolling along the quayside, its curved digger blade filled with rusting chain. 'We'll find out,' I said.

Perhaps it took a half-hour to get the chains attached to the van. Dronsky and I sat together in the Kamka drinking coffee with our own thoughts. Perhaps Ilya was thinking of home and his wife with the leg badly injured in the late Civil War and the two children that I had come to think of as part of my family. For myself, I felt the desolate emptiness of failure. Failure to protect Natalya. Failure to protect Abby, even when a threat had been issued, when Jay's bed had revealed an Afro-American rubber child's doll.

While the tractor's chains clanked and slithered across the quayside I smoked and drank coffee and forced the image of those floating strands of hair through some process of wish-fulfilment. Every faint recreation of the image made it easier to see them as a man's longish, rough-cut hair, lifted from the skull by rising currents and bubbles of trapped air. But I didn't believe a word of it. In my heart, I knew the body in the van's cab was a woman. In my heart, I knew it was Abby.

It was an hour before the chains began to tighten and take the strain. I was out of the Kamka, running across the edge of the quay as the van's roof tipped forward and the back rose, water streaming from it.

I think I wanted to scream at them to take care, to do their grisly job with the care and respect Abby Cunningham deserved. Perhaps I *had* begun to shout because Dronsky's hand was on my shoulder. I felt it tighten but he said nothing. What was there to say?

Silently now we watched as the tractor backed away from the water's edge. For a moment the van raked the cement lip of the quay as the back wheels came over the side, then it was being hauled slowly backwards, pouring water, and I ran forward to the passenger window.

Isobel Bridger's face stared up at me, the plumpness drawn from it by death, her hair slicked back as it had never been on public view in its carefully coiffed life. Dronsky and Rakovsky were standing beside me. 'Is it who you expected?' the militia captain said.

I shook my head. I think my voice would not have raised past a croak of intense relief at this point.

'What about the other one,' Rakovsky shone his flashlight through the grille and into the back of the van. 'Better luck there?'

My stomach fell as I saw a bare foot and the darkness of a black bundle above it. Behind us two militiamen were opening the back doors. Without any awareness of movement I was standing there, Dronsky beside me. The torch flashed and jumped jerkily into the van. I heard Dronsky grunt. The body, barefoot for some reason, lay on its side. The whole inside of the van was like a miniature theatre stage, alive with the effects of dripping water. More water streamed from the hair and open mouth of Miles Bridger.

58

I MISLED YOU. I misled Abby. A terrible lust and a desperate guilt can exist together. Lukas Roop enjoyed what he was doing. I saw that on the screen. That he was afterwards guilty, even apologetic, now seems to me to be natural. Was that because I knew him? Was it because he had led a life of deprivation almost beyond belief? Was it because of the ugliness of his mother? Or the terrible hand chance had dealt a lonely child when it had lodged him in the same house as one of the greatest serial murderers ever? Is that why I'd tried to keep him tucked away in my mind as an accessory? I don't know. But I now know that I was wrong. Lukas, who had left the dolls, had not left them in ritual apology for what someone else had done. The dolls were his own apology. He was the man who could savage Abby as Joan Fowler and Jay had been savaged. But he was also a man who felt a desperate need to apologize afterwards.

I misled you, as I misled myself. He is not, of course, the soft absorbent victim of his own experience I painted for you. Sasha is certainly somewhere involved. But the *spirit* in this, not in the business of selling children into slavery perhaps, but in the business of murder, of achieving, as Potanin would say, *satisfaction*, that spirit is Lukas. That much I saw on the film.

When the phone next rings I know it's going to be him, brothers. The extent of my failure makes my heart thump, my eyes fill with tears. I could never have saved Natalya . . . never saved Joan. But I might well have saved Jay. And I might yet, might just yet, save Abby.

I am staring at the dark blue plastic phone, somewhere in that sleepy, drifting half-world still not susceptible to the probings of science, when it shrieks its summons at me.

I know it's him.

I pick up the phone carefully. Wet my lips. 'Vadim,' I say. 'Constantin Vadim.'

There is a long pause which signals to me that it's him. When the voice comes it is soft, polite. 'Constantin,' he says.

I ask him who it is calling. Ask him to give his name, from some macho need not to give him the satisfaction of knowing I was hanging on the line.

'When we were at Primary 36,' he says, 'I'd always hoped we could be friends.'

'Where are you?' I was trying to control my voice, control my anger.

'At the hangar, of course. But Constantin . . .?'

'Yes?'

'Better come alone. You understand me, of course.'

'I do now.'

59

O N THE HIGHWAY out of the city I was stopped by a roadblock. As I was showing my papers, Pinsk came hurrying up. 'We've had a call from him,' I said. 'He wants me there alone.'

The football head rolled from side to side. The eyes narrowed unhappily. 'You mustn't do it Chief,' he said. 'Let me go with you. I can stay back, come in at the last moment if you need me.'

'He's not weak in the head,' I said. 'He'll be prepared for something like that.' I didn't need to add that if he were seen it would be the end of Abby's life.

I climbed back into my Kamka and drove on towards the helicopter base. Where the road winds above it, I stopped and turned off my lights. I was looking down now on the dark, humped-back hangar and Lukas's long barrack hut beside it. It was set in a cleared area of woodland that made futile any attempt to approach it unseen. I switched on my headlights, drove slowly down the hill so that a watching Lukas had time to see there were no police vehicles backing me up, and, without extinguishing the lights, brought the Kamka to a halt ten metres from the main building.

I got out and walked towards Lukas's hut. No illusions left. I was of course an easy target. The back of my neck tingled and sweat gathered in the dip just below my lower lip. But it was my doing that Abby was held now. I had tried to beat a confession out of Lukas when only a fool would have confessed. And that act, that night up on the lake, had renewed a thirty-year-old guilt. Had taken me back to Primary 36, to the memory of my own crude child's pity and my own crude child's guilt that I had not done more to defend him against the bullying taunts of people like Roy. So thereafter I had defended him against Abby's suspicions, certain that, at the lake, *I* had become the bully. Certain in my own mind that a man could not be victim and fiend at the same time. Not realizing that the contradiction of that lay in a dozen textbooks, lay in the life of Andrei Chikatilo.

But all that had fallen away now. I wanted Abby safe and I wanted Lukas in my power. I wanted to know exactly what had happened that night that Natalya disappeared. I wanted every detail in his own words. And if he escaped into the woods he knew so well, I wanted him hunted down and brought to me. He deserved dogs.

In the headlights of the Kamka I could see the door of Lukas's hut was open, swinging easily in the slight breeze. My footsteps sounded crunchingly across the gravel. My back now was to a line of high window ports along the top of the hangar. If Lukas crouched there with his wolf-gun . . . I stepped inside and a shiver of relief passed up my back. I faced danger from one direction only now, from the front. I was armed myself, of course, with a pistol in a standard militia shoulder holster and another on my waist belt. I switched on the lamp and dropped quickly down beside a low table, my hand on the pistol in my shoulder holster.

The light threw shadows everywhere, of broken, torn or mangled dolls. The wolf's head jeered from its hook. A pair of wolfskin mittens lay like paws upon the table. Several dolls, those with the most damaged, distorted faces, had been given golden tresses which somehow emphasized their ugliness. It took me a moment or two to realize that they were meant to be *Rusalki*, the dead maidens who, in the old Slavonic belief, returned to abduct and torture and maim the living. And perhaps it was as a Rusalka that the androgynous Lukas saw himself, dancing naked in make-up and wig that night I had so nearly killed him. A northern Rusalka who taunted and tortured her victims before death.

As I stared at the figures, some with torn mouths, others with just one eye, I seemed for a moment to get into Lukas's head, to see his mother as he saw her, as a vicious Rusalka who had tortured him as a child and continued to haunt him now. And something else came home to me, with a powerful rush. If I'd thought more of what the old woman with the mice had said on one of my visits to her – Christ, if I'd simply thought more – I would have him now, safe from the harm he could still do. *This man you're seeking*, she had said, *is someone who has every reason to hate women. This man has learnt at the feet of a master.* And that master of course was no metaphoric figure. That master was the gentle-seeming occupant of the upstairs apartment, murderer of fifty-two women and children, Andrei Chikatilo himself.

*   *   *

I have chosen to come alone because I sense that is the only way Abby will remain alive. I'm not working on anything rational here, brothers, as you'll soon enough see. Just on the feeling that Lukas believes there's nothing left for him but to avenge his past, and all the past has done to him. And that the present personification of that wretched past is *me*. If I'm wrong, of course, Abby dies. If I'm right perhaps she still dies – but in the middle of it all there's just one small glowing chance that he'll be diverted by me, diverted long enough for me to shoot him dead. Because I don't intend him to outlive this night . . .

I was out on the gravel forecourt again and I could now see that the Judas panel, set in the hangar's vast double doors, was ajar. An invitation to enter. An invitation that might be accompanied by the blast of the lupara and a single ball big enough to stop a grown wolf dead in his tracks.

I sidled up to the small green-painted door. I could go back to the Kamka and call up a commando unit from the naval base. Nobody would think that much less of me. A sensible move in the circumstances. Or I could step over that low wooden sill – into the huge cold vault of the hangar. And what?

It's not courage that drives me on – it's guilt. If we had done things Abby's way, she wouldn't be in Lukas's hands now. And I wouldn't be trembling on the edge of finding some excuse to desert her.

Then suddenly, I couldn't think any more. I stepped forward over the wooden sill. It was as cold as I expected. I looked up. Moonlight entered through the line of small angled windows high in the barrel roof. I could discern the shapes of pale naked figures leaning on the balcony rails. If they had been chattering and laughing and pointing down at me, I would have hardly been surprised. In this great ribbed and vaulted cathedral the figures looked like some medieval depiction of porno-blasphemy: *The Naked Whores Prepare to Dance for the Abbot and his Monks.*

In great metal-skinned hangars like this footsteps ring out. There was, I saw immediately, no way to hide my presence or disguise my whereabouts on this vast concrete floorspace. I stood and switched on my flashlight.

Very slowly, I let the beam climb the inside of the hangar until it reached the gallery where the dolls, enlivened by the play of light, postured and posed behind the rail.

I cleared my throat. 'Lukas . . .' My voice rebounded from the sides and roof of the hangar. 'Lukas, it's Vadim. It's Constantin.'

I heard the soft shuffle of someone moving about above me even before the echo of my own voice died. I moved the torch beam slowly along the gallery but there was no human movement visible among the frozen figures of the dolls.

For a moment, I stood listening. Somewhere there was another noise too, a noise made by human throat and lungs. I put a meaning to it, perhaps because I wanted to, as a woman struggling with a gag. In a mad surge of hope I called out to her. 'Abby . . . are you there?'

As I called I was already running across the hangar floor, climbing the staircase in the half darkness. At the top I stepped into a shadowed patch to listen.

'Constantin,' a voice said from the forest of expressionless faces in front of me, his voice close. 'You tried to kill Sasha,' he said with that false and terrifying calm of the true psychopath.

'Is he here?' I said. I was thinking only of the presence of a second opponent but Lukas seemed unaware of that.

'I tried to treat him,' he said, 'but he was slowly bleeding to death. If I hadn't got him to the Lermontov, he would have been dead by now.'

I passed the beam back and forth across the dolls' faces. 'Let Abby go,' I said. 'You have me. Let her go.'

'Abby Cunningham is dead,' he said. 'You tried to kill Sasha. I killed her.'

I was stunned off guard. 'Where is she?' I said. 'For Christ's sake, where did you leave her?'

Even standing here I knew that his laugh was satisfaction at the anguish in my voice.

'Or perhaps she isn't dead. Perhaps she'll die with us. As part of the spectacle. It's what Andrei Chikatilo said. He wrote to me when he was in prison, Constantin. A man, he said, is remembered by spectacle and nothing else. I never knew what he meant until his trial when he became the most famous face in Russia.'

He was close to me, I knew that. The faint scuff of soft shoes or maybe even bare feet led my eye further down the gallery. I turned off the torch and knelt, hoping to catch some movement in the faint steely gleam of moonlight from the port windows high above us. But there was nothing. There must have been a hundred, perhaps two hundred figures on the gallery, mostly naked, but some few dressed or partly dressed.

'Now watch,' the almost disembodied voice said. 'Watch and wonder.'

A movement, a flicker of light like a firefly passed over my head. I had time to register a violent shuffling from the forest of dolls. And then suddenly Abby's voice in a scream freed from the gag. 'Run, Constantin! Get out while you can!'

At that moment the Molotov cocktail hit the hangar doors and erupted into yellow flame.

And then as I charged between the dolls, sweeping them over as I headed for Abby's voice, fireflies flickered through the darkness in all directions, exploding among groups of dolls, erupting among packing-cases or igniting the old banners of the 351st Regiment that hung from the ceiling.

'On midsummer nights we celebrate with flame,' his voice intoned.

I slid to a stop, my spine icy with fear. Those were the words of the old Slav Kupalla burial ceremony: the call to sacrifice a woman to accompany the dead hero on his journey into the night.

The flames were leaping like a Kupalla dancer now and the lethal stench of burning latex was already searing the back of my throat.

As combustible material went up in every direction, the swirling smoke and the hollow roaring of the flames had scattered my sense of direction. Panic rose in me. I had minutes now, seconds even to save Abby – or to save myself. A clutch of models stood facing me. The fire had not yet reached this part of the gallery. There was a chance the staircase would be still free of flame.

I ran forward. Burning sections of the regimental banners were now dropping from above, swooping and falling in the hot air like great, blazing snowflakes. When the far end of the gallery floor collapsed I knew I was near death.

In all that noise and smoke and flame a single scream might not have been heard. But my ears selected it from the crashing sections of gallery and the roar of burning.

I ran towards it. I was no longer saving my own miserable skin. I ran towards that thin human voice in the inferno and burst through a parliament of already melting dolls.

Four women sat round an iron table. Chins were casually rested in the heel of hands. Cigarettes held between long fingers. Only one was capable of movement. Strapped to her chair Abby was choking on the thick fumes. I tore off grey duct tape and pulled her to her feet. I no longer even thought of danger from Lukas and his lupara. As sections of the gallery floor fell away, groups of dolls would plunge through, their articulated arms raised in horror. Images of burning shipwreck overwhelmed me. When the floors collapsed, it was the deck; when the burning regimental flags dropped into the inferno, they were the sails. And me, I was a matelot helping a woman through the crashing beams to safety.

Clean air burst over us like a deck wave. We fell onto the gravel apron. We scrambled away from the building, then rolled across the gravel as if we had landfall on a moonlit beach. I clasped one of Abby's hands.

Heat throbbed from the metal building. Whole parts of the roof sheeting now glowed a dull red. When the hangar doors collapsed we were presented with a blazing interior in shape like one of those English boilers in the Lermontov basement. Inside Lukas stood looking up at the gallery. We could hear nothing but he was shouting and shaking his fists in triumph.

There was still one clear narrow passage through the burning wreckage. If I shouted loud enough he *could* still just get out.

I must have started forward but Abby's hand closed hard round my wrist. I turned to look at her. 'What good would it do?' she said.

I stopped. A full Russian trial, deposition taken by someone like Pasko, questions about Natalya, her lifestyle, her sexual orientation . . . Abby was right. We stood there together and watched him dancing and mouthing up to the gallery where he thought we were, watched him until in a sudden, shocking moment his hair caught fire and he fell to his knees, his arms extended until he and everything around him blazed towards the roof.

Trust me, brothers. Revenge is not *that* sweet.

60

THEY WERE KEEPING Abby overnight at the Lermontov to check for damage from inhaling latex smoke. When I looked in to see her she had been lightly sedated. She lifted a bandaged hand in what I have come to think of as a V.I. Lenin salute and gracefully passed out again.

Two floors above is the secure area of the hospital, a place with a permanent militia guard and barred windows. At the desk placed in the entrance a young militiaman and a nurse sat, heads together, only moving apart when I showed my warrant card.

'Mr Roop is being treated for severe loss of blood, Inspector,' the nurse said severely. 'There's someone in there with him already. The doctor said only one visitor at a time.'

'Tell the doctor I'm not a visitor,' I said, walking past her. 'Look, no fruit, no flowers, I'm here as a police officer.' I'm not sure how I looked with my torn and charred clothes. Wild, I suppose, and wild-eyed with lack of sleep. I didn't mean to glare at her but she visibly trembled.

'Just a few minutes then, perhaps,' she summoned the courage to say and I turned into the small private room.

Sasha Roop lay propped up in bed with massive bandaging round his right shoulder and drip lines into his wrists. His eyes, slitting wearily, flew open wide when he saw who it was. 'You lay a hand on me and I'll lodge an official criminal complaint,' he said in panic.

'How will you do that?' I said casually. 'Dead men tell no tales.'

'You're a madman,' he said.

Dronsky was seated beside the bed, a notebook on his knee. 'He's ready to give a statement, Chief,' he put in placatingly. 'He's not going to give any trouble.'

'You've reminded him of his rights?'

'Every one.'

'Including section 233 of the March 2015 Criminal Justice Act?'

'The clause that specifies hanging for multiple homicide. I did, Chief.'

'Let's hear what he has to say, then?'

I leaned back against the wall and caught the cigarette Dronsky flicked adroitly to me.

'Lukas is dead. You're not going to make me plead guilty for what he did,' Sasha said, dragging himself higher in the bed. 'I'm not falling for that.'

I stood staring down at him until his black eyes looked away. I knew now that he was not the initiator I'd imagined him to be. I knew, from the security film, that Lukas was more than capable of acting alone. But I didn't know exactly what Sasha's part had been, how much he knew about Badanova and the trade in children.

He fell back on the pillows. 'I didn't kill anybody,' he said.

I didn't remind him he was prepared to kill me. But I found I wasn't interested in that. I'd been there, I'd seen what happened. It was Natalya's abduction I needed to know about. Her abduction and her death.

'Let's have it from the beginning,' Dronsky said quietly. 'All of it.'

Sasha looked down at his drips, then up at me. 'None of this needed to have happened,' he said bitterly. 'I had a good business. I was doing well . . .'

I could hardly believe it. The man was running with self-pity.

'It was my maniac of a brother,' Sasha said. 'I trusted him to do a simple job for the *vlasti*.'

'The bosses? Which bosses?'

'The governor of course, General Badanov – and his wife. She was always the strong one in that couple. She briefed me.'

'To do what?' Dronsky said, looking up from his notepad.

'I'd done jobs for the general ever since we were in the air force together . . .'

'And got three months' community service in the Lermontov morgue for one of them,' I said.

He dropped his eyes. 'This job was straightforward enough. It was a surveillance. Just keeping an eye on Joan Fowler and . . . your wife.'

'Keeping an eye on them?'

'They were doing something the governor didn't like. Getting under their feet is the way I understood it. But I told Madame Badanova, I'm a businessman, I have a factory, I don't slink around corners spying on people.' He paused. 'She had ways of insisting.'

'So you put Lukas onto it.'

'He loved every moment of it. Going to the Nunnery for the lectures . . . He got so close to Joan Fowler she offered him a job. Of course, I checked with Badanova to see if it was OK. She couldn't have been more pleased.'

'OK,' I said impatiently. 'That night, that Saturday night?'

He shrugged and winced at the pain in his shoulder.

'That Saturday night they ran off the road. They had these children in the back that they'd collected from the hulks.'

'This is just Joan Fowler with Lukas driving, right?' Dronsky said.

'That's it. It was the night of the last big blizzard. At Intersection 33 they went off the road. With seven prison children in the back they couldn't call the militia – so Joan Fowler called your wife, Dr Vadim.'

'And when she arrived there . . .?' Dronsky said.

'When she arrived there, Lukas had already lost his head. He was obsessed with women of course. You have to understand he was two sides of a coin. Polite and helpful . . . until he boiled over. That night he'd been sitting in the van with the American woman for two hours. Finally, the soft-headed prick couldn't keep his hands off her.'

'And when my wife arrived,' I said, 'he attacked her as well.'

'By then he'd gone berserk. The other side of the coin. He'd tied Joan Fowler to the steering-wheel of the van. He overpowered your wife and tied her too. Then he used her medical bag to give them both a shot. He was a medic during army service. He knew about these things.'

'All this you knew nothing about, you're telling us,' Dronsky said from the corner.

'Nothing. Not a word. I swear.'

So far I think I believed him.

'He drove the van with the kids in the back into the disused factory building on the corner of Intersection 33. Then he loaded Joan Fowler and your wife into the Kamka and drove them back home to the hangar. He got me up in the middle of the night. When I found he had the two women in the back I've never been so frightened in my life.'

'Perhaps. But what did you *do*?' I said.

'What was I to do? Call the militia? Release them?'

'You called Badanova.' I took a light from Dronsky and leaned back against the wall. 'That's what you did.'

'Not yet. I knew I had to get the women as far away from the hangar as possible. We drove them down to the Clinic garden. I slipped into the morgue in cleaners' overalls and mask, easy enough that part, and went in through the tunnel to let Lukas in from the garden.'

'What did you think he was going to do then?'

'I told him to do nothing. To secure them down there and come back with me. *Then* I phoned Badanova.'

I let the silence fall. In the hall outside the room I could hear the mutter of the nurse and the young militiaman.

'Badanova went crazy,' Sasha said. 'She arranged for someone to pick up the children and deliver Lukas's van back to the hangar. Then she came over. I don't mind telling you I was scared out of my wits.'

'How did she want you to handle it?'

He looked from me to Dronsky. I could see him swallow.

'What did she want him to do, fuck your mother!'

'This was not me. Nothing to do with me.'

I must have made some movement because Sasha cringed away. 'She wanted them killed,' he said. 'She wanted them killed and disposed of as soon as possible. She only talked to Lukas. She wouldn't talk to me. He only told me afterwards. She gave him the two women . . .'

'*Gave* him,' I said, sickened.

'On condition they were dead at the end. And never seen again.'

Dronsky fumbled in his back pocket and pulled out a flask. He unscrewed the cap and passed it to me. 'Let me just take his statement, Chief. You go home.'

I let the hot liquor run down the back of my throat. On condition they were *dead at the end*. 'I'm staying,' I said. I wanted all the detail. I needed it. 'But Badanova's troubles with Lukas hadn't finished?'

Sasha shook his head. 'Joan Fowler had left her car at the hangar at the beginning of the evening. When Lukas drove it to North Bay, the madman left a doll in it . . . And another dressed in Dr Vadim's clothes here in the Lermontov. I thought Badanova would have us both killed, Lukas *and* me.'

How I wished to God she had.

'What saved us,' Sasha said, 'was when your wife disappeared from the Clinic boiler-room. When Lukas told us we thought she'd escaped down the tunnel.'

'And how did Madame Badanova react to that?'

'The first few hours was total panic. Badanova had a light plane ready to fly her to the West somewhere. We were all ready to run and then nothing . . . Nothing happened at all. We couldn't understand. Didn't understand it until the body was found, until . . .' he caught my eye and corrected himself quickly, 'until Dr Vadim was found by you and the FBI woman.'

'So why didn't it finish there? Why was Jay Dellerman next?' Dronsky said.

'I was out of it by now. Madame Badanova was dealing direct with Lukas. Jay had served her purpose.' He turned to me with a smirk that disappeared quickly. 'She'd persuaded you to steal the votes. But Jay was an American. Independent. When Badanova decided Jay would always have something to hold over her, she set Lukas on her. She gave him Jay Dellerman.'

Again that verb. She *gave* him Jay Dellerman!

'And Abby Cunningham?' Dronsky said.

'Lukas had broken the leash by then. He took her because he wanted her.' He looked at me unblinkingly for the first time. 'He took her because he wanted *you*.'

He wanted the friend of the school bully. The man who had battered him half to death on the frozen lake. I wished to God now I had gone further. I wished to God I hadn't let that faint niggling Western self-doubt prevent me. I could never have saved Natalya but I could have saved Jay and the unspeakable sufferings of Abby in the last twenty-four hours.

Abby slept under sedation until six that morning, giving me time for a couple of hours' sleep on an examination couch next door. For the moment she was being held for possible delayed shock and treatment of a deep burn the size of a rouble where boiling latex had dripped onto her shoulder. I could see her through the slatted window as I approached the open door to her room. She was sitting up in the white sheets, her brown shoulders naked, the white gauze and plaster dressing covering the top of her right upper arm. Angled in her mouth, like a jauntily held cigarette, was a thermometer.

I stopped in the doorway. I didn't think she'd seen me. She was scribbling on a large white notepad. After a second she looked up, working the thermometer into a more comfortable position in her mouth, then lifted the pad. It read: *The black chick says thanks a trillion.*

I smiled and came into the room. It hadn't escaped me that she seemed only able to communicate real feelings via the black chick put-down. Sitting on the bed, I took her hand.

'I thought they'd given up those things a decade ago,' I gestured to the thermometer. 'I thought they stuck them in your ear now.'

She removed the glass tube and handed it to the nurse who had just entered the room. 'No orifice is safe,' she said.

I kept hold of her hand. 'You OK?' I asked her.

She nodded. 'You?'

'Yuh, I'm OK.'

She forced a laugh. 'You look like a goddamned scarecrow.'

'We're nearly there,' I said. 'Sasha's coughed. He's signed a statement.'

'Dronsky filled me in.' She gave a wry smile. 'I guess you're back on the case.'

'Do we talk?' I said.

'No avoiding it.'

'How do we start?'

'I think we start by closing the door.' She threw back the sheet before I could stop her. The hospital nightdress was high on her thighs as she swung her legs down from the bed. She crossed the room and pushed the door closed and adjusted the venetian blind on the glass panel.

'I need a drink,' I said.

'Do this sober.' She walked slowly back towards the bed. 'For the first time in your goddam life, Constantin, do this sober.'

The tone shocked me. 'What are you saying? What are you telling me?'

She stood, one hand holding her upper arm just below the gauze dressing. 'I knew Natalya,' she said. She took a deep breath, like a swimmer about to dive. 'I met Natalya when she came to Moscow for a week in January.'

I all but reeled backwards. 'At the medical conference?'

'There was no medical conference.'

'Ah . . . No medical conference.'

She shook her head.

'What was there instead?'

407

'Natalya came to a meeting with Charles Fearless, head of FBI section in Moscow at that time.'

My head felt like the inside of a tumble-drier, ideas rolling unstoppably. 'Your predecessor. A meeting. What about?'

'Natalya knew that children were disappearing from the camp at Nivka. Possibly other camps as well. She didn't know who was behind it but she knew what was happening.'

'But she said nothing to me, for Christ's sake!'

'No . . .' She drew the word out.

I couldn't control, couldn't even understand the turmoil boiling in me. 'Was Joan Fowler there? At this meeting in Moscow?'

'No.' Abby walked back to sit on the bed. 'Joan was hugging the shadows. Staying clear in case she and Natalya found themselves forced to take action alone. I realize now that was the strategy they'd already decided on if the FBI refused to help.'

'Queen of Heaven, take it slowly. What did Natalya tell you when she came to Moscow?'

'She told Fearless and myself that she had reason to suspect there was a trade in children. From Kola juvenile penal colonies to the West.'

'She never revealed the fact that this was information Potanin had supplied to Joan?'

'No. If she had I would have treated Potanin differently. But Natalya did say she believed information on the trade was being blocked at a high level in the American consulate in Murmansk.'

'Was that what triggered the FBI checks in Boston that finally revealed Bridger's wife's bulging bank account?'

'You have it,' she said. She took a sip from a glass by the bedside. 'Natalya also suspected a high-level Russian involvement here. She thought Mayor Osopov. As we discovered, she could have gone higher to the regional governor himself.'

All this Natalya knew, and had said nothing! All this she had spent hours discussing with Joan – but said not a word to me. 'Do I really have to take this sober?' I said.

She seemed to read my mind. Perhaps the abrasive hurt of exclusion was clearly written on my face.

'If it helps,' she said, 'I think Joan swore Natalya to absolute secrecy. If the FBI in Moscow wouldn't agree to intervene, they were prepared to steal consular funds, to intercept penal convoys. You can see that, Constantin. You can see her making Natalya swear.'

I looked away. Sworn to absolute secrecy against me? Had that really been necessary, I was wondering, or was the secrecy part of another, deeper bond between them?

'In Moscow,' Abby said, 'Charlie Fearless claimed he was less than convinced by what Natalya was telling us. Perhaps he didn't want a big case blowing open in the last month or two of his time in Moscow.'

'But he knew children had been found dead with a K tattoo in the US.'

'He knew that. But he insisted it wasn't relevant to this matter. He preferred to accept the official Russian view that these children could have come from any of a dozen juvenile camp regions with the K code.'

'You didn't?'

'No. I thought Natalya's information pointed to a Kola connection. In the week before Fearless retired, I took a risk and applied, through the All-Russian Procurator's Office, for an investigation of the tattoos in the Kola region.'

'And you applied for me to run it.'

'Yes, I applied for you. I planned this would give Natalya an unofficial signal that *something* was being done. If I was forced by Washington to pull out of the investigation, all I've done is authorize an investigation into the K tattoo. Nothing special to Kola – I got going militia investigations in Krasnoyarsk and half a dozen other places beginning with K.'

'You know how to cover your ass.'

'We ran checks on Natalya as soon as she arrived in Moscow. They were good. Very good. We ran checks on her husband.'

She sat back on the bed and crossed her legs under her like an Eastern mystic. Except normally they don't have legs like that.

'Are you listening?' she said.

'I think so. I still need a drink.'

Then Abby did a strange thing. She pressed the button and when the nurse came in she asked for a half-litre and two glasses.

'That bad, is it?' I asked her.

'This husband . . .' Abby said slowly, 'was an unusual man, apparently. A sort of mix of very bright and . . .'

'Pretty dumb.'

She shrugged a half-agreement. 'A lot of talent . . . and definitely honest.'

'But not much in the way of stable, solid character.'

She nodded. 'A drinker . . .'

The nurse came in and put down the half-litre and two glasses. I unscrewed the cap and poured. 'A drinker, you were saying . . .' I handed her a glass.

'All of which made him . . .'

'Something of a maverick?' I suggested.

Her face hardened. 'Maverick? No. That's too self-appreciative. More of a liability. Unreliable. Likely to jump to conclusions, right or wrong. Shakespeare would have got him in one line.'

'One *word*,' I said. 'But I'd never use it in front of a woman.' I tipped my glass in her direction. 'You know, Abby, for some reason, my ears are burning.'

'Drink up,' she said. 'It doesn't get easier.'

'All this and you still offered me the job . . .' I poured myself another thumb, looked at the glass and filled it to the brim. Beaded bubbles. Winking, they disappeared into the flat surface of the spirit.

I waved the bottle towards Abby. She covered the top of her glass with her hand. 'In Moscow, Natalya had said she thought the rot went deep and maybe even very wide. I needed to be sure that the investigator wasn't one of them. As Natalya's husband, you qualified. You were the only member of the militia I could be sure of. You were not buyable. And the chances were you'd soon start kicking up dust.'

'And as soon as the dust was rising, as soon as you saw which way it was drifting, the real investigators would move in? You and Dronsky had already teamed up.'

She nodded. 'We'd worked one case together in Moscow and got along fine.'

'So everybody knew,' I said. 'Natalya, Dronsky, your bosses, they all knew why I was being offered the job.'

She hesitated. 'We discussed it, yes.'

I scowled. 'It would have been fun to have been there.'

She ignored that. 'To their great relief you turned it down.'

I remembered Madame Badanova's delight that I had said no. She put it over as surprise and admiration that I had stood up to her husband. 'I did exactly what they wanted me to do.'

Abby shrugged. 'Within a few hours the job had become irrelevant,' she said. 'Natalya and Joan were missing.'

'And you didn't think it worth filling me in when you arrived in Murmansk.'

'I remembered the check we ran. The maverick husband . . .'

I shook my head. 'Not maverick. It's too self-appreciative, remember?'

'OK,' she took a pull at her vodka and grimaced. 'You might as well have it all. If I'd had things my way, I wouldn't be telling you this now. At this stage, there seemed to be no point in you knowing.'

'But Dronsky insisted.'

'Right. Listen, I have a lot to thank you for.'

'Forget it.'

'I'm not here to fight, Constantin. I cut you in on the investigation, remember?'

'Only because again Dronsky insisted, right?'

'I still cut you in.'

'Cut me half-in,' I said. 'Cut me in half.'

She paused. I think there was real pain in her eyes. 'So much was riding on it, Constantin. Washington was insisting we first identified which Russian toes they were before we stepped on them. They were even afraid the whole thing was being run by Moscow, by one of the Presidential candidates.'

'Then thank God it turned out to be a quiet little *provincial* piece of profitable obscenity, after all.' I emptied my glass.

'I promise you,' she said. 'Badanova will be brought to Moscow for trial. That's a promise direct from the Procurator's Office. She won't walk, Constantin.'

'You have to find her first,' I said. 'You have to extradite her. How many countries in the world have an extradition treaty with *us*? I don't blame them, we're a pariah nation. A *maverick* nation. But face the facts, Agent Cunningham, you're not going to get Badanova back for a Moscow trial. Together or separately we've blown the case.' I turned away. This was no good. I knew I just wanted to hurt her. Holding the bottle and glass in one hand, I opened the door. Not looking at her, I said: 'I'll say goodbye.' And, as an afterthought, 'Get well soon, uh?'

In the hour that followed, walking the early morning streets of the city, I wasn't sure I could take much more.

61

THE EFFECTS OF that sort of beating can last a lifetime if you let them. At most, I had been allowed to do no more than dance on the very edge of the investigation. I went back to the apartment. Abby wouldn't be back today. I had a shower and put on a robe and made some coffee. I sat on the sofa and turned on *Kola Round-up*. Have I mentioned before that the morning round-up has a particularly tedious pre-title sequence. Maybe not. But it's important. The eyes don't really focus as they show these shots of wealthy tourists salmon-fishing or the Northern Fleet putting to sea (that's footage from when it was capable of putting to sea). The eyes don't really focus as last week's pages get ripped from the calendar. Until the music stings and today's date comes spinning through the salmon-fishers to stop centre screen. May 15th. I lifted my coffee-cup. May 15th. Why should that date set those electrical charges racing round the brain again?

This time the connections sparked quicker. And suddenly I had information Abby hadn't. In Badanova's former campaign headquarters, in the Admirals' Palace, the last scrawl on the basement wall had been: *Alexei – my birthday tomorrow. May 15th, 2017.*

In the panic of that terrible dawn I had missed, completely missed the significance of the date. *My birthday tomorrow, May 15th* meant that Alexei and the other children had been there yesterday morning. Maybe only been removed an hour or two before I had been there. Removed in a hurry.

To where, then? Transported to the West? But how could that be when there were blocks on every road out of Kola, when every train, every aircraft, passenger and cargo, had been checked from the moment Badanova had gone missing?

So by ship? By one of the hundreds of ships, from river boats to the vast ore and chemical tankers, that used the Kola Gulf? But shipping schedules aren't that flexible. Not like a car or bus. If the children had been moved early yesterday in panic, it didn't mean a ship could just weigh anchor and sail away. It was there to load or offload cargo. It had fuel to take on. The crew, as likely as not, had to be dragged out of the seamen's bars along the docks. With a big ship you couldn't just make a head of steam and sail away. Not until the provisioners had finished with her. The little boats that chugged back and forth restocking the ships at anchor. The provisioners.

Suddenly I remembered. I threw clothes on. There was a chance here, a glimmer of hope. A hope I could work on.

I applied at the Lermontov Registry for his name. Igor Gerasimov lived in Murmansk. Over on North Bay. Better than that, he was working as a cleaner in Men's Surgical, stomping around on his cheap wood and leather foot effectively enough to mop floors and carry buckets.

He was a small wizened man, with dirty blond hair and a grin that showed broken teeth. We sat in a visitors' room furnished with stained red sofas and coffee-tables with 1950s boomerang legs.

'It's not a day I'll forget, Inspector,' he said, lifting his wooden foot and waggling it towards me. 'No . . . you'll agree the day a man has his foot cut off in the middle of a blazing ship is not a day he's likely to forget. Especially as she needn't have done it.'

'You mean it was unnecessary?'

His small head reared up. 'It was necessary, all right. I was trapped under a metal bar that would have taken oxyacetylene to cut. I meant she needn't have risked her life as she did. She could have run straight past the wheel-house, and left me to burn with the rest of the ship.'

'But she didn't.' I found it difficult to speak. Natalya? Of course she didn't!

'The whole wheel-house was alight by this time. No fire-suit, nothing. She came in and asked me, calm as a summer sea, did I agree to lose the foot? I said yes and that was it. A big shot of something and she did it. The medics told me we were last off the ship. Suddenly they look up and they see this blonde woman dragging me along the deck.'

His eyes had filled with tears. Too many to notice that I was almost as far gone. He leaned forward. 'You know who she was?'

I nodded.

'The one that went missing that same day. And I don't even remember her name.'

'Natalya Vadim,' I said. 'I was married to her.'

He gave me all the information he could. And it was enough. A small provisioner like the boat he worked on ran errands out to the bigger ships, five, ten times a day. They took chilled beef, fresh vegetables, medicines, fruit, any sort of supplies they were asked to carry. But children? Never that he remembered.

He sat there thinking. 'But the *Sword of Stalingrad* did.'

'Go on,' I said.

'The *Sword*'s a provisioner like us. Like we were. Running goods out. I had a mate on board. He told me they used to get double money for a quick trip carrying kids. He reckoned it was for adoption in the West. Nice kids, a bit lost, not really knowing what was happening to them. Not entirely legal some of these adoptions because the double rate was definitely hush money. Not a word to immigration, was the message.'

'Did he tell you which ship they were delivering to?'

'To some of the fancy cruise ships that do the Norwegian fjords. They're motor vessels rather than ocean-goers. No more than two hundred passengers. First-class cabin service. You've got one in port at the moment that uses the *Sword* for provisioning. Liberian registration. It's called the *Arctic Fox*.'

I called Abby. This was no time for grudges, no time to go it alone. Some things, at least I had learnt. Throughout the afternoon I briefed the coastguard and the port militia. By early evening we were ready to go. The timber-hulled, single-smoke-stacked provisioner the *Sword of Stalingrad* was docked in the old port just down river of the harbour-master's tower. It had already been secured by Pinsk and half a dozen men.

When Abby and I arrived we were conducted down a rusting accommodation ladder to a musty, ill-lit hold. Silent, we stood there while Pinsk held the sacking aside. As our eyes became accustomed to the light we could see that two-tiered bunks lined each side of the narrow ship. A child of anything from five to ten or eleven slept on each one, slept chained by the wrist to the bunk posts. I could hear the depth of Abby's breathing as we stood while the children muttered and shuffled in their sleep. Now and again a child pushed himself up on his elbow and stared at Abby in sleepy confusion before he dropped back onto the mattress.

I felt her take my hand. 'Jesus Christ, Constantin . . . How could they?'

I had no answers.

She let go my hand. 'Jesus Christ,' she said again, but now Abby was speaking more than half to herself, 'I never thought that at the beginning of the twenty-first century, I'd be investigating *slavery*!' She stopped. 'God knows how much suffering there's been already,' she said almost to herself.

'Or how many died afterwards,' I said. 'At the hands of their *owners* in New York or London or Paris . . .'

We stood for a few moments longer, watching the sleeping children.

'I've sent for a bus and half a dozen women officers,' Pinsk whispered from behind us.

I was watching one child, a dark-haired boy of about ten, as he tossed and turned in his sleep. 'For God's sake, make sure they're taken straight to the American Orphanage,' I said.

Abby glanced at me sideways and nodded. 'Whatever the legal complications – we'll sort them out later.'

We climbed the iron accommodation ladder and reached the captain's cabin through a narrow passageway between piled sacks of vegetables and flour, crates of fruit and cartons of cigarettes, wine, beer and canned goods. Over a high sill we stepped into a narrow, iron-ribbed space with a bunk, a washbasin, a small cupboard and a life-size poster of a sleek nude on the wall.

The captain, Gleb Morosov, sprang up from the bunk as we entered. Pinsk had already sketched out to him the trouble he might be in and he had a desperation to co-operate that would warm any policeman's heart.

'Comrade Inspector,' he said, 'Senior Police Official Cunningham, I swear I believed the children below were boarding this vessel of their own free will.'

'They were chained down, you fleabag!' I said.

'For their own safety only,' he said unctuously. 'Aboard ship, young children like that can run into all sorts of trouble.'

Abby's lip curled.

'I am not an immigration officer,' the captain spluttered on. 'Obviously I didn't ask for papers. My job is to take provisions out to the ships at anchor . . .' As he spoke, he was shuffling around the narrow cabin trying to insert himself between Abby and the nude poster on the wall.

'You have a contract to supply the motor vessel *Arctic Fox*. Who was it signed with?' Abby asked him.

'One of the ship's officers. A Turkish gentleman I think. It's a list, nothing more. There are no signed agreements in the provisioning business.'

'And what about the people business?' Abby said.

He looked down, breathing heavily. 'Believe me, there was no compulsion.'

I thought Abby was going to lunge at him. But she swallowed hard. 'How did they arrive?'

'The children were delivered to me here by truck during mid-morning. Normally we would have taken them across to the *Arctic Fox* within the hour. But as luck would have it, a transmission sleeve had slipped. It had to be welded back into place – which is why we were still berthed here when Lieutenant Pinsk arrived.'

I stopped him with an index finger in his chest. 'We aren't interested in your part at the moment, Captain,' I said. 'We'll go into that later. Just now, what we want from you is to get under way and make your delivery to the *Arctic Fox*.'

We stood in the cramped wheel-house of the *Sword of Stalingrad* while it shook and shuddered as it made steam. The captain bit on his lip and turned away from the wheel. 'We're ready to move off, Inspector,' he said in a subdued voice.

'Let them know,' I said.

He took a mobile from the rack in front of him and punched buttons. 'Gleb Morosov,' he said into the phone. 'We're ready to move off.'

The man at the end of the line said something and Morosov assured him, in reply, that he had a full complement of goods. Moments later we pulled away from the dock and began to chug out across the water in our own cloud of oil smoke and steam.

I looked at Abby. 'This is it,' I said.

She was looking out at the dark shapes of the merchant shipping dotted across the waters of the gulf, their navigation lights glittering at stern and bow. Without turning towards me she nodded slowly. 'Yes. This is it, Constantin.'

I followed her line of sight. We had emerged now, past a line of warehouses to starboard. The motor vessel *Arctic Fox* seemed to ride the water, each deck striated with blazing lights. Behind it the hills rose, still white-topped with the last of the year's snows.

While we watched, the lights suddenly dimmed as if a dense bank of mist had floated between us and the other ship. I could see movement on the deck. 'What's happening?' Abby said.

'This is what they do. This is what they always do,' the captain said.

I peered out across the water. 'Jesus Christ,' I said under my breath. 'Look at them!'

Abby lifted the nightscopes that hung round her neck. I could hear her mutter of disgust. She ducked out of the strap and passed the scopes to me. With every metre the figures on the *Arctic Fox* were clearer, men of all ages, fat and thin, tall and short, crowding the deck rail of the motor vessel with a sickening eagerness.

We were within fifty metres and I could make out individual faces when a bright white light shot up from the darkness of the gulf and fell towards the low hills on the other side of the river. At almost the same moment two powerful beams of light sliced the darkness and marine engines whined into acceleration. Out of the mist on either side two coastguard cutters moved towards the *Arctic Fox*.

I felt I could almost hear the shocked gasps of alarm. On the deck above us men were reeling backwards, their arms up to shield their eyes from the coastguard searchlights. When the first coastguard tear-gas shell popped on the deck, a chaotic scramble for cover now replaced the eager scuttling of the men along the rail.

As we came alongside I heard shouts in both American and English accents, words of German, French, Italian, Spanish . . . the languages of Western Europe.

Armed members of the coastguard stood at all the stairheads. Abby and I remained on deck while the men shuffled past us, their hands in a sort of loose chained handcuff. Mostly I was struck by the ordinariness of them. There were no slack mouths or raddled, debauched faces. They were men you might meet, I'd guess, any day in the more expensive districts of London or New York or maybe Hamburg or Munich, oddly younger than I think I expected. Most of them hung their heads and tried to turn their faces away from the flashlights of photographers who had by now reached the scene. Some even, mostly the English-speakers, I noticed, protested and threatened they would call their embassies or sue for false detention. False detention! In Russia, mind you!

As they descended the aluminium steps towards the coastguard cutter, one of the passengers, his hands chained, had fallen, was perhaps nudged into the icy water. He was allowed to kick and scream and gasp for life for a few moments. An escorting coastguard even stretched out a leg and put his seaboot on the man's head, pressing him down below the cold black water. When he came bobbing up, he was choking, close to death. They hauled him up casually by the chain between his wrists. He screamed in pain. The other paedophiles, watching from the cutter, or from halfway down the aluminium steps, looked on in open-mouthed terror.

Below decks Pinsk took us through an exhibition saloon decorated with sculptures and huge pictures of young children. One set caught my eye: a number of children secured by rings to the wall. I saw tortured faces and the weals of a whiplash across their backs. A ship's store had magazines, posters and videos for sale along with a collection of cuffs and neck-irons. Even branding-irons with interchangeable initialling.

'The captain's not prepared to say anything,' Pinsk said, 'but I've found a crewman who's talking. He says that, in the last few years, Russian children have been the big seller in the market-place. He says that the auctions were held here the night the ship set sail. You could buy yourself a child for your own private use. Or you could use the services of a dozen or so others on the cruise back. We're talking about a lot of very rich people.'

'I think I'm going to be sick,' Abby said. 'I don't want to see any more of this. Let's go straight into the saloon.'

It's rare, in a policeman's day, in a policeman's life, that you see something that is so uplifting, so deeply satisfying as the sight of the long line of men being checked off by a coastguard officer before being marched up to join the others on deck. But it was not the shuffling, defeated look of the men that made my stomach lurch. It was the single woman about halfway down the line.

This was not a Badanova I had ever seen before. She wore a roll-neck sweater and dark trousers. No make-up and hair that hung limp. Standing in line with the rest of the crew, her wrists chained, I saw her reaction when we entered. Not the flicker of fear I had hoped for. Instead a stare of malevolence and fury – and that contemptuous pride that I should have seen in her before, and didn't.

The line moved forward. She stopped by me. 'My nemesis,' she said, with an air of stage sadness. 'And I thought you were my golden boy.'

I had nothing to say to her. This was no time for magnanimity in victory. She and her husband had put in motion the events that had killed Natalya. A coastguard pushed her forward. I felt Abby's hand on my arm. I turned my back.

We followed Badanova up to the deck. Pinsk had told the coastguard we wanted her separated from the captain and crew and that the militia would take responsibility for her from now.

I saw Badanova cock her head. I saw a gleam in her eyes, or what we call a gleam, a narrowed calculating look as she walked along the deck to the aluminium steps. A minute ago I could have killed her myself – but now I didn't want this one to go the way of Lukas or Bridger. Not yet. In a moment of revelation, I saw that what would hurt Badanova most of all would be the squalor of a prison cell . . . What she would find near-impossible would be to take all the humiliations of the Russian legal process, all the haranguing and cross-questioning and forced admissions of a trial.

She had come to the same decision. I saw her take a step forward. 'Keep hold of her,' I screamed at Pinsk. But it was a full second too late.

She pitched forward with a sudden, unnatural elegance, her chained hands lifted like a diver above her head. The surface gulped and rearranged itself. I saw the kick of her legs that drove her down into the black water. I could only think of the man who had fallen earlier, half dead with cold when they had pulled him out less than a minute later.

It was impossible not to feel cheated. When the coastguard brought her up ten minutes later there was not the remotest possibility of revival. I remembered her words in her sumptuous penthouse apartment. 'You would never guess it now, Constantin, but at one time I swam for the USSR at the Montreal Olympics.'

62

THERE WAS A big turnout for Abby at the airport. Roy, of course, would never miss a chance like this. His office had assembled the press and broadcasters. While we waited for her and Dronsky to arrive, he was busy, in pinstripe suit and club tie, filling in details about his part in the whole affair.

When he saw me he charged across the concourse and grabbed my arm. 'I'm in my element,' he grinned. 'I tell you, these veks . . .' he thumbed over his shoulder to the media. 'If it suits them they'll believe anything you tell them!' He swung me round by the arm. 'They're carrying a story on your personal part in cracking this case. We don't want all the credit to go back to Moscow. Listen, when the US Senate's Special Commission on Aid comes to Kola, I'm appointing you security adviser for the duration of the visit . . .'

I held up my hands.

'No? How about head of Homicide?'

'Forget it, Roy . . .'

'OK . . . Perhaps that offer needs a rethink. In the meantime will you take director of Murmansk Dynamo? You've got to have something. I owe you, *bratkin*.'

'Listen Roy, for a lot of reasons this is not my big day. We'll talk later.'

'Sure. But remember one thing, Costya, if you remember nothing else. You are now talking to Mr Clean. We're putting the bad old days behind us. That means burying a lot of dirt, if you follow me.'

I looked up to see Pasko standing nearby. His uniform looked better pressed than usual. 'Where does he figure on your gift list?'

'I'm planning to appoint him head of Regional Security.'

'Under Pasko it'll be a straight revival of the old secret police. This isn't burying dirt, Roy, it's spreading the muck on top.'

Roy turned me round with a tight grip on my arm. He gave me

that contrite schoolboy look that I knew so well. 'OK Costya,' he said. 'Who would *you* choose for head of security?'

'Pinsk,' I said, without hesitation. 'He's your man.'

'A lieutenant?'

'Make him up to major. He's worth it.'

Roy looked grumpily from under his eyebrows. 'And I suppose he's honest, too, fuck your mother.'

I saw the lights approaching a kilometre or more distant down the long road that links the city to the airport. Giving Abby's limousine a few more seconds, I began, very slowly, to flick my lights.

Dronsky, in the driving-seat of the limousine, slowed cautiously and pulled to a halt when he recognized me. 'What are you doing out here, Chief?' I could see a slightly worried look on his face.

'It's bedlam in there. I want a few words with Abby,' I said. 'Some unfinished business.'

Dronsky looked at Abby. 'Sure,' she said. She knew, I think, what I was talking about.

I got out of the Kamka and changed places with Dronsky. 'I'll drive it to the airport and leave it in the parking-lot,' he said.

The road was quite narrow here, without a hard shoulder, and I followed Dronsky's tail-light for a while until I found a place to pull over. For a moment, we sat staring at the lights of the airport, hazy in the early summer mist. Beyond the terminal buildings a big jet raced across the front, appearing and disappearing between the trees until it lifted and was swallowed in low cloud.

I knew there was no time to waste. I half turned so that I was looking at her in profile. 'Tell me about that night.'

'The night we got drunk together?'

'You know that's what I'm talking about. What happened?'

'To you or me?'

'To both of us.'

'Let's start with you. You fucked a black woman for the first time in your life.'

It took my breath away. 'And you?'

'Me? I guess I became the most screwed-up Special Agent in the FBI – and we have a few.'

'Screwed-up?'

'For a couple of hours, I was in seventh heaven, Constantin. I was having a whale of a time.' She gave a short laugh. 'Remember?'

I heard the echo of that first language test she had given me over the video link in Governor Badanov's library. 'I remember,' I said.

She pursed her lips. 'The only problem was that it all stayed with me. Along with a lot of guilt and stuff like that. Worst, I suppose, of all, I couldn't tell you.'

'You told Dronsky though.'

'I had to tell someone. That's a phrase I've heard a time or two before. But I really felt it. I had to tell someone.'

I was half turned in the big car. I was looking not at her eyes but at her wide-etched mouth. When I raised my head, I felt the question, like a spark, leap the distance between us.

She felt it too. 'If that's what you want,' she said quietly. 'It's OK with me.'

I reached forward and put my hand behind her neck, bringing her mouth to mine. For a moment I let it rest there. Then, with my tongue, I pressed her lips open.

I felt her response in the movement of her lips, felt the extraordinary headiness as our tongues wove together. Then she pulled back – her mouth, not her body. 'You're sure about this?' she said. 'I wouldn't like to fuck you up more than you are already.'

I sat back. 'Sure as I am about anything,' I said.

Abby reached for the door. 'Then we'd better climb in back,' she said. 'Even this car doesn't have the leg-room to get my clothes off in front.'

At the airport car park I stayed in the driver's seat as she got out. 'Buzz down your window,' she said as she slammed her door closed.

I did it.

She bent slightly forward. 'Take a vacation with me. We could fly to New York,' she said. 'No strings.'

'Maybe sometime.'

She kissed her fingers into the air. 'Fucking Russians.'

'Good for nothing else.'

She reached through the car window, caught my ear and twisted it. 'I have a month's leave this fall. Don't forget.'

She had turned away before she could see me shake my head. As she passed through the swing doors, the noise poured out round

422

her. I stayed long enough to see her join up with Dronsky, then crossed over to where he had left my Kamka.

Inside the lobby, the Murmansk Dynamo brass band had struck up *My Way* . . . Roy had his arm round Abby, guiding her through to her plane. With his free hand he was conducting the band. When they reached the last barrier she half turned in Roy's encircling arm, twisting her neck to look back towards the swing doors. She couldn't possibly have seen me.

EPILOGUE

T HEY OPENED THE museum at the old Nunnery on 7th November 2017 to remember the hundredth anniversary of the Communist Revolution. The American government had donated the Nunnery when they moved into their new glass and steel consulate on the waterfront. Abby, I know, was prominent in persuading Washington that this was the right way to dispose of the old building.

The Nunnery is now known as the Natalya Vadim Museum. As an institution it's unique, devoted entirely to the impact of our bitter past on the forgotten armies of the *children* of Russia. Its scope is, quite simply, to record honestly those sufferings of our children which, in other parts of Russia, have been swept under the carpet. It is an archive, of film and document, for historians to examine what went on here in one single part of Stalin's vast Soviet Union, an archive that reaches right up through the Yeltsin period to the myriad, unrighted wrongs of the present.

Our new governor, Roy, was not at all enthusiastic about the idea. But it was made clear to him that, if he was looking for Special Aid status for Kola, he had no choice.

Dronsky was behind another, less welcome, donation. Against all my pleas, V.I. Lenin has been appointed the museum cat. He stalks his new domain with the arrogant certainty that, from such an institution, he can never be removed. We often come across each other when I visit the museum as one of the board of directors. Our practice is to pay little attention to each other. But if we pass in a quiet corridor, a raised hand is usually reciprocated by a discreetly raised paw. Or vice versa.

Believe me, brothers, it's the closest we'll ever get.